Robin Waterfield is an internationally acclaimed scholar and author, whose publications range from academic articles to children's fiction. He has some forty books to his credit, including *Xenophon's Retreat: Greece, Persia and the End of the Golden Age*, *Why Socrates Died: Dispelling the Myths* and *Dividing the Spoils: The War for Alexander the Great's Empire*.

Kathryn Waterfield is a writer specializing in Greek history. Formerly with the Interdisciplinary Center for Hellenic Studies and the Department of History at the University of South Florida, she also spent several years at the Tampa Museum of Art, working with their Greek and Roman antiquities collection.

D0685412

The Greek Myths

Stories of the Greek Gods and
Heroes Vividly Retold

Robin Waterfield

and Kathryn Waterfield

Quercus

First published in hardback 2011 by Quercus
This paperback edition published in 2013 by

Quercus
55 Baker Street
Seventh Floor, South Block
London
W1U 8EW

ISBN PB 978 1 78087 748 8
ISBN EBOOK 978 0 85738 413 3

10 9 8 7 6 5 4 3 2

Text and plates designed and typeset by Ellipsis Digital Ltd

Printed and bound in Great Britain by Clays Ltd. St Ives plc

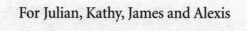

For Julian, Kathy, James and Alexis

Contents

Creation

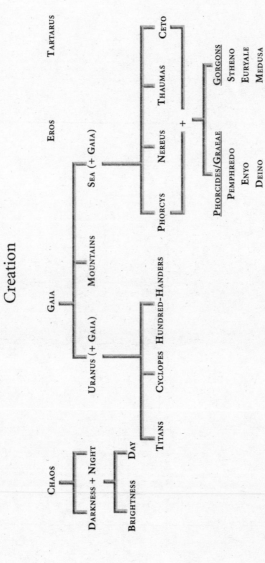

The Olympian Gods

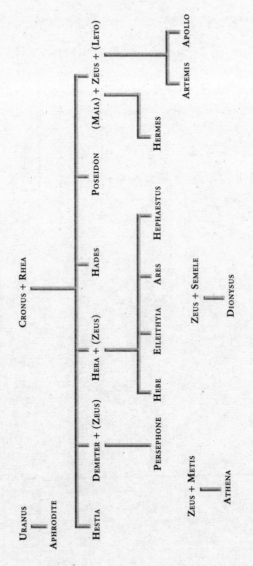

Introduction

The book you hold in your hands contains a retelling of the traditional Greek myths and legends. You will meet all the famous and familiar stories (and hopefully some new ones), but you may also find some unfamiliar details. Retelling the Greek myths is not a simple matter, above all because very few, if any, of the myths exist in a single version. Often, in fact, there are downright contradictions between extant versions of a tale. There is no such thing, then, as the definitive version of any myth; in fact, the more famous a story became, the more versions there were of it.

This variability is essential to the Greek myths. They did not exist in single, monolithic, or 'authentic' versions. Consider the work of the great tragedians of Athens in the fifth century BCE – Aeschylus, Sophocles, and Euripides. They took the traditional tales and tweaked them for their own reasons – often to make a political or ethical point relevant to their immediate audience. As long as the heart of the story remained unchanged, or was intact in the background, writers were free to add and subtract as they chose.

This is how the stories retain their vitality. By the same token, Ovid's often fanciful retellings in the early years of the first century CE; or Ariosto's adaptation of the Perseus myth in *Orlando furioso* (early sixteenth century); or the 1967 *Star Trek* episode 'Who Mourns for Adonis'; or Wolfgang Petersen's 2004 movie *Troy*; or Rick Riordan's series of Percy Jackson books for children; or the thousands of other examples that could be given – all serve to perpetuate in their own ways and for their own purposes the vitality of the ancient Greek tales of war and adventure, magic and miracles, love, jealousy, murder, rape, and revenge.

The ancient Greeks loved stories – so much that they illustrated their walls, temples, high-end tableware, ceremonial armour, and even their furniture with artwork that was intended to tell tales. But for them the stories served additional purposes, over and above entertainment. When they told the myths to their children, they expected them to be educational as well as exciting: to teach about the nature of the gods and goddesses, and about their awesome powers; to illustrate right behaviour for mortal men; to see that, though the gods are relatively omnipotent, and Fate is unavoidable, it is still a mortal's wilful activity that brings disaster down on his or her head. Other myths served more straightforwardly to give emotional power to the foundation of a community, to make a religious ritual more meaningful, or to speculate about the origin of the universe.

No myths endure unless they give a community an underlying layer of meaningfulness. Nevertheless, the ancient Greek myths and legends have proved to have the astonishing ability to transcend their origins, the particular cultural contexts in which they arose, and be relevant within our societies today, as if they tapped into some deep layer of the human mind. For us, it has been a pleasure and a privilege to enter the stream of classical myth, to allow it to flow through us and, we hope, to excite and engage further generations of readers.

ROBIN AND KATHRYN WATERFIELD

Hope for Humankind

The Population of the Earth

The gods were bored, becalmed in the ocean of time. It's all very well being immortal, but time does start to weigh heavily after a few dozen millennia. Each of them had his or her own provinces and powers. Aphrodite was the embodiment of sexual attraction, but she had long ago exhausted all the possibilities of fun among her fellow deities.

Boredom isn't stillness; boredom is sameness. The gods' lives flowed on with endless monotony; no century was really any different from any other century, and there was no prospect that the next century would be any different from the last. They needed amusement and entertainment, but it wasn't just that: they found themselves longing even for opposition. Opposition would spark interest, create twists and knots in the smooth unwinding yarn of the years.

They decided to populate the earth. It would be the great experiment. Perhaps this would give their lives meaning; if not, they could always scrap that attempt and start again. Zeus, king of the gods, enjoined his extended family to get busy, and they fell to their task with relish. Before long, they had moulded all the creatures of the earth out of clay. Once all had their shapes, the gods gave Prometheus the job of equipping each species with its powers.

Now, Prometheus was a Titan, one of the elder gods who had been overthrown by Zeus and his fellow Olympians. The Titans, led by Zeus' father Cronus, had not given up without a struggle, but they had lost the war. Prometheus' brothers, Menoetius and Atlas, had been severely punished – Menoetius cast down into the dungeons of Tartarus, and Atlas, the largest of the Titans, forced to carry on his shoulders the burden of the heavens for all eternity.

But Prometheus had persuaded his mother Themis, the goddess of right and order, to side with Zeus during the war, and so he and his twin brother had escaped punishment and were living in the palaces and high halls of Olympus, along with the other immortals. Prometheus was smart, his mind endlessly shimmering with ideas and schemes. His brother was quite the opposite. In fact, Epimetheus was . . . average. He could carry out assigned tasks well enough, but lacked creativity and moved dully. He was inclined to make mistakes if left to his own devices.

So Zeus gave the job of equipping the animal species to Prometheus. But Epimetheus was jealous: 'You get all the fun jobs,' he complained. 'Let me have this one.' When Prometheus hesitated, Epimetheus said: 'When I've finished, you can inspect my work. You'll have the last say.'

Prometheus agreed on these terms, and Epimetheus set to work. To some creatures he gave strength, but not speed; others, those he left weaker, he made fleet of foot. Small ones were protected by their ability to take off into the air, or burrow inside the earth; large ones were protected by their sheer size.

Some had tusks or claws, while others had thick hides to save them from tusks and claws. Their outsides were designed in various ways to shield them from the extremes of heat and cold to which they would be exposed. Their insides were designed to cope with all the various foodstuffs of the earth, with no species in danger of exhausting its supply: some preferred roots, others leaves or grass, and yet others the blood and flesh of weaker creatures. But then the weaker creatures gained the boon of deep hiding places and many offspring, while the stronger ones produced fewer.

Epimetheus was pleased with his work. He had ensured the perpetuation of all species. His masters would be delighted. But first he had to satisfy his brother. And Prometheus *was* pleasantly surprised. His brother had indeed done a good job. He inspected all the animal prototypes, hearing Epimetheus' explanations and nodding in agreement. But there, right at the end: there was the problem.

Lost in the shadows and dust of Epimetheus' workshop, Prometheus found a neglected clay form. Naked, with no hoofs or claws, no speed or strength, no natural home for refuge, no ability to live well on raw food, no impenetrable hide – nothing. This lump of clay had nothing. But it was time. The day appointed by Zeus for the population of the earth was at hand.

'What about this one? What are your plans for it? Anyway, what is it?'

'It's a human being,' replied Epimetheus, close to tears as he realized his foolish mistake. 'And I have no plans for it. I just forgot it, and now I've used up all the powers we were given. There's nothing left for it.' Prometheus thought for a little while. 'All right. There's nothing to be done now. Zeus wants the earth populated right away, with *all* the species, and we'll just have to let this . . . *human* . . . fend for itself for a while. Meanwhile, I'll try to think of something.' And so, out of the gods' boredom, the earth was populated with all the animal species.

The gods were truly delighted with their new toys. Every aspect of life on the earth came into existence on that day. Goodness was henceforth defined as whether the brief part danced by a creature on the earth's stage was pleasing in the gods' eyes. It amused the gods to remind their creatures, in various ways, who their masters were, and to test their goodness. Just when everything was going well, they would cause a flood, or earthquake, or famine, or personal disaster. And they devised more and more complex dances for their toys.

Prometheus pondered ceaselessly the problem of what to do to ensure the survival of human beings. He felt a strange kinship with these creatures, as though he had made them himself. He felt that they had the potential to resemble himself and his brother – to reach the same heights of brilliance and depths of criminal negligence. But, as things were, their lives were little better than those of the dumb beasts around them. They soon learnt to huddle together in caves, to afford themselves some kind of protection rather than going out in search of food one by one, but still it wouldn't take long for the other creatures of the earth to eliminate these defenceless men. As a first measure, then, Prometheus simply invested them with his own essence.

It came like a bolt of lightning, illuminating the dark places. It came like the most beautiful dawn, rising up out of the sea. It came like a two-edged sword, dividing and yet forging the possibility of a higher union. It was called intelligence, and with intelligence came speech. At first, the sounds they made were meaningless and confused, but they slowly developed articulate words. By agreeing among themselves which sounds stood for which objects, they established means by which they could communicate and pass on knowledge about the world, starting with their own safety. They began to develop rules to govern their behaviour, so that they could live together peaceably, without preying on one another.

But with Promethean intelligence, these first men (for there were as yet no women) also gained the ability to fear the future and felt the need to protect themselves against mere possibilities. Now, the gods were not aware that the intelligence of these human creatures had been the gift of Prometheus; they assumed that this was their special ability, just as other creatures were strong or swift or otherwise formidable. But they were quick to see its potential. Men now feared the future, and the gods had the power to make the future better or worse. So, they said, let's make it so that men have to ask us, to beg us, to plead with us, for the better instead of the worse. And let's make it so that they have to ask us in the right way, otherwise we shall just ignore their requests. This idea pleased all the gods. It would afford them endless amusement.

So the gods invented sacrifice. Men were to pray to them for what they felt they needed, and their prayers were to be wafted up to the heavens by the smoke of sacrifice. The sacrificial victim should be something valuable, a gift freely given to the gods. The richer the sacrifice, the thicker the smoke, and the better the chances that the gods on Olympus would smell the prayer. But none of this was going to happen unless men had fire.

Prometheus was not slow to understand the importance of fire to his wards. Fire could make up for his brother's carelessness by giving humans the essential tool for their survival and development. They could cook their food to make it digestible;

heat kilns to make pottery; keep warm in winter; forge metals. Fire is the key that opens all these doors and lays the foundation of human life. Without it, there is no possibility of advancement or civilization. With it, and with Promethean intelligence, who knew whether men might not become as gods themselves? At any rate, fire would be the foundation of a civilized and communal life, which would protect them from other creatures.

So the gods came down from the palaces and high halls of Olympus to earth, to see that this idea of theirs was carried out in the right way. With Prometheus himself acting as the champion of his people, the negotiations were soon over. Zeus would give men fire, and in return men were to sacrifice to the gods, giving the gods the best bits of the sacrificial victim. 'And let what is done here today be final,' Zeus proclaimed, his voice like thunder, echoing from the surrounding hills. 'This is the Day of Fire!'

An unblemished cow was found for the first sacrifice. Zeus left it to Prometheus to divide the beast into two halves, a portion for the gods and a lesser portion for men. Ever anxious to look after the interests of men, whom he loved, Prometheus the prankster played a trick on Zeus. He wrapped all the fine bits of meat in the cow's stomach, so that it resembled a gigantic haggis, which should contain only offal; and he covered the cow's skeleton with a layer of gleaming fat, and stuck the hide back on, to make it look an attractive whole. And Zeus chose the fair-seeming, but less nutritious portion. Not that he or the gods needed meat; they wanted only the smoke of a sweeter sacrifice.

What was done there that day was final, as decreed irrevocably by Zeus. For ever afterwards, the gods had to be satisfied with receiving the lesser portion of every blood sacrifice, with the smoke bearing it up to the palaces and high halls of Olympus, along with the prayers and petitions of mortal men. For so it was done on the Day of Fire.

But Zeus was furious when he discovered the trick, and decided to wipe humankind off the face of the earth. He would not do this by flood or famine or overwhelming disaster. He wanted them to suffer, and he wanted Prometheus to see them suffer. He simply withdrew his offer of fire. Without fire, and without the arts and crafts that fire could supply, humankind would die out. It would take time, as the other creatures preyed on them, but that would only make it more interesting, and a more fitting punishment.

Prometheus chose a desperate expedient. He knew the consequences, knew that he was destined to be the wounded healer. He accompanied the rest of the gods back to Olympus, and immediately stole into the workshop of Hephaestus, the blacksmith god. There was always fire to be found there. Concealing and preserving the precious flower of fire in the stalk of a giant fennel plant, he brought it down from heaven to earth. It was still the Day of Fire: what was done that day was final. Prometheus gave fire, life, and civilization to mankind, and it could not be taken back. Men raised high the burning brands and danced all night in celebration. They were safe now; they would survive, and even, in ages to come, make themselves the dominant species on the broad face of the earth.

But the wrath of Zeus fell fiercely on Prometheus. Hephaestus forged adamantine chains and Prometheus, bound, was dragged from Olympus down to earth, to the Caucasian mountains. There he was splayed out naked, and pinned to the rock by his wrists and ankles with the adamantine chains, which for security were driven lengthwise through the centre of a mighty pillar and deep into the bedrock of the mountain. He had no chance of escape, but that was not the worst of it. Every day a gigantic eagle came and tore open his stomach and gorged on his liver; every night the wound healed again, to feed the monstrous bird the next day. There was no end to this torment: Prometheus was immortal. Death could not limit his pain, and he was sustained only by the joyful thought of how much grief he had caused the gods.

Even the gods' anger abates in time. After thirty thousand years had gone by, Zeus reprieved the tormented trickster, sending his favourite son Heracles to kill the eagle. True, Prometheus was still unable to move, but half of his agony was over. In gratitude, he gave Heracles information that would help him complete one of his labours, as we shall see.

Still the remorseless years rolled by, and the time came when Zeus conceived a desire for the sea goddess Thetis. This was the moment Prometheus had been waiting for, for he knew a secret: that Thetis was destined to bear a son who would be greater than his father. If Zeus was the father, then, his son by Thetis would overthrow him, just as Zeus had overthrown his own father Cronus. He bargained the information for his release, which Zeus allowed him, provided that he never again made trouble. He was to wear a garland for ever, encircling his head in remembrance of the chains that had bound him. Prometheus was content to sink into obscurity: along with his intelligence, his human wards had inherited the power to tease and trouble the gods. His work was done.

For the theft of fire, Zeus punished Prometheus, but men suffered his wrath as well. Of course: he couldn't allow such a direct threat to his authority to pass as if unnoticed. But the time hasn't yet come for that tale. Let's turn now to the immortal gods. Let's leave humankind, for a while, with some hope.

2

The Ascent of the Olympian Gods

In the Beginning

Speak to me, Muse. Give me words to recount the miraculous births of the gods, from the very beginning until now, the regime of Father Zeus. In the beginning, there was . . . nothing. Picture it as a gap, a void filled with swirling movement, not emptiness. There was nothing that held together, nothing distinct, nothing measurable by any form of measurement. There were no borders or limits, but within the void appeared Gaia, the Earth, just as when building a house the foundation comes first.

And in the depths at the lowest extent of deep-rooted Gaia was Tartarus, the place of punishment, the world beneath the world. Earth and Tartarus emerged spontaneously, but Love is the fundamental creative force. Love, coeval with Gaia, governs the subsequent stages of creation.

Gaia and Tartarus were surrounded by the darkness of night, but Night blended with Darkness and bore Brightness and Day. And so time came into being, measured by the onward-rolling day and night. By herself Gaia, the Earth, bore Uranus, the

Heaven, to cover her completely. Heaven lay with Earth, and she conceived and bore Ocean, the water encircling the continents of Earth, and Tethys, the waterways within the continents of Earth.

From the prolific mingling of the waters the earth was clothed, and from the mingling of Earth and Uranus there emerged, among many other children, the Titans, twelve in number: Cronus and Rhea, Hyperion and Theia, Iapetus (the father of Prometheus), and the rest of the gods of old. Their names now are mostly unfamiliar, for these were the days of yore. Under the rule of Cronus the world was of a different order, and it is not easy to comprehend it, except to say that it was primitive.

Wide-shining Theia bore for Hyperion the blazing sun, the radiant moon, and the rosy-fingered light of dawn, which gently fills the sky even before the sun rises. Helios the sun-god drives his golden chariot from east to west, and sails in a golden vessel each night on Ocean back again to the east. Helios had a son called Phaethon, the gleamer, who was allowed by his father, in a moment of weakness, to drive his chariot for one day, much later in the earth's history. But none apart from Helios can control the blazing chariot drawn by four indefatigable steeds, and Phaethon hurtled to earth in a ball of flame. Much of the earth's surface was scorched and became desert, and the skin of those dwelling there was burnt black for all time. Phaethon's sisters were turned into trees, and the heavy tears of grief they shed for their brother solidified as amber.

In later times, sisters Selene, the moon, and Eos, the dawn, fell in love with mortal men. Endymion was a shepherd, who slept each night in a mountainside cave in Caria. Selene caught a glimpse of him from on high, and as her pale gleam fell on his features she fell too, such is the force of love's attraction.

Every night she lay with him while he was cradled in sleep, not knowing that his reality was stranger than any dream. Selene loved him so much that she could not bear the thought that he would age and die. She implored Zeus to let him remain as he was, and the father of gods and men granted Endymion eternal youth and eternal sleep – except that he awoke each night when Selene visited him to satisfy her longing.

Eos enjoyed numerous affairs, for once she went to bed with Ares, and in jealous anger Aphrodite condemned her to restless ardour. One of those with whom she fell in love was the proud hunter, Tithonus, as handsome as are all the princes of Troy; and she begged Zeus that her mate should live for ever. Zeus granted her wish, but the love-befuddled goddess had forgotten to ask also for eternal youth for her beloved. In the days when their passion was new, the graceful goddess bore Memnon, destined to rule the Ethiopians for a time and meet his end before the walls of Troy. But as the years and centuries passed, Tithonus aged and shrank, until he was no more than a grasshopper, and Eos shut him away and loved him no more. If asked, he would say that death was his dearest wish.

And Helios too dallied for a while with a mortal maid, Leucothoe by name. He thought of nothing but her, and for the sake of a glimpse of her beauty he would rise too early and set too late, after dawdling on his way, until all the seasons of the earth were awry. The god had to consummate his lust, or the chaos would continue. He appeared to her as her own mother, and dismissed her handmaidens, so that he could be alone with her. Then he revealed himself to her; she was flattered by his ardent attention and put up no resistance. But when her father found out he buried her alive by night, so that the sun might not see the deed, and by the time morning came there was nothing he could do to revive his beloved. But, planted as she was in the soil, he transformed her into the frankincense bush, so that her sweet fragrance should please the gods for all time.

Now, Uranus, the starry sky, loathed his children – not just the twelve Titans, but the three Cyclopes, one-eyed giants, and the three monstrous Hecatonchires, each with fifty heads and a hundred hands. Every time a child was born, Uranus seized it and shoved it back inside its mother's womb, deep in the darkness of Earth's innards.

In the agony of her unceasing labour pains, Earth called out to the children within her, imploring their help. But they were still and cowered in fear of their mighty father, all except crafty Cronus, the youngest son. Only he was bold enough to undertake the impious deed. He took the sickle of adamant that his mother had forged and lay in wait for his father. Soon Uranus came to lie with Earth and spread himself over her completely. Cronus emerged from the folds where he was hiding, wielding his sickle, and with one mighty stroke he sliced off his father's genitals and tossed them far back, over his shoulder.

The blood as it scattered here and there, and spilled on the soil, gave rise to the Giants and the Furies, the ghouls who sometimes, with grim irony, are called the Eumenides, the kindly ones. They protect the sacred bonds of family life, and hunt down those who deliberately murder blood kin. They drink the blood of the victim and hound the hapless criminal to madness and the blessed release of death. They are jet black, their breath is foul, and their eyes ooze suppurating pus.

But the genitals themselves fell into the surging sea near the island of Cythera and were carried on currents to sea-girt Cyprus. From the foam that spurted from the genitals grew a fair maiden, and as she stepped out from the white-capped waves onto the island grass grew under her slender feet. The Seasons attended her and placed on her head a crown of gold, and fitted her with ear-rings of copper and golden flowers; around her neck they placed finely wrought golden necklaces, that the eyes of all might be drawn to her shapely breasts.

Her name was Aphrodite, the foam-born goddess, and there is none among men and gods who can resist even her merest glance. She is known as the Lady of Cythera and the Lady of Cyprus; and henceforth Love became her attendant.

Cronus, the youngest of the children of Uranus, usurped his father's place as ruler of the world – but inherited his fear, the typical fear of a tyrant. For his parents warned him that he in his turn would be replaced by one of his sons. Each time, then, that a child was born to Rhea, his sister–wife, he swallowed it to prevent its growth. Five he swallowed in this way: Hestia, Demeter, Hera, Hades, and Poseidon. Pregnant once more, Rhea appealed to her mother Earth, who promised to rear the sixth child herself. And so, when her time came, Rhea went and bore Zeus deep inside a Cretan cave, while to Cronus she gave a boulder, disguised in swaddling clothes, for him to swallow.

In the cave on Mount Dicte, the infant Zeus was fed by bees and nursed by nymphs, daughters of Earth, on goat's milk, foaming fresh and warm from the udder. Young men, mountain-dwelling Curetes, wove outside the cave a martial dance and clashed their spears on their shields to cover the sound of infant wailing. As he grew older, Amalthea, the keeper of the goat, brought the boy all the produce of the earth in an old horn.

And so the mountains of Crete are sacred ground, and even now the Cretans summon the god by means of dance, and he replenishes their hearts and their crops. And Zeus flourished and grew in might, but in his heart he nurtured his mother's dreams of vengeance.

War against the Titans

Zeus laid his plans with skill and cunning – with his witchlike consort Metis, whose name means 'skill' and 'cunning'. There was nothing this shape-shifting daughter of Ocean and Tethys didn't know about herbs, and she concocted for Zeus a powerful drug, strong enough to overcome even mighty Cronus. Together, and with the help of grandmother Earth, they drugged Cronus with narcotic honey. And while he was comatose they fed him the emetic.

The result was exactly as intended: Cronus vomited up in order first the boulder, still wrapped in mouldering rags, and then Zeus' brothers Poseidon and Hades, and then his sisters Hera and Demeter, and finally Hestia, oldest and youngest. For the forthcoming war – for war was inevitable – these were Zeus' bosom allies. Cronus, for his part, was joined by all his fellow Titans and their offspring, with the notable exception of Themis, for right was on Zeus' side and victory was destined to be his.

Zeus made his headquarters on Mount Olympus in northern Greece, while Cronus chose Mount Othrys, a little to the south. This was the first war in the world, and there has been none like it since. For ten years the conflict raged ceaselessly and without result; for ten years earth and heaven resounded and shook with the frightful din of battle. Neither the Titans nor the Olympians could gain the advantage.

Long ago, in the early days of the war, Prometheus, resident on Olympus with his mother Themis, had offered Zeus some advice. Still imprisoned deep within Gaia were the Hundred-handers and the Cyclopes. Zeus considered them too monstrous, too hard to control, but now he was desperate to break the deadlock. He extracted from them the most solemn oath, that if he released them and armed them, they would be his grateful allies. The former could hurl boulders the size of hills with their hundred hands, while the latter, cave-dwelling smiths, would create for Zeus his weapon of choice, the thunderbolt – the missile that accompanies a flash of lightning. And at the same time they made weapons for his brothers in their forge: a trident for Poseidon and a cap of invisibility for Hades. The earth, the seas, and the heavens resounded as hammers met anvils; the sparks were as the stars in the sky.

Now Zeus sallied forth from Olympus, the acropolis of the world, and confronted the enemy face to face. Hurling lightning and thunderbolts in swift succession, he overwhelmed the enemy. The land blistered and blazed with fire and the waters boiled; steam and flame rose and filled the sky. It sounded as though Earth and Heaven had collapsed into each other with a ghastly crash. It looked as though all the subterranean fires of the earth had boiled up from the depths and erupted on the surface of the earth.

The heat of Zeus' missiles enveloped the Titans, and the blazing lightning blinded them. Meanwhile, Aegicerus, half goat and half fish, the foster brother of Zeus from the Cretan cave, blew a trumpet blast on his magical conch-shell and sowed panic in the Titan ranks. And now the Hundred-handers played their part. As thick and fast as hailstones, huge boulders rained down on the Titans, darkening the sky and crushing even Cronus. Overcome, the Titans were bound and sent down to the gloom of Tartarus, from where nothing and no one can escape but through the pardon of the Ruler of All. It is like a gigantic jar, with walls of impenetrable bronze, and its entrance is stopped with three layers of darkness and guarded by the Hundred-handers. It is the place of uttermost punishment, lying as far beneath the earth as the heaven is above it. Nine days it would take a blacksmith's anvil to fall from the edge of heaven to the earth, and a further nine days still to reach Tartarus. But easy though the descent may be, the return journey is impossible.

And so the sons of Uranus mostly pass from our knowing, for no bard sings in praise of the defeated. The noble but misguided Atlas, for allying himself with his uncle Cronus, is forever compelled to shoulder the tremendous burden of the heavens. The female Titans – Leto, Memory, Tethys, Phoebe, Themis, Theia, and Rhea – were allowed to remain under the upper sky, honouring the will of loud-thundering Zeus. Leto bowed to his desire and on the sacred island of Delos bore him the twin deities Artemis and Apollo; Memory lay with Zeus and from her were delivered the divine Muses, nine immortal daughters, patronesses of culture and all the arts; and Themis gave birth to the three reverend Fates, whom the unfortunate castigate as blind hags.

Among the Muses who dwell on Mount Helicon, the province of Calliope is epic poetry; of Clio, history; of Urania, science; of Euterpe, the music of the pipes; of Melpomene, tragedy; of Thalia, comedy; of Terpsichore, lyric poetry and dance; of Erato, love poetry; and of Polymnia, sacred music.

Sweet Muses, delighting in song and dance, but they know also that true sadness may inspire poets to their greatest work, and like all deities they are proud of their domain. The nine daughters of Pierus of Pella challenged the goddesses to a singing contest, and were turned into chattering magpies for their presumption when they lost. And once Thamyris of Thrace, the foremost musician of his age, desired to sleep with the Muses, all nine; and his eyes, one blue, one green, sparkled at the thought. The Muses agreed – if he could demonstrate his superiority to them as a musician. He lost the contest, and they took his eyes from him along with his talent. There is a lesson here for a pious man, if he takes the time to ponder it. It's a fool who vies against the immortals.

Of the three Fates, Clotho sits with her spindle and whorl, twisting and spinning out the thread that is assigned for every creature from birth to death. At her left hand, her sister Lachesis, the dispassionate apportioner, marks the length of the thread. By their side stands the implacable Atropos, ready to cut the thread at the chosen point and bring a life to an end. Just as the Fates determine the length of mortal life, so also the ancient goddesses decide how long prosperity, health, and peace are to last. And know this: if the length of a life is already determined, men must act with courage, for they will die anyway when it is their time.

War against the Giants

The Titans were defeated, but still there were challenges to Zeus' rule. Not long after – but after many centuries of human time – he had to face the Giants, born of the blood of Uranus. The Giants had various forms and features, just as do the children of men, except that in place of legs they had the sinuous strength of huge snakes, and they were wild and shaggy all over. They were a force for disorder and chaos, rapists, thieves, and murderers, and they could not be allowed to co-exist with the new order. Things came to a head when the Giants rustled the cattle of Helios, the sun-god. It was the last straw. War was declared, and the uncouth and unkempt Giants stormed heaven with boulders and burning brands.

There were so many of them that Zeus could not handle them alone, and for the first time the gods worked together as a team. Even so, they could not prevail against the hostile mob. For it was foretold that the Giants could be defeated only by a force that included a mortal. But no mortal then alive would last more than an instant against the Giants: this was not yet the Age of Heroes. It would be like pitting a candle flame against a tempest. And the Giants, knowing this, were sure of their final victory.

Zeus concocted an awful plan. The only human ally he wanted was Heracles, but Heracles had not yet been born. Zeus reached into the future and pulled Heracles back through time to help against the Giants. To Heracles, it seemed a lucid dream, one never to be forgotten – a dream filled with fire and pain and awesome deeds. In desperation at Zeus' cunning, Gaia sought a unique herb that would give her foul children true immortality, even against Heracles. But Zeus, learning of her quest, forbade the sun and the moon and dawn to shine, so that Gaia could not find the plant and Zeus plucked it for himself.

The greatest of the Giants was Alcyoneus, who could not be killed while he was in touch with the land from which he had sprung, the Pallene peninsula. Heracles shot Alcyoneus with his bow, but no sooner had the Giant crashed to the ground than he sprang up again, reinvigorated. Heracles was at a loss: again and again he shot him, and every time the same thing happened. Then wise Athena told him Alcyoneus' secret, and summoned indomitable Sleep, and the giant fell into a deep slumber. While he was asleep, Heracles laid hold of him and dragged him off Pallene. The Giant awoke, briefly struggled, and breathed his last.

But Porphyrion, equal in might to his brother Alcyoneus, and the leader of the Giants, overwhelmed the goddess Hera and began to rip off her clothes, desiring to take her against her will. Zeus stunned the savage Giant with a thunderbolt, and Heracles finished him off with his bow. Dionysus, surrounded by wild animals and riding into battle on a donkey whose braying cowed his enemies, smote Eurytus with his thyrsus staff, while foul Clytius fell before the flaming brands of the dread witch-goddess Hecate. Mimas died horribly, his body boiled by molten metal poured from Hephaestus' crucible.

Fearsome Athena buried Enceladus under Sicily, and then turned to Pallas; she flayed him alive and wore his raw skin, sticky with blood, as a shield. Poseidon broke off part of the island of Cos and crushed Polybotes with it. Hermes, wearing Hades' cap of invisibility, killed Hippolytus, and Artemis did away with Gration. Apollo shot out the left eye of Ephialtes, while Heracles' arrow lodged deep in the other. The Fates, wielding massive clubs of bronze, crushed the skulls of Thoas and fierce Agrius. The rest were scattered by Zeus' thunderbolts and, to fulfil the prophecy, shot down by Heracles as he raced after them on his chariot. Gaia implored Zeus for the lives of her children, but he was not to be swayed. There should be none to challenge him.

After bitter war, peace came to Olympus. For a brief while, the heavens were untroubled, and Zeus began to make provisions for his newly acquired realm. But then there arose a new contender for the throne of the world. Gaia was saddened by the defeat and death of her offspring, the Giants, born of the blood of Uranus. But she had to admit that Zeus was proving himself a worthy king. She devised for him one final test, so that all might see his kingly qualities, or his humiliation.

Out of her most hidden depths Earth heaved forth a terrifying monster. A hundred snake-heads sprouted from Typhoeus' shoulders, and the forked tongues flickering from their mouths matched the fiery flashes from two hundred eyes. But the sounds the gigantic creature emitted were the worst: not just the hissing of snakes, but the baying of hounds, the bellowing of bulls, and the roar of lions; not just recognizable and comprehensible sounds, but sounds that were never heard before or since, that had meaning, but no meaning anyone could grasp. The part-human, part-serpentine body of the beast was as strong as a mountain, and he advanced on Olympus with his confidence high, ready to institute a new and terrible order for gods and men.

At the sight of the monster all the gods fled from Olympus to Egypt and disguised themselves as innocuous animals. But Zeus came down from the high mountain to meet the challenge. Had there been onlookers, it would have seemed as though the land and the sea were consumed by a horrific storm. Swollen purple and black clouds shrouded the battle, and all that could be seen were flashes of fire and lightning, and the billowing and surging and whirling of the clouds. The noise was abominable – the crashing of the thunder, the crack of lightning, the hiss of flames extinguished in the sea, the cries of pain from Typhoeus, magnified a hundred times by a hundred howling heads.

Zeus attacked without mercy, blinding the creature with fire and shrivelling his heads black with lightning. Typhoeus leapt into the sea to extinguish the flames that erupted all over his body, but Zeus smote him again and again, until the rocks of the battlefield melted like wax, the sea boiled, and the tormented, smoking ground shook and cracked open black and gaping maws. And Zeus finally hurled the monster into the greatest of these chasms all the way down to Tartarus, and piled Mount Etna on top and pounded its roots deep into the ground, to contain Typhoeus for ever. Only once in a while is he able to wriggle a bit, causing little-knowing mortal men to say that the Sicilian volcano is rumbling.

But the sounds of the volcano are no more than faint echoes of his voices of old, and its power the merest sliver of Typhoeus' former strength. All he left behind were his children, the winds of destruction and the many-headed monsters: Cerberus, the hell-hound that guards the entrance to the underworld, with his three savage heads and tails of venomous serpents; the nine-headed, marsh-dwelling Hydra; two-headed Orthus, protector of the red cattle of Geryon; and the Chimera, whose foreparts were those of a lion, but her tail was a living serpent, and a goat made up her trunk, and all three heads hissed and roared and spat with indiscriminate fury.

Zeus and His Brothers

Zeus had cleared the world of the most potent forces of disorder and chaos, a burden that would also fall on some of the heroes of later time, in proportion to their lesser abilities. By force of arms, he had confirmed his right to the high, golden throne of heavenly Olympus.

In order to ensure ongoing stability, every major domain of life on earth was given into the care of one of the gods, so that each had his or her unique province and none should be dissatisfied. Above, there spread the wide heavens; below, the misty underworld stretched down to Tartarus, the place of woe; between lay the surface of the earth. Great Zeus, the wielder of the thunderbolt and lightning, took for himself the heavens and the halls of Olympus, but treated his two brothers as equals. Dark Hades became lord of the underworld, while horse-loving Poseidon gained the surface of the earth, and especially its waters.

And so Zeus is the cloud-gatherer, the hurler of thunderbolts, the shining lord of sky and weather. Men pray to him for many things, for all the other gods obey his commands; but especially they pray for sufficient rain to impregnate the earth, so that their flocks fatten and their crops multiply.

From high Olympus he looks down on the earth and ponders its fate. Effortlessly, he raises a man up or brings him low, makes the crooked straight and humbles the proud. The earth trembles at his nod. If he descends to earth, he comes as a flash of lightning, and the scorched ground where he alights from his chariot is sacred. His majesty is second to none, and he may also appear as a soaring eagle, aloof and magnificent. He speaks to mortal men through the rustling of his sacred oak at Dodona; the oracle at Olympia is his, and the four-yearly games there are sacred to him.

Men think of Poseidon as the trident-bearing lord of the sea, and they pray to him for safety, for they and their craft are puny, and he is mighty and of uncertain temper. But he is also the earth-shaker, the maker of earthquakes, when the very land seems to ripple like the sea and yearn to be water. And he delights in horses, for a free-running horse flows like a mighty wave, with muscles gleaming and tail streaming. All he has to do is stamp a hoof, or strike a blow with his trident, and sweet water gushes from solid rock. His wife is Amphitrite, who dwells in the booming of the sea and the whisper of the sea-shell, though he had children by many another nymph and goddess too.

Poseidon drives over the sea in a chariot drawn by horses with brazen hoofs and golden manes, and at his approach the waves die down and the sea gives him passage.

What can be said about Hades? No living man has ever beheld his face, and the dead do not return from his mirthless domain. He is the invincible one, for death awaits all; with his staff, he drives all in their time into the echoing vaults of his palace. No one knows for sure where the entrance is to his subterranean realm. Some say that it is in the far west, where the sun goes down to darkness; others that certain caves or chasms conceal an entrance.

Through the gloom of his underworld realm flit the feeble remnants of men of old, pale spirits, gibbering and forlorn, and dust and mist is all their food; and the River Styx, never to be re-crossed, surrounds the domain of Hades, as Ocean surrounds the continents of the earth and the Milky Way surrounds the heavens. Charon the ferryman, dreaded by all, transports the dead across the river to their eternal home, if they bring the coin to pay him. Otherwise, they remain as pale ghosts, whimpering feebly on the banks of the river and imploring all-comers for a proper burial; but those who come are only the dead themselves, and can help no more.

This is the doom that awaits us, except for the few, righteous or unrighteous. Those whose brief dances have pleased the gods are allowed to dwell for ever on the Isles of the Blessed, or in the Elysian Fields, where temperate breezes gently stir meadow flowers, nurtured by sweet springs and showers. But warmongers and tyrants, murderers and rapists, perpetrators of all foul and abnormal crimes against the gods or hospitality or parents, are cast into the depths of Tartarus and suffer endless torment. Hades is the lord of the dead, but his lady Persephone shares his powers, and the souls of the dead are judged by three stern judges: the two wise sons of Europa by Zeus, Minos and Rhadamanthys of Crete, and Aeacus, son of Zeus and Aegina. And Hades is also Pluto, the giver of wealth, because all crops arise out of the under-earth, and he bears rich minerals deep in his secret places.

3

The Gods of Olympus

Zeus the King

The regime of Zeus is marked by order. Essentially, the world is stable: goats are not born to men or cows, but only to goats, and deformed monstrosities – hybrid creatures, or distorted versions of the species – are no longer born, or only rarely. The sun rises where it should day by day; the seasons follow in an orderly fashion. This was the change that marked the end of the era of Cronus and the beginning of our familiar world. And it was the job of many of the heroes to tame the world.

The will of Zeus is that the world should continue as a stable entity, as long as the dominant species, human beings, recognize the power of the gods and revere them aright. And the will of Zeus is so dominant that none of the other gods dares to violate the limits he has set. Just as no single one of the natural elements of earth, water, fire, and air prevails in our world, so the power of one deity cannot usurp pride of place. Each of the gods is, on his or her own, invincible. If Aphrodite prevailed, the world would be nothing but copulating couples; if Ares prevailed, the madness of war would be all that we know. But this is not the case, not while Zeus is in command. Balance is preserved, even if, in their suffering, mortal men find this hard to see.

The gods that dwell with Zeus on high Olympus are these: Aphrodite, primordial deity; Zeus' sister–wife Hera, and his other sisters, Demeter and Hestia; and the children of Zeus: Athena, Ares, Hephaestus, the twins Apollo and Artemis, Hermes, and Dionysus. These are the immortal gods who dwell on Olympus, and ichor flows in their veins. They are many, but their purpose is one: to carry out the will of the Father of All. He has no need to move from his throne. He rules by wisdom, but he brooks no disagreement. Even his wife Hera, when she displeased him, had her hands bound with golden chains, and was suspended from heaven on a rope, with anvils attached to her feet. The strength of Zeus is such that it surpasses that of all the other gods put together, and they dare not oppose his will, even if they desired to.

Hera

Sister–wife of lord Zeus, white-armed Hera preserves the sanctity of marriage and guards the keys of wedlock. Unlike him, she has no time for the frivolity of extra-marital affairs. She is held in respect as the golden-throned queen of heaven, and she is called cow-eyed, for she looks on the world with stately and serene regality; all mortal queens should aspire to be like her. She it is to whom women pray for a good marriage, and for healthy offspring, for along with her daughter Eileithyia, Hera is the goddess of childbirth.

Though she sleeps with her husband – and it is said that meadows bloom beneath them as they make love – she renews her virginity each year by bathing in a spring at Nauplia. She is

virgin, wife, and matron, and all womanly life is hers. When
Heracles was born, Zeus brought him to Hera to suckle, hoping
thereby to make his favoured son immortal. But the strapping
babe bit her nipple, and in shock Hera pushed him away. The
divine milk spraying from her breasts formed the Milky Way,
though some fell to earth and from the rich drops sprouted
pure-white lilies.

Though Hera is known to be the faithful consort of the Ruler
of All, yet the tale is told of Ixion, king of wide lands in Thessaly, who fell prey to his passion for the fair queen of heaven
when he came to the hallowed halls of Olympus, invited guest
of Zeus himself. For Zeus had offered to purify Ixion after he
had killed his father-in-law. Ixion sought to betray his host,
another heinous crime, but Zeus was not caught unawares, and
fashioned a replica of his wife from mist. This cloud, Nephele,
lay with Ixion, who believed he made love to Hera.

But disaster comes to all who seek to deceive the gods. For
his transgression, for desiring golden-sandaled Hera, though he
lay not with her in truth, Zeus had him lashed to a fiery wheel,
which revolves through the universe for eternity.

As for Nephele, though she was more form than substance,
yet she conceived from Ixion and bore Centaurus, a son to break
a mother's heart, for he honoured neither men nor the laws of
the gods. He coupled with the mares on Pelion's slopes and
fathered the race of Centaurs, half-man and half-horse, with
strong appetites for carnal pleasure and destruction.

Hestia

Hestia is the firstborn of Cronus and Rhea. Hers is the hearth
and its sacred fire, the source of life and prosperity to every

home and every settlement, and her dark hair flows with rich oil. Her seat is at the centre of every home there has ever been. When land grows scarce and younger brothers band together to seek a new home abroad, they carry with them the sacred fire of the mother city, to bless their venture. Although she was wooed by her brother Poseidon and her nephew Apollo, she swore on the head of Zeus to remain a virgin, so that she would dwell equally and impartially at the heart of every household. She has no need of a temple, for the hearth fire of every community and household is her sanctuary, a place of rest and asylum, from which none can be turned away. She it is who oversees the introduction of new members of the family, and at their leaving she is extinguished and renewed. But the exemplary goddess never leaves Zeus' wide halls, and little rumour or fable of her has reached the ears of man.

Demeter

Demeter is the goddess of cereal crops – of lovely wheat and barley, oats and rye. Without her blessing, mortal men face sure starvation, for her fare is staple in every culture. She watches over the ploughing and the sowing, the reaping and the threshing, and the storage of crops. She is every ear of grain on every stem that has ever grown. She is the foundation of law and morality, for without food in their bellies men turn to crime.

Now, Demeter had by Zeus a daughter, and she loved Persephone with all her heart. But Zeus promised the maiden goddess to his brother Hades, dark lord of the underworld. One day, Persephone was out gathering flowers with her friends, the Ocean nymphs, in the garden of the gods. And Gaia, the Earth, put forth a new flower, never before seen, of especial beauty, the narcissus; and the sweetness of its fragrance made the earth smile and the seas laugh aloud.

Persephone, straying from her friends, found the precious flower. But when she reached out her hand for the pale bloom, the earth split open and Hades emerged on his chariot and snatched her away. The maiden's cries to her father fell on deaf ears. No one heard her, none of the gods, save Hecate in her distant cave, conjuring spirits. And in a moment Persephone's screams of terror faded as Hades bore her down, down into the depths of the underworld – but a last, faint cry came to the ears of her mother, borne by a kindly wind.

Demeter lit two torches in the fires of Etna, and for nine days she roamed the broad earth over hill and dale, denying herself sleep and rest, but nowhere was her daughter to be found. All she found was a bunch of dried narcissus blossoms lying on the healed earth. Poseidon took advantage of her distress to press his suit, and when Demeter changed herself into a mare to avoid his attentions, he became a stallion and had his way with her. And in due course of time she gave birth to a wonderful stallion called Arion, and a daughter whose name is known only to the initiated.

On the tenth day sombre Hecate came and told her what little she knew – that her daughter had been abducted. Together they went to Helios, the sun-god, who sees all, and he explained that it was the will of Zeus that Persephone should be the bride of his brother Hades, and consoled her with the thought that Zeus' equal was no mean husband for her daughter.

But Demeter was not to be consoled, nor was she of a mind to give up. She wanted nothing now to do with the gods of Olympus, who had betrayed her and her daughter. She disguised herself as a mortal and roamed over the earth ceaselessly, in grief and despair. Only Hesperus, the evening star, could persuade her to quench her parched throat with a little water. For mother and daughter are inseparable, and are ever worshipped together.

At last she came to Eleusis, where Celeus was king, and seated herself by the Maiden's Well in the shade of an olive tree. There came to the well to collect water the daughters of Celeus, and they addressed her with the respect due to her venerable years. For Demeter had disguised herself as an elderly woman named Doso, a refugee from pirates. And in this matronly guise, she begged for work.

Lovely Callidice answered her: 'Our mother Metaneira has but lately borne a son. No one in this town would turn you away, for your demeanour is stately and godlike, but let me ask her. She would appreciate help in rearing our brother Demophoön.' When the girls returned from the well, Metaneira was delighted and told them to bring Doso back home. And the goddess followed them, her heart grieving and her head veiled. But when she stood in the doorway, Metaneira looked up and for a moment saw her as a goddess, only to dismiss the vision.

The weeks and months passed, and in the goddess's tender care the babe grew bonny and blithe. For by day Demeter anointed him with divine ambrosia, and at night she buried him in the embers of the fire, for she knew how to make him immortal. Her heart was filled with the joy of tending to the boy, though she yearned ceaselessly for Persephone.

But one night Metaneira saw Demeter burying her son in the coals and screamed out loud for sheer terror. In fury, Demeter snatched the boy from the fire and cast him aside. 'Fools! Ignorant mortals!' she cried, revealing herself in her godhood. 'I would have made your son deathless, but now he shall be no more blessed than others, except that he has been nursed by a goddess. For I am Demeter, and all worship me.' And she commanded the people of Eleusis to build her a temple, where her mysteries would be celebrated for all time.

But Demeter mourned her missing daughter with fresh tears, and devised a terrible punishment for gods and men. Crops were stillborn in the barren soil, or, if they appeared at all, it was only to wither with blight. First their cattle died, their sheep and goats, and then human beings themselves were starving to death. Moreover, the gods were not receiving their due in sacrifices, for there was nothing for men to give.

This was intolerable to Zeus, and he sent many-hued Iris, the rainbow messenger of the gods, arcing down to where Demeter sat in Eleusis. 'Come back!' implored Iris. 'Let Zeus the cloud-gatherer make you welcome once more in the high halls of Olympus!' But Demeter hardened her heart and shut her ears. She vowed that never again would she tread the paths of fragrant Olympus unless she could do so with her daughter at her side.

Taking matters in hand, Zeus sent swift-darting Hermes to escort Persephone out of the underworld and into the light of day – to rejoin her mother. 'Come with me,' he said, 'or all mortal men will perish, whose lives are but the shadow of a dream, and the gods will have no one to honour them.'

Hades understood, and turned to his bride, who was seated beside him, as befits the queen of the underworld; but still in her heart she pined for her mother. 'Go, my dear!' he said. 'Console your sorrowing mother. And when you return, you shall have high honour as my wife.' But he did not entirely trust her to return of her own accord, and he gave her the sweet seed of a pomegranate to eat, the forbidden food of the dead, so that she was bound to come back, and not to dwell for ever on Olympus with her dark-cloaked mother.

Hades loaned Hermes his own chariot, and Hermes sped with Persephone by his side to Eleusis. The reunion of mother and daughter was as joyful and tearful as may be imagined – but suddenly Demeter pulled out of their embrace, sensing a trick. 'Tell me, daughter,' she asked, 'did you eat anything while you were there in the underworld? If you did not, you will be free to dwell with me and the immortal gods for ever on Olympus. If you ate even the slightest morsel, you are bound to return, to live as Hades' bride in the underworld for a third of every year; for so the Fates have ordained it. And for that time, the soil shall be barren in its mourning.'

So it is. Demeter returned to Olympus and the fields began once more to produce their rich harvests. And Triptolemus, the son of Celeus, received from her the gift of agriculture, and became her missionary. On a chariot drawn by dragons, he travelled the earth, teaching men how to cultivate the soil. But the time comes every year when Persephone goes back to dread Hades and takes her seat beside him as his bride, with sombre Hecate as her handmaid. On earth, the fruits begin to fade and the leaves of the trees to fall; but when she returns to the light of Olympus and the upper world, the flowers bloom afresh and roots spread deep and wide in the fertile soil.

So Demeter has the respect of the gods who live on Olympus, and dwells there for ever in high honour. Once she took a human lover, Iasion, in a thrice-ploughed furrow, but hard-hearted Zeus blasted the man with his thunderbolt for his boldness. And she too was once angry with a mortal man and punished him. Erysichthon, grandson of Poseidon, took twenty of his men, full giants in size, to cut down trees to make a banqueting hall, and

chose trees from a grove beloved of the goddess. When the tree
nymphs cried out loud in their pain, she appeared to him as
her own priestess and tried to dissuade him, but he rashly threatened her with an axe. 'Away!' he cried. 'Or I fix my keen blade
in your flesh!'

For his greed and impiety she cursed him with insatiable and
relentless hunger. However much he ate, he was never satisfied,
and his flesh never filled out, until he shrank to no more than
skin and bones. Hunger lay deep in his belly, and he ate everything in his house, including the cat, so that the vermin ran
free. And then he was reduced, the son of a king, to begging at
the crossroads for stale crusts and rancid refuse. Beware the
gods! May care and moderation be your watchwords!

Aphrodite

Sing of Aphrodite, all you Muses! Sing of her pale loveliness,
that no man can resist! Sing of the fair-crowned, laughter-
loving goddess, born in the foam off Cyprus, wife of Hephaestus
and lover of grim Ares! For her the seas grow calm, the
meadows put forth flowers and butterflies, the storms abate.
For her gardens bloom. In her train wild wolves and panthers
follow with adoration in their eyes and tails wagging in sub-
mission. The dove is hers, blessed, smiling Aphrodite, weaver
of charms, and her attendants are the Graces and Eros, who
is Love. Hers is the allure of sex, hers the magic girdle that
makes any woman irresistible. Sometimes she cares not where
she finds a lover, but sex within wedlock is her first domain
and lawfully begotten children; and the first prostitutes were
women of Cyprus who denied her divinity and were henceforth
compelled to bear the shame of selling their bodies to all and

sundry. For the goddess may bring honour, but she may also bring disgrace.

Now, Pygmalion was horror-struck by these whores, and denied himself a wife or the pleasures of the marriage bed. But he made a statue of ivory, as white as snow, and made it more beautiful than any living woman. So lifelike was the statue that you would have sworn it had merely paused for a moment before continuing on its way. And Pygmalion fell in love with his creation, kissed it and caressed it gently for fear of bruising its pale loveliness, and called it Galatea. He brought it gifts and love tokens, and dressed it in the finest clothes and jewellery.

It was the day of Aphrodite's festival, and everyone turned out for the procession. Pygmalion accompanied his offering at the altar of the goddess with a prayer, which he dared not utter aloud. But kindly Aphrodite understood his need and the flame flared bright on her altar. When Pygmalion returned home, he greeted his statue with a kiss – and it seemed to him that she was warmer, softer than before. Cautiously, but with rising anticipation, he looked into her face and saw beautiful eyes shining back at him with equal measures of love and astonishment. He touched her breasts, caressed her body. She was alive! His unspoken prayer had been answered! Praise be to the goddess!

The grandson of Pygmalion was Cinyras, and he in his turn had a daughter called Myrrha. Though courted by many for her beauty, Aphrodite inflamed Myrrha with an unholy passion for her father, for her mother had boasted that her daughter was more fair than the goddess. Myrrha lay awake night after night, wrestling with this demon, consumed by her ungodly passion. Eventually, with the help of a servant, she consummated her love in the secret spaces of dark night. When Cinyras found out that he had been sleeping with his own daughter, he was terrified and filled with anger. To hate one's father is a lesser crime than to love him like this. As she fled from his wrath, Myrrha prayed to the gods for deliverance, and was turned into the myrrh tree, for ever shedding bitter tears. But Myrrha was pregnant and the child continued to grow inside the tree, until his day came. The baby boy was born, and tended by nymphs, and his name was Adonis.

The child, so unlawfully begotten, was so lovely that Aphrodite wanted to keep him for herself, and she hid him in a chest, and gave him to Persephone for safekeeping. But Persephone peeked inside the chest, and wanted the child for herself. The cries of the quarrelling goddesses came to the ears of Zeus on Olympus, and he decreed that the boy would spend a third of the year with each of the two goddesses, and a third of the year wherever and with whomsoever he chose. And fair Adonis chose to stay with Aphrodite for that third of the year as well.

Adonis grew up to be the ideal of young masculinity, and Aphrodite's heart was pierced. Love shook her mind like a storm wind falling on tall trees. She was so much in love that she shunned the lofty halls of Olympus, and lingered no more in the shade on soft pillows, but joined her lover every day in his hunting, until her fair skin was darkened and scratched.

But one day, when Aphrodite was not with him, Adonis was fatally gored by a wild boar, the most savage and unpredictable of the huntsman's quarry. Even the best have been known to fail, and this boar was sent by Ares, Aphrodite's jealous lover. Aloft in her chariot, trim-ankled Aphrodite heard the youth's dying groans and raced down, only to find him a corpse. With a prayer to Persephone, she sprinkled nectar in a death rite on the boy's spilled blood, and a delicate flower sprang up. Like

Adonis, the anemone clings poorly to life and spreads its frail beauty for but a brief spell. And ever after women mourn in the name of Adonis the uncertain swiftness of life's passing.

Adonis was not the first mortal man to receive the fair goddess's love, but his wretched predecessor had been a puppet manipulated by divine intrigues. Zeus wanted to teach sly Aphrodite a lesson. She had proved very expert at causing other gods to fall for humans, but she had always stood apart from such unions herself. So the lord of gods and men showered handsome Anchises, who tended cattle in the hills above Troy, with the essence of virility. So smitten was the golden-haired goddess that she would let nothing stand in the way of their love. She returned straight away to Cypriot Paphos, to her great temple, adorned with star and crescent moon, and there the Graces bathed her and anointed her with divinely perfumed oil of ambrosia, heavenly in its sweetness. But deep in her aching heart she knew that Anchises was a mortal, due to die.

That night she found her beloved alone in the hills. She appeared to him in the form of a ripe young virgin, and the moonlight silvered the swell of her breasts. Anchises met the passionate longing in her gaze; he loosened her willing girdle and, all unknowing, made love to a goddess. When he awoke, Aphrodite showed herself to him in her true form, and he was afraid and cast down his eyes. He knew that those who sleep with goddesses lose their potency ever after. But she said: 'Fear not! For the beds of the gods are not unproductive, and I shall bear for you a son, Aeneas. He shall be raised in the mountains by nymphs, and his children's children will rule the earth!' And so it came to pass. Aeneas escaped from the sack of Troy, bearing his father on his back, and, after many adventures, founded the seven-hilled city of Rome. But Anchises boasted of his night with Aphrodite, and was crippled for his arrogance.

Without Aphrodite, the weaver of snares, Paris would never have won fair Helen, whose face launched a thousand ships. Without Aphrodite, Hippomenes would never have loosened the girdle of majestic Atalanta. The stately daughter of Schoeneus of Boeotia delighted in nothing so much as hunting. She let all her suitors know that she would wed only the one who could beat her in a cross-country race. She was fair of face and slender of body, so her suitors were many, but none could defeat her, and for all the price of defeat was death. Often she would give the hapless man a head start, and then run after him and kill him when she caught up; for they ran bearing shield and sword. It was not that she hated men, but an oracle had warned her to beware of marriage.

But Hippomenes, son of Megareus, loved the tall maiden and was determined to wed her. He brought with him three golden apples, imbued by Aphrodite with irresistible charm. When he and Atalanta raced, he rolled one apple in front of her and, tempted, she picked it up. This delayed her, but soon she caught Hippomenes up again – and he rolled the second apple. And then the third was enough to allow him to reach the finishing line before her. True to her vow, she happily married Hippomenes, but her foolish husband forgot to thank Aphrodite for the gift of the apples. In punishment, the slender-ankled goddess had the two lovers comport themselves with passionate indiscretion in the shrine of the Mother of All, who turned them for their sin into sexless lions to draw her chariot. So the oracle was true that told Atalanta to beware of marriage. By such stories as these we may come to some little understanding of the power and nature of the gods.

By Hermes, Aphrodite bore Hermaphroditus. One day, the

youth was wandering in the hills of Caria when he came across a beautiful pool, limpid and fresh. It was the home of the nymph Salmacis, and she was unable to resist her desire for the handsome lad. When he undressed and entered the pool to bathe, she stripped off her clothes and joined him. The virgin boy was frightened and tried to fight her off, but Salmacis clung to him and entwined herself around him. 'You shall never escape me!' she cried. 'May the gods hear my prayer: let us never be separated!' From then on they became as one being, but with both male and female attributes. In his distress Hermaphroditus cried out to his parents, that they should curse the pool. And ever thereafter, any man who steps into the pool emerges less than a man.

By Dionysus Aphrodite bore Priapus, the lecherous god of gardens. With his gnome-like figure and enormous, swollen phallus, he scares all evil from the gardens of those who worship and pray to him, and his curses fall on those who presume to trespass on ground that is under his protection. He it was who taught infant Ares first to dance, and only then to make war.

Ares

When men meet in hand-to-hand combat, as they frequently do in this Age of Iron, there is Ares. His domain is not strategy, not distance killing, but the frenzy, the rage, the screaming madness born of the stark immediacy of killing or being killed, when you can smell the breath and salt sweat of your adversary. Ares *is* the madness, and he is the most feared and hated of the gods, for there is no one and nothing, save only Father Zeus, who can control his lawlessness.

At the same time there is no god to match him for virility, for only men of courage can be possessed by him, while others shrink and flee. Golden-helmeted, bronze-armoured, strong-fisted Ares launches himself eagerly at every battlefield, and if he is seen by mortal men, it is as a dark storm hovering over the combatants, and he moves with the muscular menace of a wild boar. He is the war whoop, and his sons are Fear and Terror, and goat-footed Pan rides by his side to panic those who are destined to be the losers. At Ares' shout the mountains tremble, the sky darkens, and all creatures run for cover.

Now, Ares, born of Hera, fathered heroic warriors on a number of mortal women, but his natural partner is and always was Aphrodite. As the Magnesian stone attracts iron, so the two of them are drawn to each other. And though Aphrodite was given by Zeus to Hephaestus, Ares scorned her marriage and seduced the fair goddess, though she was not unwilling. None knew of their affair, but in time they were seen by Helios, the sun-god, who told lame Hephaestus. In his wrath, the cuckolded god went straight to his workshop, and made a net of gossamer strands, so fine that they were invisible even to immortal eyes, and so strong that not even the god of war could break them in his rage. It was as though the net were made out of the strength of non-things: the stillness of dawn, the sinews of the winds, the potential of an acorn, the sound of a bluebell. And he cunningly fastened the web-like trap to Aphrodite's bed.

Then Hephaestus took his leave of lofty Olympus and pre-tended to go to the island of Lemnos, his beloved retreat. Ares wasted no time. As soon as he saw the blacksmith god limp away, he went straight to Aphrodite and found the goddess bedecked with flowers. The lovers retired without delay to the bed chamber, anticipating joy; but when they sank down upon the cushions and turned to each other, Hephaestus' magic net closed around them and pinned them where they lay, naked in each other's embrace.

Hephaestus returned on cue and found the lovers lying there, and the sight was as a sword in his heart. He cried out in his pain and bitter anger: 'Father Zeus, and all you gods! Come and see how Aphrodite despises me for my lameness and incapacity, and takes as her lover Ares, just because he is a fine figure of a god. But at least I have my revenge. I shall keep the two of them trapped there, until Father Zeus has returned to me all the gifts I gave him as the bride-price of Aphrodite. He owes me: it's because of him that I'm lame and despised.'

While the goddesses stayed away out of modesty, all the gods ran up to see the sight, and roared with laughter at the plight of the lovers. Seeing Aphrodite lying naked there, they gazed lustfully on her, and bold Hermes declared that it would be worth the netted humiliation to spend time in bed with the beautiful goddess of love. But Poseidon begged Hephaestus to free them, and promised that he would be paid all that he felt was his due. And so Hephaestus freed the lovers, and Ares fled in shame to Thrace, while Aphrodite retired to her temple at Paphos, where the Graces attended her and restored her wounded pride.

Hephaestus

Hephaestus is the god of fire, an outsider, unkempt and accustomed to mockery. He works in his underground forges while the other gods are idle, as if he were of another caste. Driven to the margins by his deformity and his work, he is the blacksmith magician, encrusted with soot and dirt from his furnace, but creating objects of extraordinary beauty and utility out of dull rock. Magicians must always work on the margins, or lose their objectivity.

Many are the marvellous and intricate devices made by the hands of Hephaestus, and all artisans, but especially metalworkers, honour him in their hearts. He is attended in his workshop by the Cyclopes, the first forgers of Zeus' thunderbolt, but also by golden automata, made by Hephaestus himself. He made the gods' homes, Zeus' aegis with its hundred golden tassels, greaves for Heracles, and a full set of armour for Achilles.

Hunched from birth, he disgusted his mother Hera, who flung him off high Olympus into the depths of the moaning sea, and the twisting of his ankle as she whirled the baby around lamed him for ever. Thetis reared him in her cave on the shores of Ocean, and he made for her jewellery of surpassing fineness. But he was angry with his mother, and wanted to humiliate her as she had humiliated him. He wrought for her a beautiful golden throne, of palpable majesty, and sent it to her Olympian palace as a present, a token of peace between them. All unwitting, Hera delighted in the ornate throne – but as soon as she sat in it, it held her fast and rose high into the air.

The enraged goddess, the embarrassed queen of gods and men, sent Ares to bring Hephaestus back to high Olympus and free her. Ares sped to Ocean on a chariot of fire, but Hephaestus beat him off with his torches, shouting in his pain and grief that he had no mother. But Dionysus was the friend of Hephaestus, and he went to visit him in his volcanic forge, and plied him with cup after cup of the finest wine, sufficient even for a god. The wine loosened Hephaestus' limbs and freed his caged anger. Dionysus escorted the drunken deity back to Olympus, slumped astride a mule, and he agreed to release his mother, if his father would grant him a favour.

Once the throne had been rendered harmless, Hephaestus begged the almighty son of Cronus to allow him to make stern Athena his bed-partner. Zeus smiled in pity and gave him permission to try, for Athena had sworn to remain inviolate. Though lame and ugly, Hephaestus approached her with brash confidence, but she spurned him, and he spilled his seed upon the ground. In later years, from the impregnated soil arose Erichthonius, earth-born king of Athens.

But Hephaestus, having failed with Athena, asked instead, as his reward for freeing cow-eyed Hera, that Aphrodite herself might become his wife; and great Zeus the cloud-gatherer granted his wish, for she was surely not a sworn virgin. But the marriage was neither of Aphrodite's choosing nor to her taste.

Athena

Sing now, Muse, of keen-eyed Athena, whom Metis bore for Zeus. But when Metis was close to her time, Zeus swallowed her, anxious lest a son be born mightier than him, who would take his place and rule over gods and men. For even the gods cannot always turn aside Fate.

But divine Athena was compelled to her birth, and in her great need sought a channel out of her father. Every avenue she explored, until she came to his head. In the extremity of his labour Zeus cried out for relief, and the halls of Olympus trembled at the sound. Even in the din-filled depths of his forge, Hephaestus heard the cries and hobbled as fast as he could to where Zeus sat on his throne, holding his head with his hands. Without hesitation, he boldly raised his axe and split open the head of Zeus, the mighty lord of gods and men, and out sprang Athena, fully formed and fully clad in golden armour, her grey eyes flashing. Lofty Olympus shuddered in fear at the power of the goddess, and the earth shrieked. Waves billowed on the sea and then fell into a dead calm, and Helios the sun-god stopped his chariot for a timeless moment in the sky, until new-born Athena unstrapped her armour, and Fear slunk out of the room.

Her appearance is that of a fair and stately woman in the prime of life, but she was born of her father, and her mind is wholly her father's; her masculine mind and her martial prowess keep her apart from the other goddesses. She has a rare beauty, but it trumpets her untouchability, and no man or god dares to approach her, for she has sworn to preserve her virginity. By accident, the Theban seer Teiresias once saw her bathing, and she placed her hands over his eyes, blinding him, though he had been woman as well as man.

Athena was the first teacher of all the household crafts that form the basis of society. She made the first ship and wagon, the first plough and loom. Perfection in craft is also hers, and so she is both the ever-near protector of the household and the owl-eyed protector of cities; if they are threatened, she will surely respond, and the snake that lies coiled at her feet will rise up hissing. She fights not with passionate rage, like Ares, but with skill and prudence; he loves danger, but she finds ways to make danger safe. She is the strategist, the leader of hosts, and Ares carries out her will. Victory and glory she holds in her hands. And Zeus honoured his beloved daughter with the gift of his aegis, for it may be cast as protection over a whole city. It is a mighty weapon, as well as a shield, for the sound of the aegis, shaken over a battlefield, is so terrible that trembling seizes the limbs of all who hear it.

There was a time when Arachne of Colophon won fame throughout Lydia for her spinning and weaving, though she was of humble birth. Even the nymphs of the mountains and winding rivers travelled far to see her handiwork, or just to see her hands at work. And when they compared her to Athena, Arachne said: 'Let her compete with me if she wants.' Athena came to her in the guise of an old woman and said: 'You would do well to heed my advice, girl. Seek only to surpass other mortals in your craft, but leave first place for the goddess. Pray for forgiveness for your rash words.' But Arachne's response was full of scorn. 'Woman, old age has stripped you of your wits!' she cried. 'See how the goddess refuses my challenge.' 'No!' cried Athena, casting off her disguise. 'She is here!'

The two set about their embroidery. The theme of Athena's work was her own victory over Poseidon in the contest for patronage of Athens, and she embellished the border with examples of the folly of mortals who challenge the gods. But Arachne showed the gods as seducers and deceivers of mortal women, and her work was perfect. Even Athena could find no fault with it, and in her pride and anger the dread goddess forced the girl to suicide. But as the maiden was gasping out her last breath in the stranglehold of the noose, Athena let her live, but as a spider, so that she could hang and spin for ever.

Apollo

All hail, blessed Leto, mother of the lord Apollo and the lady Artemis! When you were pregnant and your time was due, you travelled the known world, seeking a safe haven where you could give birth. But dread of Apollo gripped all the lands, and only the humble island of Delos was willing to accept you – and him. For the barren island had nothing to distinguish it, but as the centre of the worship of the golden youth it has attained wealth and eternal fame. And before it was rootless, a wandering isle, but in gratitude you fixed it in place.

Sacred also to Apollo is Delphi, which lies at the centre of the universe, for Father Zeus released two eagles from the opposite ends of the earth and there they met. When the lord Apollo came down from Olympus to find a site for his oracle, he came to Crisa and slew the she-dragon under snow-capped Parnassus and made the place his own. Crisa came to be known as Delphi, because Apollo, in the form of a dolphin, brought Cretan sailors to land there to serve as the first priests of his oracular sanctuary

Nowadays, young maidens serve as Apollo's Sibyls. But though Apollo speaks through the mouths of maidens elsewhere as well, he declares the law most clearly from Delphi, and the heavens there are filled with light that gleams on the precipices of the Shining Rocks and sparkles on the crystal waters of the sacred spring. For he is the source of the light of law, education, and civilization. The lyre is his, and his minstrels play sweet music that soothes the savage breast; for poetry, as we bards know well, is the sister of prophecy.

Rich in gold is Apollo, with golden lyre and golden bow, golden locks and golden tunic. But he is vast, a god who is great enough to contain multitudes. He is the far-shooter, for he must stand apart to do his work, and as well as the lyre, he lays claim to the bow. Sweet music is his, but also the paean – *Ie Paian* – sung in triumph or as a war-cry. He is the god who both spreads the miasma of sickness and disperses it. He is gentle and violent, fair of face and dark of brow, healer and destroyer. Praise the god in his greatness! May he grant us only good and avert all evil in our days! Whoever knows Apollo is raised to greatness; whoever does not know him is bound to be of lowly estate.

Now, Athena, stately goddess, invented the pipes to imitate the sweet, keening sound of the dirge the Gorgons made to mourn Medusa's death. She delighted in the reedy tone, stepping lightly in time. But as she was playing the pipes one day, she caught sight of her reflection in a pond, and hated the way she was disfigured by the straps that bound the pipes to her face. Away she hurled the loathed instrument, and it flew to Phrygia. There it was picked up by a Satyr, Marsyas, who learnt to play so sweetly that the clouds wept with sadness at the plaintive melody.

In pride at his accomplishment, Marsyas challenged Apollo to a contest, pipes against lyre. 'So be it,' agreed golden-haired Apollo, 'and let the winner do whatever he likes with the loser!' Marsyas spent some time in contemplation, listening to the source of sound, and when he played it was as if he had heard the secret song of the world. Apollo himself, with his lyre, could do no better – but he was a god, and tolerated no such insult as Marsyas' challenge. He flayed all the skin from Marsyas' body, and the Satyr's tears formed the river that still bears his name.

Many are the tales that are told of Apollo. Ever fair and ever young, he has loved and been loved by many a maiden and youth. He loved Daphne, fair nymph, daughter of the river Peneus. His passion for her was as none before or since, for he had sneered at the arrows of Eros, saying that *his* aim was more true; in response the god of love simply loosed a single barb at the golden god. Even he, the healer, had no cure for this sickness. But Daphne had sworn to remain a virgin, and repulsed his advances. She was loved also by Leucippus, the son of Oenomaus, who dressed as a woman to join her throng and be close to her. So Apollo, in his jealousy, put it into Daphne's head to bathe in the river. Poor Leucippus! He desired to see her nudity, but not that she should see his. When he refused to undress and swim with the other girls, his deceit was revealed, and in their outrage Daphne and her friends pulled him into the river and drowned him.

But Apollo was not to be put off, and he pursued her as a hunter pursues a hare, though she ran from him as a lamb flees a wolf. Away she sprinted, but the god sped close on her heels. In desperation she prayed to her father for release from her beauty, so that she should suffer wrong no more. Peneus had no quarrel with Apollo, but he honoured his daughter's vow of chastity, and in an instant her prayer was answered. Even as she was running her limbs stiffened and her toes sought the darkness of the earth. There, in her place, stood a laurel tree. But Apollo loved her still, and made the laurel his sacred tree. Even now the winners at the Pythian games of Delphi receive no material reward but a garland of berried laurel – and the blessing of the god.

Apollo also loved Cassandra, princess of Troy, and when she agreed to give herself to him, he rewarded her with the gift of prophecy. But then she insulted the god by changing her mind. Apollo asked her for one last kiss, and when she turned her face up to him he spat a curse into her mouth. Ever thereafter she was doomed to prophesy in vain, for no one believed a word she said and all took her for a madwoman.

Apollo loved Hyacinthus of Sparta too, and it was their pleasure to anoint themselves with olive oil and test each other's athletic prowess. Once Apollo took into his hands the weighty discus and hurled it true and far. Hyacinthus in his joy ran after the discus, laughing, to pick it up and take his turn at the fair sport. But the Spartan prince had spurned the advances of Zephyrus, the west wind, and in his anger Zephyrus turned the discus back. It struck Hyacinthus full in the face, and he died cradled in Apollo's arms.

Two exalted sons were born to Apollo: the healer Asclepius, and the minstrel Orpheus. Coronis was loved by Apollo, and was pregnant with their son Asclepius; but the white raven, Apollo's bird, saw her lying with another, and told his master. Quick-tempered Apollo seized his bow and shot her dead. But he could not bear that his son should die as well, and even as Coronis lay on the pyre, the mighty god snatched his son out of the flames and his mother's womb, and brought him to the cave of the Centaur Cheiron, for him to raise the boy. But he changed for evermore the raven's colour from white to black, a bitter reward for the bearer of bitter tidings.

Meanwhile, Asclepius grew up to bear his father's gifts as a healer, and even to surpass them, for the time came when the lady Artemis asked him to heal her follower Hippolytus, the son of Theseus, though he was dead. Peerless Asclepius exerted all his skill and at last the young man breathed again – but as a mortal Asclepius had breathed his last, for Zeus blasted him with a thunderbolt for violating the laws of nature. But Asclepius was taken into the heavens, and is the patron god of medicine, beloved by many for his healing power.

Apollo, however, was furious at the killing of his son, and in revenge his swift arrows soon found the hearts of the three Cyclopes, Hephaestus' assistants, makers of Zeus' thunderbolt. But the will of Zeus is not to be scorned, and the son of Cronus, the cloud-gatherer, was ready to hurl Apollo down to Tartarus, to be imprisoned there for ever. But kindly Leto intervened, and instead Apollo was sentenced to serve for one year under Admetus, king of Thessalian Pherae.

Now, Admetus had but a short time to live, and Apollo took pity on his master and begged the Fates to stay his death. The Fates agreed – provided that someone could be found to take Admetus' place. No one was willing, save only loyal Alcestis, his wife, and Admetus accepted her sacrifice. But Heracles wrestled Death himself for the life of fair Alcestis, and won, and restored her to her husband.

Orpheus, son of the far-shooter by the Muse Calliope, was such a gifted musician that, as he sang and played on his lyre, the breezes stopped to listen in, wild beasts followed tamely in his train, and the trees bent down their lofty crowns to hear the sweet strains. Orpheus loved the beautiful oak-nymph Eurydice, and the charm of his music won her heart. But on the day of their wedding, the very day, she was being pursued by Aristaeus, the lustful god of bee-keeping and olive-growing. Deep into the woods she plunged to escape him, where she was bitten by a snake and died.

The world has seen no grief like that of Orpheus. He dared to descend into the underworld, and sang his request to grim Hades and his veiled wife Persephone. At the sound of his song, Cerberus pricked up his ears, Tityus' vultures raised their gory beaks, Sisyphus sat on his boulder and listened. Entranced, the dark deities laid aside their habitual indifference and heard his heartfelt plea, and allowed Eurydice to return from the dead. There was only one condition: Orpheus was not to look back at her until they had left the halls of Hades. Long, dark passages they traversed, and at last they were on the threshold – and just then Orpheus glanced over his shoulder for his beloved, whose footfall behind him he could no longer hear. Immediately, Eurydice lost substance and fell back from whence she had come.

However much he pleaded, however long he lingered on the

banks of the Styx, foul river of the dead, gloomy Charon refused to ferry him across a second time. Orpheus left the banks of Styx and wandered disconsolate in Thrace, choosing wilderness to spare lives, for many would have died from sorrow on hearing his songs of mourning. Only the birds of the air and beasts of the earth suffered the shafts of his bitter strains. But Maenads too choose the wilderness when Dionysus possesses them, and a band of them found him asleep and mistook him for an enemy. They tore him to pieces, and his head and lyre, still lamenting, floated down the Hebrus to the restless sea. But he and his beloved Eurydice were never again separated.

Artemis

As Apollo stands apart, so too does his twin sister Artemis. She is the Mistress of Animals, and her pleasure is in wild and remote places; and she is a chaste virgin, disdainful, undefiled, and free. Men are not to her liking, and as a girl she begged her father Zeus for chastity, and that she should be as great a deity as her noble brother. And great Zeus granted her every desire.

She ranges with her attendant nymphs over shady hills and the windy heights of virgin wilderness, unsullied by man. Pan gave her Arcadian hunting hounds, the best of their kind, and she deals death with arrows crafted by the Cyclopes that well fit her silver bow. She wears the horns of the cold, chaste moon on her headdress. She is the overwhelming and fearsome presence within untamed lands, where mortal men find how puny they are, and as she passes through the moonlight the hills tremble and the valleys with them, and all beasts cry and howl. She is the V of flying geese and the yellow glare of a lynx's eye. She is the All-Mother, the protector of all young creatures, and some she allows to live, while the weaklings are culled. She abides on the margins, at change-over points, especially when girls become women, and women become mothers.

The people of Thebes gave Leto great honour as the mother of the twin deities Apollo and Artemis, but arrogant Niobe, wife of King Amphion, disagreed. As the daughter of Tantalus and granddaughter of Atlas, she claimed that her lineage was greater than that of Leto. She also bragged that, since she had borne and raised a greater number of children, her life was more filled with blessings. And she might indeed have been the happiest of mothers, if only she had not boasted of it.

For the insult to their mother, Apollo and Artemis removed Niobe's blessings: Apollo shot down her six sons, while Artemis did the same with her six daughters, except one called Chloris. The twanging of their bows mingled with the screams of the dying, and the corpses remained unburied for nine days. Niobe was turned to stone and carried away by a tornado to her native Lydia, where her tears still trickle from the obdurate rock of Mount Sipylus.

Apollo and Artemis again avenged Leto's honour when huge Tityus, the son of Earth, tried to rape her as she was on her way one day to Delphi. The twin deities hunted down the giant, and when they found him they riddled him with their arrows. Down to Hades he lurched, where his body is spread out massively over the ground, and on either side sits a vulture, feasting for ever on his liver.

Actaeon of Thebes, learned in the lore of the forest, was relaxing at midday after a morning of good hunting. He loved his aunt, Semele, but she was the beloved of Zeus, and jealous anger swelled in the breast of the great god, father of gods and men. He put it into the mind of Actaeon to take his rest, all unknowing, in a grove favoured by Artemis, where the goddess came to be bathed by her attendant nymphs in a limpid pool of cool water, sheltered by a cave. No mortal man sees Artemis naked and lives! While the nymphs screamed at the sight of a man and tried to cover their mistress's nakedness, she rose to her feet, majestic and unafraid, and revealed all her glory to him in his last moments as a mortal man.

With a mere flick of her wrist, she splashed him lightly with water from the pool, and before the last drops had rolled like tears down his cheeks, antlers were already sprouting from his head. The stag dropped onto all fours and fled, while Actaeon's own hounds gave chase with slavering jaws. He tried to shout at them, to calm them as he had in the past, but instead of their master's voice, they heard only the bellowing of a terrified stag. Soon they caught him and brought him down, and the pack leader's powerful jaws closed over his windpipe and gripped tight, until the stag breathed no more.

With none to command them, the rest of the pack set to and tore him to pieces, who had once been their beloved master. And Artemis, Mistress of Animals, was pleased, for the purity of the goddess is not to be tainted, even by 'accidents'.

Callisto spent her days and nights in the mountains of Arcadia, hunting and living wild with Artemis and her nymphs. But she was very fair, and desire flared in Zeus' heart and loins. He came to her, taking on the appearance of Artemis, as she rested alone one day in a dell. Too late did the maiden discover his trick when he forced his embraces on her. She fought back, but no mortal or god can resist the power of Zeus. The weeks and months rolled by, and the time came when Artemis called on all her followers to bathe with her, for there was no man to see them. Callisto blushed and hesitated, but she had no choice, and her nakedness made her pregnancy plain for all to see. Artemis in anger turned the maiden into a bear and banished her from her entourage; and the bear gave birth to a son, Arcas, who was raised by Maia, the mother of Hermes. But later Callisto wandered into a forbidden sanctuary of Zeus, and was about to be killed by Arcas himself, for he had become a masterful hunter; but Zeus took pity on his former lover and translated her into the heavens as the Great Bear constellation.

Orion was a mighty hunter, the son of Poseidon, and lover of Eos, the dawn light. So vast and fleet of foot was he that he could cross valleys at a bound and his father endowed him with the ability to walk on water. But once, drunk on Chios – for the island produces the best of wines – he raped the king's daughter, and for this sin he was blinded. He took a young boy onto his shoulders, and commanded him to lead him eastward; and as the sun rose, Eos shone her light straight into her lover's eyes and cured him, and he returned to Crete, where he was awarded the unique honour of hunting in the company of Artemis and Leto.

So successful was he at clearing the earth of the ferocious beasts that preyed on men's flocks and livelihoods, that he fell to boasting. 'There's no creature,' he cried, 'that I could not bring down with my strong spear or my swift arrows!' Zeus' brow darkened at this foolish boast, and in anger he sent against Orion a giant scorpion. The contest was over as quick as the flick of the monster's tail. Zeus raised the victor to the heavens, and, at Artemis' request, did the same for Orion; and in the heavens the scorpion chases Orion for ever. Orion, however, chases the Pleiades, the seven daughters of Atlas after whom he had lusted in life. For seven years he had pursued them, until Zeus in his mercy made them stars.

Hermes

Many tales are told too of crafty Hermes, son of Zeus by the nymph Maia. From the moment he came into being, his restless nature was plain. It is said that, on the very day of his birth, he found and killed a tortoise, scooped out the soft flesh, and strung the hollow shell to make the first lyre. Then, that same night, he stole the cattle of the archer-god Apollo. To mislead any who should give chase, he drove the cattle backwards, while walking backwards himself and disguising his barefoot baby prints with oversized sandals, strapped to his feet like snow-shoes.

Having corralled the cattle, he invented the fire-stick, and used it to light a cooking fire on which he roasted two whole cows, and ate them. Then he returned to the cave of his birth and clambered into his cot, cooing innocently. But Apollo guessed who the culprit was and threatened to toss the baby down into Tartarus. At first Hermes lied – 'I'm just a baby! How could I have stolen any cattle?' – but then he confessed, and to be reconciled with Apollo gave him the lyre. Apollo took the instrument as his own, and in return made for Hermes the three-pronged caduceus wand, the living, golden staff that will be his symbol and sign for ever.

Hermes is the god of the sudden and unexpected, the elusive and edgy. He governs thievery, trade and bargaining, messages and mischief, invention and inspiration. He is the trickster and the eternal adolescent, for he comes when least expected, and not always when called. He is the restless god of magic and of luck, his countenance never still. He is the god of borders and crossings; the guardian of flocks, which stray without his guidance; and the wayfinder, into whose hands travellers commend themselves. He appears out of the blue, bringing good fortune or a message from the gods, perhaps in the form of a lucid dream; or he snatches a dying man and guides him to the underworld. For the journey between life and death takes but an instant. When a sudden silence falls or joy thrills a heart, there is Hermes; unanticipated opportunities for love or fortune are his gifts.

Some say that Hermes fathered Pan, goat-footed deity of the mountains and valleys, of the remotest crags and peaks and meadows, and the sweet sounds of his reed pipes echo in the canyons in the late afternoon as the shepherds call their flocks. Pan invented the pipes when he lost the nymph he was chasing and turned his attention instead to the reeds where she had hidden. Another musical maiden he loved was Echo, who could imitate any sound in the world. When she spurned him, he drove some shepherds insane, and they tore the fair nymph to pieces; but Earth buried each scattered piece of her, and still the secret places where her parts are buried return the sounds of others. Pan is the god of shepherds and the hunter of small animals, of the kind that keep men alive during their months of vigil, watching over their flocks in the hills and mountains. But he is also the bringer of panic, when flocks – or men in battle – for no reason stampede and turn to frantic flight. And he was called Pan, 'All', for he was pleasing to all the gods, but especially to Dionysus.

Dionysus

Sweet Muse, tell at last of twice-born Dionysus. His mother was Semele, daughter of Cadmus, whom Zeus loved. But when Hera found out, in her jealousy she plotted her rival's death. She appeared to Semele in the guise of her aged nurse and persuaded her that, as the bedmate of the Ruler of All, she should be the equal of Hera – that Zeus should appear to her as a god, not as a mortal man. And Semele listened to the goddess's honeyed lies, for she wanted to know the greater pleasure of lying with a god not in human form.

When Zeus next came to her in his earthly disguise, she teased her lover and made him promise to do whatever she asked. Her request, of course, was for him to reveal himself. The great god hesitated, for he knew what would happen. But he had given his word and came blazing to her bed. As Hera had planned, Semele was consumed by the brilliance of Zeus' majesty, but the cloud-gatherer took up his unborn son from her lifeless womb and sewed him up in his thigh, from where he was born again when his time came. Later on, Dionysus went down to Hades to recover his mother, and she dwells now for ever with the blessed gods on Olympus.

Dionysus is the god of viticulture and wine, a joy for mortal men, and hence of ecstasy and liberation from the conventions of society. He is the sap of life, the blood throbbing in the veins, the sweet burst of the grape in the mouth. He is the god of the theatre, for men permit themselves to release their emotions, for better or for worse, when absorbed in the marvellous productions of playwrights. Dionysus is known as Bromius, the rebel, and his robe is as gorgeous as any girl's.

His gift is freedom, and so little regard has he for what men call 'law' and 'custom' that his followers, the raving Maenad women, are said to tear apart wild animals and eat them raw, when they are possessed by the god and endowed with superhuman strength. They drink his blood as wine, and eat his flesh. For the other gods keep their distance, but Dionysus possesses his followers completely and is wholly possessed in return. Clad in fawnskins and clutching the sacred thyrsus staff, entwined with ivy and topped with a pine cone, they revel with wild abandon in the countryside to the sound of the pipes and the cymbal, grasping poisonous snakes with immunity and petting tame panthers. Meanwhile, the horse-eared Sileni and goat-bearded Satyrs who attend the god go about their lustful business.

Many a tale is told of the fate suffered by those who resist the entry of his shocking and unconventional religion. When Lycurgus of Thrace drove his followers off the mountain, great Zeus, the father of Dionysus, blinded the man for his blindness. And when all the women of Thebes thronged to the hills and forests to worship the god, King Pentheus persecuted them, and for his pains was killed by his own mother and sisters. The fool spied on their worship and was discovered, but the women failed to recognize him in their god-induced frenzy. They tore him limb from limb as easily as they would a rabbit, relishing their gruesome task as a sign of their devotion to the god.

And in Boeotian Orchomenus the daughters of Minyas refused to acknowledge the god's divinity and join the other women in the countryside. They preferred to stay indoors, as they believed good women should, and get on with their weaving. Dionysus appeared to them as a girl to warn them of their folly, for the god is not without pity, but they ignored him. He drove them mad, and one of them tore her own baby to bits.

In the course of his missionary travels, spreading the word of his religion, Dionysus came to Athens. There he taught King Pandion the art of nurturing the vine and turning its fruit into blessed wine, but some drunken peasants, not appreciating the divine gift of the god, thought their king had poisoned them. They killed Pandion and hid his body. His daughter Erigone, led to the woodland grave by her father's faithful dog, hanged herself in grief from a sturdy branch. But Dionysus always retaliates. He drove the women of Athens mad, and for ever after they propitiate the god by hanging little fetishes of Erigone in trees and setting them to swing.

Once, as a youth, Dionysus was captured by pirates as he walked on the shore, and they were pleased, for they thought him the son of a king and worth a fine ransom. They bound him with strong rope, but the ropes fell in worthless coils to the deck of the ship. When the pirates remained heedless of this warning, further signs appeared: the ship's hull flowed with sweet wine; vines and ivy, thick with fruit and blooming flowers, entwined the mast and the sails; and phantom shapes, as of tigers and panthers, prowled the deck. Then the god became a lion and devoured the ship's captain, while the rest of the sailors leapt into the sea and were turned into dolphins. Only the helmsman survived, for he had recognized the god's divinity, and carried him safely over the waters to his holy haven, the lush island of Naxos.

On high Olympus, the gods are attended at their golden feasts by Hebe, daughter of Zeus and Hera, for she is the ideal of young nubile womanhood, loyal to her elder kin and dedicated to their service. But Zeus' special cup-bearer is Ganymede, once the mortal prince of Troy, so fair of face and form that Zeus could not resist his charms and had him carried up to Olympus by a whirlwind, though some say Zeus bore him off himself, in the form of an eagle. The lad's father Tros was grieved, for he did not know where his son had gone; but Zeus sent Hermes to give him the glad tidings that Ganymede was held high in Zeus' honour and would remain youthful for ever.

As further recompense for his loss, Zeus gave Tros immortal horses, the pick of his shining herds. And so fair Ganymede stands devotedly by the throne of Zeus, ready with the golden cup of sweet nectar. And Hebe modestly supervises the feasting and ensures that all appetites are satisfied at the banquet table of the gods.

These are the gods and goddesses who dwell for ever in bliss in the halls of high Olympus. The tales that are told about them imbue them with traits like our own, as though they were simply many times more powerful and wise than mortal men and women. Yet one unbridgeable chasm is set between them and creatures of mere flesh and bone: the gods cannot die! They are eternal and carefree, while men soon wither and die like leaves from a tree, and their lives are filled with toil and sorrow. The gods are, then, finally incomprehensible to mortal minds, just as a monkey cannot understand a man, and that is why we speak of them in parables. The storyteller's job is to shed light, no more.

4

The Age of Heroes

The Flood

There have been several ages of man, or at least of creatures that we might recognize as human. But in between each age, a cosmic catastrophe more or less destroys the human race, and leaves little memory of the preceding age, and little continuity between them. Such is the history of man: progress cut short by catastrophe. So will it always be, until men learn to worship the gods and the earth aright.

First, in the era of Cronus, came the race of golden men, each sprung fully mature from the earth. They had no need to work, or even to cook, for Earth put forth all her bounty freely, and it was theirs for the taking. Nor did they fall ill or grow old: they remained in their prime, and just died one day gently in their sleep, returning to the earth from which they had been born. Of these men and their life of leisured ease no trace remains, unless any of them linger as kindly ghosts upon the earth. It's hard to say even if they were like us in form, whether we would recognize them as human beings, since they were born from the earth, not of human mothers; for there were as yet no women. They preceded the formation of all animals by Zeus and the Olympian gods, and they came long before Prometheus' gift of fire, by which we measure the foundation of the human species. For the earth was still very young.

But the next two races of men – the silver and the bronze, the first two races that benefited from Prometheus' gift of fire – proved unsatisfactory. The men of silver were fair but witless; immature and irresponsible until they were a hundred years old, they then promptly died. And while they lived, like children, they abused one another and failed to recognize the gods. In due course of time Zeus did away with this race, but the bronze one that followed was little better. They were hulking men, with huge bodies; many had thick hides of bronze. They had limited intelligence, and delighted only in war, until they wiped one another off the face of the earth, and now they dwell for ever in Hades.

Zeus sent a flood to finish off these brutes, but Prometheus ensured that the human race would continue. His son Deucalion and Epimetheus' daughter Pyrrha repopulated the earth, and thereby became the ancestors of the next race, the race of heroes. Many of them too perished untimely in war or other ventures, but the earth thrived for a while, and there are many tales of the heroes to be told. Humankind had at last fulfilled the potential bestowed on it by Prometheus. But now, by a simple process of degeneration, we live in the Age of Iron, when human life is nothing but toil and suffering and early death. That's all the Age of Iron has to offer. The gods no longer linger with mortal men on earth, as they did in the time of the heroes, but have removed themselves in carefree abandonment of the human race. Truly the poet sang: 'Best not to have been born at all, or else to die as early as possible.'

Let one story of the hateful men of bronze suffice for them all. Lycaon, king of Arcadia, had many sons, and they were notorious for their subhuman savagery. By then Zeus had in any case endured enough of the depredations of their kind, and he visited Lycaon and his sons in the guise of a poor pilgrim, to see for himself how wicked they were. At the king's banquet table, they served him the flesh and intestines of a recently slaughtered child. Zeus in disgust pushed the dish away and departed at once. He was now determined to eliminate the race of bronze; they had no redeeming features. He saw that the heart of that race was a pit writhing with serpents and maggots, and that if they were ever good it was only out of fear of him. So he gave them reason to fear him.

First, he locked up all the warring winds in a cave, so that they might not scatter the clouds, save only the wet south wind, whose beard and misty-white locks dripped with rain, and storm clouds hovered on his brow. The rain that fell smelled of promise and decay, but it was heavy enough to flatten crops within a few hours, and then flood the fields. Zeus called upon his brother Poseidon to help, and the earth-shaker commanded all the rivers to overflow their banks. The flood waters tore down trees, bore away cattle and men, houses and wagons. Streams became torrents, torrents became mighty rivers, rivers became lakes. Before long, even the tallest towers had vanished beneath the surging waves, and the whole surface of the earth was sea. Fish swam among the branches of trees, and turtles paddled where goats had grazed. Many of those who survived drowning later succumbed to starvation, since there was little food to be found anywhere.

But Deucalion was a rarity, a righteous man in the Age of Bronze, taught well by his father Prometheus. The Titan warned him of the impending deluge, and Deucalion built an ark, no more than an oversized chest, and stocked it with provisions for himself and his wife. The curious vessel bobbed along, at the mercy of the wind and the waves, and on the tenth day it struck one of the two peaks of Mount Parnassus, which were now lone islets in the endless expanse of sea. There Deucalion found a sanctuary of Themis, and he and Pyrrha prayed in tears for the restoration of the human race. And the goddess taught him, saying: 'You and your wife are to veil your heads, and as you walk from my sanctuary, throw behind you the bones of your mother.'

The two of them, husband and wife, deliberated for a while about what the goddess might mean. Then they left the sanctuary, tossing over their shoulders behind them stones, the bones of the all-mother Earth. And immediately, as each stone landed on the earth with a thump, it softened and took shape. Those that Deucalion threw sprang up from the mountaintop as men, and those that Pyrrha tossed were women. All other creatures emerged from the warm mud as the waters receded. So all the men of the next era, the Age of Heroes, descend from Deucalion or some other fortunate survivor. For there were a few, but only a few. The will of Zeus was carried out.

The Line of Deucalion

Deucalion and Pyrrha also had a son Hellen, from whom all the Greeks, the Hellenes, are descended. In their blood are mingled the spirits of both Prometheus and Epimetheus. The sons of Hellen were Dorus, Aeolus, and Xuthus, whose sons were Ion and Achaeus. And so the tribes of the Greeks are the Dorians, the Aeolians, the Ionians, and the Achaeans.

Aeolus had many sons and daughters, who became in their turn the forebears of heroes. Some tales are told of his sons. Salmoneus got ideas above his station, and began to style himself Zeus. He rode around in a chariot that had been equipped, farcically, with bronze jars and pine torches, to imitate Zeus' thunder and lightning. Zeus hurled him down into Tartarus, to suffer eternal torment, and he annihilated his followers, for many had obeyed the mad king's injunctions to bow down and worship him. Only his daughter Tyro was spared, for she had fallen out with her father over his delusions. Poseidon lay with her in the curl of a wave, and she became the mother of Pelias and Neleus, while to her husband Cretheus she bore Aeson, Pheres, and Amythaon – heroes all, but their children were even mightier.

Poseidon slept too with Aeolus' daughter Canace, and one of their sons was Aloeus, whose wife Iphimedea was also loved by Poseidon. Two strapping sons she bore him, Otus and Ephialtes, but they shared the arrogance of Salmoneus and resolved to overthrow the reign of Zeus and the Olympian gods. By the age of nine, the boys were nine fathoms tall and nine cubits wide. They feared only Ares, god of war, but through treachery they bound him in fetters and imprisoned him in an inescapable jar of bronze. Through treachery also the whereabouts of Ares was revealed to Hermes by the giants' stepmother, and he released his brother, the god of war. When Otus and Ephialtes began their assault on heaven, by piling up mountains – Ossa on lofty Olympus, and Pelion on Ossa, a monstrous ladder by which to ascend to the heavens – they were summarily destroyed by the war god, cast down in a tangle of bloodied and broken limbs. For the new breed of men, the descendants of Deucalion, had almost as deep and wide a vein of hubris in their souls as their brazen predecessors.

The famous Sisyphus was another son of Aeolus, but his fame rests on the torment devised for him. It was said that, despite being married to Merope, one of the seven daughters of Atlas, he secretly visited Anticlea, the wife of Laertes, and that she conceived Odysseus from the union, but concealed the fact and passed the baby off as Laertes'. But Sisyphus' crime was this. Zeus was in love with Aegina, daughter of the river Asopus, and abducted her to the island that would bear her name, keeping her there as his concubine. Asopus searched everywhere for his daughter, but could find her nowhere. It was Sisyphus who told him the truth, and for this Zeus sent Death to him. But Sisyphus wrestled with Death and bound him fast; and the natural order of things ceased, for no one now could die. But dark-browed Ares released Death from his fetters and handed Sisyphus over to him.

The son of Aeolus made one last attempt to cheat death: he forbade his wife to perform the customary funeral rites, so that Charon could not let him cross the river Styx and join the rest of the dead in the underworld. But Sisyphus had no more tricks to play, and eventually he died in earnest. Suspecting that he would try to escape again, Hades devised for Sisyphus a terrible punishment. Unceasingly, he is compelled to roll a heavy boulder up a hill; when he reaches the top, the boulder rolls back down again to the bottom, and Sisyphus has to begin again. Thus men should know not to anger the gods.

The Argonauts and the Golden Fleece

Athamas, son of Aeolus and king of Boeotia, took as his wife Nephele, the cloud, and she bore him two fine children, a boy and a girl, Phrixus and Helle. But Nephele returned to the sky, and Athamas took as his second wife Cadmus' daughter Ino, who had nursed Dionysus. Ino hated her stepchildren, and determined to do away with them. Her opportunity came when throughout Boeotia the crops failed. The failure itself was Ino's doing: she had persuaded all the women to spoil the seed in their husband's stores, so that it wouldn't sprout.

Athamas sent to Apollo at Delphi to ask what he had to do to stop the famine, but the envoys too were Ino's men, and they returned saying that, according to Apollo, the only remedy was to sacrifice Phrixus. The boy nobly agreed to his own death, if it would bring life to others, and Athamas, tears streaking his cheeks, was just about to comply with the god's terrible command, when Nephele snatched up her children and took them into the sky. When Athamas learnt the truth, Ino hurled herself and her son off a cliff, but Dionysus made sure that his old wet-nurse did not die, and transformed her at the moment of her death into the sea-nymph Leucothea.

Meanwhile, Nephele placed the children on a golden-fleeced ram, the offspring of Poseidon when he had mated as a ram with Theophane in the guise of a ewe. Away sped the magical ram eastward through the sky, but, as he passed the narrow strip of water that divides Europe from Asia, sweet Helle lost her grip and fell into the sea. Hence the strait is known as the Hellespont, the Sea of Helle, in memory of the wretched girl. But her brother flew on, knowing why both tears and the sea are salty.

On and on, over the south coast of the Black Sea he flew, until he came to Colchis, where King Aeëtes, son of the Sun, made him welcome. In thanksgiving for his deliverance, Phrixus sacrificed the fantastic ram to Zeus, and gave the fleece to Aeëtes, who hung it on an oak tree in a grove sacred to Ares, and set as its guard a fearsome serpent, whose eyes never closed in rest. But Aeëtes had been warned against strangers bearing, or bearing off, a golden fleece, as a sign that his reign would come to an end, and he killed Phrixus to avoid this destiny, not knowing that he was not the stranger to whom the oracle alluded.

So might matters have rested for ever, were it not for the villainy of Pelias, son of Tyro, in distant Greece. At the death of Cretheus, brother of Athamas, he usurped the throne of Iolcus from its rightful king, his own brother, Aeson. In fear, Aeson smuggled his son Jason out of the city, and sent him to the hills, to be brought up by the Centaur Cheiron. But Pelias was afraid of Jason, for he knew of an oracle that foretold his death at the hands of a descendant of Aeolus. Even though Aeolus had many descendants, the field was narrowed down by an oracle that was more precise, if somewhat bizarre: 'Beware of a man with one sandal!'

When Jason came of age, he returned to Iolcus. On the way he came to a river whose water was swollen by rain. An old woman stood helpless beside the raging torrent, and Jason took pity on her and offered to carry her across. Unknown to Jason, the old woman was Hera in disguise, and henceforth he found favour in her eyes. But the current was strong and his burden not so light; the mud of the stream-bed sucked off one of his sandals, and the turbulent water carried it away downstream.

Jason limped into the palace of Iolcus, wearing his single sandal, and Pelias was terrified. Jason demanded the throne of Iolcus as his birthright, now that he was a fully grown man, and Pelias agreed, on one condition: that Jason was to bring back the golden fleece from Colchis. Pelias saw this as a chance to get rid of the young pretender once and for all, but Jason, mighty hero and confident youth, saw a quest worthy of his mettle, and agreed to undertake the task.

But how to reach Colchis, which lay at the edge of the known world? No one had yet invented a vessel that was capable of such a long voyage. Jason called on the goddess of craft, the lady Athena, and begged her to solve the problem. The quick-witted goddess thought for a while and her thoughts readily acquired shape. She infused her knowledge into the mind of the artisan Argus, and the ship he constructed was called the *Argo*, whose name means 'swift'. But the goddess herself fashioned the prow from the living oak of Zeus' oracle at Dodona, and endowed it with the power of speech.

The journey would be long and dangerous, plying unknown waters past unknown lands filled, most likely, with lawless monsters. It was exactly the quest that the heroes of Greece had been waiting for, and Hera urged their hearts to respond eagerly to Jason's call for crew to man the sleek vessel and share the hazardous journey. Before long, Jason had a full complement of fifty men, all of them fine warriors and sage counsellors, surpassing all others in their skills.

Heracles was there, and Idas, his rival in size and strength, who once fought Apollo himself for the right to bed fair Marpessa; and Meleager and Menoetius, bold hunters and men of war. So was Peleus of Aegina and his comrade Telamon of Salamis, who matched oars on either side of the bow. The soothsayers Idmon and Mopsus accompanied the Argonauts, as did Euphemus, son of Poseidon, who could run so swiftly over the surface of the waves that his feet remained dry. Neither Castor the horseman nor his twin brother Polydeuces the boxer could resist the challenge, and the shape-changer Periclymenus too made his special skill available to Jason. Tiphys was the helmsman, while far-seeing Lynceus took the prow, and Orpheus himself carried the beat for the oarsmen.

After leaving the Greek mainland, their first adventure took place on the island of Lemnos, inhabited only by women and ruled by Queen Hypsipyle. The Lemnian women had neglected the worship of Aphrodite, and in punishment the goddess had made them emit a smell that repulsed their husbands and drove them into the arms of their slaves. All Greek men assume the right to sleep with their female slaves, but the Lemnians ignored their legitimate families, and set up new homes. In retaliation, the women killed or banished all their menfolk. By the time the Argonauts got there, the women had not known men for some time. They refused to let the Argonauts land until they had promised to tarry with them. The heroes stayed a full year, before Heracles tore them from their life of ease and they continued on their way; and many fine sons and daughters were born on the island of Lemnos.

They stopped next at the Cyzicus peninsula, where they helped the king defeat some earth-born giants who were terrorizing his people, the Doliones. After celebrating their victory with a feast, the Argonauts cast off, but adverse winds drove them back to Cyzicus in the night. Their new friends mistook them for enemies in the darkness and driving rain, and a fight took place in which Jason himself killed the king, and many other Doliones died. In the morning, the king's daughter hanged herself in grief, and the heroes were prevented from leaving by storms, until Mopsus used his powers to divine the will of the gods, and told them they must sacrifice to Rhea. Only she, ancient goddess, could heal the terrible wounds.

They were still far from their destination when they lost Heracles. He was so strong that he had broken an oar, just by pulling on it, and the voyagers made land at Cius where he could find timber for a replacement. But while he was ashore, cutting and shaping the trunk, his beloved Hylas disembarked to draw water. Far he wandered into the forest, until he came to a pool of crystal water. But when he knelt down at the water's edge and looked into the pool, he saw no reflection of his face. Closer and closer he leant down – and then, in the depths, he glimpsed a bevy of the most beguiling and beautiful girls he had ever seen. He was never seen again; the water nymphs had made him theirs. But Heracles spent so long searching for his lost boy that the rest of the heroes carried on without him, and still the hills and forests around Cius echo the name of Hylas, as if from the lingering cries of Heracles.

In Bithynia they stopped to consult blind Phineus, the most famous soothsayer in the world. Because he was such an outstanding seer, and knew too much of the gods' minds, Zeus himself had blinded the old man and set the Snatchers on him, black-winged monsters with the faces of hags, swift as the storm wind. In return for his advice Phineus charged the heroes with driving off the horrid monsters. For every time he sat at table, they swooped down and stole the food from under his nose, or befouled it, and the man was wasting away.

The Argonauts succeeded in chasing away the Snatchers, and in gratitude Phineus gave them good advice about how to win their way through the hazards that still awaited them. Above all, he told them how to escape the Clashing Rocks at the entrance to the Black Sea, which came together faster than the wind and crushed all shipping. Even dolphins were sometimes caught in the granite jaws. Phineus told them to release a dove to fly between the rocks, so that they could time their own passage. They did as he suggested, following the dove, and the bird lost its tail-feathers to the rocks, but the surge of the waves rebounding from the looming cliffs prevented the passage of the *Argo*.

Now the rocks were closing in on the heroes again. They could see the grain of the stone and the spray dripping from the menacing face of the dark cliff. But Hera herself, Jason's protectress, held apart the jagged precipices while they scraped through, as the rocks crashed together for the last time, taking only the tail end of the stern.

After further adventures, the heroes reached their destination, Colchis. Aeëtes superficially made them welcome, but secretly recognized in Jason the stranger foretold by the oracle, the one who would bring his reign to an end. Jason politely asked him for the fleece, and explained the circumstances of the quest he had been set by Pelias, but Aeëtes saw this only as a way to engineer Jason's death. He promised him the fleece if he succeeded in carrying out two tasks. But the tasks were meant to be impossible: even if Jason somehow managed to survive the first one, the second would surely kill him; and once Jason was dead, Aeëtes planned to do away with the rest of the Argonauts.

It was a good plan. What Aeëtes didn't know, however, was that his daughter Medea had fallen head over heels in love with Jason. Hera and Aphrodite between them had slyly seen to that, by supplying Jason with a potent love-charm. Jason surreptitiously gave the charm to Medea as one of the guest-gifts he had brought for her and her father. The young woman couldn't understand it: she had hardly met him and yet she knew she did not want to see this quietly confident stranger die. There was something about him . . . Medea was a useful ally: she was a priestess of Hecate, skilled in sorcery and charms known only to the wicked and the wise.

Jason's first task was to sow a field with dragon's teeth. It sounded easy enough – but the field had to be ploughed by a team of fire-breathing oxen with lethal bronze hoofs and aggression to match. Medea made a salve for Jason which would temporarily protect him from fire and metal. Jason boldly disrobed and smeared his body; naked and gleaming, he approached the oxen unscathed. Staring them in the eyes, he bowed them to his will. They submitted to the sturdy yoke, and he ploughed the field, scattering the dragon's teeth from his helmet.

But no one – except cunning Aeëtes – expected what happened next. No sooner had the dragon's teeth been sown than fully armed warriors sprang from the soil and formed up to attack Jason. Medea, looking on, was terrified: she hadn't anticipated this and had no potion prepared that would save her beloved from the warriors' spears. But Jason was equal to the task. Thinking quickly (and, if he did but know it, imitating Cadmus), he picked up a boulder and tossed it into the hostile throng. Supposing they were under attack from their own midst, the warriors fell to fighting among themselves, and the slaughter continued until none remained.

So Jason had survived his first test. The second was simply to take the fleece – but in order to do so he first had to get past the sentinel and into the thicket where the fleece was hanging. Medea brewed a drug and gave it to Jason. 'This will put the creature to sleep,' she said, 'but it has to take it in deeply. You will have to let it swallow you.'

Jason steeled his nerves and did exactly as she had told him. Clutching the phial of potion, he approached the monster – it was larger than a warship, and venomous spume dripped from its mouth – and let it swallow him whole. As soon as the drug began to take effect, the dragon vomited Jason up from the disgusting depths of its stomach. Then it lay down beneath the tree that held the fleece, and fell fast asleep. Once he had recovered his composure and rinsed the vile stench from his limbs, Jason took the wonderful fleece down from the tree where it was hanging, and ran straight for the *Argo*, with willing Medea holding tightly onto his hand. All his men were waiting there, for the soothsayer Idmon had guessed Aeëtes' designs and warned Jason that they must make a swift departure.

Aeëtes speedily set sail in pursuit. But Medea had taken her little brother Aspyrtus with her as well and she devised a terrible way to delay her father. As they were sailing from Colchis down the Phasis river to the sea, she killed Aspyrtus, chopped his corpse into pieces, and threw it limb by limb over the side of the ship. It took Aeëtes a long time to retrieve enough of the body to ensure that the boy could be given a proper funeral, a father's first priority. So the Argonauts made their escape.

Their route back to Thessaly, to claim the throne of Iolcus from Pelias, was tortuous. Storm winds and adverse deities often drove them from their path, even to the waters of Ocean. On Crete, they encountered Talos, the tireless guardian of the island, capable of striding around it three times in a single day. A survivor from the Age of Bronze, he was invincible – except that there was a patch of ordinary skin on his ankle, unprotected by bronze. Medea brought all her powers to bear, and uttered curses and charms that caused the monster to slip and graze his ankle on a sharp rock as he was seeking boulders to hurl at the Argonauts. 'Keep away! Keep away!' he shouted. But then, like a tall tree that has been hewn in the forest, Talos swayed on his feet. Looking down, he saw the ichor flowing out of his wound like molten lead, and crashed lifeless to the ground, shaking the entire island and causing a freak wave that threatened to swamp the *Argo*.

The eastern slopes of Pelion loomed ever larger as the *Argo* sped towards her destination. Jason knew that, despite his recovery of the fleece, Pelias had no intention of handing the throne over to him when he returned. His uncle had already killed Jason's remaining close kin, and the hero understood that only one of them would survive this clash. He confided his concerns to Medea, and she hatched a plan to get rid of Pelias for good.

When they got close to Iolcus, they beached the ship out of sight, and Medea went on ahead, disguised as a priestess of Artemis. Before long, she had befriended Pelias' daughters, and had found out that their greatest desire was for their elderly father to be young again. They were enjoying their royal luxury, and didn't want to see it come to an end soon. Medea told them that she knew just what to do.

For nine days and nine nights she searched high and low on her dragon-drawn chariot for the herbs she needed, and plucked them without metal in moonlight to preserve their powers. Then, to convince the gullible girls that she knew what she was doing, she demonstrated her skill on an aged ram. Wide-eyed with horror, Pelias' daughters looked on as she slit the ram's throat, drained it of blood, and then put the body in a cauldron of elixir made from her special herbs and roots. Three times she circled the cauldron righthandwise, and three times lefthandwise. After a while, the girls were astonished to hear a gentle bleating from inside the cauldron – and Medea pulled out a lamb!

Certain of Medea's skill, the very next day the girls persuaded Pelias to accompany them to Medea's chamber. As soon as they were inside, two of them seized their father's wrists, while the third slit his throat. The hot blood gushed out and Pelias collapsed to the ground, with a look on his face more of puzzlement than pain. The girls couldn't wait to stuff his body inside the cauldron. Three times they circled the cauldron righthandwise, and three times lefthandwise. But in the night Medea had drained the cauldron and replaced the rejuvenating elixir with useless soup. Needless to say, the sorceress too had disappeared overnight.

All the heroes reassembled for the magnificent funeral games in honour of the dead king. The winners were Zetes and Calaïs in the long footraces – but then, as sons of the north wind, they had a distinct advantage; Castor won the sprint, while his brother Polydeuces totally dominated the boxing event; Telamon outthrew all-comers with the discus, as Meleager did with the javelin; Peleus wrestled all his opponents to exhaustion, even fair Atalanta; Iolaus easily won the chariot race, and of course no one could match Orpheus at the lyre.

But Jason did not take part, for he was not there. The killing of an uncle, however wicked he had been, polluted Jason and Medea with the miasma of sin, and they had to leave Iolcus in the hands of Pelias' son Acastus. Otherwise, the pollution would spread and infect the whole city with pestilence and famine. They settled in Corinth and lived there for a few years in peace, until Jason decided that, in order to improve his position, he should put aside his foreign wife and marry Glauce, the princess of Corinth, daughter of King Creon. Medea seethed inwardly with rage and jealousy, but disguised it well. 'This is the right decision,' she said, 'for you and for our children.' But she was lying through her teeth. She sent Glauce and Creon presents for the wedding, a gorgeous robe for Glauce and a crown for Creon, and they accepted the gifts with joy.

No sooner had they donned these items of clothing than the

poison with which Medea had imbued them went to work. Glauce's robe began to burn her, and she tried to rip it off, but it clung to her like a second skin. She ran shrieking to the nearest water – still known as Glauce's spring – and hurled herself into the pool, seeking relief. But it was no good. Her flesh blistered and her blood boiled, and she died in sheer agony.

Meanwhile, Creon's crown tightened on his head like a vice, and still it went on squeezing, until his skull was crushed and the grey matter of his brains puddled on the ground below the throne where he slumped. Medea then slit her own children's throats, to spite Jason, and flew off in her dragon-drawn chariot to Athens, where she had been offered refuge by King Aegeus. And apart from the rumour of an attempt on her stepson Theseus' life there, the ill-famed sorceress passes out of the memory of man.

As for Jason, some claim that he took his own life, grieving over the murder of his children. Others say that he never recovered his luck, and one day, as he entered the temple of Hera, the cracked stern-piece of the *Argo* he had dedicated there in gratitude fell from its plinth and killed him. Those who have been chosen by the gods for great deeds rarely live to a peaceful old age.

The Calydonian Boar Hunt

The Fates attend all those who bleed and dream – the heroes of legend no less than us. Fair Althaea, descended from Aeolus, was cousin and consort of Oeneus, king of Calydon in Aetolia. But one night Ares himself, the god of war, came and lay in love with Althaea, and in due course of time she gave birth to a son, and she called him Meleager. But when the boy was no more than seven days old, the implacable Fates paid her a visit and predicted that Meleager would die when a particular piece of wood in the fireplace had burnt up. 'We have allotted the same span of life,' said the ghastly crones, 'to your son and to this log.' Naturally, Althaea snatched the blazing log from the fire and, once she had extinguished the flames, she hid it away in a chest that only she knew about. And the boy grew to be a hardy warrior, strong and proud.

But Fate cannot be averted. The chain of events began when Oeneus angered the lady Artemis, chaste Mistress of Animals. In his folly, he sacrificed to all the other gods, but ignored or forgot her. She sent a boar to ravage his land – and not just any boar, but a monstrous brute, as large as a hulking bull, capable of uprooting whole trees as it pawed the soil for food. Meleager, expert with javelin and spear, summoned a true band of heroes to help him hunt down the beast. Peleus and Telamon came, Castor and Polydeuces, Jason, the inseparable pair Theseus and Pirithous, Admetus, the soothsayer Amphiaraus, and many others. There also arrived the fair huntress Atalanta, whom Hippomenes one day would wed by guile – but, for now, no sooner had Meleager set eyes on her than he fell in love.

So they set out after the rampaging boar. They found traces of it everywhere: fallen trees, trunks gashed by tusks, acres of ground churned into a useless mess, trampled crops. All other wildlife had fled in terror. For seven days they tracked it, hardly resting even at night. The rocks and logs of the harsh wilderness served as their only pillows, leaves were their mattresses, and a gibbous moon was all their illumination.

At last they had the beast boxed up in a thicket, and they spread their strong nets to prevent its escape. But a boar is easily enraged, and fights back when threatened. For all their stature as heroes, several fell, gored in the groin or the belly by its savage tusks, bright blood staining the leaf-strewn ground. Eupalemon and Pelagon fell, and so did Hyleus, Hippasus, and Enaesimus, while Eurytion was killed by accident, when Peleus sped his spear too hastily into the dark and tangled thicket. But then, with a bellow of rage, the monstrous creature charged into the open – straight at Nestor of Pylos. No one even had time to shout out a warning, and it looked as though his doom was assured, but he cannily used his spear to vault into the safety of a tree's branches.

Despite the encouragement Nestor shouted down to his comrades, it looked as though the boar would prevail, and even escape to continue its destruction of Calydon. But then Atalanta drew back her trusty bow, and the arrow grazed the boar's back and lodged in the folds of its neck. The sight of red blood made Ancaeus bold. 'Let's see what a man can do,' he boasted. 'This is no work for women.' As the boar charged at him he let fly with his spear, but missed. The enraged beast ripped out his bowels with its tusks, and he fell, gasping out his last breath along with his steaming entrails on the blood-stained ground. Then Meleager stepped up and released his javelin; it took the beast through the mouth and brought it crashing in a cloud of dust to the ground, instantly dead.

The hide and tusks belonged by right to Meleager, as the killer of the boar. But to honour the first strike, and because he desired her, he gave the spoils of the hunt to fair Atalanta. But his uncles were there, the brothers of Althaea, and they taunted him for being less than a man. Meleager's mettle was up, and his father's blood flowed dark and strong in his veins. Before any of those present could draw breath, his mother's brothers joined the scattered corpses on the hunting ground.

In the depths of her grief, Althaea went to the old chest, the one in which she had hidden the log all those years ago. She removed the log from its hiding-place and threw it on the fire, calling upon the Furies as avengers of kindred slaughter. Meleager immediately felt a burning sensation deep within, and he faded and died as quickly as an aged log burns in the fire.

But Althaea repented of what she had done, and tore her cheeks, and hanged herself in sorrow deeper than the sea, while her daughters were turned by Artemis into guinea hens, and mourn their brother for ever with plaintive cries. Gorge and Deianeira were spared at the request of Dionysus, for Deianeira was destined to become the second wife of Heracles; but Gorge bore Tydeus from incestuous union with her father.

Io and the Danaids

The great city of Argos, rich in horses and cattle, is in the care of Hera, as Athens is of grey-eyed Athena. Now, Io was the daughter of the river-god Inachus and a priestess of Hera at Argos. As Night's chariot winged its way across the sky, and the bright foam from his horses' mouths settled on the earth as dew, Io was troubled by dreams in which she seemed to hear a voice. 'Foolish girl,' cajoled the voice, deep and serene. 'Why do you guard your virginity, when you could have the greatest of lovers, Zeus himself?'

Night after night the dreams returned, and eventually she gave in to their insistent clamour. When Zeus visited her, she opened to him not just her arms, but also her heart. But his behaviour had aroused the suspicion of Hera, and she came in search of him. Just before she caught the lovers, Zeus detected her approach and changed Io into a cow, as a concrete plea of innocence: 'There's no one here, just this cow.' But Hera could feign innocence as well as her husband, and she asked to keep the cow herself. Zeus had no choice but to let her take it.

Hera summoned Argus, an earth-born giant with a hundred eyes that could see in all directions, already famous for making the district safe against lawless monsters. She tethered Io to an olive tree within her sanctuary, and set Argus to guard her, giving him the gift, or curse, of sleeplessness, so that none of his eyes would ever be tamed by weariness. But Zeus sent Hermes to free Io from captivity, and once the wily god had lulled Argus the all-seeing to sleep with his soothing pipes, he promptly cut off his head. But Hera retrieved Argus' eyes and put them in the tail of her favoured bird, the peacock.

Hera's dark rage had not yet run its course, however, and she sent a gadfly which tormented Io so badly that she wandered, as a cow, all over the earth, denied rest by the irritating bug. Every time she imagined it had gone, it would return and prick her with its sting. At last she came to Egypt, where with a mere brush of his fingers, Zeus restored her to human form; and when her son was born, she called him Epaphus, because she had been impregnated by the tender touch of Zeus. The royal lines of Egypt and Phoenicia, of Argos, Thebes, and Crete, all look back to Epaphus as their ancestor.

In Egypt, the great-grandsons of Epaphus were Danaus and Aegyptus, fathers respectively of fifty daughters and fifty sons. Danaus hated his brother, and took himself and his daughters off to live in exile in Argos. Aegyptus, however, naturally expected that his sons would marry their cousins and followed them to Greece. This was a reasonable expectation, and Danaus was not in a position to stand in his brother's way – except that he ordered his daughters to kill their husbands on the very night of the mass wedding, before their husbands had taken their virginity.

The vile deed took place as planned – or almost as planned: one of the Danaids, Hypermestra, could not go through with it. She spared her husband Lynceus and their descendants became the rulers of Argos. But her sisters couldn't avoid marriage for ever. Danaus arranged a footrace for all their suitors, and the first across the line took his first choice of woman, the second chose second, and so on, until all forty-nine were accounted for. Nor could the Danaids avoid punishment for their terrible crime: in Hades they are condemned eternally to try to prepare their bridal baths by fetching water in sieves.

Perseus and the Gorgon

Hypermestra, the Danaid who spared her groom, bore him a son. They called him Abas, and he in his turn had two sons, Proetus and Acrisius. These brothers fought even in the womb and later divided the realm of Argos between them, with Acrisius becoming lord of Argos, and Proetus king of Tiryns. Acrisius had a daughter, Danae, while Proetus had several daughters, whose terrible ten-year madness is a lesson in not insulting the gods. For abusing her temple, Hera caused them to dress like slatterns, and to wander the hills imagining themselves cows. The wise shaman Melampus cured them and received in return a share of Proetus' kingdom and a princess bride to bear his children.

Now, Acrisius loved his daughter Danae, but naturally he wanted a son and heir for Argos. He consulted far-shooting Apollo at Delphi, and the news was bitter: he would have no sons, and a son born of his daughter would kill him. They say that love conquers all, but Acrisius let fear overcome love: he imprisoned his dear daughter within an underground chamber of bronze, leaving only a narrow aperture through which Danae took her meals and breathed sweet air. But Zeus conceived a passion for Danae, and no prison made by the hands of man can keep him out. He turned himself into a shower of liquid gold, and poured himself through the slit. Thus the great god lay in love with Danae.

In due course of time a secret son was born, and Danae named him Perseus. The baby lived with his mother inside their brazen dungeon, but one day Acrisius heard the metallic echoes of the young boy at play, and Danae's secret was discovered. Acrisius laid ungentle hands on his daughter, demanding to know who the father was. 'It was Zeus!' she cried, but Acrisius didn't believe her. He locked both mother and child in a wooden chest and tossed them into the sea, so that he would be absolved of their deaths. But the frail vessel caught in the net of a fisherman called Dictys, and he took Danae and Perseus to his home on the island of Seriphos and let them stay with him. The years passed and Perseus grew up lithe and sleek; it was clear that he was favoured by the gods.

Now, honest Dictys' brother Polydectes, the king of Seriphos, lusted after fair Danae. But confident in the protection of her son, she always spurned his unwelcome advances. Polydectes therefore decided to get rid of Perseus, and the proud youth foolishly made it easy for him. Polydectes invited him, along with all the important men of the island, to a banquet, supposedly to elicit contributions for the wedding of Pelops and Hippodamia. Every man was to provide a horse, but Perseus was not rich enough to own one. The young man nervously quipped that he could as easily bring Polydectes the head of the

Gorgon as a horse. Seizing his opportunity, Polydectes held him to his word: he was to fetch the Gorgon's head. That would remove Perseus from the scene for a long time – perhaps permanently – and in the meantime Polydectes could have his way with Danae.

Perseus' quest began in despair. He knew about the Gorgons: there were three of them – Stheno, Euryale, and Medusa – and they had originally been the beautiful daughters of Phorcys and Ceto, children of Earth and Sea. Stheno and Euryale were fully immortal, but Medusa was as a mortal woman, only far more fair. So Medusa fell foul of Athena. She claimed her looks rivalled Athena's own beauty, and she further angered the chaste goddess by coupling with Poseidon in her holy sanctuary.

For punishment, all three Gorgons were turned into stubby-winged monsters, with drooling and engorged tongues, tusks projecting from their mouths, decaying skin, and poisonous snakes for hair. They were creatures from a nightmare, and Medusa's once-alluring eyes turned all who looked directly at them into stone, for ever.

So Perseus wandered to a lonely part of the island and sat down to think. Gulls wheeled and cried overhead in the salt breeze. And there came to him two mighty gods, Hermes and Athena, telling him to have no fear. 'But what can I do?' he said. 'I can't just confront the Gorgons.' The gods agreed, and recommended an oblique course.

'Did you know that the Gorgons have sisters?' they asked. 'If anyone knows a sister's weaknesses, it's another sister. You should find the Graeae, and compel them to tell you how to defeat the Gorgons.' They told him about the three Graeae, who had been born and lived as crones, hunched with age, as grey and chilling as the foam of the sea from which they came; and forestalled his next nervous question by giving him directions for finding them.

When Perseus reached the distant seashore where the Graeae lived, he asked them at once for help. 'But who are you?' demanded Pemphredo, staring in his direction out of eyeless sockets, ghastly to behold.

'It's a young man,' croaked her sister Deino. 'I've got the eye, so I can see.'

'Give it here, then,' rasped Pemphredo. There was a soft sucking noise as Deino prised the slick orb out of her socket and handed it to her sister. The eye sank into her head with a squelch, and after taking stock of Perseus she passed the eye over to her other sister, Enyo. 'Swap you for the tooth,' she said. 'I've still got a bit of raw octopus left to chew.'

As Perseus submitted to the scrutiny of the strange creatures, he blushed – but an idea occurred to him. He could see that the Graeae had only the one tooth and the one eye between them, and depended on them utterly. Slowly, carefully, he edged closer to the grizzled women. His moment came when both the eye and the tooth were in transit from one Graea to another: Perseus grabbed them and stepped back. The shrieks of the crones were terrible to hear – at once like a seagull's harsh scream and the wind keening over storm waves. 'Give them back, give them back, give them back!' they cried.

'No!' said Perseus. 'Not until you tell me how your sisters can be defeated.'

At first the Graeae refused, out of loyalty to their kin. Perseus, calling their bluff, began to walk away with the hostage bits, his feet crunching on the shingle, but he hadn't gone far when they called him back and agreed to help him. He pressed the eye and the tooth into the unseeing hands of Deino, and the grizzled creatures burst into sing-song voice.

'Far distant is the home of our sisters,' they said, 'on the western shores of Ocean, close to the entrance to the under-world. Months will pass in the journey, or even years, unless you have some magical means of transport. And beware! Their senses are very acute: it would be best to be invisible. Further-more, even if you succeed in decapitating our sister Medusa, what will you do with the head? You can't leave it uncovered, because it will turn everything that looks at it – including you, perhaps – into stone for ever.'

Perseus found their advice distinctly unhelpful. His task seemed even more impossible than before. 'So I've got to be able to fly,' he said, 'and be invisible, and safely transport the Gorgon's lethal head. Unfortunately, I can't do any of these things.'

'But fortunately,' said the Graeae, 'we know how you can acquire these abilities. After the transformation of our sisters, Poseidon entrusted certain items to some of his daughters, the sea nymphs. He was worried in case the Gorgons might run amok and terrify the world, so he had to leave the means of their destruction in safekeeping.' And they told Perseus how to find the nymphs.

Away he sped on his mission, and the nymphs saw in him a true hero and graciously loaned him a cap of darkness, a pair of winged sandals, and a special satchel. Hermes gave him a wickedly sharp sword, and when he drew it from its sheath a cold wind whistled across the blade, and it showed no reflection of the moon's shining.

Perseus flew with his sky shoes to the edge of the world, near the source of the vast river Ocean that sweeps around the continents of the earth, and found the foul Gorgons asleep. Once he had spotted them from on high, he donned his cap of invisibility and swooped down. Acting on the advice of Athena and Hermes, he used his bronze shield as a mirror, to avoid the direct gaze of Medusa. Even with this handicap, he managed to cut off her head cleanly, with one slice. Immediately, through the Gorgon's severed neck, leapt her children by Poseidon: the winged horse Pegasus, and the horse's human twin, Chrysaor, the father of Geryon.

All this turmoil awoke Medusa's sisters, and the snakes on their heads seemed to have the power to penetrate the aura of invisibility with which he was surrounded. Perseus quickly stuffed the head into the satchel and flew off, while the hideous twins screeched and raved futilely, and their serpent hair writhed and hissed. As he flew over the desert of Africa, drops of blood fell from the satchel and the ground thus inseminated gave birth to all the poisonous snakes that dwell there.

When Perseus reached the coast of Palestine, an extraordinary sight greeted his eyes. A young woman was struggling helplessly against chains that bound her to a jagged rock, so close to the water's edge that salt spray mingled with the tears on her face. The curious hero landed, tucked away his cap of darkness, and made enquiries in the local town. The woman was Andromeda, the daughter of the king, Cepheus. And it was he, her reluctant father, who had ordered her to be bound and left for a savage sea monster to devour, because this, he had been told, was the only way to stop its ruinous raids on his land. The monster had been sent by sea nymphs, because Andromeda's mother had boasted that her daughter was more beautiful than them. Sometimes, the sins of the mother are visited upon the daughter.

Perseus was so taken by the girl that he was inclined to agree with her mother's assessment of her charms, and he began to negotiate with Cepheus: the hand of Andromeda if he could get rid of the monster. The bargain struck, Perseus didn't hesitate. He returned straight away to the rock and freed fair Andromeda . . . just in time, for already they could see the creature breasting the foam, forging a furrow in the sea towards them as straight as a plough in soft and stoneless earth.

Perseus rose into the air on his winged sandals, and drove the creature mad with fury by hovering just out of reach of its snapping jaws. Time and again he returned to earth, each time to collect ever larger boulders, with which he stunned the monster and drove it off. He and Andromeda returned in joy to the palace, already committed to each other, but when Perseus claimed his prize, Cepheus' brother Phineus objected, for he wanted Andromeda for himself. He lured the young man into an ambush – but nimble Perseus found time to close his eyes and yank the petrifying head out of its satchel.

Perseus swept Andromeda into his arms and together they flew back to Seriphos. There they found Danae and Dictys huddled fearfully at an altar, to which they had fled for refuge. Both, in their different ways, had been abused by the king, and they greeted the returning hero with tears of hope. Perseus strode into Polydectes' palace, the uninvited guest, the bringer of death. He found the king at banquet, surrounded by his supporters, in his lofty reception hall.

'And did you get me the Gorgon's head?' the king taunted. Perseus reached in and pulled the ghastly object out of his satchel, while averting his gaze. Polydectes and all the others were instantly turned to stone, the mocking laughter frozen for ever on their sneering lips. A quick smile flitted across Perseus' face.

After he had returned the magical objects to Hermes, Perseus gave the Gorgon's head to Athena, who set it in the middle of her aegis for ever. She is a terrible goddess, and anyone who sees her as she is freezes in awe and fear. Then the young hero returned with Danae and Andromeda to Argos. Acrisius, hearing of their arrival, fled, but Perseus set out in pursuit. He caught up with his grandfather in Thessaly, and the two were reconciled, but there is no escaping the word of Fate. Perseus agreed to take part in an athletic competition, and the discus that he threw accidentally struck and killed Acrisius. Polluted even by this unintentional murder, Perseus exiled himself from Argos, but took nearby Tiryns as his seat after his great-uncle Proetus' death. He also founded golden Mycenae, and in both places the Cyclopes built the massive defensive walls for him, which still stand after all this time.

Bellerophon

As Perseus stands to Argos, Theseus to Athens, and Heracles to the Peloponnese as a whole, so Bellerophon stands to Corinth, the greatest of its heroes. His grandfather was Sisyphus, and his mother had been loved by Poseidon, whose child she said he was. But he was compelled to leave the land of his birth after accidentally killing a brother, and he settled in Tiryns, under King Proetus.

The handsome youth attracted the fancy of the queen, Stheneboea. She began by flirting with him in secret, which was tolerable, if uncomfortable, but in the end she demanded an assignation. Bellerophon refused her, but hell truly has no fury like a woman scorned, and Stheneboea told her husband that Bellerophon had tried to rape her. Blinded by his desire for revenge, Proetus sent Bellerophon to his wife's father Iobates, king of Lycia, with a sealed letter containing Stheneboea's charges – and the request that Iobates get rid of his young visitor, permanently. In order to encompass his death, Iobates therefore set him to cleanse Lycia of its plagues. By rights, any one of the tasks should kill him. Iobates could only win: either Bellerophon would die, or, if he succeeded, Lycia would at least have been freed from terror.

Bellerophon, however, was beloved of the gods. Poseidon gave him his son Pegasus, the white, winged horse that had sprung from Medusa's severed neck. But Pegasus was wild and untamed, and nothing Bellerophon could do would make the proud steed obedient to his commands. Keen-eyed Athena, noticing the boy's trouble, and wanting to help, came down by night from Olympus with a magic bridle, and with this he was able to mount and control the splendid creature. After a bit of practice, he found that he could fire his arrows with deadly accuracy, while gripping the flanks of the winged horse with his knees and thighs, and he soared up to the heavens and swooped towards the earth in delight. As he sped through the air, his dark cape flowed gracefully out behind him, and peasants working in the fields stared up at the sky in awe and amazement.

All his labours met with success. First he shot down the fire-breathing Chimera, dread offshoot of Typhoeus, which was ravaging Iobates' land – three deadly arrows in quick succession, one for each of the creatures that made up its body. Then he expelled the wild Solymi, the first inhabitants of Lycia, and drove them into the mountain fastnesses where they still live. Finally, he quelled the Amazons, for the warrior women were raiding Iobates' territory.

Having singlehandedly done all that Iobates wanted, Bellerophon set out in triumph back to the king's palace. But the
treacherous king, true only to Proetus' request, sent a strong
force of his men to conceal themselves and take the young hero
unawares. Not one of the ambushers returned alive, and at last
Iobates was forced to recognize that Bellerophon was under the
special protection of the gods. He realized that his daughter had
been lying, and in recompense gave Bellerophon half his
kingdom and another daughter's hand in marriage. When she
learnt that her shamelessness and lies had been revealed, Stheneboea killed herself rather than live with the humiliation.

But being dear to the gods is not a sufficient shield against
arrogance. Men encompass their own destruction. Bellerophon
took it into his head one day to ride on Pegasus' back up to
heaven, to remonstrate with the gods about the injustice of life
on earth. Who among us has not wished to do such a thing?
But the great steed, mindful of his father, refused to have anything to do with such a foolish enterprise, and bucked his rider
off to the ground. Bellerophon broke both hips and spent the
rest of his life as a wretched cripple. Perhaps in the end he learnt
wisdom, but the storytellers do not say.

5

Thebes in the Age of Heroes

Cadmus, Europa, and the Foundation of Thebes

Cadmus, son of Agenor, was king of Tyre, and grandson of Epaphus. He had a sister called Europa, who was so fair of face and form that her beauty came to the attention of Zeus. The son of Cronus changed himself into a magnificent white bull and drew near her. The maiden was fascinated by this bull: so massive and powerful, and yet so gentle. Quelling her fearful fancies, she approached the majestic creature and stroked its panting muzzle. The bull breathed the scent of saffron, and when it bowed its forelegs to the ground, the girl sat, sideways but secure, on its back.

Immediately, the bull raced for the coast, and Europa clung on in terror. The magnificent creature plunged into the sea and swam forcefully for the island of Crete. When they came ashore, Zeus shed his disguise as a bull and had his way with her. And she bore him Minos, the wise king of Crete who became a judge of the dead, as did his brother Rhadamanthys.

But Agenor sent his sons to find her, for he had no idea where she had gone, so silent and swift had Zeus' abduction been. Phoenix he sent north, where he founded the Phoenician race; Cilix futilely searched in the east, and settled at last in the land known since as Cilicia. Cadmus was sent west.

Arriving in Greece, he made his way to Delphi to ask Apollo's advice. The golden god told him that Europa's destiny was not his concern, and enjoined him to follow the first cow he encountered after leaving the Delphic precinct. He was to found a city wherever the cow first took her rest. After a while, he did indeed come across a cow, and she lumbered to her feet as soon as she saw him. She set off east, and Cadmus followed, and founded the great city of Thebes where she took her rest. In proper thanksgiving for the end of his travels, he decided to sacrifice the cow, and he sent his men out to find water. But a formidable dragon, a pet of Ares, guarded the spring, and many of Cadmus' men were ripped apart by the vicious creature's fangs, or crushed in its coils, until Cadmus himself came up and slew it in its pride with a rock that broke its skull.

The cow was duly sacrificed to Athena. In return the keen-eyed goddess gave Cadmus some advice: to honour Ares and the previous occupants of the land by sowing the serpent's teeth in the ground. But as soon as he planted the razor-sharp teeth, armed warriors sprang up from the tilled furrows.

Responding out of sheer instinct, Cadmus wrapped his muscular arms around a boulder resting at the edge of the field and lobbed it into their midst. The warriors, more like automata than thinking men, supposed that one of their number had done it, and fell to fighting among themselves.

In the end, only five of the Sown Men remained, and from these five are descended the five noble families of Thebes. But Athena and Ares reserved half the teeth and gave them to King

Aeëtes of Colchis, who found a use for them when Hera's favourite Jason came to his land.

Zeus awarded Cadmus as his wife Harmonia, daughter of Ares and Aphrodite, but first he had to work as Ares' servant for a year, in recompense for the slaying of the dragon. All the gods and goddesses, including the Muses and the Graces, came to the acropolis of Thebes, to celebrate the wedding. Among the bride-gifts for Harmonia was a marvellous necklace, made for her by no less a craftsman than Hephaestus, to be a priceless heirloom for her descendants. But an heirloom is not only precious: it carries the fortune of the family down from one generation to the next, whether that fortune be good or bad.

As well as a son, Polydorus, the royal couple had four daughters: Semele, who became the mother of Dionysus; Ino, who nursed Dionysus and tried to do away with Phrixus and Helle; Autonoe, mother of the hunter Actaeon whose love Semele spurned; and Agave, who along with Autonoe was driven mad by Dionysus and tore her son Pentheus to shreds with her own hands and teeth. At the ends of their lives, Cadmus and Harmonia became serpents themselves, while their spirits live for ever in bliss in the Elysian Fields. But after Polydorus the throne of Thebes passed to Cadmus' doomed grandson, Pentheus, who, as we have seen, brought about his own destruction by resisting the rites of the twice-born god of liberation.

Oedipus

A terrible plague held the land of Thebes in its deadly grip; the crops were stricken with blight and the people began to die of disease and starvation. For in Greece the line between a good year and a bad one is very fine. As is proper for the king in such times, Oedipus consulted the oracle at Delphi, and was told that Thebes was polluted by the murder of Laius, the previous king, for the murderer was still at large.

And Oedipus swore a terrible oath, that the murderer should be found and punished, whoever he was, with the most terrible punishments. He should be stripped of his family and belongings, flogged, and driven from the land to live out his days as a rootless beggar. No one was to talk to him; no one was to offer him shelter or the warmth of Hestia's fire; no one was to feed him. If he survived, he would be gnawed for ever by guilt and serve as prey to passing brigands. But who was the guilty man?

After the death of Pentheus, the rulership of Thebes had descended into chaos. Eventually Labdacus began a new line, but he too died resisting Dionysus, and the throne passed to his infant son Laius. As often happens, the young king's regent, a man called Lycus, usurped the throne. Now, Lycus' niece, Antiope, was loved by Zeus, and gave birth in secret to twin boys. But knowing that Lycus would see them as rivals and kill them, she left the infants at the city gates. They were taken in and brought up by a childless shepherd couple, whom they charmed with their infant smiles and dimples. The happy peasants named them Amphion and Zethus.

Out together one day, the young men met a dishevelled and distraught woman, whom at first they took to be a runaway slave. After questioning her, however, and finding out that she was Antiope, they began to suspect the truth about their origins. Both boys looked remarkably like this strange woman. But just then Lycus' wife Dirce arrived with an armed escort, to haul Antiope back to Thebes, back to the life of constant torment and humiliation to which Dirce subjected her.

Zethus and Amphion questioned the shepherd and his wife, and the truth came out amid many tears. The boys saw it now as their duty to save their true mother from Dirce's hands. Zethus was in favour of taking immediate and drastic action, but the gentle musician Amphion needed persuading. In the end they avenged their mother's long years of distress by having Dirce tied to the horns of a bull and dragged to her death; but sweet water sprang from the face of the rock at the place of her death in Thebes, and the spring still bears her name. Lycus received no further punishment beyond banishment. Amphion and Zethus also banished Laius, who was on the threshold of adulthood. They ruled together, but not amicably, and their reign was beset with woes.

Zethus was married to Aedon, and Amphion to Niobe, whose foolish boast led, as we have seen, to the massacre of her children, and endless sorrow. But even earlier her children had been at risk, victims of the jealousy of her sister-in-law. Aedon determined to kill one of Niobe's children, but mistook the child's bed at night and killed her own son. When she realized her terrible error, she prayed to be taken from this earth. Her prayer was answered, and she became the first nightingale.

Amphion and Zethus are remembered as secondary founders, after Cadmus, of the seven-gated city of Thebes. They enlarged the city and built its defensive walls. Nor did they just supervise the building, as kings generally do: the massive stones were summoned and leapt into place under the spell of Amphion's lyre. On their deaths, Laius returned from exile and resumed the throne of Thebes. During his exile, Laius had been taken in and made welcome by Pelops, king of Elis. But when he left he abused the sacred bonds of friendship and hospitality by abducting Pelops' son Chrysippus, with whom he was in love.

But Chrysippus killed himself for shame, and Pelops called down the curses of the gods on Laius and his descendants for the death of his beloved son.

Later, when Laius was king of Thebes, he consulted the oracle at Delphi to learn if his wife Jocasta would bear him any children, and he was told that, if he truly wanted to protect the city, he should avoid having children, and also that, if Jocasta did bear him a son, that son would kill him. And Apollo made it plain that Pelops' curse was the cause.

But Laius in his folly ignored the oracle, and in due course of time a son was born. In an attempt to avoid the unavoidable, Laius ordered him exposed on a nearby mountain, with an iron pin driven through his ankle. Needless to say – for the curse had long to run yet – the slave who had been given the job of abandoning the baby in the wilderness gave him out of pity to a kindly shepherd. The countryman passed the child on to Polybus, king of Corinth, and Polybus brought him up as his own. The boy's wound recovered, but ever after he was known as Oedipus, Clubfoot.

Years later, Oedipus began to suspect that he was not the natural son of King Polybus and Queen Merope. He paid a visit to Delphi and asked the oracle who his parents were. The oracle, as often, didn't reply directly, but told him that he must never set foot on his native soil, since he was destined to kill his father and marry his mother. Naturally, Oedipus chose never to return to Corinth, which he took to be the country of his birth – and he set out on the road from Delphi that led to Thebes, walking easily, with his long, dark hair tied up with a fillet, and his brow furrowed with concern. It seemed he had a hard road ahead of him.

It's well known that crossroads and junctions are places of danger and mystery, where ghosts congregate and Hecate rules. Oedipus arrived at such a place just as a chariot came clattering up, the driver and passenger unconcerned for the young wanderer with whom they shared the narrow road. To avoid being crushed, Oedipus leapt aside onto the rough shoulder, but then he sprinted alongside the chariot, shouting angrily and grabbing for the driver. At this, the passenger, an elderly man with cold eyes, struck him hard on the head with a whip. In an instant, quick-tempered Oedipus pulled the man from the back of the chariot and killed him for the insult. It was, of course, his true father, Laius, though Oedipus had no idea that he had just fulfilled the first part of the prophecy. Ironically, Laius had been on his way to Delphi to ask whether the son had survived, whom he had abandoned so long ago.

When Oedipus reached Thebes some time later, he found the city mourning its dead king and afflicted by the Sphinx – a monstrous creature with the face of a woman, the body of a lion, and the wings of an eagle. It had blocked the gates to the city and set about terrorizing all who sought exit or entry by demanding the answer to a riddle it had learnt from the Muses: 'What goes on four legs at dawn, two legs at midday, and three legs in the evening?' The beast proceeded to devour all who failed to give the right answer, and the city was soon threatened with losing all of its best and brightest, for many tried but none could find the solution.

Queen Jocasta's brother Creon was acting as regent since the death of Laius, and was desperate enough to offer the throne of Thebes and his sister's hand in marriage to anyone who could rid the land of the riddling pest. Oedipus, confident in his wits, boldly confronted the Sphinx at the mouth of its cliff-top cave.

'"Man" is the answer,' he said. 'As an infant, he crawls; as an adult he walks on two legs; and in the evening of his life he supports himself with a cane.' In anguished surprise at the abrupt end to its deadly game, the Sphinx hurled itself with a blood-curdling howl off the precipice. Oedipus gained the throne and married Jocasta. Apollo's words had come to pass.

Ignorance can be bliss, and for many years Thebes and Oedipus thrived. He and Jocasta had two sons, Eteocles and Polynices, and two daughters, Antigone and Ismene. But then the plague struck, and in his blindness Oedipus cursed the man who had brought pollution down upon his people by murdering King Laius.

At this point, Polybus died, and a messenger arrived from Corinth, offering the now-vacant throne to Oedipus. But Oedipus refused: he was mindful of the prophecy, and still thought that Polybus and Merope were his parents. But when he explained his refusal, the messenger, in all innocence, told him not to worry, because in their childlessness Polybus and Merope had adopted him. 'I know they aren't your true parents,' said the messenger, 'because I am the very shepherd who took you in when you had been abandoned as an infant in the hills.'

A trifling snowball gathers further bulk as it rolls down the mountainside, until it becomes a devastating avalanche; just so, the evidence accumulated, until the truth was unavoidable. Oedipus was himself the cause of his people's suffering, and he had indeed killed his father and married his mother, as the oracle had foretold. Jocasta hanged herself in horror at her incest, and on discovering her lifeless body, still warm and swaying, Oedipus blinded himself with a brooch torn from her robe. Creon became regent again, and blind Oedipus locked himself away in the recesses of the palace.

But there still remained plenty of energy in Pelops' curse. Alone in his self-imposed prison, Oedipus' tortured mind was prey to irrational fears and fantasies. Though he did not forgive himself, he was well looked after by his sons, Eteocles and Polynices.

One day, after making a sacrifice, they brought a special treat for their father. Rather than the usual poor cut of meat, they presented him with a meaty haunch served on a silver plate that had belonged to all the kings of Thebes since the time of Cadmus. But in his madness Oedipus took this as a cruel reminder of his condition, as a king brought low and denied luxury. He shouted for the gods to take note, and over the haunch, now turned sacrificial victim, Oedipus called down Pelops' curse afresh on the heads of his own sons. He doomed them to divide their kingdom with the sword, and die at each other's hands.

The Seven against Thebes

So the Theban princes, Eteocles and Polynices, Oedipus' sons and brothers, came of age. They both wanted the throne of Thebes, and adopted a compromise that was bound to fail, whereby each of them would rule for a year, while the other made himself scarce. Eteocles ruled first, with Polynices spending the year in Argos, at the court of King Adrastus. As insurance, he took with him the family heirloom – the fabulous necklace made for Harmonia by Hephaestus. Nevertheless, at the end of the year, Eteocles refused to give up the throne. Power had gone to his head.

During his year of exile Polynices had married one of Adrastus' daughters, and the Argive king now promised to help restore him to his throne. After all, there was far more point in having a king as a son-in-law than a homeless exile. Adrastus assembled an army that was led by seven champions: himself, Polynices, Tydeus, Capaneus, Hippomedon, Parthenopaeus, and the soothsayer Amphiaraus.

Amphiaraus at first refused to join the expedition; he knew by divination that he would not return from it. He went into hiding, and his absence threatened to abort the effort altogether. But his wife was bribed by Polynices with the cursed necklace of Harmonia. She revealed her husband's hiding-place, and Amphiaraus bravely accepted his fate. The Seven descended on Thebes as wolves descend from the hills in winter to steal defenceless lambs. They were seven only, but they were a match for seven hundred ordinary men.

Their route took them past Nemea, where they found Hypsipyle, the former queen of Lemnos. A victim of warfare, she was bound in servitude to the local king, Lycurgus, as the nursemaid of his infant son and heir. Adrastus' troops were short of water, and Hypsipyle offered to show them the way to a spring. She laid the cradle containing her young charge on the ground, but while she was away a serpent came and devoured the child. When the Seven had quenched their thirst, they returned to a scene of bloody horror, with the mangled remains of the baby scattered on the ground or dribbling out of the monster's mouth. Too late, they killed the serpent. But to honour the baby who died so that they might quench their thirst, they instituted games that are still held today, once every two years.

The heroes found the seven-mouthed city of Thebes well defended; seven warriors had volunteered to hold the gates against the enemy. The Thebans were not defenceless lambs, after all. The Theban seer Teiresias foretold that the city would not fall as long as one of the descendants of the original five

Sown Men sacrificed himself. If this happened, said Teiresias, the debt incurred by Cadmus' killing of Ares' dragon would finally have been paid off, and the city would survive the assault. Menoeceus willingly sacrificed himself on the very spot where the dragon's lair had been, but still it seemed that the fate of the city hung in the balance.

The Seven met the seven Theban champions in single combat to decide the war, one at each of the city's gates. It was an outright victory for the Thebans. Of the attackers, only Capaneus succeeded in scaling the walls. But once he reached the top he crowed that not even the fire of Zeus could stop him – but it did, because dark-browed Zeus struck him with a bolt of lightning for his arrogance. Even Tydeus died, though he was a favourite of Athena. When he was fatally wounded by Melanippus, the goddess flew down from Olympus to administer a potion of immortality to the dying warrior, and transport him afterwards to bright Olympus. But Amphiaraus, who hated Tydeus, killed Melanippus and gave Tydeus his brains to eat. 'In this way,' he suggested, 'you will gain the dead man's spirit, and live.' Amphiaraus' grim design was realized: when Athena saw her favourite at his obscene meal, she withdrew in disgust, and Tydeus died a mortal's death.

Of the Seven, only Adrastus and Amphiaraus survived the failed siege of Thebes. They fled the battlefield. Adrastus made it safely back to Argos, but the earth gaped before Amphiaraus as he was driving his chariot away. Still in a fury at the doomed expedition, he welcomed death at a gallop and kept a firm grip on his bright-maned horses as they plunged into the underworld. Henceforth Amphiaraus is worshipped as a superhuman healer, who visits men and women in their dreams and instructs them in their cures.

As for the two brothers, Eteocles and Polynices, they traded blows and wounds in a fight that was so close and fierce that in the end they both died. It was as well that their mother was no longer alive to see the pitiful spectacle and their father's curse fulfilled.

Creon, once again the emergency ruler of Thebes, gave orders that Polynices and the rest of the aggressors from Argos were not to be honoured with burial. But Antigone could not abide this sin against her dead brother. Her sister Ismene counselled caution and obedience, but Antigone pushed her aside and defiantly gave Polynices at least the symbolic burial of three handfuls of dust thrown on his corpse. She preferred the unwritten law of the gods to Creon's edict, and was prepared even to suffer death for it. Creon had her walled up, to starve to death, but Haemon, his son and Antigone's betrothed, broke in to rescue her. Finding that she had hanged herself with her girdle rather than face a slow and painful death, he slew himself on the spot with his sword. And Creon's wife did the same when she heard of the death of her son. Creon was well repaid for ignoring the gods' wishes.

But Thebes did fall ten years later, to the sons of the Seven, led by Amphiaraus' son Alcmaeon. Teiresias saw that this time the destruction of the city was inevitable, and ordered its evacuation, so that at least human lives would be spared. But his daughter Daphne was captured, and sent by Alcmaeon to Delphi, where she became the first of the Sibyls – the first of those who can open themselves up to Apollo and speak for him.

Alcmaeon also paid his mother back for her treachery by slitting her throat and taking the necklace of Harmonia. As a matricide, the Furies hounded him from place to place, but he gained temporary shelter in Arcadia, where he married the king's daughter Arsinoe, and gave her the necklace. But he was a murderer, a matricide, and soon a plague descended on Arcadia. Knowing himself to be the cause, he left, seeking purification for his sin.

On the advice of an oracle, he sought a land on which the sun had not shone when he killed his mother. Eventually, he found a place that fitted this description at the mouth of the river Achelous, where silt carried down the river had formed new land, and he married fair-flowing Callirhoe there, the daughter of the river-god.

But Callirhoe had heard of the precious necklace, and insisted that Alcmaeon return to Arcadia and get it back. He did so, pretending that he had to take the necklace to Delphi to complete his purification, but when Arsinoe's brothers learnt of the trick, they killed him and retrieved the accursed bauble. Callirhoe prayed that her young sons might immediately be old enough to take their vengeance, and the gods granted her prayer. The curse of the necklace at last came to an end when the boys, so suddenly elevated to young manhood, gave it to Apollo at Delphi.

6

Mycenae in the Age of Heroes

The Curse of the House of Atreus

The royal house of Mycenae suffered no less than the Labdacid house of Thebes from the effects of a deadly curse. It all started with Tantalus, son of Zeus and king of Mount Sipylus in Lydia. What everyone knows about Tantalus is that he is 'tantalized': his punishment in Hades is to stand up to his chin in a pool of water, which sinks into the ground every time he tries to drink from it, while above his head a tree laden with all the appetizing fruits of the world raises its branches out of his reach every time he tries to pluck one of the fruits. But what did he do to get there?

The trouble was that he was too familiar with the gods. He used to dine with them, he was privy to their counsels, he hobnobbed with them on a daily basis. Familiarity, as we know, breeds contempt, and over time Tantalus got to know the gods so well that he began to doubt their powers. It was said that he stole some nectar and ambrosia from Olympus, the food and drink of the gods, and distributed it among mortals. He gave mortal men a glimpse of heaven, though they called it a dream, a hallucination. He might have been punished for that alone, but his crime was far worse, far more hideous.

The method he chose to test their powers was perverse in the extreme. He invited them all to dinner, all the great Olympians, and served them up a special dish. He had chopped up his own son Pelops and cooked the body parts in a rich sauce. The gods sat down to table and addressed their dinner – but all of them immediately pulled back in horror, proving their powers of discernment. All, that is, except for Demeter, who, distracted and pining for her daughter – it was the time of year when the pale queen was dwelling in the underworld – chewed and swallowed a juicy chunk of the boy's shoulder before realizing her mistake.

Appalled at what Tantalus had done, the gods took pity on the roasted youth, and in a rare show of unity and cooperation, they worked together to restore Pelops to life. The only difficulty was the bit that Demeter had eaten; and so ever after Pelops had an ivory shoulder, the first prosthetic, designed by Hermes and fashioned by Hephaestus. For his abominable meal Tantalus was sent down to Hades, to be denied food and drink for ever – and, like Sisyphus, Tityus, and Ixion, to serve as a warning to future criminals.

When Pelops was grown up, he migrated from Asia to the southern part of Greece, the part that still bears his name: the island of Pelops, the Peloponnese. His sister Niobe also left her native land to marry Amphion of Thebes – but she was fated to be carried lamenting back home to Lydia, and to weep cold tears there for ever. Pelops came in the first instance to win the hand of Hippodamia, daughter of Oenomaus, who was a son of Ares and king of Olympia. Now, Oenomaus was known to be an outstanding chariot-racer, and he would give his daughter away only to the man who could beat him in a race all the way across the Peloponnese from Olympia, over some of the most rugged terrain Greece has to offer. Thirteen brave men had already tried, but all had failed, and their heads were fixed above the doors of Oenomaus' palace. For he loved his daughter himself, and wanted no other man to possess her.

Pelops was beloved of Poseidon, and the earth-shaker supplied the young hero with a magnificent chariot for the race. Even so, Pelops was not at all sure he could win, given that Oenomaus' horses, as was well known, could outstrip Boreas, the north wind. Oenomaus' groom was called Myrtilus, and his father was the god Hermes. Oenomaus should have known better than to trust a son of the god of thieves and trickery.

Before the race, Pelops suborned Myrtilus by offering him half the kingdom he would gain by winning. Myrtilus agreed, and sabotaged Oenomaus' chariot by changing the metal linchpins – the pins that joined the wheel to the axle – for realistic-looking pins of wax. So the day of the race arrived. It was Oenomaus' practice to give the suitor a head start, and then catch up and kill him. And every suitor carried Hippodamia in his chariot, because the game that Oenomaus liked to play was that his daughter was being abducted, and that he was giving indignant chase. So off set Pelops and Hippodamia, and before long Oenomaus set out after them, with no reason to think that there wouldn't soon be a fourteenth head adorning his doorway.

No sooner had his godlike horses got up to full speed than the fake linchpins gave way. Oenomaus crashed to the ground amid a jumble of smashed wood and jagged metal, and was dragged by his horses over the rocky ground to a bloody death. Though Hippodamia grieved over the death of her father, she accepted the rules: she was Pelops' prize.

Myrtilus met them at the wreckage, to gloat over his success. And he seemed to think that his half of the kingdom included Hippodamia, because he began to molest her. Pelops leapt on the false groom and bound him fast. Myrtilus promised to leave Hippodamia alone, and reminded Pelops that he was owed half the kingdom, but Pelops was in no mood to listen.

The highest cliffs he knew were on the east coast of the Peloponnese, and at the earliest possible opportunity he drove over there with his prisoner. He made sure that the man knew what was about to happen, smiled at the dread on his face, and pushed him over the edge. Myrtilus plummeted hundreds of feet to his death, and the sea is named the Myrtoan Sea after him. But all the way down, as Myrtilus fell, he cried out a curse on Pelops and his descendants. And a true curse from the son of a god is always effective.

Atreus and Thyestes

Pelops ruled the kingdom of Olympia for a good many years, until he and his family almost came to believe that Myrtilus' curse had no power. Now, an oracle had proclaimed that a son of Pelops should be king of Mycenae, but when his two eldest sons, Thyestes and Atreus, went to the golden citadel to claim their inheritance, they fell murderously out with each other. It was Hermes' doing: angry at the death of Myrtilus, and determined to implement the curse, he sent a shepherd to Mycenae, bearing a golden lamb that had miraculously been born in his flock. The lamb was a clear token of kingship, and Atreus' claim to the throne was confirmed by the fact that the shepherd gave it to him, not his brother. In fact, the 'shepherd' may have been the god Pan in disguise, acting on his father Hermes' instructions.

Atreus immediately began to prepare for his coronation ceremony, but Thyestes had not given up. He seduced Aerope, his own brother's wife, and she gave him the fabulous lamb in secret. All the nobles and commons assembled for the glorious ceremony – and it was Thyestes who appeared with the lamb and was crowned king.

But the contest was not over yet. Zeus favoured the kingship of Atreus, and he sent Hermes to whisper in Atreus' mind. Atreus listened, and knew that the words came from a god. He declared to the people of Mycenae that his right to the throne would be heralded by a portent far greater than a mere golden lamb. And Zeus caused all the heavenly bodies to turn back on their paths. Thyestes had no choice but to recognize Atreus' greater claim.

So Atreus was king of Mycenae, and Thyestes was banished for his crimes. The first thing Atreus did was drown Aerope for her sin, but still he stored the bitter bile of vengeance in his heart. He pretended to forgive his brother, and invited him back to Mycenae for a feast of reconciliation. And for the main dish of the feast, he took and cut up Thyestes' sons. The heavens darkened and the sun hid its face at the crime, but Thyestes, all unknowing, ate heartily. At the end of the meal, he sat back, satisfied, and asked to see his sons. Then Atreus uncovered a serving-dish that held the boys' hands and feet and heads, for their father to see. Thyestes leapt to his feet, vomit spewing from his mouth, and kicked over the table, crying out a curse: 'May your house fall as surely as this table!'

Once more Thyestes left golden Mycenae, and went to dwell in Sicyon. Still looking for ways to be avenged on his brother, he consulted an oracle, and was told that he would father a child by his own daughter, Pelopia, and that the boy would grow up to be the instrument of his vengeance. Thyestes was appalled – he wanted revenge, but not like that – and he fled back to Sicyon; but on his way he stumbled at night upon Athena's sanctuary, where an all-female rite was being conducted.

But Athena's priestess soiled her robe with the blood of the sacrificial victim, and left the sacred precinct to wash it in the nearby stream. She undressed not far from where Thyestes was hiding. There was no moon, but in the starlight he caught glimpses of the swell of a young breast and the shapely curve of a thigh, until he was consumed by lust. He leapt out and raped the young woman in the darkness. It was, of course, Pelopia, his own daughter, though neither of them recognized the other in the dark and the frenzy of the moment.

When the child was born, Pelopia wanted nothing to do with it. She cast it away from herself and ordered it to be left for wolves and carrion crows in the mountains. But kindly shepherds found the baby and kept him alive with the milk of their goats, and so he was called Aegisthus. And when the baby was weaned, they took it to Atreus in Mycenae, and he raised the child as his own, as blind to his fate as all mortals are.

The years passed, and Atreus' sons, dour Agamemnon and red-haired Menelaus, grew and flourished. So did their foster brother Aegisthus. But the feuding sons of Pelops continued their bitter rivalry. Once more Atreus pretended to be reconciled with Thyestes, and invited him to his hilltop palace at Mycenae. He had filled the boys' ears all their lives with tales of the wickedness of Thyestes, and Aegisthus determined to kill the man he took to be his uncle, to repay Atreus for raising him.

They met in a secluded place and Aegisthus drew his sword against his father – the very sword that Pelopia had abandoned in disgust along with her unwanted infant. But as he raised it in the air for the killing thrust, Thyestes cried out: 'That sword! It's mine! I lost it years ago! Where did you find it?'

It was indeed the sword he had lost on the night of the rape. The awful truth came out: Thyestes and Aegisthus recognized each other as father and son, and sent for Pelopia to learn the truth. But the news could hardly bring her joy or relief from her long years of guilt and grief; she seized the sword and killed herself with it. Aegisthus took the weapon, streaked black with his sister–mother's blood, to Atreus and showed it to him as proof that his brother was dead, so that Atreus would lower his guard. And when the king went off alone to perform a thanks-giving sacrifice, Aegisthus killed him and restored his father to the throne of Mycenae. Agamemnon and Menelaus fled.

But even after all this slaughter the curse had not been drained of energy. Some time later, Agamemnon and Menelaus succeeded in expelling Thyestes from Mycenae for the last time, and he passes out of our knowing, for he lived out the rest of his life in exile on the lonely island of Cythera, sacred to Aphrodite. And Agamemnon ruled Mycenae wisely and well, while Menelaus was king of Sparta – until the outbreak of the Trojan War.

The End of the Atreid Curse

The two sons of Atreus, Agamemnon and Menelaus, were central to the Greek war effort against Troy. In a sense, you could say Menelaus caused the war – certainly there was grumbling from both officers and men along those lines – and Agamemnon was the commander-in-chief of the Greek forces. For ten long years the war was fought, and its outcome was uncertain until the very end. But the Greeks did what they had to do to win, and then they came back home. Back in Mycenae, Agamemnon was greeted by the full force of the family curse, now working out its evil in his generation.

Agamemnon was married to Clytemestra. It was an illustrious union: the king of Mycenae and the daughter of Tyndareos of Sparta and Leda. Her egg-born sister was Helen, sometime wife of Menelaus, and her brothers were Castor and Polydeuces, who would become the Heavenly Twins.

Now, as we shall see, Clytemestra could well claim that Agamemnon was guilty of the death of their own daughter Iphigeneia. For all the years that Agamemnon was away at war, her daughter's fate poisoned Clytemestra's mind and heart. She had other children – Orestes, Electra, and Chrysothemis – but even by the end of the war they had not reached maturity. And she took as her lover Aegisthus, son of Thyestes and killer of her father-in-law, Atreus. Aegisthus had long wooed her, but Agamemnon left behind a trusted bard to keep his wife from harm.

When the time came for open rebellion against her husband, she had the bard abducted and abandoned on an empty island, to perish of heat and thirst; and then she went willingly to Aegisthus' bed. It was a poor exchange, Agamemnon for Aegisthus, but Clytemestra's father Tyndareos had once forgotten to sacrifice to Aphrodite, and the vengeful goddess filled his daughter's heart with infatuation.

By the time Agamemnon arrived back in golden Mycenae, Aegisthus' and Clytemestra's minds were made up. For seven years, they had been living together as man and wife, and as king and queen, and their sinister plans for the rightful king had long been laid. Clytemestra greeted him with apparent affection, as a returning hero, and even though Cassandra foresaw what was going to happen, why should she speak out? No one would believe her. For Agamemnon had brought back, among other rich booty, the Trojan princess, the truth-teller no one believed, now the king's concubine.

Clytemestra led her husband into the palace, where, as a good wife would, she had prepared a bath for him, to cleanse the dust of travel from his body; and Agamemnon laid aside his weapons. Under the pretence of a romantic reunion she sent the servants away; she would bathe the newly returned king with her own hands.

For a moment she hesitated: he had become so toughened by ten years of warfare that he seemed invulnerable, and somehow magnificent. But she stiffened her resolve, and no sooner had he risen, dripping, from the relaxing warmth of the water than Clytemestra entangled his limbs in a sheet, and trapped him as effectively as a proud stag in a net. Aegisthus emerged from concealment and together they stabbed him to death, rejoicing in the gouts of gore that soiled their clothes and rapidly reddened the sweet water of the bath. And then they slaughtered Cassandra too. Iphigeneia was avenged, and the black cloud of the curse closed in on the palace of Mycenae.

Now, Orestes, the only male child, was away from Mycenae at the time. In fact, it was Clytemestra herself who had sent him away, uncertain whether Aegisthus might not think it in his interest to rid Mycenae of the last male Atreid. When he heard of Aegisthus' and Clytemestra's coup, Orestes stayed away, and grew safely to manhood in Phocis. He knew all along that he was bound to avenge the murder of his father, even if that meant killing his mother, and Apollo himself, through his oracle at Delphi, assured him that it was the right thing to do.

In due course of time, Orestes returned secretly to Mycenae with his friend Pylades, son of the king of Phocis, and, with the help and encouragement of Electra (but to the horror of Chryso-themis), they killed both Clytemestra and Aegisthus, hardening their hearts and calling on the ghost of Agamemnon to witness the piety of their awful deed. And so the dream came true that had appeared to Clytemestra when she was pregnant with Orestes: that she suckled a snake, which drew blood as well as milk from her breast.

But the horrible Furies pursue anyone who commits murder within the family, and they harried Orestes, until the guilt gnawing at his mind drove him quite insane. During one of his lucid moments, he begged Electra to take him to Delphi. Apollo assured him that he would be cured, and sent him for trial at Athens, where Athena herself held court. And the wise goddess freed him of guilt and ordered the Furies to plague Orestes no more. She is a great goddess, whose vision pierces veils, and the power of her word ended the curse that had afflicted the family for four generations and caused the worst crimes known to man.

7

Athens in the Age of Heroes

The First Athenian Kings

At Athens the bards sing of their first kings, but no one now knows all their names or stories. The earliest kings of whom we know something were these five: Cecrops, Erichthonius, Pandion, Erechtheus, and Aegeus, who was the father of Theseus.

Cecrops is remembered as the original founder of Athens. In his time, a dispute arose between Poseidon and Athena as to which of them should be the guardian of the city. Mighty Poseidon took up the challenge and struck the solid rock of the Acropolis with his trident, and a fresh-water spring burst forth, a great boon for the city. But Athena caused the first olive tree to sprout, and the olive is the foundation of Athenian prosperity. The prize was hers, and in her honour the city came to be called Athens, though the earth-shaker too is held in high esteem there.

Like Cecrops and all the early Athenian kings, Erichthonius was born from the earth and the lower half of his body was serpentine. He was born, as we have seen, when Hephaestus, lusting after Athena, spilled his seed on the receptive ground. Athena, however, gathered up the strange infant and kept him safe in a chest, and set a guard of two snakes over the baby, which coiled their lengths around his infant limbs. Athena gave the chest to the dew-bright daughters of Cecrops for safekeeping, and warned the young women – Aglauros, Herse, and Pandrosus – not to look inside. But curiosity got the better of them, and after one glance they became deranged and threw themselves off the Acropolis to their deaths. After this, Athena brought Erichthonius up herself, until he was ready to take up his kingdom.

Pandion, who succeeded Erichthonius as king, had two daughters, Procne and Philomela. Procne was married to Tereus, king of Thrace, and lived there with him, and bore him a son, Itys. But when Philomela, her beloved sister, came to visit, Tereus violated her and, to make sure she wouldn't tell anyone, cut out her tongue and locked her away in a hovel deep in a gloomy forest, telling Procne that her sister had unexpectedly fled. For it was fated that he should die at the hands of close kin, and Tereus had already killed his brother out of fear. But Philomela was undefeated: she wove the story into a tapestry and, using sign language, told the servant who attended her to take the work to her sister. Procne understood the tale spun by her sister's loom, but patiently bided her time.

The time came for the women of Thrace to celebrate the mysteries of Dionysus in the countryside, away from the restricting conventions of populated places. Procne seized the opportunity to rescue her sister from the forest, and she brought her back to the palace and hid her in her quarters. The two sisters plotted ghastly revenge: they killed young Itys, cooked him, and gave him to Tereus to eat. Too late Tereus realized what meat had been laid before him, and in a murderous frenzy he chased the women through the palace.

But the gods intervened and transformed them into birds to escape him. Procne became the nightingale, and ever mourns her dead son at night; while the swallow Philomela, trying to tell of her sorrow with her tongueless beak, succeeds only in producing an incoherent gurgle. Tereus, however, with his high-crested helmet and his sword, became a hoopoe.

Pandion, as we have seen, the devotee of Dionysus, was killed by drunken peasants. The fate of Erechtheus, Pandion's son and heir, was scarcely better. In his time, baneful war first came to Athena's city, wielded by Eumolpus, son of Poseidon and king of Eleusis. And the gods told Erechtheus that the city would fall, unless he sacrificed one of his daughters. Erechtheus and his wife, crushed by the terrible burden of their duty, gave their consent, so that the Furies would have no pretext for persecuting them. In the ensuing battle, Erechtheus himself killed Eumolpus, but for his pains was killed in his turn by Poseidon, who cracked open a chasm in the earth with his trident and hurled him inside. From the earth came this half-snake king, and to the earth he returned.

Erechtheus had three other daughters of whom stories are told. Oreithyia was loved by Boreas, but his suit was rejected: Erechtheus had no desire to ally himself and his city with the cold north wind. But Boreas was true to his violent nature. He found the fair maiden gathering flowers on the banks of the Cephisus, and whisked her away to his mountain fastness in Thrace, for all that her sisters tried to hold her back. There she bore him Zetes and Calaïs, sons who did justice to the noble lineages of both their parents: as Argonauts, they drove off the Snatchers, and, at the funeral games of Pelias, they were the celebrated winners of the long footrace.

Another daughter, the bewitching Procris, was wedded to Cephalus, the son of Herse by Hermes, and they loved each other so truly that they swore never to have sex with anyone else. But saffron-robed Eos, the dawn's faery twilight, was in love with Cephalus, and persuaded him to test his wife's fidelity. 'I would not have you break your vow to your wife,' she said, 'unless she breaks hers first.' And she disguised Cephalus as a stranger, burdened him with precious gifts, and sent him to seduce his own wife.

Each day he increased his offer to her, and each day she faithfully refused to lie with him. But his stupid persistence was duly repaid. When she eventually gave in to the 'stranger', he revealed himself, and in shame she ran away to Crete, to the court of King Minos. And Minos too fell in love with the enchanting young woman. But Minos had been cursed by his wife Pasiphae, so that whenever he had sex he would emit foul little snakes and tiny scorpions. Procris cured him, however, and in return he gave her gifts that Artemis had given him: a javelin that never missed its mark and flew back to the thrower's hand, and a hound that always caught its quarry.

With the hound at her heels, and the javelin in hand, Procris returned to Athens disguised as a young nobleman, a fanatical hunter. She and her husband became friends, and spent many days together in the mountains, searching for game.

Naturally, Cephalus began to covet the remarkable hound and the incredible javelin. Daily he offered more wealth in exchange for them, and each time Procris refused to trade. But at last she said, 'Give me what's between your legs!' Cephalus was somewhat taken aback by his friend's suggestion, but his longing for the hound and the javelin was such that he would do anything.

In the bed chamber all was revealed, and husband and wife were reconciled. But secret distrust was still rotting the foundation of their marriage. Cephalus used to go out hunting with his lady's infallible javelin, and after the heat of the chase he would lie down and beg any clouds in the sky to hurry his way, to give him shade. But an attendant took him to be calling for a woman called Nephele – the name means 'cloud' – and confided his suspicions to Procris. The next time Cephalus went out hunting, she secretly followed him, and hid close by in the bushes while he took his rest. But a twig-snap alerted the keen hunter to the presence of an animal, or so he thought. Without a moment's hesitation he hurled the unerring javelin at the bush, and the javelin, which pierced the heart of its target, returned with bloodied head to Cephalus' hand.

Cephalus banished himself from Athens for the slaying of his wife and went to live in Thebes for the period of purification. When he arrived there, with his hound, he found that the Thebans were being harassed by a fearsome man-eating fox, too crafty and too fast for any of their hounds to catch. 'Watch this!' said Cephalus. But the magical fox could not be caught. Round and round they went, the hound endlessly closing in on the endlessly elusive fox . . . As we shall see, it took Zeus to resolve the stalemate, and he did so in order to enable his favourite son Heracles to be born.

Another daughter of Erechtheus was Creusa, who was ravished and abandoned by Apollo, but bore him a son, Ion. Not wanting her father to know that she had a child out of wedlock, she left Ion to die in a remote cave, but Apollo cared for his son, and sent Hermes to rescue him and take him as a foundling to Delphi, where he worked in the holy precinct as a humble servant. Years later, Creusa and her husband Xuthus, son of

Hellen, came to Delphi to enquire about their childlessness, and Xuthus was told by the god to take as his son the first person he met as he left the temple. And so Ion returned to Athens and became the revered ancestor of Ionian-speaking Greeks.

The Labours of Theseus

Next among the legendary kings of Athens was Aegeus. He and his wife had as yet no heir for the kingdom, so he went, as is usual, to the sanctuary of Apollo at Delphi, to ask whether he would have children, and what he should do about it. The oracle's reply was oblique and puzzling: 'Leave the wineskin's mouth unopened until you get home.'

On the way back from Delphi to Athens Aegeus stayed for a while with Pittheus, king of Troezen. At an evening's banquet Aegeus shared with his friend the confusing message he'd received from the god. Pittheus thought for a while, and then ordered his servants to see that every wine cup remained full, especially that of his noble guest. And once Aegeus was good and drunk, he bedded him down with his own daughter Aethra. But on the same night that Aethra lay with Aegeus, she lay also with the god Poseidon, and so her child was the son of both the earth-shaker and the king of Athens.

Before leaving Troezen, Aegeus instructed Aethra that, if she bore a male child, she was to bring him up without telling anyone who the father was, and send him to Athens when he was able to raise a certain rock by himself. Under the rock Aegeus had hidden a pair of sandals and an ivory-hilted sword, as tokens by which he would be able to recognize his son. In due course of time Theseus was born, and the birds fell silent in awe at his birth.

The years passed, and red-haired Theseus grew to young manhood, skilled in the ways of battle and council chamber. One day he was out hunting in the hills near Troezen, and he thought that a hare he was chasing had taken refuge under a boulder. With some effort, he managed to lift up the boulder – only to find no hare, but, mysteriously, a valuable sword and a pair of sandals. He replaced the heavy stone and went quickly to fetch his mother, to show her the cache. Aethra realized that the time had come for her son to go to his father in Athens. So with the sword at his side and the sandals strapped to his feet, Theseus set off to meet his destiny.

To reach Athens, Theseus was bound to take the dangerous coast road around the Saronic Gulf. This untamed territory was infested with unscrupulous killers and robbers, who rejected the sacred laws of hospitality towards strangers. This would be an epic journey for the young man, and a test of his mettle as a hero and a future king. First, near Epidaurus, he was set upon by the Man with the Club, as the beetle-browed brigand Periphetes was called. One blow from the club of this hulking son of Hephaestus was enough to send all those he encountered to the dank halls of Hades, lord of shades. But Theseus dodged the blow, seized the club – and found that one blow from him was enough to crush Periphetes' skull as well. Then he continued on his way.

The region around the Isthmus was under the sway of Sinis, a son of Poseidon. Gigantic and terrible, he had devised an appalling death for anyone he caught on the road. He would bend down two young pine trees until their tops were close together, tie his captive's ankles to one tree and his wrists to the other – and then let the saplings spring upright, ripping his victim limb from limb. Theseus gave the Pinebender a taste of his own deadly medicine.

Just west of Megara, in the district of Crommyon, an enormous, man-eating sow, said to be under the control of a witch, was terrorizing the inhabitants. No one dared leave home to work the fields or attend a ceremony at a temple, for fear of becoming the bristling monster's next meal. Theseus fearlessly hunted the sow down in the low hills and killed it – and as it died, the aged crone who was its keeper faded away to nothingness.

The domain of monstrous Sciron lay a little further on, between Megara and Eleusis. The cliffs here soar high and sheer from the sea, and the road clings tentatively to the precipice. Sciron had the habit of blocking the narrow way and forcing passersby to kneel and wash his feet in a basin of water. As if the humiliation wasn't enough, while they were crouching down he dealt them a mighty kick that sent them tumbling down the cliff and into the sea below, where a giant turtle ate them. Theseus saw through Sciron's foul ruse and played the victim, but as he bent down he seized hold of the man's legs. He flipped him over his shoulders and into the churning sea hundreds of feet below, where the hungry turtle was waiting.

Just beyond Eleusis lived a brigand called Cercyron, a son of Hephaestus. His favourite pastime was to compel travellers to wrestle with him. He claimed falsely that those who beat him were allowed to continue on their way – but in fact none could defeat him, and he fought them to the death. Theseus was the first to out-wrestle him. He picked the huge highwayman up off the ground, held him aloft for a moment, and smashed his body down onto the ground, which bristled with sharp rocks.

Finally, Theseus had to pass crazy Procrustes, whose name means the Stretcher. Not far from Athens, Procrustes had blocked the road with a bed upon which he compelled all travellers to lie. If they were too long for the bed, he took up his axe and chopped them down to size; if they were too short, he took up a mallet, made for him in Hephaestus' workshop by the Cyclopes, and flattened them into a perfect fit. But Theseus, taking Procrustes' measure, grabbed the lunatic and pinned him on the bed. It was the killer's turn to die; Theseus hacked off bits of him until he was just the right size.

Having cleared the coast path of its many dangers, Theseus arrived in Athens and presented himself, as Aethra had suggested, at the royal palace. But it so happened that Aegeus was away at the time, negotiating with potential allies for the forthcoming war with Crete. The young hero was greeted by Medea, who had fled from Corinth to Athens after ruining Jason's life and killing their children, and was now married to King Aegeus. The sorceress recognized the young man as Aegeus' son, and realized what a threat he was to her own son. Medus would never inherit the Athenian throne with Theseus around. So she sent Theseus off to certain death on the coastal plain of Marathon.

The fields and low hills of Marathon, north-east of Athens, were being terrorized by an enormous bull. This was the same bull that led to the ruin of Cretan Minos . . . but we shall have that story soon enough. Many men had fallen beneath the savage hoofs and deadly horns in their failed attempts to subdue the beast. But Theseus wrestled the bull to the ground and hobbled it, and drove it in triumph back to Athens, where he sacrificed it to Apollo. Aegeus was back in Athens by then, and held a banquet to celebrate the capture of the bull. But he hadn't recognized his son yet, and Medea advised him to do away with this mysterious stranger, lest he try to take the throne. 'If you agree,' she said, 'I'll provide you with some wolf's-bane right now, and you can put it in his wine.' But when Theseus lifted his cup to acknowledge his hosts before drinking, his cloak fell away from his shoulder, and Aegeus glimpsed the ivory hilt of his sword. He dashed the poisoned chalice away from Theseus' hand and, to Medea's chagrin, amid tears of joy Aegeus publicly recognized Theseus as his son and heir.

Theseus and the Minotaur

Theseus and Aegeus were together at last, and they spent their days getting to know each other during a brief time of peace. But before long Athens was attacked by King Minos of Crete, one of the sons Europa had borne for Zeus. Prior to Theseus' arrival, Minos' son Androgeos had paid a visit to Athens, and had mightily impressed everyone with his athletic prowess. But Aegeus suspected that Androgeos had secret dealings with Pallas, Aegeus' ambitious brother, who sought the Athenian throne for himself and his sons. The Athenian king had therefore sent Androgeos off to test his strength against the Marathonian bull, and the bull had, as expected, gored and trampled the young man to death. In retaliation, grief-stricken Minos launched an invasion.

He landed first at Megara, where Aegeus' other brother Nisus was king. Now, Nisus had a bright lock of immortal hair growing on his head, and as long as it was there Megara would be safe. But his daughter Scylla had offended queenly Hera, and in retaliation the cow-eyed goddess sent Eros to make the girl fall in love with her enemy. As Scylla looked out from the walls of the town, her eyes fell on Minos, and Eros' arrow pierced her heart. A trusted servant delivered her message to the Cretan king, and he sent her in return a false token of his love, a many-stranded necklace of weighty gold. Knowing what she had to do to win her man, she cut off her father's magic lock while he slept and sent it to her purported lover. But Minos ruthlessly rejected her, sacked the city, killed Nisus, and then sailed off for Athens.

It didn't take Minos long to subdue Athens, and, as recompense for the murder of his dear son, he imposed a heavy penalty on the city. Every year, seven noble youths and seven noble maidens were to be chosen by lot and sent to Minos' palace in Cnossus. Once there, they were to enter the amazing labyrinth that Daedalus had built under the palace. At its heart lived the fearsome Minotaur; none who entered the labyrinth ever returned.

What was the Minotaur? A horrid hybrid, with the legs and body of a man, but the shoulders and massive head of a bull. It was, indirectly, a member of Minos' family. In order to help Minos carry out his obligatory annual sacrifice to Poseidon, the sea-god himself had sent him a bull from the sea – all white, flawless, and massive. So perfect was the bull that it seemed to Minos a waste to do away with it, and in his folly he selected a less perfect sacrifice for the earth-shaker's altar.

This had angered Poseidon, and he cursed Minos' wife Pasiphae, daughter of the sun, with a perverse lust for the gorgeous bull. She called on the skilled craftsman Daedalus to find a way to allow her to couple with the creature, and he constructed a hollow cow of wood. He covered the frame with hide to fool the bull, and Pasiphae squirmed herself into position inside the dummy cow. Soon the handsome bull came and fulfilled her twisted fantasy. The result was the Minotaur.

Minos was so disgusted and ashamed of his wife's behaviour and the offspring of her foul union that he had Daedalus construct an elaborate labyrinth under the palace, and the mazy multitude of winding ways was so confusing that even its maker was hard put to find his way around it. And at the heart of the maze lived the Minotaur, chained and hungry, raging in its squalor.

The ingenious Daedalus was a cousin of Aegeus, from a minor branch of the Athenian royal family, but he had fled Athens after killing a nephew, and had fetched up in Crete, along with his son Icarus. Endowed by the gods with a clever mind and hands to match, he was the most skilled inventor and craftsman of this or any other age. The statues he sculpted were so lifelike that you would swear they breathed and moved; he built temples and altars, and he invented all the basic tools of carpentry and building to help him and his successors in their work. For his part in helping Pasiphae to consummate her obscene lust, Minos imprisoned Daedalus and his son. But the prison walls had not been built that could contain the master. 'Minos may control the land,' said Daedalus to Icarus, 'and he may control the seaways; but the sky is beyond his reach.'

Within his cell, Daedalus fashioned for himself and his son strong wings. Great eagle feathers covered a light wooden frame, which could be strapped to the arms. The feathers were coated with wax, both to glue them to the frame and to make them strong enough to bear the weight of a human being. When all was ready, the two of them, man and boy, perched on the window ledge of their lofty prison and launched themselves into the air.

Daedalus' latest invention was astounding: human beings could fly! As they began to flap and glide their easy way towards Sicily, Daedalus warned Icarus to steer a middle course. 'The peril stands equal, my son,' he said. 'If you fly too low, the hungry waves may lick up and drown you; but if you fly too high, the sun may melt the wax which binds your wings together. Fly not too high, my son!'

Again and again the anxious father had to warn his son about the danger, and every time Icarus obeyed at first, but soon began to experiment, as teenagers will, with the limits of his father's marvellous invention. He swooped and soared to his heart's delight, and Daedalus was pleased to see that the wings were sturdy enough to stand this much stress. But in such hazardous ventures, one mistake is all that is needed. Icarus rose too high in the sky, preparing for a joyous dive. The wax melted, the feathers fell off, and the boy plummeted headlong to his death in the sea.

But Daedalus was revenged on Minos. Shortly after the time of our story, Minos went to Sicily to recover Daedalus and punish him. Daedalus went into hiding, but Minos cunningly took with him to Sicily a conch shell, and he offered a princely reward to anyone who could pass a thread all the way through the windings of the shell.

Now, the only one who could do it was Cocalus, king of Acragas, and the way he did it was to tie the thread to an ant, which then worked its way through the tortuous channels of the shell. But this was a trap: Minos knew that only Daedalus could have thought up the business with the ant, and so he knew that the fugitive prince was in Acragas. When Minos confronted Cocalus, the king greeted him kindly, and suggested a bath to wash the dust of his journey from his royal body, with his own fair daughters in attendance. And when Minos stepped into the bath, Cocalus had his daughters pour boiling water over the Cretan king, who died in horrible agony.

*

At the time in question, Minos defeated the Athenians and imposed the indemnity of the seven youths and seven maidens, to be sent into the labyrinth as a sacrifice to the Minotaur. Young Theseus was grieved to see his new-found father humbled so, and was enraged by the city's loss. The people of the kingdom were assembled, and fourteen names were read out amid the cries and wails of heartbroken parents and siblings. But while all the other young men and women had been chosen by lot, Minos chose Theseus himself, for he wanted Aegeus to suffer the loss of his newly discovered son. But Theseus was glad to go, for he intended to do away with the Minotaur and rid Athens once and for all of the indemnity.

The fourteen victims were hustled onto the black-sailed flagship of Minos' victorious war fleet and set sail on a favourable breeze. In the course of the voyage, Minos began to lust after one of the young Athenian women, but Theseus stood up to him and protected the terrified virgin. 'And who are you,' thundered Minos, 'to prevent a son of Zeus from having his way?' 'A son of Poseidon,' Theseus snapped back, and challenged Minos to prove that Zeus really was his father. 'I will if you will,' said Minos, and he called upon Zeus to send thunder, as a sign that he recognized him as his son. A massive peal of thunder rumbled and shook the heavens, and then Minos hurled a ring into the depths of the sea, challenging Theseus to recover it, if he truly was the son of Poseidon.

Nothing daunted, Theseus leapt into the foaming waves; for heroes recognize no limits. None expected to see him again, but dolphins came and bore him to the undersea palace of his father Poseidon, where the brother of almighty Zeus sat on his throne with Amphitrite at his right hand. Amphitrite presented her stepson with Minos' ring, and gave him a beautiful cloak and a crown that Aphrodite had once given her. And Theseus, endowed thereby with the aura of Aphrodite, was escorted back to Minos' ship by Poseidon's assistant Triton, whose massive, scaly bulk belied his gentle nature. Theseus clambered back on board, miraculously dry. If Minos was concerned, he kept his fears to himself. No sooner had the ships docked at the harbour of Cnossus than Ariadne, the Cretan king's beautiful daughter, hurried down to greet her father. But as soon as she cast eyes on Theseus, standing tall and proud on the prow of the flagship, she fell in love with him. Ariadne crept out after dark and whispered her love to Theseus through the barred window of the rough quarters shared by the young Athenian captives. The hero eagerly returned her words, for she was surpassingly fair – and potentially useful.

Theseus' greatest problem was this. Even though he was unarmed, he was confident that he could kill the Minotaur – after all, nothing had been able to resist him so far – but first he had to find it. The maze was famously complex, designed to baffle the human mind and heart. A man could get lost in there for ever, and wander futilely and in increasing terror until death overtook him. So when the time came for him and the other young Athenians to enter the labyrinth and confront the Minotaur, Ariadne secretly slipped him a spool of shining thread, which he could unwind as he worked his way through the maze, and rewind on the way back.

The fourteen young men and women stepped into the gloom of the labyrinth, but their sinking hearts recovered when they saw the confidence of their champion's stride. He led the way, and they crept through the maze behind him. Time and again they found that they had come to a dead end, so they rewound the thread back to the last junction and tried a different route. At last, by eliminating all the dead ends, they drew closer and closer to the centre, until they could hear the snuffling and stamping of the monster and let the noise pull them fearfully forward in the gloom. The closer they came, the worse the stench that assailed their nostrils – the miasma of the Minotaur's rotting victims and waste.

As soon as the beast caught their scent, it raised its muzzle and blasted the stale air with hot breath, that issued like a wet cloud from its red-rimmed nostrils. It began to tug at the leg-irons that chained it to the solid rock and prevented escape to the world above. When the beast caught sight of them, it seized some of the massive boulders that were lying about the floor of the cavern and began to hurl them at the terrified youngsters. But Theseus told the rest to stay well behind, while he boldly advanced and fought the creature singlehandedly, man against monster. Before long the Minotaur was gasping out its final breaths in a pool of blood on the rocky ground, battered by the same rocks it had hurled at Theseus.

It was a simple matter to escape the foul dankness of the labyrinth: all they had to do was follow Ariadne's thread back to the entrance, where she anxiously awaited them. Gulping sweet life into their lungs along with the clean, bright air, they sprinted for the harbour. After scuttling all the rest of Minos' ships to prevent pursuit, they leapt aboard the black-winged flagship in which they had come, and set sail safely for Athens. Everyone had reason for joy, and Ariadne anticipated soon being Theseus' royal bride.

The fugitives spent the first night on the island of Naxos. But Athena appeared to Theseus in a dream, and commanded him to continue his voyage immediately, and to leave Ariadne there on the island. For she was destined for a higher station. Theseus did so, but reluctantly, with a last lingering look at the fair maiden; but the orders of the gods are not to be disobeyed. When Ariadne awoke in the morning, she was frightened and bewildered, but the god Dionysus appeared before her and said that she was destined to be his wife, and promised her fidelity. And Father Zeus made her immortal, so that she would never know death or age, and could live for all eternity with her husband. The veil between mortality and immortality is fine, but so strong that only Father Zeus, king of gods and men, can part it for an instant.

So the young Athenians continued their voyage home. Now, on the day Minos took him and the others from Athens to become fare for the Minotaur, Theseus had promised his father that, if he managed to destroy the beast and return, he would hoist white sails on the ship, to replace the morbid black ones which had carried him away on his deadly mission. But caught up in the joy and anticipation of a victorious homecoming, Theseus forgot to change the sails. Day after day, Aegeus had climbed to the highest point of the Athenian Acropolis to keep an anxious but hopeful vigil and watch for the sign of his son's safe return. And at last he saw the ship on the horizon – but black sails, not white, snapped in the wind.

His son was dead; he had no reason to go on living. Aegeus cast himself to his death off the Acropolis. But others say that he saw the black sails from the cliffs of Sunium, and there threw himself into the sea which now bears his name, the Aegean.

King Theseus

By this unhappy accident, Theseus gained the throne of Athens, but it was not a smooth succession. Aegeus had long been feuding with his brother Pallas, and now Pallas gathered a mighty force to seize the throne. With his sons as his generals, he prepared to attack Athens. But Theseus got wind of his plans, launched a surprise counterattack, and eliminated the threat once and for all. So Theseus protected his people, and they prospered under his wisdom.

Theseus' best friend was Pirithous, king of the Lapiths in Thessaly. Pirithous was a son of Ixion, and also of Zeus, who had mounted Ixion's wife in the form of a noble stallion. Pirithous and Theseus became friends when the Thessalian tried to rustle some of Theseus' cattle. Theseus set out in pursuit and caught up with the thief – but Pirithous turned and offered him friendship instead of enmity. From then on the two were inseparable, and shared a number of adventures. Usually, but not always, their concern was to tame the earth, to make it a place where human civilization and culture could flourish.

Together they led an expedition against the Amazons, who dwell in distant Scythia, on the edge of the world, and they abducted the Amazon queen Antiope, who bore Theseus a son, Hippolytus. But then Theseus cast Antiope aside and chose Phaedra, daughter of Cretan Minos, to be his lawful wife. No one treats a proud Amazon queen like that and gets away with it! Antiope summoned her sisters and they attacked Athens in force; but the Amazons were repulsed, and Antiope died from her wounds.

Hippolytus grew up fair and strong in his father's halls, and became a devotee of Artemis. He loved nothing better than running with hounds and other hunters, bare-chested and sweat-soaked in the hills; and he swore that he would remain chaste all his life, in imitation of his goddess. But Phaedra's heart was filled with an abominable love for her stepson, and then, when he refused her, with cold fury. She went to Theseus and told him that Hippolytus had tried to rape her. Theseus called on his father Poseidon to destroy Hippolytus, and a bull emerged from the surf of the sea and attacked the young man as he was driving his chariot. The horses bolted and Hippolytus was dragged along the ground to his death. At the sight of his mangled body, Phaedra killed herself for shame – but Hippolytus was miraculously resurrected by Asclepius, and for this unnatural act Asclepius was blasted by Zeus the cloud-gatherer.

Now, Pirithous was betrothed to Hippodamia, daughter of Atrax of Hestiaeotis, and the time came for the wedding to be celebrated. Pirithous arranged a splendid wedding feast, and invited not only all his fellow Lapiths, but his distant kin the Centaurs as well, who dwelt near by in the mountains of Thessaly. The servants, obeying orders, served the shaggy Centaurs milk to drink; but the tempting scent of the sweet wine the Lapiths were drinking inflamed the wild half-men, and they pushed their milk aside and seized flagons of wine instead.

At first, the Centaurs became boisterous, then unruly, and finally they tried to rape the Lapith women. Tables were overturned, women were being dragged off by the hair. Their screams mingled with the confused cries of the Lapiths and grunts of the Centaurs as they hauled their reluctant victims away. The Lapiths armed themselves with whatever they could grab – cups, cushions, knives – while the Centaurs wielded trees that they uprooted, and boulders that they snatched up in their powerful arms.

The conflict that broke out at the wedding spilled out of the house and became more formal warfare, to be resolved by battle only when Theseus came to help. In the course of the fighting many heroes fell, including the noble Lapith Caeneus, the brother of Hippodamia. He had been born as Caenis, a girl, but she granted her favours to Poseidon, who in return granted her a wish. And her wish was to become a man, and immortal. But despite his immortality, the Centaurs hammered Caeneus into the ground with tree trunks, and sealed him inside for ever with a massive boulder.

Even the noblest heroes can act like fools under the influence of Eros. The most notorious escapade which Theseus and Pirithous got up to involved two bungled abductions. The young men set their hearts on making daughters of Zeus their own. Theseus chose Helen, daughter of Zeus and Leda, while Pirithous aimed even higher, for Persephone, wife of Hades. They succeeded in abducting Helen from Sparta – she was just a young girl at the time, and they found her dancing naked by the Eurotas river with her friends – but Theseus left her in Athens and immediately set out to help his friend with Persephone. Helen's brothers, the divine twins Castor and Polydeuces, took advantage of his absence to regain their sister – and at the same time they kidnapped Aethra, Theseus' mother, to be Helen's handmaid.

Pirithous' attempt on Persephone was even more of a disaster, though he foolishly entertained the idea that, since he and Persephone shared Zeus as their father, the cloud-gatherer would look kindly on the endeavour. When they arrived in Hades' palace, the dark-cowled god made them welcome, but his heart spoke other words, for he knew their designs. And so he bade them be seated – but as soon as Pirithous took his seat on an intricately carved bench, the stone softened and moulded itself around him, and then hardened again, so that he was utterly trapped. Theseus' help was as vain as Pirithous' struggle. The Athenian king was compelled to leave his friend for ever in the underworld, as one of the dead, condemned to an eternity of grief and remorse.

Back in Athens, his adventures over, Theseus proved to be a wise and good king – but such qualities do not make one immune from treachery. By such means his cousin Menestheus usurped the throne of Athens and banished Theseus to the island of Scyros, where in due course he died. His body was found broken at the bottom of a cliff, and no one knew whether he had fallen or been pushed.

8

Heracles

The Birth of Heracles

Electryon, king of Mycenae and son of Perseus and Andromeda, went to war with the Teleboans, who had killed his sons and stolen his cattle. While he was away, he left Amphitryon in charge of Mycenae, and signalled his trust in his young nephew by giving him his daughter Alcmene, who was so beautiful that men thought they were in the presence of Aphrodite herself, the subduer of men. But Electryon told Amphitryon that he was to leave Alcmene a virgin until after he returned from his expedition, and Alcmene agreed: no sex until her dead brothers had been avenged.

But a terrible accident occurred. Electryon found the missing cattle before he had avenged himself on the Teleboans. He sent for Amphitryon and together they began to drive the herd back to Mycenae. But during the drive one of the cows ran amok. Amphitryon hurled his club at the creature's head, but it bounced off the horns and struck Electryon instead, killing him instantly. When Amphitryon got back to Mycenae, the priests told him he had to leave, in case his blood-guilt polluted the city, and he chose to go to Thebes.

So Amphitryon went to Thebes for purification, taking his wife with him. But Alcmene still refused to let Amphitryon into her bed until her brothers had been avenged. A homeless exile, Amphitryon was not up to the task alone: he needed the help of his host, Creon of Thebes. But Creon was preoccupied by a deadly fox that was devastating the countryside. Each month one young man was sent out after the fox, and was never seen again. To make matters worse, everyone knew that the fox was destined never to be caught. Creon promised help, but only once the fox had been dealt with.

Just then, Cephalus arrived in Thebes. The Athenian needed purification from blood guilt as well, after accidentally killing his wife with his infallible javelin. Tainted by its deadly deed, the javelin had been left behind, a dedication in a temple, but Cephalus still had his hound. They set out after the fox – the infallible hound against the fox that could not be caught. An impossible situation developed, a paradox: the hound was bound to catch the fox, but the fox could not be caught. But Father Zeus grew bored of watching the endless chase. He resolved the riddle by turning both fox and hound to stone, and they stand there still.

Creon was now free to help Amphitryon and together they marched out against the Teleboans. The chief problem was that the Teleboans could not be conquered as long as their king, Pterelaus, was alive, and he could not be killed. He sported a magical lock of golden hair which kept him alive. But it didn't require Zeus to solve *this* riddle. Pterelaus' daughter fell in love with Amphitryon and betrayed her father. She cut off the golden lock and he immediately died. The city fell, and Amphitryon punished the Teleboans for killing Alcmene's brothers.

When Amphitryon returned victorious to Thebes, he was at last allowed to lie with his wife, but there was something he didn't know. Alcmene had just been honoured by a long and fulfilling visit from Zeus. The great god had appeared to her as Amphitryon and slept with her, before revealing himself to her and giving her a golden goblet as a gift. Not only had he slept with her, but he had persuaded Helios, the sun-god, to rein in his stallions so that the sun would not rise in the morning, and the night would be prolonged to three times its normal length. So much potency did Zeus want to sow in fair Alcmene.

Now, Zeus' nocturnal visit took place on the same night as Amphitryon's return, and Amphitryon too slept with his wife. In due course of time, then, Alcmene bore twins: Heracles and Iphicles, begotten respectively by Zeus and Amphitryon. It was a hard birth, but Hera, the goddess of childbirth, showed no pity. Zeus, knowing that his son was due to be born, announced that whoever was born on that day should rule all those around him. Hera saw an opportunity: 'Do you swear to that?' she said. 'Whoever is born today shall rule his neighbours?' And Zeus, failing to perceive his wife's trick, nodded his head in solemn assent.

Straight away, Hera left Olympus for earth. She did two things. First, she delayed Heracles' birth, but accelerated that of his cousin, Eurystheus of Tiryns, so that Eurystheus should rule Heracles and not the other way around. And so it turned out. Second, furious with Zeus for yet another affair, no sooner had Heracles been born than she sent two slithering vipers into Alcmene's chamber, intending their poisonous fangs to make short work of her husband's bastard baby. But the mighty infant grasped a snake in each of his chubby hands and squeezed them to death.

Alcmene was frightened now, and dared not suckle the baby in case she aroused Hera's wrath. She took the baby out of the palace and abandoned it in the maquis, most likely to die. But Zeus sent Hermes to bring the infant secretly to Olympus and ensure that he sucked at the breast of Hera herself, so that, despite being mortal, Heracles should attain godhood. But the baby bit the great goddess's nipple and she thrust him away in pain, and Hermes brought the baby back to Alcmene and persuaded her to raise him herself. 'Be of good cheer,' he reassured her. 'Your child shall know greatness.'

Heracles grew like a young sapling in an orchard. As a youth, he had the best teachers for everything: Linus for music, the son of Apollo and Psamathe; Eurytus for archery; Amphitryon for chariot-driving; and Autolycus, the father of Anticlea, for wrestling. But in a fit of anger Heracles killed Linus. The teacher struck the student, as teachers will, for a mistake – and Heracles picked up the stool on which he was sitting and struck him back. The young hero was banished from Thebes to the slopes and gorges of a nearby mountain, where he killed a lion that was preying on the cattle of Thespius, the king of Thespiae. In gratitude, Thespius let the young man sleep with all his daughters, and there were fifty of them, each more fair than her sisters. Thespius could recognize a hero when he saw one, and wanted his grandchildren to inherit something of that spirit.

Heracles engineered his return to Thebes by offering to do Creon an immense favour. Thebes at the time was subject to Orchomenus, and paid the king of Orchomenus one hundred oxen every year, a heavy burden. But Heracles led the Theban army out into the field and inflicted a decisive defeat on the people of Orchomenus, though Amphitryon died in the battle. Creon gave Heracles his daughter Megara to wed, and she proved to be a loyal wife and sensible mother.

The years passed in peace. Heracles grew in strength and Megara bore him fine children, who were the delight of their parents. But heroes are not destined for peace. Hera hadn't finished persecuting the son of Zeus – she would never finish, until his death – and from high Olympus she sent a fit of madness down into the home of Heracles and Megara. Suddenly, the house seemed strange to Heracles, as though it were the home of some enemy. It was filled with foes, and he hunted them from room to room, slaughtering as he went.

When Athena saw what was going on, she raced down from Olympus and hurled a stone at Heracles' head. He dropped unconscious and sprawled on the floor, blood matting his thick-curled hair and beard. When he came to his senses, he found that the corpses that littered the rooms were not those of hostile strangers. Megara and his children lay on the floor, their lives ripped from them with appalling savagery.

Horror-struck, Heracles went weeping to Delphi to seek the advice of Apollo. The god told him that he had to serve his cousin Eurystheus, king of Tiryns, for twelve years, and carry out whatever tasks he should set him. And the gods had Eurystheus set him hard labours, well nigh impossible, for Heracles was a man of great power and had to be tested greatly. But Apollo also declared, though not to Heracles himself, that at the end of this time Heracles should become immortal, not just for ridding the world of many evils, but especially for having aided the gods in their battle against the Giants.

The Twelve Labours of Heracles

The first batch of Heracles' labours all took place in the Peloponnese. At the time, it was a wild and unruly place, as was much of the world, but Eurystheus seized the opportunity to make it safe, with Heracles as his heroic agent. For the first labour, Eurystheus demanded the skin of a lion that was ruining men's livelihoods in the hills around nearby Nemea. Now, this lion, the offspring of the Chimera, had been raised by Hera specifically to be a trial for Heracles. Sword blades bent on its impenetrable hide, and clubs, such as the one Heracles carried, simply bounced off. When Heracles drew close to its lair, the lion sprang at him from a dark thicket. Its claws and fangs ripped Heracles' flesh, but he flung aside his weapons, knowing how useless they were, and wrestled the creature with his bare hands. The fight was fierce, but brief, as Heracles locked his arms around the lion's neck and strangled it to death.

After staunching his wounds, he used the creature's own razor-sharp claws to flay the otherwise uncuttable hide. And ever after Heracles wore the lionskin as his armour, with the jaws agape over his head as a helmet, the mane falling around his neck, and the rest of the pelt draping his powerful shoulders. He is known to all by his lionskin, his bow, and his club – a brigand's attire. For Heracles tamed the world, but he was not tame himself.

For the second labour, Heracles was sent to kill the Hydra, a serpentine water monster living in the marshes of Lerna, near Argos. Again, Hera had nurtured this vile offspring of Typhoeus, hoping that it would end the life of her husband's bastard favourite. The creature writhed out of the turbid water to meet him, its nine heads hissing and snapping and spitting deadly poison. Eight of the heads were mortal, but one was immortal. Heracles confidently crushed one of the Hydra's heads with his club, and slime and scum and blood sprayed in all directions – but then *two* heads, equally ghastly and dangerous, sprang up in place of the one he had crushed. And a gigantic crab emerged from the swamp, another of Hera's pets, whose enormous, snapping claws threatened to disembowel the hero.

Ducking beneath the Hydra's hissing mouths as they snaked towards him, Heracles first smashed his club down onto the crab's shell. No one but he could have even cracked the adamantine carapace, but one blow left the monster twitching feebly in the shallows, its dying claws snapping at thin air. Hera was so fond of it that she translated it into the heavens as the constellation Cancer.

Meanwhile, Heracles was struggling with the Hydra. Its body was entirely invulnerable, and its heads multiplied themselves if attacked. He clearly couldn't manage alone, and he summoned his loyal companion Iolaus, the son of his twin brother Iphicles, from their camp. If Hera could cheat by sending two monsters at once, he was allowed an ally. Hera was desperate for the hero to fail: if he failed at any one of the labours set him by Eurystheus, even Zeus could not allow him to become immortal.

Heracles and Iolaus danced around the Hydra, nimbly dodging the gouts of poison that spewed from its mouths. Every time Heracles' club struck off or crushed one of the Hydra's heads, Iolaus immediately seared the stump with a blazing torch, to prevent another two heads from sprouting up.

Finally, Heracles was left with only the immortal head. He struck it off with his club and buried it for ever under an enormous rock. The monster's corpse lay jerking spasmodically in the turbulent water, oozing deadly poison from the cauterized stumps of its necks, and as it died it seemed as though scores of snake-like vapours wriggled through the waters of the marsh away from the corpse. But with an eye to the future – an unseeing eye, as it turned out – Heracles dipped the heads of his arrows in the venom.

For the third labour, Eurystheus asked Heracles to bring him a hind that lived on Mount Cerynea in Arcadia. This was a marvellous creature, with golden horns, despite being female. The hind was harmless, but the task was still peculiarly difficult, for the gentle animal was sacred to Artemis. Anyone who harmed it would incur the wrath of the goddess, and she had proved with Actaeon and others just how terrible her wrath could be. For month after month, Heracles chased the hind over hill and dale, looking for an opportunity to capture it.

Many times he could have killed it from a distance with an arrow, but every time he crept up on it, the wary creature bounded away, and it was incredibly swift. In the end, he gave up trying to capture it with just his bare hands. It was impossible; he might as well try to make rope from sand. He took careful aim and barely grazed the hind with an arrow – just enough to slow it down – and then captured it and slung it across his shoulders to carry back to Tiryns. Artemis intercepted him and demanded to know what he was doing with her hind, but Heracles, thinking quickly, explained that he was on a mission for Eurystheus, as commanded by Artemis' brother Apollo.

For the fourth labour, Heracles had to round up an enormous boar that was devastating the land around Mount Erymanthus in north-west Arcadia. Not a root or blade of grass or ear of grain remained, and the monster was as big as a bull, but Heracles had to bring it back alive. He tracked the ferocious animal to its den and enticed it out. For days, they parried each other's attacks, but the boar was always too swift and too strong for Heracles to trap in his nets. Eventually, high in the mountains of Arcadia, he found the solution. He drove the monstrous beast into a snowdrift, which halted it in its tracks long enough for Heracles to stun it with his club. Then he wrapped it in his nets, hauled it up onto his shoulders, and made his way back to Tiryns. The boar was so hideous and menacing, even when muffled in Heracles' net, that when the hero entered Eurystheus' palace, the king promptly scurried off and took refuge inside a large storage jar! Heracles despised him for his lack of spirit, and held the boar snout first above the mouth of the jar, so that the cowardly king got a good look at the fearsome beast. 'And yet you are my master,' sneered the hero.

On his way to Mount Erymanthus, Heracles happened upon another adventure – and a further sign that he was a man of destiny. He stopped for the night at the cave of the Centaur Pholus, and it turned out that this was a fated as well as a fateful visit. Dozens of years earlier, Dionysus himself had given Pholus a large jar of wine, with instructions that it was not to be opened until Heracles paid a visit. Pholus sank the jar into the ground for safekeeping and forgot about it; now, as a good host, he opened it. But the fragrant aroma attracted all the rest of the Centaurs from his tribe, and they stormed Pholus' cave in their mad greed for the sweet wine. Heracles successfully defended the cave mouth and drove them off with flaming brands and arrows, and then set out in pursuit of the rest.

Some of the Centaurs he tracked all the way to Thessaly, where they took refuge in the cave of their wise cousin Cheiron. Heracles attacked them there, and in the course of the siege Cheiron himself was wounded by one of Heracles' poison-tipped arrows. This was the last thing Heracles wanted, and what made it worse was that Cheiron was immortal, the son of Philyra, one of the daughters of Ocean, and Cronus in the form of a horse. He could not die, only suffer unimaginable torment as the poison spread and seared his whole body from inside. In his agony, he appealed to Zeus for relief. Even Zeus couldn't just cancel Cheiron's immortality, but he banked it for Heracles in the future. So Cheiron could die and be free at last of pain.

After attending sorrowfully to the Centaur's burial, Heracles returned to Pholus's cave in the Peloponnese, where further horror awaited him. While the hero was away, the Centaur had busied himself burying his slaughtered fellow tribesmen, consigning them to the worms and the gods. He then set about tidying the cave and collecting all Heracles' spent arrows. He held one shaft lightly between thumb and forefinger, turning it this way and that, marvelling that something so slight and slender could fell something as great as a Centaur. But in the course of his musing, he accidentally dropped the arrow, point first, onto the fleshy spot just above his hoof. Before long the Hydra's venom had done its lethal work. The two Centaurs who were the best and noblest of their kind were dead, innocent victims of their race's weakness for wine.

For the fifth labour, Heracles travelled to Elis, in the northwest of the Peloponnese, where Augeas was king. Augeas was rich in cattle and owned huge numbers of them – but their stables had never been cleaned out and were deep in accumulated ordure. Heracles' job was to muck out the stables within a single day. This was an impossible task, and Eurystheus fully expected Heracles to fail. But the canny hero found a solution to the messy problem: he diverted two rivers through the stables, and their rushing waters did the job for him with daylight to spare.

Now, Augeas had also promised Heracles a tithe of all his cattle if he should succeed, but he reneged on his promise and drove out of Elis both Heracles and his own son Phyleus, who was ashamed by his father's behaviour and took Heracles' side. They were received in the home of Dexamenus of Olympia, and in return Heracles did him a favour. His fair daughter was being harassed by the Centaur Eurytion's unwanted attentions, but just one of Heracles' arrows curbed the creature's ardour for ever. This was also the occasion when Heracles instituted the games at Olympia, by measuring out the length of the stadium where the footraces were to be held: he took a deep breath and sprinted until he had to draw breath again, and that was the length of the stadium.

For the sixth labour, Eurystheus sent Heracles to Stymphalus, a town in north-east Arcadia. There was a beautiful lake there, overlooked by mountains and bordered by wooded shores – but the woods had been taken over by a flock of terrible birds, which could shoot their feathers like deadly arrows. Heracles could not expect just to enter the dark forest and shoot them from their lofty perches: the foliage was dense and their camouflaged plumage hid them well. But Athena gave him a bronze rattle, which Heracles dashed repeatedly against a mountain. The clamour spooked the birds and sent them soaring from their treetop roosts, squawking in alarm. And while they were circling in the open air, too frenzied to fire their feathers, Heracles shot them down with his trusty bow.

The final six labours sent Heracles all over the world – and even under it. The seventh took him to Crete, where he had to bring back to Tiryns the gift of Poseidon that Minos had rejected: the perfect, lusty, white bull with which Pasiphae had mated. Heracles lassoed it, swam back to the Peloponnese with the bull in tow, and drove it with his club to Tiryns. After Eurystheus had seen the bull, to verify the completion of the labour, the sacred beast was set free to wander where it would. It ended up near Athens, on the plain of Marathon, where it wreaked havoc (as we have seen), until Theseus caught it, tamed it, and sacrificed it to Apollo.

For the eighth labour, Heracles travelled to Thrace, to fetch the famous mares of King Diomedes, a warlike son of Ares. On the way he lodged as a guest with King Admetus of Pherae, and this was the famous occasion when he wrestled Death to restore to life Alcestis, the king's wife. Then he continued on to Thrace.

Despite appearances, Diomedes' mares were scarcely ordinary horses: their preferred food was human flesh. There were four of them, so that Heracles stood no chance against them, but he had expressly been forbidden to take his nephew Iolaus or anyone else to help him. He had to manage by himself. But he had had plenty of time to think up a plan that was simplicity itself. As soon as he arrived, he picked up Diomedes himself and flung him into the mares' paddock. While the creatures were gorging themselves on their erstwhile master, he crept up on them and bridled them. Since it was Diomedes who had trained them in their man-eating ways, his death released them from the spell.

The horses allowed themselves to be harnessed to a chariot, but they were hardly tame, and they shot off in entirely the wrong direction, to the north instead of the south. In Scythia they encountered bitter weather. Heracles burrowed under his lionskin to rest, but while he was asleep the horses, which had been rooting around in the snow for something edible, were silently spirited away, leaving only the chariot yoke to which they had been harnessed.

The next morning, Heracles went in search of his lost horses, and came upon a cave where there lived a curious creature. The elegant form of a beautiful woman ended not in legs, but in a viper's tail. Echidna was her name, and she confessed to hiding Heracles' horses, but refused to part with them until he had slept with her. She conceived three boys, and before he left Heracles made her a magnificent bow. Whichever of his sons, when they grew up, could draw the bow would be the ruler of the land – and it was the youngest, Scythes, who managed the feat, and became the first king of Scythia.

Finally, Heracles drove the horses in triumph back to Tiryns, where Eurystheus dedicated them to queenly Hera and set them free.

For the ninth labour, Eurystheus ordered Heracles to bring him back the golden war-belt of the Amazon queen Hippolyta, as proof that he had rid the world of the barbarous trouble-makers. The belt had been made for Hippolyta by the war-god Ares himself, and rendered its wearer invincible. The Amazons, warrior women who live by themselves and take in men only for pleasure and procreation, make their home in Scythia, at the northern edge of the world, and are famed for their martial prowess.

Heracles and his allies (including Peleus, Telamon, and the ever-loyal Iolaus) lay in ambush for the queen's sister Mela-nippe, captured her, and then sent a message to Hippolyta, demanding the belt as ransom for their captive. Hippolyta sent the belt back with the messenger straight away, but she had no intention of giving it up, or of sacrificing her sister. The Greek heroes were about to re-embark, prize in hand, for the voyage back to Greece, when the Amazons attacked. The battle was fierce, but it was an utter defeat for the warrior women. Telamon slew Melanippe, while Heracles himself killed Hippolyta. He took the magic belt back to Tiryns, and even now it is displayed in the temple of Hera at Argos.

On his way back from Scythia with the belt, Heracles stopped at Troy – and fell into another adventure. It so happened that he found Hesione, the daughter of the Trojan king Laomedon, helplessly bound to a rock, the unwilling victim of a sea monster. In retaliation for Laomedon's failure to pay him his due for building the walls of Troy, Poseidon had commanded the sea to rise up and flood the farmland up to the city walls; and he had sent the foul, fanged beast to devastate the remaining land and bring the king to his knees. Laomedon consulted an oracle and was told that he would have to sacrifice Hesione, but he was not resigned to this course of action alone. He also announced that whoever could save his daughter from death and free the land from the monster would receive as his reward immortal horses. These were the noble steeds that Laomedon's grandfather Tros had been given by Zeus in compensation for the loss of his son Ganymede, whom Zeus loved and took up to Olympus.

Wise Athena and the Trojans built for Heracles a sturdy barrier close to the shoreline. Heracles hid behind it and waited for the monster to emerge from the depths of the sea. When it came, it opened wide its stinking jaws to swallow Hesione, and the fair maiden swooned from the stench. But Heracles leapt out of his hiding-place and dived into the monster's gaping mouth. The surest way to kill it was from the inside, disgusting though the prospect was. Once he had stabbed the monster to death and hacked his way out of the horrid pile of flesh and intestines, the waters receded from the Trojan plain. Heracles freed Hesione and restored her to the arms of her parents, and sailed back home with the horses. But Laomedon cheated and gave him not the immortal mares of Tros, but ordinary horses. He would pay for it.

For the tenth labour, Heracles had to drive back to Tiryns the red cattle of Geryon. There were many obstacles. For a start, Geryon lived on the island of Erytheia, which was situated as far west as it is possible to go, where the sun sets and the entrance to Hades is located, on the far side of the river Ocean, that none dare even think of crossing. Then Geryon himself – the offspring of Chrysaor and Callirhoe, the daughter of Ocean – was a terrible creature: three huge human bodies tapered down to a single waist, from which three pairs of legs sprouted, and the whole was topped with heads of such hideous ugliness that he resembled his grandmother, the Gorgon Medusa, thrice multiplied. Finally, his cattle were tended by a gigantic cowherd and a savage two-headed dog, Orthus, another of the dread children of Typhoeus.

There was no way that Heracles could get to Erytheia without help. The island is so mysterious that many people deny its existence altogether, or consign it to the realm of myth. Helios the all-seeing sun would know of its whereabouts, so first Heracles had to travel to the far east, to catch the sun just as he rose. But when Heracles consulted him, Helios refused to help – until Heracles notched an arrow to his bow and threatened him. Then the bright shiner gave Heracles a fabulous golden cup, which would convey him to the western edge of the world.

No sooner had Heracles embarked in the cup on Ocean than the river threw up choppy waves with which to swamp the hero. This time it was Ocean's turn to feel the force of Heracles' dark-browed anger and the power of his threats. He promptly subsided, and conveyed Heracles in his cup from the far east to the far west. The voyage took months, or it might have been instantaneous, but once Heracles reached Erytheia, he was on familiar ground: there was only a trio of horrible monsters to deal with.

He made short work of killing all three. He shot down the gigantic cowherd from afar with his arrows, and did the same for Orthus when it charged at him, both jaws slavering in anticipation of meat. Then he advanced on heavily armoured Geryon with his sword. The first stage was the hardest: killing one of the bodies while parrying the thrusts of the other two; but once the first torso lolled back dead, like a drooping poppy, Heracles made short work of dispatching the other two.

Then he re-embarked on the Cup of Helios, taking the cattle with him, as red as the setting sun. He made land at Spain and set out for Greece, driving the cattle before him. But first, to commemorate his remarkable voyage, he set up two pillars, one on either side of the strait between the Mediterranean and the Outer Seas. What was beyond was beyond; out there, on the perimeter, there are no stars.

It was a long drive back to Greece, and Heracles had several adventures on the way. In the land of the Celts he was attacked by the local tribesmen, who came at him in such numbers that he soon ran out of ammunition. In desperation, he prayed to his father Zeus, who sent a rain of slingshot-sized stones, which Heracles used to repel his attackers. The plain near Massilia is still littered with the stones. A little further on, two lawless sons of Poseidon, Ialebion and Dercymus, tried to steal the amazing red cattle from Heracles, but succeeded only in encompassing their own deaths. Their only claim to fame is to have fallen before the might of Heracles.

Continuing south, Heracles passed with the cattle into Italy. On the future site of Rome, the fire-breathing brigand Cacus, a son of Hephaestus, stole some of the cattle while Heracles was asleep, and dragged them backwards into his cave, so that their hoof prints seemed to lead in the opposite direction. Heracles was baffled, and reluctantly set out with the remaining cattle, even though returning without the full complement might not count as a completed labour. But just as he was setting off, the lowing of his cattle was answered from the depths of the cave by a bellow from one of the stolen calves. Heracles assaulted the rustler's stronghold, throttled him, and recovered his stolen livestock.

From Italy Heracles crossed over to Sicily, where Eryx, king of the western half of the island, challenged him to a wrestling match, with the cattle as the prize. Foolish Eryx, to listen to Hera's whispering and think he could win! Heracles threw him to the ground three times for the match, before killing him. And then at last Heracles returned to Greece. When his epic drive was over and he reached Tiryns with the cattle, Eurystheus was fully satisfied, and sacrificed them to Hera.

The eleventh labour was just as challenging. Far in the west lived the three Hesperides, the daughters of Night. Their life's work was gardening, and they lived in bliss, singing and dancing and tending, above all, to one particular tree in their grove. This tree, the wedding gift of Earth herself to Zeus and Hera, produced golden apples whose sweet flesh gave eternal youth. But the tree was guarded by the dragon Ladon, which was coiled, ever sleepless, around its roots; and Ladon was sibling to the dreadful Gorgons.

Again, as with the island of Erytheia, Heracles' first problem was finding the way there, since the garden of the Hesperides was situated beyond the knowledge of men. He first visited the nymphs of the river Eridanus in the far north, where the river's waters mingle with Ocean. They didn't know the way, but they sent him to find the sea-god Nereus, who like all his kind was both wise and a shape-shifter. He would impart the information, however, only if Heracles managed to maintain a grip on him, whatever form or forms he changed into.

Heracles tracked Nereus down to a deserted shore. The hoary old deity was easy to recognize, because he was impossible to recognize. His features and form shimmered and dissolved even as Heracles looked at him; he was never quite what he was, always in the process of becoming something else. But Heracles knew what he had to do, and grabbed hold of him. Without a moment's hesitation, Nereus changed into a lion – but Heracles' grip remained firm. Then in the blink of an eye he became a writhing serpent, then fire, then water – but still Heracles kept hold of him, and at last Nereus had to concede defeat, and he told Heracles where he could find the garden of the Hesperides.

It was clear from what Nereus said, however, that the task was quite beyond even Heracles' abilities. It wasn't just that the apples were guarded by Ladon, but that the garden itself was unreachable, hidden behind veils that were not of this world. So Heracles wandered in dejection, and his aimless feet brought him to Egypt and Libya. In both places, he continued his work of pacifying and civilizing the earth. Busiris, the king of Egypt, had the unpleasant habit of slaughtering all visitors to his land at the altar of Zeus. Heracles let himself be bound and taken, a meek prisoner, to the altar – and then exploded into action, bursting his bonds and killing Busiris and all his attendants, freeing the land from foul tyranny.

Antaeus, the king of Libya, was a giant, the son of Earth and Poseidon, and he wrestled to death any and every visitor to his realm. His mother's merest touch made him invincible. If any opponent did manage to throw him, that only brought him into contact with the earth and renewed his energy. So many men had failed to defeat him that he had used their skulls to construct a temple to his father. Heracles began by wrestling Antaeus in the normal way, attempting to throw him to the ground, but he soon understood what was going on. It reminded him of a dream he had once had, in which he was battling the Giants on the side of the gods . . . He held Antaeus above his head, off the ground, and as the giant weakened, Heracles slowly crushed him to death with his bare hands.

But these adventures were mere distractions. On and on Heracles roamed, seeking advice, and at last he ended up in the Caucasus mountains, where Prometheus lay chained to the solid rock, waiting by night for the eagle to return every day to eat his liver. Heracles shot the eagle with his bow, and in gratitude Prometheus advised him to seek out his brother Atlas, whom Zeus had punished by having him support the sky on his back for ever, to keep earth and sky apart. Atlas knew where the garden of the Hesperides was, and it would be easy for a Titan like him to go and get the apples.

Heracles journeyed west again until he found Atlas standing firm, with the sky resting on his head and clouds veiling his shoulders. He explained the situation to the Titan, and asked for his help in gaining the golden apples. 'I can help, certainly,' said Atlas. 'But what will you do for me in return?' Heracles made various offers, none of which were acceptable. But the Titan had his own suggestion. 'I'll get the apples for you,' he said, 'if you shoulder my burden while I'm away.' Heracles agreed, and with a grunt took the sky on his shoulders and head, while Atlas disappeared over the horizon.

Time passed, but Heracles' task required all his attention and he didn't notice its passage. Eventually Atlas returned, and indeed he had the apples with him. But the liberated Titan was reluctant to take on his great burden once more. 'I'll take the apples to Eurystheus myself,' he offered enthusiastically.

'Fair enough,' said Heracles. 'You've well and truly outsmarted me, and now I'll have to carry the sky for ever. But, first, let me get a cushion for my aching head. Just take the sky for a moment, and then I'll take it back.' Of course, no sooner had Atlas shouldered the sky again than Heracles picked up the apples and left. Atlas fumed with helpless rage, but soon Heracles was beyond the range of his complaints. And so Eurystheus gained the far-famed apples – but they were not his for long. Athena declared that they were too sacred to be part of the dismal world of mortals, and she took them back to the faery land of the Hesperides.

The twelfth and final labour was the hardest, as Heracles' shade admitted to Odysseus, when the much-travelled man summoned him up from Hades. He had to fetch up from the underworld three-headed, snake-tailed Cerberus, offspring of Typhoeus. Cerberus was a kind of valve for the entrance to Hades' realm: he would greet new arrivals with canine obsequiousness, fawning on them and wagging his tail; but should any of the dead try to depart, the hell-hound turned savage and devoured the wretched ghost. But Heracles pinioned the creature and dragged him away on a triple-tied leash, though Cerberus snarled his reluctance every inch of the way. The dark lord Hades and his lady Persephone protested at the removal of their watchdog, but Hermes explained the situation and promised that Cerberus would soon resume his post. In the palace of Tiryns, Eurystheus once again took cover in his big jar, and only peeked out to confirm that Heracles had succeeded in this, his final task. And then the hero, true to his word, returned the hound to Hades.

Heracles, a living man, had entered the underworld and come back again, against all the odds. Only Orpheus and Theseus would ever match such an extraordinary feat. Before entering the underworld, Heracles had taken one of the cattle from Hades' own herd, and sacrificed it as a blood offering to propitiate the underworld deities. Hades' cowherd Menoetes tried to stop Heracles stealing the cow and Heracles would have killed him, had Persephone not ordered the two apart. But the vapours of the blood of the sacrifice summoned up shades with information for Heracles, and so he met the ghost of Meleager, the son of Ares and Althaea. And though it was scarcely usual for a living person to enter into a contract with one of the dead, Meleager gave Heracles his sister Deianeira, daughter of Dionysus, as a wife, to replace Megara, for whose death Heracles had now at last atoned.

Heracles the King-Maker

Heracles' trials had by no means finished with the end of the twelve labours and betrothal to Deianeira, his destined bride. No hero ever suffered as Heracles suffered. No body bore the scars that Heracles bore, or endured so much mental pain. For as he surpassed all others in excellence, so his life-path surpassed all others in difficulty.

One piece of unfinished business lay with Augeas. Heracles' fifth labour had been to clean the stables of the Elean king, and Augeas had promised him, as a reward if he succeeded, a tenth of his cattle. He didn't expect the hero to succeed, and when it came to it he refused to pay up. So when Heracles was free of his labours, and living in Argos, he returned to Elis to seek his revenge, and to install Augeas's son, honest Phyleus, on the throne in his place.

Heracles arrived in Elis at the head of a considerable army. The battle was short but fierce. Heracles' brother Iphicles died in the fighting, cut down by the Moliones, armoured twins joined at the hip; but Heracles was close at hand and they did not long outlive their victim. The mission was a complete success: the city was taken and Augeas killed, and Phyleus assumed the throne instead. Iphicles' funeral was suitably lavish.

This was not the only major military expedition Heracles organized in those days in the Peloponnese. He also launched an all-out attack on Sparta for the sake of a murdered kinsman. Once Oeonus, one of Heracles' nephews, was passing the mansion of the king of Sparta, a man called Hippocoön. One of the king's mastiffs set upon the traveller, who naturally picked up a stone and threw it at the dog to keep it at bay. But Hippocoön's sons took this amiss. Angry words turned to fisticuffs, and then daggers were drawn. Before long Oeonus lay dead in the dust, and the mountains looked on impassively.

Once again Heracles summoned his friends and allies. At first Cepheus of Tegea was unwilling to leave his city undefended, but Heracles needed him and his twenty sons as allies. The son of Zeus called upon Athena for help and the great goddess gave him a lock of the hair of the Gorgon Medusa. One of the daughters of Cepheus was to raise this serpent lock high from the city walls three times in her hand, and this would serve as a sure shield for the city and protect it from all harm.

Then Cepheus agreed to join Heracles' expedition, but so valiantly did his sons fight that almost all of them were killed, along with their father. Even Heracles was wounded in the hand, the sign of a rare lapse of self-confidence. But Sparta fell.

Heracles killed the king and all twelve of his sons, and installed
Tyndareos (descended from the Titan Atlas) on the throne in
place of Hippocoön.

Heracles Becomes a God

Meleager's ghost had promised Heracles the hand of his sister
Deianeira, but first Heracles had to win her. She had a rival
suitor, no less than Achelous, the river-god, whose courtship of
the girl had been persistent: he had appeared to her as a bull, a
snake, and a composite creature, half bull, half man. In fact,
fair-girdled Deianeira was about to give in when Heracles arrived.

For the wrestling match that would decide her future husband, Achelous chose the form of a bull. He pawed the ground
and charged at Heracles, but the mighty hero stood his ground
and took the force of the bull's charge. He seized the bull's horns
and twisted with all his might to force the creature to its knees.
So strong was Heracles, and so fierce the resistance of Achelous,
that with a sickening crack one of the horns snapped off in
Heracles' hands. At last the scales of the fight tipped in Heracles'
favour as the bull's strength slackened, and then it was only a
matter of time.

Once Achelous had admitted defeat, he and Heracles
exchanged horns. Achelous wanted his broken horn back, and
in return gave Heracles the Horn of Amalthea – the very horn
of plenty with which Zeus had been fed in infancy in the Cretan
cave. This magical horn had the property that it never ran out
of food or drink; every time it was emptied, it filled right up
again with all the good things of the earth. Heracles' household
would indeed prosper.

So Heracles took his prize, his new wife, back to Argos. Along the way they were joined by the Centaur Nessus, one of the last of his kind – and, as it turned out, true to his nature. At one point, the trio had to cross a raging river. Nessus invited Deianeira to ride across on his back, and Heracles accepted the kind-seeming gesture. But as soon as they reached the far bank, while Heracles was still on the other side, the Centaur attempted to rape Deianeira.

Alerted by her screams, Heracles looked up. The width of a river was nothing to such an expert marksman, and Heracles' poison-tipped shaft took deadly effect. Nessus's blood poured from the wound and mingled with his seed, which had spilled on the ground during the bungled rape. Before Heracles had time to wade across the river and rejoin Deianeira, the Centaur advised the naive young woman to gather some of this potent mixture. 'It's a love potion,' he gasped, as his life ebbed away. 'We Centaurs know about such things. It will stop Heracles loving any other woman.' A wonder it seemed, and she collected a phial of the fatal drug, but told Heracles nothing about it.

Heracles and Deianeira lived long and happily in Argos, and Deianeira bore two fine children, Hyllus and Macaria. But Heracles' amorous nature got the better of him, and he fell in love with Iole, princess of Oechalia, daughter of King Eurytus. For it was fated that she should be the instrument of Heracles' death and deification.

Beautiful Iole had many suitors, and Eurytus arranged an archery competition, with his daughter as the prize. The final round pitted Heracles against his old teacher, for Eurytus had taught him archery in his youth. Two stout bows were drawn back; two swift arrows were notched; and they let fly, master and pupil. Iole herself went to fetch the target and carry it back to the contestants: by a hair's breadth, Heracles was the winner.

But in a shameless display of unsportsmanlike conduct, Eurytus refused Heracles his prize, and the lionskin-clad hero returned trophy-less to Tiryns, nursing black vengeance in his heart. It was not Heracles, however, who was destined to take the life of the Oechalian king. Eurytus went on to challenge Apollo himself to a test of bowmanship, and lost both the contest and his life.

Now, after a while one of Iole's brothers, Iphitus, came to Tiryns in pursuit of some horses, thinking that Heracles might have stolen them (as in fact he had). He had been searching all over the Peloponnese. In Messenia he had met Odysseus and had given him Eurytus' far-famed bow as a gift, knowing that his father's treasure was in good hands. When Iphitus came to Argos, Heracles feigned innocence. He treated the young man well and lodged him. But in the course of a drunken dinner, when Iphitus accused him of rustling the horses, Heracles picked him up and hurled him to his death from the high point of the city. Iphitus' dying screams brought Heracles to his senses, and he realized what he had done – killed a guest, one who had done no more than speak the truth – and all guests were under the protection of Zeus. Another fit of madness had caused another change in the life of Heracles and his family.

The murder ran the risk of polluting the city, and who knew what plague or pest the gods would send in retaliation? Once again Heracles became an exile. This time he chose to take his family to Trachis, a town in central Greece, north of Delphi. On the way, the refugees were set upon by Cycnus, a son of Ares, who made his headquarters a cave near the sanctuary of Apollo at Delphi, and was living by stealing the sacrificial victims worshippers brought there as the price for consulting the oracle.

Heracles and Iolaus did battle with Cycnus, but Ares himself came down from Olympus to support his son, and the heroes were driven off. Before long, however, with Athena's encouragement, they rallied and returned to the fray. Cycnus soon lay dead on the ground, while over his body Heracles and Ares fought, and the heavy silence was broken only by their grunts. They were so evenly matched that they might be fighting still, if father Zeus had not broken the contest up by hurling a thunderbolt between the two contestants. Ares limped back to Olympus; never before had a mortal held his own against the god of war. But then Heracles was on the way to becoming a god.

After leaving his family at Trachis, Heracles went to Pylos, intending to receive purification from the king, Neleus, and to stay there for the prescribed period of time, until there was no further risk of pollution from Iphitus' death. But Neleus refused to purify him from his sin, and Heracles, brow darkened with anger, swore vengeance. The spirit of a true warrior is never broken by a mere setback. Heracles left, but only to gather an army and return.

Now, Neleus had twelve sons by Chloris, the only surviving child of Niobe, and one of these sons was Periclymenus, the shape-shifter. It had been foretold that Pylos would never fall as long as Periclymenus was alive. One by one Neleus' sons were cut down in the battle, but Periclymenus' constant changes kept him alive, and he wreaked terrible slaughter among Heracles' allies. Finally, he changed himself into the form of a bee, and rested on the yoke of Heracles' chariot; but even from afar Heracles recognized the bee as Periclymenus, and shot it – a superhuman feat of bowmanship.

A full-scale battle developed, with some of the gods involved as well: Athena and Zeus fought alongside Heracles, while Hera, Hades, and Poseidon supported the other side. And Heracles, whose achievements were rapidly becoming more and more remarkable, more and more godlike, succeeded in the course of the fight in wounding Hera in the right breast and Hades in the shoulder. The poison from his arrows caused them great pain, but of course they could not be killed. They made their way back to Olympus, where they were tended by Apollo.

And in the end Neleus was defeated and killed, and the only surviving son, Nestor, inherited the throne of sandy Pylos and his father's hatred of Heracles. It is said that Nestor lived to such a great age because Apollo gave him the years that had been allotted to his brothers, before Heracles cut them down.

But still Heracles had not found the release of purification from the sin of killing Iphitus, and now his body was ravaged by foul boils and abscesses. He went to Delphi to find out what to do, but the Sibyl there was appalled at the state of the man, who bore the marks of a murderer and a brigand all over his body, and refused to reply. In anger and disgust, Heracles ran amok and attempted to plunder the sanctuary of its treasures, including the sacred tripod on which the Sibyl sat to utter her dark words of prophecy. If she would not look into the future for him, he would use her tripod to establish his own oracle elsewhere. But Apollo could not allow this, and he came down in person from high Olympus, and wrestled Heracles for the tripod. Once again, however, Heracles held his own against one of the great gods, and once again Zeus had to break the contest up.

At the command of Zeus, Heracles was sold to Omphale, queen of the Lydians, to serve as her slave for three years, as the period of purification. Hermes himself, the god of commerce, negotiated the sale. For all this period of time, Omphale kept his lionskin and weapons for herself, while he was forced to dress as a woman, and do woman's work such as weaving inside the palace. Nevertheless, she had a child by him – a son called Lamus.

Just like Iobates with Bellerophon, she set him to clear the land of pests. First, he expelled the Itoni, the first inhabitants of Lydia, who were resisting the rule of Omphale's house. Then he dealt with Syleus, a foul-mouthed landowner who compelled passersby to work in his vineyard. Heracles pretended to go along with the game, but instead of harvesting the swollen grapes, he swiftly drank up the wine store and started destroying the vineyard with his mattock. When Syleus and his daughter came up to protest, Heracles killed them and burnt the vineyard.

Finally, he had to get rid of the Cercopes, two mean little dwarfs who played spiteful tricks on people. Heracles travelled to Ephesus, where the Cercopes had their lair, and began to search for them. Although he often got close, they always evaded him, and all Heracles heard were irritating giggles receding in the distance. But malice and wisdom tend not to coincide in the same mind. At last, exhausted, Heracles lay down to rest – and the mischievous Cercopes crept over to where he lay under a tree and began to steal his weapons. But men like Heracles sleep with one eye open, and he grabbed them before they could race away.

Heracles found a stout pole and tied the dwarfs to either end of it, as a way of carrying them off to permanent confinement. Now, the Cercopes had known for a long time – their mother had drummed it into their youthful ears – that they should beware of a black-bottomed man. And when Heracles began to carry the imps away, they at last understood the bizarre prophecy. Suspended as they were by their heels upside down from the pole, they got a good look at Heracles' bottom – and, indeed, it was black – black with wiry hair! This caused the

Cercopes no end of amusement, and they began to make crude jokes about Heracles and his black bottom. 'Which wooded hills are cleft by a valley you'd never want to walk in?' 'What's black, hairy, and gases strangers?' 'I spy with my little eye something beginning with "b".' That kind of thing. But good men laugh well, and Heracles enjoyed the jokes so much that he let them go. They have never been seen since, and the rumour is that they tried to play a practical joke on Zeus and were turned into monkeys.

After he had completed his three years of penance in Lydia, Heracles made his way back to Greece up the western coast of Asia Minor. He had a bone to pick with Laomedon, king of Troy. He had rescued Laomedon's daughter Hesione from certain death at the jaws of a sea monster, but Laomedon had cheated. Instead of giving Heracles the promised reward, the immortal horses of Tros, he had given him ordinary horses.

Now, this was not the kind of deception that could last: as soon as the horses began dying, Heracles knew he had been cheated. So he returned to Troy with eighteen ships to claim his proper prize by force. While Heracles marched with his men towards the city, Laomedon made a sortie and attacked the ships, beached and vulnerable on the shore. On his way back to Troy, however, he fell into an ambush set by Heracles and his allies. Laomedon was killed, and then the heroes assaulted the city. Telamon was the first to force his way inside, and received Hesione as the prize for his valour. All of Laomedon's sons were killed, save only Priam, whom Heracles, in a final act of king-making, set on the throne of Troy.

So Heracles set sail from Troy, flushed with victory, and in possession of the immortal horses. But now it was the time of Hera's greatest folly – her final attempt to ruin the life of her husband's beloved son. She called on Sleep, and he wove his magic on Zeus, and the father of gods and men fell into a deep slumber. While he was asleep, Hera summoned up a savage storm, which separated Heracles from his companions and drove him south to the island of Cos.

At first, he was made welcome there by King Eurypylus, who persuaded him to stay by offering him his daughter Chalciope. As others had before him, he wanted the blood of the hero to flow in his grandson's veins. And indeed Heracles did sire a fine son on Chalciope – Thessalus, the future king of the island – but not before he and Eurypylus had fallen out. The king drove Heracles from his palace, and the battle was so hard fought that Zeus had to rescue his son to protect him from an untimely death. He transported Heracles to a peasant woman's hut, where the hero found refuge and escaped in humiliating disguise, wearing her clothes. But later he returned in force, killed or expelled all the members of Eurypylus' family, and established his own dynasty instead.

Finally, after a prolonged absence, the gods allowed Heracles to resume his life in Trachis. But Zeus punished Hera for her presumption by suspending her from heaven by golden chains, with anvils on her feet. He had to convince her that her long hostility to his son was futile, for he was destined to become a god.

After all this time, Heracles' passion for Iole had not diminished, and he returned to Greece still determined to win her, and to complete the unfinished business at Oechalia. Eurytus was dead, but his surviving sons would pay for their father's treachery. Heracles returned at the head of an army and sacked the city of Oechalia – destroyed it so thoroughly, in fact, that today no one is sure where it lay. Eurytus' sons all died in the massacre, and Heracles brought Iole into his home as his beloved concubine.

Heracles organized a splendid sacrifice, a thanksgiving offering to the gods for his victory at Oechalia. In a display of solidarity, Deianeira wove a gorgeous robe for him to wear at the ceremony. Thinking to rid her husband of his foolish infatuation with Iole, and ensure that his love for her remained lifelong, she poured the potion of Nessus over the robe, and it soaked into every fibre of the cloth.

Heracles wore his splendid new robe with pride as he approached the sacrificial fire. But before he had even begun the holy rite, the robe began to cling to his body in an uncomfortable fashion, warmed by the flames of the fire. And then it began to ravage his flesh with its acid. The more he tried to rip the garment off, the more closely it moulded itself to his limbs, like a murderous second skin.

Desperate for the release of death, Heracles had himself carried in agony to Mount Oeta. While his men were busy building a huge funeral pyre, the inconsolable Deianeira seized a sword from one of her attendants and fell on it. Grimacing through his pain and grief, Heracles told Hyllus, his son by Deianeira, to marry Iole in his place.

Then the great hero lay back on his pyre, his head pillowed by his club, and commanded his men to light the fire. But none would obey – none wanted the responsibility of sending a son of Zeus to his death – save only loyal Poeas, a shepherd. As his reward Heracles gave him his mighty bow; and so his bow and arrows would come a second time to Troy, for it was fated that a vital contribution to the sack of Troy would be made by the bow of Heracles.

As the sun rose, the mortal part of Heracles burnt away and

descended into Hades, but his spirit was taken up to Olympus by Athena, where Zeus gladly accepted him among the company of the gods, and blessed him with eternal life and youth. He ordered Hera to lay aside her grudge and Heracles married her daughter by Zeus, trim-ankled Hebe. They live for ever in bliss as gods among gods.

9

The Trojan War

The Marriage of Peleus and Thetis

The course of Peleus' life was as troubled and tortured as that of many a hero. Perhaps one of the gods or goddesses bore a grudge against him, or wanted to test him. His birth, on the island of Aegina, was propitious. His father was the king, Aeacus, a son of Zeus whose insight and advice were so sound that he came to be a judge of the dead in Hades. The family seemed to be blessed with all the good things of life.

Now, Aeacus was married to Endeis, the daughter of the wise Centaur Cheiron, and Endeis was the mother of Peleus. But Aeacus lusted after Psamathe, the daughter of Nereus, and though at first she resisted his advances by turning herself into a seal, his persistence wore her down, and she became his concubine. She bore him a fine son, called Phocus, who grew up alongside Peleus, but the house was sorely divided, for Endeis loathed this bastard offspring of her husband, and was forever plotting ways to do him harm.

In time Endeis' bitterness seeped into her son's brain and curdled it, and for the sake of his mother Peleus resolved to do away with his half-brother. Peleus' best friend was Telamon, prince of the neighbouring island of Salamis, and they planned and executed the deed themselves. Phocus was a keen and outstanding athlete, always practising for some competition or other. They joined him out in the fields for one of his training sessions, and while Telamon struck Phocus on the head with a discus, Peleus swung a double-headed axe into his spine.

As soon as the deed was done, the mist cleared from Peleus' mind, and he came to his senses; regret overwhelmed him like a storm wave, and remorse gnawed at his wits. He took himself away from his native island, and travelled the length and breadth of the land, searching for someone who would take him in and offer him purification. But only when he came to Phthia did the king there, kind Eurytion, extend a hand of welcome. And when the period of purification was over, Eurytion gave Peleus his daughter Antigone and a share of his kingdom.

But Peleus was fated not yet to find peace. When he and Eurytion joined the other heroes for the Calydonian boar hunt, he accidentally killed his new friend. The boar had taken refuge in a dark thicket, and no one knew exactly where it was. Peleus heard a noise in the underbrush; the boar was so enormous, and so fierce, that a second's delay could make the difference between life and an appalling death from the creature's tusks. Already several good men had fallen, gored in the groin or the stomach, watching their innards steam on the ground before the blessed release of death closed their eyes. Peleus hurled his trusty javelin without further pause, but it was Eurytion's blood that stained the earth.

Once more, then, Peleus had to leave the place he had made his home and take to the road as an unclean murderer, searching for surcease. This time he ended up in Iolcus, where Acastus, the son of Pelias, was king, and offered him lodging for the period of his purification. While Peleus was there, he competed in the funeral games for Pelias, where his only rival for victory in the wrestling was, to his masculine shame, Atalanta.

But Astydamia, the wife of Acastus, fell in love with the handsome visitor and tried to seduce him. When he spurned her advances, a hellish fury overtook her. First she told Antigone that Peleus was thinking of abandoning her in favour of a more promising marriage with the daughter of Acastus. Even Antigone's suicide did not sate Astydamia's desire for evil. Next she destroyed Peleus' livelihood by sending a ravening wolf against his flocks. Finally, she told her husband that Peleus had tried to rape her, and Acastus believed her.

Now, Acastus could not simply kill the man he had just purified, so he took his erstwhile friend out into the wilderness of Mount Pelion. They hunted all morning, and when they lay down in the shade to rest, Acastus hid Peleus' sword – a unique weapon, crafted by Hephaestus himself – in a shrub, and left him there defenceless against the creatures of the wild. All he could do was clamber into the branches of a tree while a band of savage Centaurs prowled below. But the wise Centaur Cheiron took pity on him, returned his sword to him, and kept him safe from his less civilized fellows.

Now, it so happened that at this time Zeus conceived a longing to sleep with the beautiful sea-nymph Thetis, daughter of Nereus. But she was fated to bear a child who would outstrip his father, however great he was, and when, as we have already told, Prometheus bargained this piece of information for his release from eternal torment, Zeus and all the gods were anxious to see Thetis married off to a mortal. None of them wanted to run the risk of being overthrown! Peleus was available, and the gods thought it would be amusing to see what happened – what son Thetis would bear for this troubled mortal.

Thetis was a goddess, and she was not best pleased by the idea of being joined in wedlock to a human being, but Zeus made it a direct order and left her no choice. For none dare gainsay the will of Zeus – or not for long. Even so, she didn't make it easy for Peleus: he had to wrestle her, to tame her, and like her father she was a shape-shifter. As fast as thought, she became a bird, a snake, a lion, a panther, and other unnamed and unnameable monsters. But throughout her transformations Peleus held fast to her, until at last she surrendered to him. He had proved himself a worthy suitor.

The wedding was celebrated on Mount Pelion, and the guest list was incredible. All the gods and goddesses deigned to descend from Olympus to attend, at least partly in relief that Thetis was not marrying one of them. Everyone was happy with the way things were. The Muses came too, and the Fates and the Graces. Nereus was there, of course, as the bride's father, and Cheiron, the saviour of Peleus, whose gift was a sturdy staff of ash, suitable for the haft of a spear. Athena herself planed the wood to perfection, Hephaestus made and fitted the long head of iron, and the rest of the gods contributed a magnificent suit of armour. But Dionysus gave a magical jar of wine that would never empty.

Into the middle of the celebrations hall limped an uninvited guest, in a foul mood at being overlooked. The goddess Strife, her frowning face lined with the weariness of her unceasing labours, stayed no more than a few minutes, but she sowed an evil that would yield countless deaths. She stood scowling in the middle of the hall where the gods and goddesses were feasting, and let fall a golden apple, wheedled from the Hesperides.

The apple was inscribed 'For the Fairest' and, as Strife had intended, Hera, Athena, and Aphrodite immediately fell to quarrelling, each claiming to be the most fair, and the rightful possessor of the beautiful bauble. The argument became so heated that Zeus had to step in and command them to be silent. He promised to find a way to resolve the matter equably, and ordered them in the meantime not to mar the wedding. The party had been spoiled, however – and a heavy doom set in motion.

As calm as the lull before a storm, the happy couple lived in Phthia, where Peleus succeeded to the throne after the death of Acastus, and ruled wisely and well. His land flourished, the rain and the winds were moderate, and no wolf terrorized his people's flocks. Each man spoke kind words to his neighbour, for peace and law ruled the land under Peleus' guidance. In time Thetis bore her husband a son, and they called the boy Achilles.

But silver-footed Thetis still resented her sojourn in the world of mortals, and longed to spend time with others of her kind, gambolling in the underwater realm, or feasting with the gods on high Olympus. If she had to be married to a mortal husband, she would at least use her powers to ensure that their son was invulnerable. And so at night she took hold of the infant and dipped him in her magic cauldron, seeking to purge all traces of mortality from him in the seething broth.

Six nights she dipped the baby thus, and on the seventh the work would have been complete. But Peleus spied Thetis at her task and his mortal eyes could see only that Thetis was dipping their child in a cauldron of boiling water. He cried out in alarm, and Thetis stopped what she was doing and flung the child away from her onto the floor. With a disdainful glare at Peleus, she stormed out of the room, and out of her husband's life, returning to her watery home. But Achilles was not quite invulnerable:

Thetis had been holding on to her child by his ankle, pinching the tiny tendon of the heel between her fingers. This last, little bit of his body had not been dipped for the seventh time into the cauldron.

The Judgement of Paris

The birth pangs were beginning, the contractions still far apart. The baby would not be born for many hours yet, and Hecuba, queen of Troy, allowed herself to doze in the spaces between pain.

Suddenly, in the dark of the night, she awoke with a start. 'What's the matter?' asked one of her handmaids anxiously, wringing the last drops from a face-cloth to cool her panting mistress's forehead. 'Nothing,' Hecuba whispered. 'Only a dream.' But the dream had disturbed her. She saw herself giving birth not to a human being, but to a blazing torch, whose flames spread and consumed the whole city of Troy. She heard cries and screams and lamentation, and saw her husband, King Priam, fall from the city walls.

The baby was born at dawn. The birth was easy, and the little boy seemed perfect, but still Hecuba was unquiet. The dream had been very powerful. As was right and proper, especially given her high station, she consulted the soothsayers to find out what it might mean, though the message seemed all too obvious. And they confirmed that the boy would grow up to cause the destruction of the city. They couldn't presume to advise her what to do, but she knew anyway.

After consulting her husband, she gave the boy – tentatively named Alexander – to trusted attendants, who took the squalling child out of the city and into the wilderness of Mount Ida, where they left him to be torn apart and consumed by wild beasts. But the first creature to be attracted by the baby's cries was a she-bear, who had lately given birth herself. She picked up the smooth-skinned infant in ungentle paws, thinking to sink her teeth into the soft flesh – and to her astonishment the baby, smelling the milk fresh on her teats, fastened his little mouth to one of them and began to suck. This she understood; the mother bear's fierceness abated, and she let the little human fill his belly until his cries stopped.

So the boy survived. He didn't starve to death, and the mother bear watched over him all that first night, protecting him from the cold and other animals. In the morning, she had to return to her own litter, but the child was sleeping peacefully. And shepherds came to that part of the mountain, following their goats as they meandered among the trees and shrubs. One of them took the infant back to his wife; they raised the boy and called him Paris.

Paris grew up an innocent shepherd boy, and his delight lay in wandering the glens of the mountains with his father's flocks. He didn't know that there was anything in the world beyond this pastoral life and, like all his fellow shepherds, felt only contempt for the city folk in nearby Troy. As far as the shepherd community of Mount Ida was concerned, the city-dwellers were good for nothing except buying their wool and cheeses.

Then one day his life changed for ever. As he was watching his flocks one morning, the god Hermes suddenly appeared to him, where a moment before there had been only rocks and grass and meadow flowers. And in Hermes' train, seeming to arise out of the ground from the flowers, there came three goddesses. There was nothing to which Paris could compare this vision. It was more vivid than any dream, and he was undoubtedly awake. And the beauty of the goddesses was . . .

well, no mortal woman that Paris had seen or even imagined came close. He knew immediately that he was in the presence of the divine.

This was the way Zeus had found to solve the contest for the golden apple that Strife had tossed among the deities celebrating the wedding of Peleus and Thetis. He chose Paris, for his innocence and noble blood and astounding good looks, to decide the contest – to make the impossible choice and decide which of the goddesses was indeed the fairest. The father of gods and men gave Hermes his instructions, and sent him down to Mount Ida with the three divine contestants.

Paris leapt to his feet and paled in terror. 'Fear not!' said Hermes, and his voice was as limpid as the mountain streams in which Paris bathed his limbs. 'We mean you no harm, but bring you great renown. For Zeus, our common father, has chosen you for a task. Do you see this apple, inscribed "For the Fairest"? Each of these three goddesses thinks that she deserves it. It's up to you to decide who gets it.'

Eventually, Paris calmed down enough to agree to do the job; he didn't seem to have any choice in the matter. He sat down on a rock, while Hermes stood aside and watched. The first to approach was Hera, and she appeared to the country boy as a woman of queenly bearing in the glow of full womanhood. A purple-bordered gown draped her majestic figure, and her hair, shining like mahogany, was wound up in an elegant coiffure. Her wide, dark eyes glanced at her competition with a look that betrayed both envy and disdain. She turned her attention to young Paris. 'If you make the apple mine,' she said, her voice ringing throughout the dell, 'I shall grant you worldly power beyond your imaginings. You shall rule vast territories, and you shall rule them securely, with no rivals to your throne.'

Paris was sorely tempted. He was just a shepherd, and here he was being offered a throne. But, to be fair, he should hear what the other two goddesses had to say as well. Athena strode briskly forward. She appeared as a keen-eyed warrior, imbued with a contained force that was ready to be unleashed at a moment's notice. Yet she had also the luminous skin and boyish leanness of a virgin. 'Should you decide to grant me the apple,' said the favourite daughter of Zeus, fixing him with her iron-grey gaze, 'I will make you invincible, not just in hand-to-hand fighting, but in all warfare. You will be the greatest general ever to lead an army. Thousands shall flock to your banner, and none shall stand against you.'

This too was a powerfully attractive offer. The decision was not going to be straightforward, and the contest was beginning to seem one of bribes, not of beauty. Paris gave Hermes an uneasy glance, as if to say 'I'm not sure I can do this'. But the god cocked his head to one side and smiled back reassuringly.

Finally, Aphrodite glided up to Paris, and she appeared as sex incarnate. With each lithe step tiny bells jingled from her gilded sandals with a sound like the tide flowing in and out on the shore at sunset. She peered at the handsome young shepherd through silken lashes, and smiled as if she knew a secret. She stood tall, with slender arms and hands, and her skin was as white as the first fall of snow, but her eyes and hair were raven black and the sunlight played in her tresses. Her flimsy dress moulded her ripe breasts and well-rounded buttocks, and hinted at further delights. The goddess leant forward and breathed in his ear: 'If you choose me, you will win the love of the most beautiful and desirable woman in the world.'

As her scent filled his nostrils, it suddenly seemed to Paris that this was where his happiness lay, not in the hazards of war or rule. What had he, a shepherd, to do with such things? This offer was more to his taste. 'But who is this woman?' he asked. 'And what does she look like?'

'She is Helen of Sparta,' replied the goddess, 'and she looks just like me. For your eyes, I have made myself in her image.'

Paris forgot his lover Oenone, so certain was he of the truth of Aphrodite's promise. His mind was swept clean: there was nothing he wanted more than the gift of Aphrodite, the weaver of snares. He indicated to Hermes that he was ready, and the three goddesses lined up expectantly. Hermes solemnly handed Paris the apple, and without a moment's hesitation Paris held it out to Aphrodite. Gracefully she took it, and with a smile of triumph. Then the four deities slowly faded away, and Paris was left with no more than the certainty that something exciting was going to happen, although he had no idea what form it might take.

The very next day Aphrodite's gift began to take effect. Priam, king of Troy, sent men out to search the countryside and bring back the most perfect bull they could find for the climactic sacrifice of a festival that was being celebrated in the city. The men chose a bull that was in Paris' keeping, and out of curiosity he followed them back to Troy. He was amazed. He had heard rumours of the greatness of the city, the wealth of its merchants, the splendour of its walls and public buildings, but the reality overwhelmed him. No sooner had he set foot in the city, however, than his sister Cassandra recognized him, and began to shout out: 'He's here! The bane of the city is here! We shall burn!' But though she spoke the truth, she had been cursed by Apollo, and no one ever believed her. They thought she was just raving, and her voice was soon lost in the joyous babble of the festival.

As is usual all over the Greek world, the festival included athletic games, and Paris, with his newly acquired self-confidence, decided to take part in a few of the events. He did extraordinarily well, beating even the local favourites, Hector and Deiphobus – his brothers, if he did but know it. Deiphobus especially was mightily displeased at being beaten by some peasant upstart; he drew his sword and Paris fled for safety to the protection of an altar. But in the tussle Deiphobus tore from Paris' neck a talisman that he always wore, and Hecuba and Priam recognized it as the token they had wrapped in their unwanted baby's swaddling clothes all those years ago. To his astonishment, the young shepherd Paris was acknowledged as a prince and welcomed back into the fold of his family. He could see that Aphrodite's spell was beginning to work. In the joy of the moment, Hecuba's dream was forgotten.

The Abduction of Helen

But who was this Helen, the gift of Aphrodite to Paris? Who was this woman, fated to be reviled down the centuries? She was indeed the most beautiful and desirable woman in the world, but Aphrodite also had a hidden motive: Helen's father Tyndareos had omitted to sacrifice to her, and she cursed him, saying that his daughters Helen and Clytemestra would be 'twice married and thrice married and yet husbandless'.

Tyndareos, the king of Sparta installed by Heracles, took as his wife Leda, the daughter of the king of Aetolia; one of her sisters was Althaea, the mother and killer of Meleager. But Leda was loved by Zeus, who came to her in the form of a swan. And in time she gave birth to four children, two by two, a pair in each egg. One egg contained the Dioscuri, Castor and

Polydeuces, while the other held Helen and Clytemestra.

Castor and Polydeuces were inseparable twins, but there was one critical difference between them. Polydeuces had inherited the immortality of his father, but Castor was fully mortal. They were two of the greatest heroes of the Age of Heroes. Together they joined the voyage of the *Argo*; took part in the Calydonian boar hunt; defeated all-comers in the funeral games of Pelias; stormed Athens to rescue their sister Helen after her abduction by Theseus.

Their greatest adventure was also their last. It began when they attended the wedding of their cousins, Idas and Lynceus, to the daughters of Leucippus, Phoebe and Hilaeira. When the Heavenly Twins arrived for the ceremony, just one look was enough for the girls to change their minds. They left their grooms dumbfounded and allowed themselves to be abducted by the handsome strangers. As if that insult wasn't bad enough, Castor and Polydeuces rustled some of their cuckolded cousins' cattle to pay Leucippus his bride-price!

Naturally Idas and his brother sought revenge. Suspecting a trap, Lynceus ran swiftly up to the top of the highest peak of Mount Taygetus, from where he could look out over the entire Peloponnese. And indeed with supernatural vision he spotted Castor and Polydeuces hiding in a hollow oak tree, waiting to spring an ambush on their cousins. Lynceus ran back down the mountain and joined Idas, and together they crept up to where the Dioscuri were hiding. And Idas, who matched great Heracles for strength, drove his spear right through the husk of the mighty tree and fatally wounded Castor.

Polydeuces leapt out and chased Idas and Lynceus to their father's grave, where they made a stand. But Polydeuces' aim was true, and his hurled spear took Lynceus in the chest. Idas tore his father's tombstone from the ground with a grunt and prepared to hurl it at Polydeuces, to bury him under it (the only way to stop immortals) – and he would have succeeded, had not Zeus intervened on behalf of his son and blasted Idas with a thunderbolt. And so Idas and Lynceus lie beside their father.

Polydeuces returned to where his brother lay dying. Tears poured from his eyes, and he prayed to Zeus that he might be allowed to die along with his dear twin. Zeus hearkened to his son's prayer, but there are some things that even Zeus cannot do, and he couldn't deny Polydeuces' immortality. Nevertheless, he found a solution, and shared Polydeuces' immortality between the two brothers, so that on alternate days the Heavenly Twins dwell in misty Hades and on bright Olympus in the company of the blessed gods. As deities it is their pleasure to protect sailors from the dangers of the deep, and sometimes they appear as pale fire clinging to the masts and rigging of vessels.

But meanwhile, ignorant of the future, there was joy in Tyndareos' palace, for he had found a noble husband for Helen. Her sister Clytemestra was already married to Agamemnon, the lord of Mycenae. There were, as can be imagined, a great many suitors for the hand of the most beautiful woman in the world: Odysseus of Ithaca, Menestheus of Athens, the grey-beard Idomeneus of Crete, Ajax of Salamis, and scores of others. All were required by Tyndareos to name the bride-price they would pay for his slender daughter.

By far the best offer Tyndareos received was from Menelaus, the noble brother of Agamemnon. But Tyndareos was worried that, whoever he chose to marry his daughter, the other suitors, proud heroes all, would cause trouble. So he made them all swear not only that they would abide by his decision, without envying the successful suitor, but also that they would, if necessary, take up arms to defend the marriage. After all, Helen had been abducted once before, when she was only a child, and she had not become less desirable over the years.

The suitors gave their word – the oath that triggered the Trojan War – and Tyndareos declared that the winner was Menelaus. He was the lucky man who would wed and bed the most desirable woman in the world. Not only that, but Tyndareos also announced that, on his death, Menelaus would inherit the throne of Sparta. He knew that his sons Castor and Polydeuces were destined for higher things. And so it came to pass, for soon afterwards Tyndareos died and Menelaus became king.

Not many weeks passed before Paris set sail from Asia to claim his prize. He had made no plans, beyond simply travelling to Sparta. Helen had been promised to him by a goddess. It would happen.

As everyone knows, nobles feel themselves closer to other nobles, even those from other cities and further abroad, than they do to the peasants of their own lands. Some pledge formal friendship with one another – a network in case of need. But even without such a pledge, it's understood that if a stranger arrives at your door, he's not to be turned away, because he's under the protection of Zeus. And if the stranger is of the same social rank as his host, he's to be treated well and given the run of the house. By the same token, it's the responsibility of the guest to show his host only the greatest respect and courtesy.

So it was when Paris turned up at Menelaus' palace at Sparta. He was made welcome, and gifts were exchanged. Above all, Paris had brought gifts for Helen, but it was not these that turned her head. Aphrodite had made Paris irresistible to her. His exotic easternness, his strange accent, his rich clothing and luxurious ways – everything about him fascinated her. And, for his part, he found that Aphrodite had indeed shown herself to him as a perfect likeness of the Spartan beauty. Passionate looks were exchanged, breasts heaved with sighs, fingers tantalizingly brushed. The lovers knew they were destined for each other, but made no further move, for fear of the wrath of Menelaus. And then Menelaus was called away to distant Crete . . .

Paris and Helen lost no time. As soon as they were sure that Menelaus must have set sail from Sparta's seaport, Gythium, they plundered the palace and left. Paris stole all Menelaus' most precious possessions – his wife, his golden tableware, his purple-dyed cloth. In the gods' eyes, Paris had violated the sacred laws of marriage and hospitality. He and his kin would have to pay. Justice would be done, reparation made.

The lovers too departed from Gythium, where Paris had left his ships, and set their sails east. In order to baffle pursuit, they lingered for a while on Cyprus and the Phoenician seaboard, revelling in eastern luxury and in the love they bore each other. But in due course of time Helen entered Troy, with death as the dowry she brought for her new in-laws, Priam and Hecuba.

The Greeks Prepare for War

While the lovers were taking their long honeymoon in Phoenicia, the Greeks got busy. The pretext for the mobilization of forces to attack Troy was the oath that Helen's many suitors had been made to swear: they were honour-bound to help Menelaus recover his bride, and they were the cream of the Greek aristocracy.

The Greek leaders were summoned by herald to bring their contingents to Aulis by a certain date, from where they would sail across the Aegean Sea to Asia. It was a huge expedition: over a thousand ships lay at anchor just off the coast, while their crews and the fighting men took their ease on land. But then, they would need a massive force to take Troy, one of the greatest cities in the known world, and well supplied with allies from Asia Minor and beyond. Menelaus' brother Agamemnon, king of Mycenae, was chosen to be the overall leader, but he was accompanied by a staff of seasoned councillors and warriors.

But two of the greatest Greek warriors were reluctant to join the expedition. Odysseus of Ithaca feigned madness, for he knew from an oracle that, if he joined the expedition, he was destined not to see his home again for many a long year. As soon as he heard that Agamemnon's agents had arrived on his island to summon him to Aulis, he yoked a plough team consisting of an ox and an ass. This was crazy in itself, because such a team would hardly plough a straight furrow. But, as if that were not enough, he then went about sowing salt instead of seed – salt that would make the land barren. But one of Agamemnon's agents was Palamedes, second in cunning only to Odysseus himself. He took from the arms of Odysseus' wife Penelope their new-born son Telemachus, and placed him in the field that Odysseus was ploughing, right in the path of the plough. Odysseus' ruse was exposed when he halted the plough to avoid killing his son; he wasn't so crazy after all. So he gathered his men and went to Aulis – but in his pride he swore to avenge himself on Palamedes.

The other absentee was even more critical. Young Achilles had the potential to be the foremost warrior in Greece. His mother Thetis had placed him under the guidance and protection of the wise Centaur Cheiron. But then she learnt that her son was essential to the fall of Troy, and that he was faced with a terrible choice: he could live a long but inglorious life, or he could go to Troy and die young and renowned.

Naturally, Thetis didn't want her son to die. She removed him from Cheiron's tutelage, disguised him as a girl, and took him to Scyros, where he was kept safe by Lycomedes, the king of the island. Achilles longed for glory, but agreed to his mother's scheme to give himself time to think: did he want it badly enough to face certain death? The young prince's presence was no secret among the womenfolk of the palace; indeed, one of Lycomedes' daughters, lovely Deidameia, gave herself in secret love to Achilles. But whenever any visitors came, everyone went along with the pretence that he was one of the king's daughters; he was known as Pyrrha, because of his fair hair.

But the agents Agamemnon sent to Scyros included some of the most clever and cunning of the Greek leaders: Nestor, Odysseus, Phoenix, and Diomedes, son of Tydeus, one of the Seven against Thebes. As is proper, they brought gifts for the king's daughters, but they had included among the cloth, perfume, and jewels some marvellously wrought weapons and armour. The girls fluttered around the gifts, trying out this or that item of jewellery or clothing – but one of the girls was more interested in the weaponry. Quietly, Odysseus picked up a horn and sounded the signal for danger. The terrified girls fled to their quarters as the alarm rang out – but Achilles seized the weapons and sprang to the city's defences.

His true nature was revealed; he cast off his disguise with disgust and went eagerly to Aulis with Odysseus and the others who had been tasked with tracking him down. He accepted the choice of a candle-brief, but glorious, life. And Deidameia wept, for she was pregnant, and suspected that she would never again see her child's father. Before long she gave birth to a boy, and called him Neoptolemus.

So all the heroes and their troops and ships were assembled at Aulis – but still the expedition could not set sail, for adverse winds kept the fleet pinned on the lee shore. Then Calchas, the wisest soothsayer in the Greek army, told Agamemnon that the wind would never abate until he had sacrificed his daughter Iphigeneia to the lady Artemis, Mistress of the Hunt. For Agamemnon, after bringing down a proud stag in a grove sacred to Artemis, had boasted that he was as great a hunter as the goddess.

So Agamemnon, lord of men, sent for Iphigeneia from his rich palace at Mycenae, saying – it was Odysseus' suggestion – that she was to marry swift-footed Achilles, the bright star of the Greek forces. Arrayed in her bridal finery and with a lovely smile of anticipation, the girl set out, and her mother Clytemestra sped her on her way, but no sooner had the girl reached Aulis than she was bound to the altar and slaughtered. Blood was shed to betoken future bloodshed; Death led the fast ships onward to Troy.

But first they were granted one more omen. Many of the leaders were gathered together and saw it. A blood-red serpent slid from beneath an altar and up a nearby tree where there were nine sparrows, a mother and eight chicks. The snake devoured the birds, starting with the chicks, and no sooner had it finished its meal than it was turned to stone. There could be no doubt that this was a powerful omen, but the Greek leaders were at a loss to explain it. Again, wise Calchas read the sign aright. It meant, he said, that the war would last nine years, and only in the tenth would they take Troy. And so it came to pass.

The Greek Landing

The Greeks made more or less directly for Troy. One important stop-off point was the island of Delos, where they picked up the three daughters of King Anius. Dionysus had granted these three young women remarkable gifts: Oeno's grapes made limitless wine; Spermo's grains of wheat and barley never failed; and abundant oil flowed thick and green from Elaïs' olives. Anius let his daughters go with the Greeks to Troy, and the army's supplies were taken care of for the duration of the war.

As the Greek fleet approached the Trojan coastline, they could see that their arrival was not unexpected: the Trojan army had come out to meet them, to try to prevent their landing. Nevertheless, Agamemnon ordered the Greeks to continue straight on, to try to force a landing. The ships' prows crunched on the shingle of the beach, and for a split second, pregnant with doom, nothing happened. For there was a prophecy that the first man to touch the soil of Troy would die. But then Protesilaus, the leader of the Thessalians, jumped from his beaked ship on to the shore.

Back home in Greece, when Protesilaus' wife Laodamia heard of her husband's death, she begged the gods that she be allowed just a little more time with him, for they had been married but one day. Her request was granted. Hermes escorted Protesilaus' ghost from the underworld, and the two lovers were together for a few hours. But when her husband left her again, never to return, Laodamia made a wooden statue of him; she spent all her time with it, and even made love to it in bed. And when her father ordered her to desist, and to burn the statue on the fire, she joined her husband in death by throwing herself into the flames. Protesilaus was cut down by Hector, the son of Priam and the Trojans' mightiest warrior; but his death paved the way for a mass attack from the Greeks. They all leapt from their ships with blood-curdling cries, and battle was joined.

The first Trojan to die was the albino Cycnus, a son of Poseidon. Cycnus was invulnerable to iron or bronze, so Achilles laid aside his weapons and throttled the man to death with the straps from his own helmet; and as he died he turned into a swan and flew off.

The force of the Greek charge was irresistible, and they drove the Trojans back in disarray to the city walls. The Greeks had succeeded in their first objective and established a beachhead. They made their camp on the shore by Troy, with the farmland plain between them and the city, two miles distant. They beached the ships safely near their tents, and protected the entire camp, ships and all, with a palisade. They dug in, but no one expected the war to last long.

Once they had established themselves, the Greeks sent envoys under a flag of truce to the city of Troy, to demand the return of Helen and to threaten all-out war if their demand was refused. Agamemnon's war council chose Odysseus, Menelaus, and the herald Talthybius to head the mission to the city. The Trojan counsellors met, and the Greek envoys addressed them at length, warning above all about the danger of hubris and asking them whether they really wanted to die for Helen.

The Trojans listened mostly in silence, but Paris had bribed Antimachus to urge the assembled Trojans to murder the Greek envoys while they were defenceless in the city. Antimachus' words met with approval among the Trojan counsellors, but noble Antenor, the king's most trusted adviser, was disgusted at such a cowardly and impious suggestion (for heralds are under the protection of the gods). He spoke out sharply against it, and argued that Helen should be returned to the Greeks – that she was not worth dying for. He failed to persuade the assembly, but at least the Greek envoys were allowed to leave. Their demand had not been satisfied, but their lives had been spared.

And so the first nine years of the war passed. Heroes fell on either side by the dozen, and ordinary soldiers by the hundred; Priam, king of Troy and father of fifty sons and fifty daughters by various wives, lost many sons, to his enduring sorrow. This too is the inscrutable way of the gods. One of those sons was Troilus, of whom it had been prophesied that if he reached the age of twenty, Troy would never fall. Swift-footed Achilles ambushed the lad outside the city as he was exercising his horses. Ares filled the Greek's soul. He dragged Troilus off his mount, pulled back his head, and slit his throat.

A major loss from the Greek side was the hero Palamedes, unjustly done to death by Odysseus, seeking revenge for his discovery on Ithaca. Ever ready with all the deceptions required in war, Odysseus forged a letter from Priam to Palamedes, offering him gold if he would betray the Greeks, and buried that amount of guilty gold in Palamedes' quarters. When letter and gold were revealed, Palamedes was condemned for treason, and ritually drowned by Odysseus and Diomedes. But Nauplius, Palamedes' father, had his revenge: he convinced Anticlea, the mother of Odysseus, that her son had died at Troy, and in abject grief she killed herself.

Hector, Ajax (the son of Peleus' friend Telamon), and the other leaders on both sides distinguished themselves. Achilles more than fulfilled his potential, and rose high in everyone's esteem; at one point, he even managed singlehandedly to quell a mutiny. The Greeks made gains, but never quite broke into the city; the Trojan defence was solid and, although they were cut off from the sea, they were able to supply themselves from inland. The Greeks were never able to put the city under siege, and were forced to engage in an endless series of skirmishes on the plain. They stuck to their frustrating task, but at the end of nine years of unbroken warfare, the position was little different from what it had been at the beginning.

Achilles Withdraws

Many prisoners were taken in the course of the war, to be made slaves or concubines to their new masters, or to be ransomed for personal profit. Among these prisoners was Chryseis, captured from a town allied to the Trojans, the fair daughter of the priest of Apollo, Chryses. Agamemnon, lord of men, took her for his own, to warm his bed and work his loom. Chryses made his way under a truce to the Greek camp, and offered Agamemnon a generous ransom for his daughter, for she was all that was left to him. But Agamemnon haughtily refused, against the advice of his staff officers.

Chryses left in despair, and from the depths of his grieving heart prayed to Apollo to punish the Greeks in their arrogance. By the rules of war a captor should accept a generous ransom, and Chryses' offer for his daughter had been more than adequate. Apollo heard the plea of his priest and sent a plague into the Greek camp. First the dogs and mules began to sicken and die, and then the disease spread to the troops. Every day dozens more succumbed, until the situation became critical: it looked as though, after all this time, the Greeks would have to abandon their effort and sail back home empty-handed.

With the men huddled together in little groups, complaining that all they could do was await a foul and pestilential death –

with the men muttering defeatist thoughts out loud for the first time – Achilles, at Hera's prompting, summoned a general assembly of the army. After pointing out how desperate the situation was, the chief of the Myrmidons wondered out loud why Apollo, the god of pestilence and disease, had made them the targets of his wrath.

He was answered by Calchas, the soothsayer. The plague would continue until Agamemnon had restored Chryseis to her father without ransom, and made a splendid sacrifice to the god. Agamemnon spat out his anger at Calchas, but, as the commander of the Greek forces, he had no choice: the good of his men had to take precedence over his own desires. He agreed to return Chryseis – but only if he was compensated. He felt that he would lose face if he lost both girl and ransom. 'Of all the Greeks,' he said, 'it's unthinkable that I should be left without my due.' Achilles vehemently pointed out that all the booty had been distributed: there was nothing left in the common pool that Agamemnon could claim as his own. 'I am the commander-in-chief,' Agamemnon hurled back. 'I'll take what I want, even if it's something of yours! None of the Greeks is my equal; I can do as I like!' He was claiming to stand to his subordinates as Zeus stands to the other gods.

The quarrel grew ever more fierce, until Agamemnon declared that as compensation for Chryseis he would take from Achilles his own favourite concubine, the captive Briseis. Achilles was so enraged by now that he began to draw his sword to kill Agamemnon, but Athena appeared to him and stayed his hand.

Instead, Achilles cursed Agamemnon in the vilest language, and declared in front of all the assembled Greeks that if Agamemnon stole Briseis from him, he and his men, the fearsome Myrmidons, would withdraw from the fighting. He knew how important he was to the eventual success of the expedition. It was not just that he had killed more of the enemy than anyone else, but also that the men had come to admire him. Not knowing that he was more or less invulnerable, they were impressed with his cool courage. Agamemnon was taking a big risk in alienating his most important ally.

Aged Nestor of Pylos, the wisest of the Greeks in council, tried to pour oil on the troubled waters. 'The Trojans would be delighted,' he said, 'if they could see you now. Agamemnon, please don't try to take the girl from Achilles; and you, Achilles, should not insult our commander like that. Respect each other, both of you.' Good words, sensible words – but both men were too far gone in anger to heed them. The assembly broke up in disarray, and swift-footed Achilles and his men returned to their tents to see what would happen next. Patroclus, Achilles' tent-mate and dearest companion, knew his friend well enough to be sure that he meant what he said. Idleness would sit poorly with Achilles, but his will was unbendable.

Agamemnon duly returned Chryseis and carried out the pro-pitiatory sacrifice to Apollo, as ordered by Calchas. But then he sent men to fetch Briseis from Achilles. The leader of the Myr-midons bade the envoys peace, because he had no quarrel with them. But he reiterated his determination to take no further part in the war. However badly things were going for his former friends, he would neither take up arms nor participate in their war councils.

Agamemnon's Dream

In his sorrow and wounded pride, Achilles called on his mother Thetis, who came from the depths of the sea and sat beside him.

She was highly favoured by Father Zeus, and Achilles asked her to persuade him to side with the Trojans and tip the scales of the war in their direction, at least for a while. Then the Greeks would learn how much they needed him.

Thetis recognized the signs that heralded the end of her son's candle-brief life, but she did as he asked. And Zeus agreed, though he knew it would get him into trouble with Hera, who favoured the Greeks; for Paris had denied her the golden apple, and in claiming his prize from Aphrodite had violated the sacred bond of marriage, which is Hera's domain. But Zeus cowed his wife into silence, and then he pondered. How should he ensure that the tide of war turned in the Trojans' favour?

The gods take their ease and play with us men, and the mind of Zeus moved into devious channels. He sent Agamemnon a dream – a lucid dream, so vivid that it seemed beyond any doubt, but it was nothing but deceit. It seemed to Agamemnon that Nestor spoke to him and said that the gods had lined up against Troy, and that if Agamemnon mustered his men and struck at once, he would easily capture the city.

At daybreak, Agamemnon summoned his staff officers to a meeting; Achilles, of course, stayed away. He described the dream to them, and they too were convinced. But Agamemnon was worried about the morale of the troops: the plague had sapped their confidence, and the business with Achilles had done no good either. If they were less than committed, the fall of Troy might not be as certain as the dream seemed to imply.

This worry was the work of Zeus, his way of robbing Agamemnon of his wits and undermining his powers of judgement. When Agamemnon next opened his mouth, he found himself saying that he would test the men by telling them it was no longer feasible for them to capture Troy, and that they should immediately return home – exactly the opposite of what the dream had advised.

The war council called an assembly of the Greek soldiers. As thick as bees they came from their tents, and Rumour blazed among them. Agamemnon addressed them, holding the staff, fashioned by Hephaestus, that he had inherited from his father Atreus, who had in his turn been bequeathed it by Pelops. As he had planned, he counselled despair and defeat. If it was just them against the Trojans, he said, their numerical superiority alone would bring them victory; the problem was all the Trojan allies. They couldn't win; they must break camp and return home immediately.

Naturally, the thought of returning home after so many years of war found an eager response among the men. Confused cries of joy filled the damp air and the assembly broke up in disarray. The men scattered for their tents, grabbed their belongings and their booty, and began to load the ships for departure. Up on Olympus, Hera was appalled as she looked down onto the swarming shore. Her favourites were on the point of throwing everything away. She sent Athena down to Troy to see what she could do. The two goddesses worked in league to countermand the will of Zeus, their anger fuelled by resentment over their rejection by Trojan Paris.

Athena found Odysseus dispirited. A cowardly retreat was not at all to his liking. And in his mind he heard the voice of the keen-eyed goddess of war as she told him not to give in to his despair, but to go among the men and try to halt the rush for the ships. Odysseus needed no second prompting; this was just what he wanted to do. He walked around the camp, and every time he came across an officer he appealed to his sense of honour and told him that Agamemnon, for reasons known only to generals, had suggested retreat only to test the men. But every time he came across an ordinary soldier, he beat him across the back and shoulders with his stick and drove him back to the assembly point.

So the men reassembled, but they were now seething with confusion and discontent, and one of their number, Thersites, a notorious troublemaker, spoke up for them. 'It's all right for you, Agamemnon,' he shouted out. 'You've gained plenty of plunder from the war.' And then he turned to the men and said: 'I think we should leave him here to enjoy his gold and girls, while we go back home. He shows us nothing but contempt, but let's see how he fights the war without us!'

His mutinous words were warmly welcomed by the men, but Odysseus was quick to act. He leapt at Thersites with his stick and pummelled him into silence, much to the amusement of the fickle crowd, who a moment before had been willing to give him a hearing. Odysseus then addressed the entire assembly, with Athena at his side guiding his thoughts. He appeased the men by agreeing that they were suffering hardship, but reminded them of the omen of the sparrows, promising them victory, but only in the tenth year of the war. And now it *was* the tenth year of the war. Nestor, whose advice had long been recognized as sound, backed Odysseus up, and Agamemnon, restored to his senses, ordered the men to eat, and then be ready to fight. Death would be the punishment for anyone preparing to leave.

The men, with their morale recovered, roared their approval and dispersed in an orderly fashion. But Agamemnon summoned his officers to attend the pre-battle sacrifice, and selected a fatted ox as the victim. He prayed for swift victory, for the destruction of Troy at his hands, little knowing how much more slaughter and sorrow the next months would bring.

Menelaus and Paris

The Greek army formed up for battle, and the Trojans came out of the city to meet them on the plain. The Trojans had heard of the disarray in the Greek camp, and were resolved to take advantage of it. For the first time ever in the war they made a full-fledged sortie, instead of merely defending their massive and impregnable walls, built by Poseidon himself. Everyone knew that this could be the decisive battle, and martial cries disguised extreme nervousness.

When the two armies were almost within bowshot, Paris, heavily armed and resplendent in a helmet adorned with leopardskin, got carried away by the excitement of the moment, and shouted out a challenge. 'Whichever of you Greeks thinks he is the best, let him come and face me, one on one!' And Menelaus, mindful of the terrible wrong Paris had done him, eagerly stepped forward into the space between the battle lines.

Reality is different from fancy, and Paris shrank back in trepidation behind the shelter of the massed Trojan soldiers. His brother Hector, the tamer of horses, berated him as a coward and reminded him sharply that the whole conflict was his fault. 'It's all right for you,' complained Paris. 'You have a martial spirit, while my talents come from Aphrodite. But you're right, and if both armies will agree, I shall fight Menelaus in single combat. In fact, let it be that the whole war is decided in this way. If I win, I keep Helen, and the Greeks must leave. If I lose, Menelaus gets back his treasure and his lady – not that she wants him any more, now that she has me.'

Hector joyfully agreed: the war would be ended today! No more bloodshed! He advanced into no-man's land, and shouted out to the Greeks the deal Paris had proposed. Menelaus had no hesitation in accepting the offer. The two sides would seal the bargain with a joint sacrifice, and Priam himself was to witness it and give his blessing to the pact.

When Helen heard of the agreement, she raced to the battlements to witness the duel. Two great heroes would fight for her in single combat! It was thrilling! She couldn't even decide who she wanted to win! Priam and Antenor also came up to the fortifications and surveyed the scene. In a fatherly gesture, Priam called Helen over to him and spoke kindly to her, blaming not her but the gods for all their misfortunes.

As they gazed out over the plain, Helen identified for the old man the heroes of the Greeks: Agamemnon, the proud commander, standing in his chariot with the sun gleaming on his armour; Odysseus, the master strategist, in his plumeless boar's tusk helmet; Ajax, who was exceptionally tall, and so terrifying to behold in full armour that men likened him to Ares himself; bold Diomedes of Argos, as furious in battle as a force of nature; Idomeneus of Crete, as sinewy as an acrobat for all his greying temples; her former husband Menelaus, with his horsehair plume waving in the breeze. She was puzzled, however, not to see her brothers Castor and Polydeuces, for she did not know that they had died not long after her abduction.

All the Greek and Trojan leaders convened between the armies for the sacrifice and oath-taking, and Priam and Antenor were taken by chariot from Troy to join them. The victims were slaughtered, libations were offered to the gods, and Agamemnon offered up a mighty prayer for all the gods to witness their oath: that Menelaus and Paris were to fight to the death, with the winner keeping all. And as they poured their libations, all prayed that the brains of anyone who broke the oath would be spilled on the ground as readily as their wine.

Priam returned to the city, for he could not bear the suspense. Odysseus and Hector marked out the duelling ground, and cast lots to see whether Menelaus or Paris would begin. Fate chose Paris.

The two champions buckled on their armour and seized their weapons. As soon as they had taken up their positions, Paris hurled his spear. His aim was true, but Menelaus easily deflected the missile with his shield. Now it was Menelaus' turn and, with a prayer to Zeus on high for revenge, he hefted his spear and threw it. It whistled through the air and struck Paris' shield straight on. Too violent for the toughened leather of the shield, the spear ripped through and into Paris' breastplate, where it lodged briefly before he shook it loose.

Menelaus leapt at his opponent with sword raised. He was looking for a single, brutal, killing blow – but the sword shattered on the rim of Paris' shield! Disappointed, but not daunted, Menelaus roared and hurled himself at Paris with his bare hands. He took a firm hold of Paris' helmet and began to drag him back to the Greek lines, choking him at the same time with the chin strap. And he would have succeeded, but Aphrodite saw the predicament of her favourite and caused the chin strap to break.

Paris had barely struggled to his feet when Menelaus seized a javelin and hurled it at him. The deadly lance sped through the air towards Paris' chest, and it looked as though the young prince's end had surely come – but Aphrodite whisked him away, off the battlefield, and set him down, safe and surprised, inside his house in Troy. Then, disguised as a serving-girl, she went up to the battlements and found Helen. 'Come, my lady,' she said. 'Your husband awaits you in his chamber.'

Helen recognized the goddess and spurned her suggestion. 'Haven't you shamed me enough?' she cried. 'Menelaus has beaten Paris, and now I belong to him again. What would people say of me if I joined Paris in his bed now?' Though Aphrodite is the goddess of sensual pleasure, she is a goddess, and her will is not to be gainsaid. 'Be very careful, Helen,' she warned. 'Otherwise, I shall arouse such hatred of you among both the Greeks and the Trojans that your life will be unsafe whoever wins the war.'

So Aphrodite spirited Helen away from the walls and into Paris' room. And while the two of them lay in love, Menelaus searched and called in vain for his lost foe. Nevertheless, it was clear that he had won the duel, and that Helen and his stolen treasure should be returned to him. By rights, the war should be over, and on both sides men dared once again to dream of a peaceful future and the resumption of normal life.

But the gods had other plans. Hera's hostility towards Troy was not assuaged in the slightest, and when the gods met in council in the lofty hall of Zeus' palace, she insisted that the war should continue, despite the mortals' solemn oath. Zeus was indifferent, but conceded to allow the war to carry on, once Hera for her part had agreed that the next time *he* wanted to see the destruction of a city, she wouldn't stand in his way. So the gods toy with the lives of men.

Zeus sent Athena down to the battlefield, to carry out Hera's plan to see the truce first broken by the Trojans. She flashed down to the plain like a shooting star, and men on both sides wondered what this omen might signify. But Athena disguised herself as Antenor's son and went in search of Pandarus, for she knew he would obey her. 'You would win praise from all Trojans,' she flattered him, 'if you were the one to lay Menelaus low. You are a great bowman! Pray to the archer god Apollo, and let fly!'

Nothing loath, Pandarus had his men conceal him behind their shields, while he bent and strung his horn-tipped bow. Then he notched a trusty arrow, the best of his quiver, and took careful aim over the top of his men's shields. With a prayer to Apollo, he let fly, and the lethal messenger of death sped through the air. His aim was true, but Athena's job was done. It was enough that the truce was broken; she did not need Menelaus to die as well. At the last moment, she deflected the arrow so that, although it pierced the king of Sparta's breastplate, he was not mortally wounded. The blood flowed freely down Menelaus' thigh, but it was only a flesh wound in his side. Agamemnon summoned Machaon, the son of the healer-god Asclepius, to tend to his brother. The skilled healer of men drew out the barbed arrow, sucked the wound clean, and sprinkled it with a balm prepared for his father by Cheiron, the wise Centaur.

Diomedes' Day of Glory

With the truce broken, both sides began once again to don armour and take their places for battle. Agamemnon reviewed his troops and called on them to be of good heart, for Zeus would not allow oath-breakers to win the war. To each of his senior officers he spoke suitable words of encouragement, or chided them if they had not so far been as prominent in the battle as they could and should have been. And so the two sides advanced across the plain once more towards each other. Grim Ares urged on the Trojan troops, while Athena instilled courage into the Greeks. And their immortal assistants, Fear and Hatred, sowed savagery in men's hearts.

The two sides met with the clash of shield on shield. Spears were stabbed through or to one side of the tall shields, and men fell to the ground, blood gushing from wounds. Groans and screams added to the clamour of fighting men. Antilochus, the son of Nestor, brought down Echepolus of Troy, with a spear thrust through the man's helmet and deep inside his skull. Elephenor tried to drag the body away, to find somewhere safe to strip it of its valuable armour; but in so doing he exposed his side, and Agenor was quick to plunge his spear in the Greek's guts.

On and on the slaughter continued, but gradually the tide began to turn, as Hera wanted, in the Greeks' favour. Here and there the Trojan lines wavered, and the Greeks yelled in triumph. Apollo urged on the Trojans: 'Greeks are not made of iron and stone!' he cried. 'Cut them with a blade and they will bleed! And see: Achilles, their greatest warrior, is not among them!' Again the battle became finely balanced; and still the carnage continued. But Athena sought out Ares and suggested that they withdraw from the battle, to leave the Greeks and Trojans to get on with it by themselves.

Now it was the turn of Diomedes to excel, the son of Tydeus who died at Thebes. He hurled himself into the thick of the fighting, and the noble brothers Phegeus and Idaeus bore down on him in their chariot. Phegeus threw his spear, but he just missed Diomedes' left shoulder. Diomedes' response was true; Idaeus fell from the chariot and lay still. Phegeus reined in the horses and leapt down to confront his foe, and he too would have died, had not Hephaestus cloaked him in darkness. For their father was his priest, and the lame god did not want both sons to die.

Diomedes was unstoppable. He was like a lion that descends on defenceless sheep, or like a spring torrent fed by snow-melt, that sweeps all before it. Even when Pandarus wounded him in the shoulder, Diomedes just had the arrow pulled out by a friend and carried on. 'Lady Athena,' he cried out in prayer, 'hear me now! Let me kill whoever it was who wounded me with his bow, a coward's weapon, for an archer stands far from the fray.' And Athena heard his prayer and restored his strength. It was as if he had never been wounded, and his lust to soak the earth with Trojan blood redoubled. But Athena warned him not to try to battle any of the gods that appeared on the battlefield, except Aphrodite.

Man after man fell to the spear or sword of Diomedes as he hacked and thrust his way through the Trojan ranks. Aeneas, son of Anchises and Aphrodite, saw the slaughter, saw that the Trojans were being pushed back, and sought out Pandarus. 'We must get that man!' he cried. 'Come with me!' Together they leapt into Aeneas' chariot, with Aeneas at the reins so that Pandarus was free to wield his spear. 'I failed with an arrow,' he muttered to himself, 'but I shall not fail with my spear. There'll be no second chance for the son of Tydeus.'

It was terrible to behold, the two fierce fighters bearing down on Diomedes. His friends urged caution, but Diomedes would hear no talk of retreat. He had already taken one chariot as booty, and was eager for another, especially since Aeneas' horses were of the noblest breed. As soon as they were within range, Pandarus let fly with his spear. The brutal bronze head burst through Diomedes' shield and Pandarus cried out in savage joy, but Diomedes had taken no wound. Now he hurled his spear, and it arced through the air and came down on Pandarus' face. Right through the nose it flew, severing his tongue completely and shattering his teeth, before projecting out from the bottom of the archer's chin.

Aeneas jumped down from the chariot and stood astride the corpse, keeping at bay all who would attempt to strip the valuable armour from his friend. But Diomedes picked up a massive boulder, greater than any two men of today could raise, and heaved it at Aeneas. It crushed his hip bone, and Aeneas collapsed unconscious to the ground.

That should have been the end of him, but Aphrodite flew to the scene, cradled her son's head in her arms, and began gently to bear him aloft and away from the battlefield. But now Diomedes surpassed even himself. Seeing Aeneas being carried off by Aphrodite, he dared to give chase. And just as the goddess was moving out of range, Diomedes bounded high in the air from his chariot and wounded her in the forearm, piercing her precious robe that the Graces had made for her. With a scream, Aphrodite dropped her son – but Apollo caught him before he hit the ground.

Aphrodite fled the battlefield with Diomedes' taunts ringing in her ears: 'What have you to do with war, lady? Flee from here!' She found Ares resting and watching the bloodshed close by, for there was nothing he enjoyed more than seeing mortals kill one another; the greater the savagery, the better. In truth, the wound was not that serious, but it was more than the gentle goddess could endure and, with ichor dripping from the gash, she begged her lover to lend her his chariot, so that she could return to Olympus. No more fighting for her! For her revenge, she would employ weapons with which she was more familiar: she was already plotting to seek out Diomedes' wife and make her fall in love with another man.

Diomedes, however, was as determined as ever. He wanted nothing more than to slay Aeneas and take his suit of armour as booty. Three times he made a killing stroke, and three times Apollo warded it off. But just as Diomedes raised his arm for the fourth time, the golden god yelled at him: 'Fool! Do you dare to challenge the gods? Give it up: there is an unbridgeable chasm set between us and mortal men!' Diomedes backed away in terror at the god's wrath, and Apollo bore Aeneas safely back to Troy, where he was tended by immortal nurses, Leto and Artemis. But Apollo made a double of Aeneas, and let the Greeks and Trojans fight it out around the unconscious body.

Still furious, Apollo sought out Ares and encouraged him to re-enter the fray. Disguised as swift-footed Acamas, prince of Lycia, Ares sought out the nobles of Troy and urged them not to abandon Aeneas. And Acamas' friend, Sarpedon of Lycia, son of Zeus and grandson of Bellerophon, lashed out at Hector: 'Are you going to let the Greeks drive us back to the city gates? You Trojans aren't pulling your weight; you're leaving us allies to do all the fighting, while you stand like sheep. Come on!' And now the battle began to turn in the Trojans' favour, with Ares moving among them and stirring them to ever greater exploits. This was unacceptable to Hera and Athena, and while Hebe prepared Hera's chariot, Athena armed herself for war. Hera cracked her whip, the gates of Olympus opened, and the two goddesses rode in glory down to the battlefield of Troy. And they went with Zeus' blessing, for Ares' lust for blood sickened him.

While Hera rallied the Greeks, Athena found Diomedes resting. 'Shame on you!' she cried. 'You are not the man your father was!' But Diomedes replied, 'I'm only obeying your command, my lady. You told me not to fight any of the gods except Aphrodite – and now Ares is fighting for the Trojans.'

'I release you from your promise,' Athena said. 'Go! Seek out Ares and do battle with him!' And she herself took the place of Diomedes' charioteer, and rode to war with him. But she wore Hades' cap of invisibility, so that Ares saw only Diomedes approaching.

The god of war hurled his spear, and the god of war never misses – unless another deity engages him. Athena deflected the wicked missile, which ricocheted harmlessly from the side of the chariot. Now it was Diomedes' turn, and he shoved his spear at the war-god's belly, and Athena put all her power behind the thrust as well, and then pulled the spear out again, dripping ichor.

Bellowing with pain and rage, Ares flew upward to heaven. His screams terrified friend and foe alike, for none had ever heard anything like it. Bitterly he complained to Zeus at the impudence of Athena, but Zeus dismissed him with angry words to find Asclepius and be healed. And he welcomed Hera and Athena when they returned from the fray, for they had forced Ares off the field of battle. Now it was man against man, Trojan against Greek, with no gods involved, and gradually, thanks to the prowess of Diomedes and others, the Trojans were being pushed back. The Trojan seer Helenus, son of Priam, took matters in hand. He commanded Aeneas, now fully restored, to rally the troops right by the city walls and make a stand. 'And you, Hector,' he shouted above the din, 'go back into the city and get our mother Hecuba to gather the women of Troy. They are to offer Athena a magnificent robe now, with the promise of a munificent sacrifice in the future of twelve unblemished cows, if she will keep Diomedes out of the city. The man is proving himself the equal of Achilles.'

Aeneas and Hector did as the gifted Helenus ordered; for when he was a baby, snakes had licked his ears. He knew the languages of all creatures of air, earth, and water, and animals make more reliable harbingers of the future than men. Once within the city walls, Hector speedily carried out his errand. But before returning to the battlefield, he sought a few moments with his wife Andromache. He found her on the battlements with Astyanax, their son, watching in dread as the fighting raged ever closer to the city gates and walls. As soon as she saw him she ran up to him in joy; and the nurse followed behind, bearing the baby boy, the light of Hector's life and Troy's hope for the future.

Andromache rested her head on the hero's chest and begged him to be careful. 'You're too brave for your own good,' she said. 'Think of me! I have no one in the world but you. Think of your son! You fight so well that all the Greeks want to see you dead. What comfort will be left for your sorrowing family after you have met your doom? The future holds only torment.'

'Don't ask me to stay away from the battle,' Hector replied in sorrow. 'I cannot; I know no other way. I do as my fathers have always done; I live and die by honour and shame. Troy will fall – this I know – and so honour is all that is left. I shall be dead, but the worst of it is that you will pass into bitter slavery.'

Hector reached out his arms for Astyanax, but the baby burst into tears and clung to his nurse. He was terrified by his father's helmet with its nodding horsehair plume and gleaming bronze. Both Hector and Andromache laughed, and forgot the horror for a moment. Hector took off his helmet and swung his child high into the air, and the boy squealed in delight. Hector kissed him, and Andromache's tears were mingled with smiles.

The fighting continued until dark brought rest to the weary combatants, though all night long Zeus' thunder rumbled in the heavens. In the morning a truce was made so that both sides could bury their dead. The Greeks also seized the opportunity to dig a trench and raise a rampart of earth and boulders to replace the palisade that had been sufficient protection for their camps and their beached ships while the Trojans were pinned inside their city. Too broad to be crossed at a leap by a chariot, the trench bristled with sharpened stakes; and the rampart was fitted with towers and well-built gates. And the Greeks indignantly refused the offer relayed by the Trojan herald: though Paris would not return Helen, he was prepared to return the treasure they had stolen from Menelaus, with interest. As Diomedes put it: 'Victory is within our grasp! We have no need of lesser offers from our enemies!'

Hector Triumphant

At dawn, the working parties of both sides assembled on the plain to gather their dead and prepare them for burial. If the corpse was that of a nobleman, it was carefully washed, dressed in a shroud, and laid out on a couch. After a suitable interval, the body was carried to the place of burial, accompanied by friends and dependants, and by women weeping and wailing the ritual lament. It was then reverently laid in the ground, to ensure safe passage across the River Styx and into the halls of Hades.

Meanwhile, on cloud-girt Olympus, Zeus called a meeting of all the gods. He chided them, and used the full weight of his authority, and the threat of eternal imprisonment in Tartarus, to force through his will. No god or goddess, he thundered, was to sneak away from Olympus and help either the Trojans or the Greeks – not by fighting for them, nor even by giving them advice. He would attend to this battle of mice himself.

The day after the mass burials, Zeus himself, father of men and gods, called for his chariot and team of divine horses, and sailed down to Mount Ida, from where he could survey the city of Troy and the Greek encampment and see that his will was done. The morning passed in inconclusive fighting – though conclusive enough for those who fell and died. At midday Zeus held up his golden scales and carefully placed in each of the pans the doom of the Trojans and the doom of the Greeks. The doom of the Greeks was heavier.

Zeus burst from Ida with lightning and thunder, and hurled them against the Greek forces. No one could withstand the onslaught: Idomeneus, Agamemnon, Ajax, Odysseus – all fell back. Only Nestor stayed on the field, because one of his horses had been wounded by an arrow fired by Paris. And now Hector was bearing down on him, and Nestor would surely have perished, if Diomedes had not raced up and taken the old man on his chariot. Together they charged at Hector, and Diomedes' spear soon found the breast of Hector's charioteer. Hector himself might well have been next, had not Zeus sent a blazing thunderbolt crashing into the ground in a ball of flame before Diomedes' chariot.

Seeing that Zeus himself was against them, Nestor cautioned Diomedes to turn back. The Argive hero was reluctant: it seemed like cowardice to turn and run. But he heeded his sage companion, and they wheeled around and joined the general rout back to the safety of their camp, with Hector's taunts ringing in their ears. Three times Diomedes was poised to turn back and fight it out with the Trojan, but every time Zeus emitted a warning rumble of thunder.

Hector was rampant. Shouting out encouragement to his men, he urged his team forward, calling on the horses by name. He felt powerful enough to take the Greeks' new trench at a single bound and challenge the new rampart; he could scent victory, close at hand. He could almost taste the smoke that would fill the air from the Greek ships he would burn. He blazed like Ares, fearsome to behold and deadly to his enemies.

Teucer, the Greeks' best bowman, tried again and again to topple Hector from his chariot, but failed. It was as though the Trojan hero were under the protection of a god. Back the Greeks were pushed, across the moat, where they made easy targets and many perished. Back they were driven, until they barely made it inside the new rampart.

As night began to fall and the fighting died down, Zeus returned to Olympus. Hera dared to chide him for stopping the rest of the gods interfering, but Zeus was adamant. 'Hector will never be checked,' he said, 'until or unless Achilles rejoins the fighting. And Achilles will rejoin the fighting only to defend the corpse of his bosom friend Patroclus. So it is; that is my will.' And the gods trembled, for they saw his plan: to place Achilles on a high pedestal of honour, as Thetis had requested, and to punish the Trojans for their sins.

Envoys and Spies

Fear stalked the Greek camp. With the Trojans encamped for the first time close by on the plain, everyone expected death and defeat the following day. Strong pickets were posted to keep watch through the night. At a gloomy meeting of the Greek staff officers, Agamemnon, a changed man in the face of defeat, agreed to swallow his pride and try to placate Achilles. 'I shall do as you say,' he said. 'I shall send envoys to Achilles, bearing great gifts: tripods, gold, women, horses, cauldrons. And I shall return Briseis to him as well, who was the cause of our quarrel. She is exactly as he left her: I have not taken her to bed. And if, with his help, we succeed in taking Troy, he will have his pick of the spoils and plunder, until his ship is filled with riches. Then, when we get back home, he shall take one of my daughters as his wife, and I shall make him a baron of my kingdom, with extensive estates of fertile land.'

Everyone agreed that this was a generous offer, and envoys were detailed to take the proposal to Achilles. The delegation, headed by friends of Achilles – old Phoenix, Odysseus, and Ajax – made its way along the shore and found the leader of the Myrmidons playing the lyre by his tent, with Patroclus as ever by his side.

Achilles greeted them warmly and made them welcome with meat and wine. Then they got down to business. Odysseus explained the situation: they faced defeat unless Achilles would take up arms again and fight for them. Agamemnon repented his rash actions, and would not only return Briseis untouched, but would give him great wealth and honour. 'This is no time for anger,' he concluded. 'Let generosity calm your wrath. Even if you still hate Agamemnon, think of the rest of us.'

But Achilles' heart remained unmoved and unmelted by Odysseus' words. Phoenix tried next, and then Ajax, but to all of them Achilles made the same reply: he would never forgive Agamemnon. The only thing that could possibly make him fight would be if Hector stormed the Myrmidon encampment and directly threatened himself and his men. Otherwise, he said, he would embark his men the next day and sail for home. The envoys chastised him for his heartlessness in condemning hundreds of Greeks to certain death, but in his terrible pride Achilles remained implacable.

Odysseus and Ajax departed in frustration, but Phoenix remained. He had been Achilles' mentor since the hero's childhood, and felt it his duty to stay by his side, and even to sail back home with him, at the cost of abandoning the rest of the Greeks. When the returning envoys reported back to Agamemnon and the war council, there was stunned silence, but Diomedes brought their attention back to the present. They badly needed information about the enemy's intentions, and Diomedes and Odysseus volunteered to sneak into the enemy camp and see what they could find out. They awoke before dawn and set out across the plain, keeping cover behind walls and trees.

But the same idea had occurred to the Trojans, and Dolon, attracted by the generous reward Hector promised, put himself forward. When Diomedes and Odysseus were about halfway across the no-man's land between the two camps, they heard Dolon coming and threw themselves to the ground. They let him pass a short distance, so that his escape route back to the Trojan camp was cut off, and then raced after him. The cowardly Dolon offered no resistance. Quaking in his boots, he told them everything they wanted to know. But once they had all the information they needed, they cut his throat even as he begged for his life, stripped him of his fine armour, and hung it in a tree to collect on their way back. Traitors could expect no less.

Dolon had carefully described for them the precise layout of the Trojan encampment, and had told them especially that a newly arrived contingent of Thracians had bivouacked at a little distance from the rest. It was foretold that if the white horses of Rhesus, the Thracian king, ate and drank at Troy, the city would never be taken. Odysseus and Diomedes just had time. They crept silently up to the Thracians as they slept, slaughtered a number of them as they lay dreaming on the ground, including Rhesus, and stole the king's horses. Diomedes was tempted to stay for more plunder – Rhesus had a fabulous chariot, decorated with gold and silver – but Athena whispered a warning to him. Just then a cry arose: someone had discovered the bodies of the men they had killed. They raced back to the Greek lines, pausing only for Dolon's bloody armour. Their material gains were slight – but the news imbued all the Greeks with new courage, and that was worth more than a hundred horses.

The Assault on the Ships

At daybreak, Zeus sent Strife down to the Greek camp. The dread goddess perched in the middle of the Greek encampment and let out a frightful wail, to stir all the Greeks to action. The two sides advanced once more into the plain, disturbing the kites from their horrid meal. Strife looked on with joy, anticipating slaughter, while Zeus gazed down unconcerned from high Olympus, for to the gods the activities of mortals are just sport. One generation dies and is replaced by another; the gods play with all alike, as careless boys sport with flies.

The battle was closely contested, but at noon the Trojan lines began to waver. Agamemnon went on the rampage, sowing death left and right. And now Antimachus paid dearly for his impious attempt to kill the envoys the Greeks sent at the very beginning of the war to present their ultimatum. For Agamemnon confronted his two sons in their chariot, and though they begged for their lives, he held no pity for them, but slew them where they stood. As a forest fire leaps forward, destroying everything in its path, so Agamemnon carried all before him, and he and his men harried the Trojans back to the city wall.

But now dark-bearded Zeus came down from Olympus to his vantage point on Ida, with his messenger Iris by his side. 'Deliver this as a message to Hector,' he commanded. 'As long as Agamemnon remains unhurt, the Greeks will dominate the battle; but once he retires wounded, I shall grant Hector the power of slaughtering the Greeks all the way back to their ships until nightfall.'

Beautiful Iris delivered the message entrusted to her by Zeus, and Priam's son heard it in his heart like an inspiration. He rallied his troops, putting fresh courage into his men all over the battlefield, but still Agamemnon seemed unstoppable. One after another he slew two sons of Antenor, leaving their mother to mourn in her chamber. But at the moment of death one of the two young men struck and gashed Agamemnon on the forearm. The Greek leader tried to fight on, but was forced to leave the battlefield to seek medical help. With a cry of encouragement to the other Greeks, he was gone.

Hector's chance had come. He urged his men to greater efforts, ordering them forward from the city gates, while he himself fell on the foe like a savage storm at sea. Ten Greek champions fell before his spear and his flashing sword. Back fell the Greeks, back and further back. They maintained good order, but all too soon they found themselves once more hard by the rampart and their camp. Diomedes and Odysseus were wounded and had to withdraw from the battlefield. Even mighty Ajax found himself slowly being driven back, and the same was happening all over the field.

Now, Achilles had been watching the action from afar, standing on the stern of his beached ship, and he saw Nestor returning from the battle with a wounded man in his chariot. He was disturbed, for it looked as though it was his friend Machaon, the son of Asclepius, and he sent his tent-mate Patroclus to find out. When the young son of Menoetius reached Nestor's tent, the old king of Pylos made him welcome, but Patroclus explained that he had only come to see whether it was Machaon who had been hurt. Now that he saw it wasn't, he would leave. His carelessness provoked Nestor to anger against Achilles, for the Greeks now needed him more than ever.

'Achilles' father Peleus sent him here to perform noble deeds,' he said, 'not to sulk and skulk in his tent. If he truly will not fight, ask him to lend *you* his armour, so that you may lead the fearsome Myrmidons into battle. The enemy will think that you are him and their courage will fail. Otherwise, I fear, all will soon be lost.'

Nestor was acting, all unwitting, as an agent of the will of Zeus. But Patroclus liked the idea. He was moved to pity by the plight of the Greeks, and could see how dire the situation was. He set out back to the Myrmidons' encampment to see if Achilles would agree. But on the way he met his friend Eurypylus, grievously wounded in the thigh by one of Paris's barbs, and he stopped to tend to him.

Meanwhile, the Trojans, foiled by the Greeks' trench, decided to abandon their chariots at its lip and press forward on foot. They formed up in five columns, and at the head of each column strode a great hero: Hector for the first, then Paris, Helenus, and Aeneas, while the allied column was led by Sarpedon of Lycia. Each column advanced against a section of the Greek rampart that they thought might be vulnerable – a gate, a stretch of less secure stonework. In answer to Trojan prayers, Zeus, surveying the action from Ida, sent a cloud of dust swirling into the Greeks' eyes.

The Trojans pressed forward with renewed vigour, and began tearing at the rampart with their hands, pulling away loose stones and earth and logs. But as fast as they removed stuff, the Greeks filled the gaps with oxhide sandbags, while raining stones and missiles down from the top of the rampart onto the attackers, as thick as hail or a snow storm.

But now the allied contingents had demolished enough of the rampart in front of them to try to clamber over it. Ajax and his half-brother Teucer ran to plug the gap, and Ajax lunged with his spear at Sarpedon. Death would certainly have met the son of Zeus had his father not protected him. Sarpedon was checked, but not hurt, and the battle raged furiously but indecisively at this stretch of the wall.

Elsewhere, however, Hector found and lifted a mighty boulder, greater than any two men of today could raise, and hurled it with all his strength against one of the gates. The crossbars gave way and the planks of the gate splintered and burst. Through the breach Hector leapt, and his men poured in after him, while the Greeks turned and fled. It looked as though he would keep his promise to burn the Greek ships.

On Ida, Zeus saw Hector's success, and felt that the day was won. He turned his attention away from the battlefield, confident that no other god would intervene in the action, for he had forbidden it. But his brother Poseidon, who had not been privy to the deliberations on Olympus, took pity on the Greeks, whom he favoured because of his ill treatment at the hands of Laomedon. He took on the appearance of the seer Calchas and rallied the weary and terrified troops. They formed a compact phalanx, an impregnable wall of shields. Hector bore down on them like a boulder rolled in a storm-swelled river, but even he was stopped in his tracks by the massed spears and swords.

The Deception of Zeus

Behind the lines, Nestor met up with Agamemnon, Odysseus, and Diomedes, returning from the beached ships after tending to their wounds. For the third time, Agamemnon counselled retreat, seeing that they could do nothing against the will of Zeus, but Odysseus told him off disdainfully for such talk, unbecoming especially in their commander. Following Diomedes' lead, the four heroes set out for the front; despite their wounds, they might give fresh heart to their men.

But the matter was not in human hands, and never had been. With Poseidon supporting one side and Zeus the other, the battle was finely balanced. And now Hera conceived the desire to disobey her husband and influence the battle in favour of the Greeks. The plan she came up with was subtle and certain. She went to her chamber, anointed her body with a rare and irresistible scent, and dressed in her most alluring robe. But still she needed to be sure. Calling Aphrodite to her side, she lied to her, for they were on opposing sides in the war. 'I'm going down to earth,' she said, 'to try to reconcile the ancient quarrel between Ocean and Tethys. I intend to get them back into bed together. That will do the trick.'

Aphrodite understood what she wanted and untied her girdle of desire, that makes all who wear it irresistible and robs both men and gods of their wits. 'Take this girdle,' she said. 'Tethys will find her lord more than willing.'

Hera smiled artlessly and took the proffered gift. Concealing it in her breast, she flew down from Olympus to the island of Lemnos, where Sleep, the brother of Death, has his abode. Offering to reward him with the golden throne that her son Hephaestus had made, she told him that she was going to make love to Zeus, and asked him to see that afterwards Zeus fell fast asleep.

Sleep was terrified: 'No, not I!' he whined. 'Once before you had me put him to sleep, while you blew up that storm to distract Heracles, and Zeus' wrath was terrible. I survived only because my brother Night hid me until his anger died down.'

'It's not the same thing at all,' countered Hera. 'Zeus won't be as furious about the Trojans as he was about Heracles.' But, seeing that Sleep was reluctant, she increased her bribe: 'If you do this for me, I shall see that one of the Graces graces your bed.'

'Swear this by the River Styx,' said Sleep, 'the only oath that is binding on the heavenly gods. Pasithea is the one I want!'

Hera swore a solemn oath, and together the two deities set off for Ida. When they reached the mountain, Sleep perched in a lofty pine, to avoid being seen by the father of gods and men, the thunderer. But Hera approached Zeus, the magic girdle slung low about her hips, and he was consumed by desire. He had never wanted any woman as much as he wanted Hera now.

'What? Here, now, out in the open on the mountainside?' exclaimed Hera in mock horror, but her almond eyes shone. 'What if someone should see us?'

'Don't worry,' replied her hasty husband. 'I shall veil us in a golden cloud, that even Helios could not penetrate.'

'Penetrate,' purred Hera. 'Now there's a word . . . ' As they lay together, the meadow beneath them bloomed with green grass and multicoloured flowers. And when they were done, Zeus lay back satiated, and fell fast asleep with his lady in his arms.

No sluggard, Sleep raced straight off for the battlefield and told Poseidon that the coast was clear: with Zeus asleep, the battlefield was his to control as he wished. The earth-shaker moved among the Greek troops, stiffening their resolve, urging them to forget Achilles, arguing that Hector could not withstand them if they worked together. In the guise of a Greek officer, he persuaded them that the best way to defend the ships was to push forward.

And so it came to pass. It was Ajax who made the crucial breakthrough. Hector lunged at him with his spear, but the point was deflected, and Ajax picked up a rock, one of the great stones used as wedges to keep the ships in place on the beach, and struck Hector with it on the chest. Stunned, Hector sank to the ground, blood trickling from his mouth. He would have died then and there, had Aeneas and Sarpedon not dragged him off the field, uncertain whether he was yet alive.

Still the battle raged, but with Hector's departure something departed also from the Trojans' hearts, as when a cat glides out of a room. Though they fought on, secretly they began to cast around for some avenue of escape should they need it. And slowly, like a tide just on the turn, they fell back step by step until they found themselves back beyond the trench.

Just then Zeus awoke. He sprang to his feet and surveyed the battlefield below. He saw the Trojans in retreat, and Hector stretched out unconscious on the ground, with men huddled anxiously around him. He knew immediately what had happened. 'Treachery and lechery!' he shouted at Hera. 'You scheming bitch! Don't you recall the times I've punished you in the past? This time I'll teach you a lesson you'll never forget!'

Zeus raged on. Hera protested that it was not she who had brought Poseidon back into the fight, but she could do nothing against her lord's anger, and even Poseidon relented, knowing that, ultimately, Troy would fall. Meanwhile, Zeus sent Apollo to tend to Hector, and the healer-god had the Trojan hero on his feet in no time. Hector's miraculous return to the battlefield was greeted with joy from his men and dismay from the Greeks, for they knew that only some god could have healed him so quickly and thoroughly. And indeed Apollo led the way before Hector, invisible, but bearing Zeus' aegis, before which no man can stand his ground. For thunder and lightning groaned and flashed from the aegis, fearsome to behold and hear.

And so once more the battle swung in the Trojans' favour, with the Greeks fleeing pell-mell back towards their ships in the face of Zeus' aegis. Once the Greeks had crossed the trench, Apollo kicked at its banks to form a causeway across which the Trojans easily flowed even in their chariots, as unstoppable as a flood tide. When they reached the rampart, Apollo simply swept it aside, as a child wrecks a sand castle on the shore. And now the Greeks had nowhere to go. Their backs were at their ships. Their aching muscles now were animated not by courage but by desperation. Men fell, dead or dying, and every moment that passed brought the end unmistakably closer.

Then Hector, in the forefront as usual – for this was the day Zeus would give him glory – reached one of the Greek ships and grasped its stern with his hand while fighting off all who came near. He called for fire, but Ajax stood near by and slew all those who came close with burning brands. But even Ajax was eventually beaten back, and then a dozen men rushed in and tossed their torches into the ship, and flames immediately caught hold and licked around the stern. It was, as Fate would have it, Protesilaus' ship.

The Death of Patroclus

This was the turning-point, the moment Zeus had been waiting for. His intention always had been to allow Hector the glory of bringing fire to the ships, but then to turn the tide against the Trojans. And so the din of battle, now so near, roused

Patroclus. He was tending Eurypylus' wound, but he left immediately to see if his tent-mate might have changed his mind. Now, surely, with defeat staring them in the face, he would agree to Nestor's plan.

'You're a hard man, Achilles,' he said. 'Surely Peleus was not your father nor Thetis your mother. No, the cold, grey sea and the harsh cliffs were your parents. But at least let me have your arms and armour, and a company of your Myrmidons, to inspire the Greeks to fresh efforts, and to make the Trojans quake at the thought that you have returned.'

Swift-footed Achilles replied: 'It's true that the fighting is now close by, but I swore not to take up arms until it reached my very camp. But I cannot hold on to my anger for ever. You may take my arms and armour, and my men – and do your best, I pray. But you must not carry the fight to the walls of Troy; that honour is for me alone. Beat the Trojans back from the ships – that's all. And then return safe to me.'

So, while Achilles told the Myrmidons to get ready and stirred their hearts for the coming battle, Patroclus put on his friend's armour, the wedding gift of the gods to Peleus: bronze greaves with silver straps, a breastplate chased with stars, the helmet with its terrifying plume, and the splendid shield. He slung the bronze sword with silver studs over his shoulder and took two of his own spears, moulded to his grip. For no one but Achilles could manage his great spear, the gift of Cheiron and the gods to Peleus.

Achilles' charioteer, peerless Automedon, prepared the chariot and team, and would drive Patroclus himself, so that for a while all should mistake him for Achilles. With a prayer to Zeus – for victory and Patroclus' safe return – Achilles sent them on their way.

Patroclus' appearance on the battlefield terrified the Trojans, and the Myrmidons under his command were fresh after days of rest. But for the Greeks, the arrival of Achilles – or so they thought – was like the clarity that follows a storm, when the light is pure and the air clean and easy to breathe. The Trojans fell back a little way from the ships, but only to rally and prepare another advance. But Patroclus led the Greeks on with blood-chilling war-cries, and they ploughed into the Trojan ranks, sowing slaughter. Every Greek officer killed his man, and the Trojan lines began to collapse.

Hector could see that the moment of victory had slipped away, and he wheeled his chariot and headed for home, calling for retreat. But the trench was not so easy to negotiate on the way back, and soon it was filled with abandoned chariots, horses screaming as they struggled to escape their shafts, and broken wheels and bodies. The din was hideous. Now it was every man for himself, as the foot soldiers fled in fear of being struck in the back or crushed under the wheels of the chasing chariots, seeking desperately for safety, shoving friends aside, tripping over fallen bodies. They were easy victims for the pursuing Greeks, and the slaughter was immense.

Only one man had the courage to stand against Patroclus, and that was noble Sarpedon of Lycia. The two of them vaulted from their chariots and prepared to duel. From Olympus, Zeus watched the two heroes and mourned, for he loved his son Sarpedon above all mortals then alive, and it grieved him that he had to die. He was tempted to use his power to fly him safely from the battlefield, but that would set an awkward precedent: all the gods would want to rescue their favourites, every time they were threatened. But the ground received hot tears of blood, shed by the immortal father of gods and men.

Sarpedon first hurled his spear, but his aim was off, and the missile flew safely over Patroclus' left shoulder. Patroclus made no such mistake: his spear plunged into Sarpedon's side, just below the rib-cage, and Sarpedon fell writhing into the dust of the Trojan plain. He breathed his last as Patroclus tugged the spear in triumph out of his body, trailing intestines on its bronze head. The Myrmidons stripped the dead man of his armour and bore it back to their camp in triumph. But Zeus commanded Apollo to collect Sarpedon's corpse, wash it with river water, and anoint it with ambrosia. And then the twins Sleep and Death were to bear him home to Lycia, where his family could bury him with all honour.

Darkness fell, but even so the battle raged on unabated in the gloom of an ill-lit night. The Trojans strengthened their ranks, but still Patroclus bore down on them in his lust for battle. Many great heroes he felled, and the Trojan lines fell back. Carried away by success, Patroclus chased the fleeing Trojans towards the city. He forgot Achilles' orders to hold back, to leave the honour of assaulting the city to him alone. The lust of battle was upon him, and it was easy to hunt down the running Trojans, striking them in the back from his chariot, or in the face if they turned to offer token resistance. He was like a raging forest fire, consuming all before him. When he reached the Scaean Gate of the city, he hurled himself at it three times in a frenzy, but Apollo repelled him, saying: 'Back, Patroclus! Troy is not fated to fall to you, nor even to Achilles!'

Just then Hector rode up to confront him, knowing now that he would face Patroclus, and win great glory if he could bring down Achilles' bosom friend. But there was no glory in the fight. At Zeus' behest, Apollo stood behind Patroclus, wrapped in mist, and struck him sharply on the back. Achilles' helmet, that had never before tasted dirt, tumbled in the dust; Patroclus' spear shattered in his hand, his shield fell from his forearm as the straps broke, and his breastplate magically unbuckled itself. Euphorbus plunged his spear from behind into Patroclus' back. Gravely wounded, Patroclus began to drag himself to the safety of his own lines, but Hector sprang forward and delivered the killing blow, sealing his own doom.

The Return of Achilles

Achilles wept. He bowed his face and poured dust and ash over his head; he lay on the ground, groaning and tearing his hair. He saw beneath the surface to the pettiness and wretchedness of human life. All his womenfolk, the war-prizes he had taken, joined in the lamentation with their ritual cries. The ripples of his agony spread until they reached his mother where she sported in the deep with sea-nymphs. And Thetis knew straight away what the cry meant: that her son's time had come, that he would never return home. She hurried to his side, as any mother would, to bring what comfort she might.

Achilles poured out his woes to Thetis: 'My dearest friend is dead, the armour has been taken that Peleus received from the gods the day he took you for his wife, and now I know that I have little time left on this earth. I must turn my back on life, for I must avenge the death of my friend and rip the life from Hector.'

'You're right,' said his mother through her tears. 'Your death will follow soon after that of Hector. It is foretold.'

'Yet even Heracles had to die,' said Achilles. 'If glory such as his awaits me after death, that will be enough. I regret my anger against Agamemnon; perhaps I might have saved Patroclus' life.

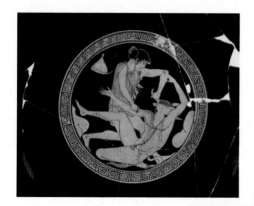

Theseus Slays the Minotaur.
Dokimasia Painter.
Red-figure cup, interior.
Greek, c. 470 BCE.

Atlas and Prometheus. Archesilas II
Painter. Black-figure cup, interior.
Greek, 560–550 BCE.

The Birth of Venus (Aphrodite). Sandro Botticelli. Tempera painting, 1486 CE.

Council of the Gods. Raphael. P

Apollo. Pistoxenos Painter or
Euphronius. Red-figure cup,
interior. Greek 500–450 BCE.

Deucalion and Pyrrha.
Peter Paul Rubens.
Oil sketch, c. 1636 CE.

Villa Farnasina, 1518 CE.

Medea. Policoro Painter. Red-figure vase. South Italian, c. 400 BCE.

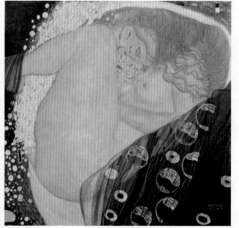

Danae. Gustav Klimt. Oil painting, 1907–08 CE.

Medusa. Caravaggio. Oil painting, 1597 CE.

Dionysus Astride a Panther. Pebble mosaic floor, from Pella.
Greek, 400–360 BCE.

The Murder of Agamemnon. Dokimasia Painter. Red-figure vase, side A.
Greek, 470–460 BCE.

The Death of Icarus. Maso da San Friano. Oil painting, 1570–72 CE.

Heracles in the Cup of Helios. Douris. Red-figure cup, interior.
Greek, 500–450 BCE.

Sleep and Death with the Body of Sarpedon. Bronze handle.
Etruscan, 400–375 BCE.

Cheiron Instructs Young Achilles. Wall painting, from Herculaneum.
Roman, 1st Century CE.

Diomedes Wounding Aphrodite. W.H.A Fitger. Oil painting, c. 1905 CE.

The Trojan Horse. Relief vase, detail. Cycladic Greek, c. 675 BCE.

The Siren Vase. Siren Painter. Red-figure vase, side A. Greek, 480–470 BCE.

Circe Transforming the Companions of Ulysses (Odysseus).
Jan van der Straet (Giovanni Stradano). Oil painting, 1570–72 CE.

The Making of Pandora. Niobid Painter. Red-figure vase, side A.
Greek, 460–450 BCE.

But the past is the past. Now I look to what brief future remains. It's better to burn out than to fade away.'

'Don't be too hasty, my son,' replied Thetis. 'At dawn I shall bring you a new set of armour, crafted by Hephaestus himself.'

Night drew over the plain, and the weary fighters disengaged. In the Greek camp, all were mourning the death of Patroclus. Achilles swore not to bury him until he had recovered the lost armour and brought back the head of his killer. And he made a dreadful promise: to slit the throats of twelve young Trojan boys beside his friend's funeral pyre. Then they bathed Patroclus' body and laid him out on a bed, shrouded in white linen. And all night long Achilles kept vigil beside the corpse, while the Greeks hardly slept, for they knew that on the morrow their champion would rejoin the fray.

Up on high Olympus, Hephaestus and his assistants were devoting the night to Thetis' request for a new panoply for her son. By daybreak a marvellous work had been wrought. The gleaming breastplate, greaves of layered tin, and close-fitting helmet with golden crest were wondrous to behold; but the masterpiece was the great shield. Five layers of metal made it safe: two of bronze on the outside, two of tin on the inside, and a middle layer of gold.

On the face of the shield was shown the whole cosmos: the earth, the waters, the heavens, and all the celestial bodies. Two cities were portrayed in fine and intricate detail by the divine blacksmith. In one of the cities peace reigned, and the people were celebrating festivals and going about their daily business; but the other city was beset by foes, and scenes of ambush and treachery, of hope and despair, seemed to flow before the eyes of the spectator. Nor was country life forgotten, with its ploughed fields and labourers, its cattle and flocks, orchards and vineyards. Young men and women danced while a multitude looked on; and around all lay impassable Ocean.

Early the next morning, Achilles received the gift with savage delight. Now he was ready for Hector. He summoned an assembly of all the Greeks, and he and Agamemnon were formally reconciled. Achilles apologized for sulking over something as trivial as a captive girl, and Agamemnon expressed regret for his high-handedness.

While the men took their morning meal, to give them strength for the day ahead, Agamemnon had gifts brought from his tent for Achilles, the gifts he had promised before: tripods, gold, women (including Briseis), horses, and cauldrons. And the Greeks performed a great sacrifice to seal the reconciliation in the eyes of the gods.

Achilles was too sick at heart to eat, and spurned all entreaties to do so. But Zeus took pity on him, and sent Athena to infuse in him nectar and ambrosia, so that he should not faint from hunger on the battlefield. Poised on the razor's edge between fury and despair, he donned his new armour, and pulled his great spear from the rack, while Automedon yoked his team of immortal horses and prepared the chariot once more.

Achilles mounted the chariot and called out to his noble steeds. For these two stallions were the offspring of Zephyrus, the west wind, and Swiftfoot, one of the Snatchers. 'Xanthus,' Achilles called out, 'and you there, Balius! Listen up! Today I commend myself to your care. Bring me back to the Greek lines, whether I am alive or dead!'

And Xanthus replied: 'Yes, we shall save you today, Achilles, but the day of your death draws ever nearer. It is your fate, and none can escape the doom that is written for him.'

'No need to prophesy my death, dear Xanthus,' Achilles

replied. 'I already know that I shall die here, far from home. But never mind that! Today is the day I shall make the Trojans suffer!'

The Death of Hector

The next morning, the Greeks and Trojans again faced one another across the plain – the same beginning as often before, but with the vital difference, to the morale of both sides, that peerless Achilles was there, in the front rank, eager for the fray. Meanwhile, on Olympus, Zeus the cloud-gatherer summoned an assembly of all the gods, including Poseidon and all the rivers and nymphs. He was concerned that under Achilles' leadership the Greeks might sack Troy before its time, and as a way of keeping things in balance, he gave the gods permission to go down once more and support whichever side they liked, while he remained on Olympus and watched.

As a result of the gods' interference, the battle see-sawed across the plain. Gradually, however, Achilles gained the upper hand. Poseidon prevented him killing Aeneas, and Apollo hid Hector from him, but by the end of the day the Greeks had driven the Trojans off the plain and back to the city walls. The gods returned to Olympus, except for Apollo, who hovered around Troy. He watched as King Priam gave the gatekeepers a delicate task: they were to hold the gates open for the retreating Trojan troops, while not allowing a single Greek to enter, especially Achilles.

They did as they were told, but Achilles still might have burst into the city, had not Agenor, son of Antenor, summoned up his courage. Despite knowing that he was no match for the Greek hero, he confronted him and delayed his advance

towards Troy, giving his men time to make themselves safe.
And though Achilles aimed a killing blow at the young Trojan,
Apollo hid Agenor in mist and swept him from the battlefield
to the safety of the city. Then he himself took on the appearance of Agenor and kept Achilles occupied at some distance
from the city while the rest raced for the gates. Troy's doom
was delayed for another day.

All the Trojans were safe inside the city? No, not all, for Hector
remained outside. Though his parents, Priam and Hecuba,
begged him from their vantage point on the walls to come inside,
to save himself, the very thought made him ashamed. But now
Achilles had extricated himself from his futile pursuit of Apollo;
realizing that he was dealing with a god, he abandoned the chase
and raced once more for the city gates. Priam saw him coming
and redoubled his appeals to his son, and Hecuba shed bitter
tears, imploring her son to save her from inconsolable grief. But
war is a cruel master. Hector remained unmoved, though in his
heart thoughts of flight competed with visions of a heroic victory.

Inexorably, Achilles drew closer, hefting his great spear on
his shoulder, his armour seeming to glow. Finally, Hector could
take it no more. He broke and ran. Achilles set out after him,
and he was famously swift-footed. Three times around the walls
of Troy they ran, pursuer and pursued, and gradually Achilles
was closing the gap, as a hound gains on a hind in flight. There
can be no doubt that he would have caught him, had Apollo
not breathed strength into Hector's limbs. From the walls of
Troy Priam and Hecuba looked on aghast and prayed helplessly
for their son's life.

Up on cloud-covered Olympus, Zeus asked the assembled
gods whether or not they should let noble Hector be laid low
by Achilles. But Athena rebuked her father, saying: 'How can

you even think of releasing the man from his doom? He is mortal; he would die soon anyway, but *this* day is fated to be his last.'

As Achilles and Hector began their fourth circuit of the great walls of Troy, Zeus raised high his golden scales. In one of the pans he placed the death of Hector and in the other the death of Achilles. Hector's doom was heavier, and Apollo immediately withdrew his support from the prince of Troy. Meanwhile, Athena appeared to Achilles and told him to rest and catch his breath, for she would go to Hector and persuade him to stand and fight.

No sooner said than done, and she appeared alongside Hector as his dear brother Deiphobus. And Hector believed her when she said that she would fight at his shoulder, that the two of them would tackle Achilles together and bring him down in his pride, as two tawny lions work together to bring down a magnificent gazelle.

So Hector stood his ground and waited for Achilles to draw close. Instead of the usual taunting – for each knew the other's lineage and prowess – Hector promised that, if he should win, he would not insult or mistreat Achilles' corpse. But Achilles replied: 'Does the wolf deal with the lamb? I'll make no pact with you. On guard!'

With these words he cast his long-shadowed spear, but Hector ducked and it passed safely over his shoulder and stuck in the earth. Now it was Hector's turn: 'You seem better at hurling words than spears,' he cried, but his spear was deflected harmlessly by Achilles' marvellous shield. He called on Deiphobus to pass him another spear, but there was no reply, for there was no one near him. And now he realized that he had been duped by a deity, and knew that his doom was imminent.

Hector bravely drew his sword and advanced on Achilles, slicing the keen blade through the air. Achilles adopted a defensive position, tucked in behind his great shield, and once more hefted his spear over his shoulder; for Athena had surreptitiously returned it to him. Hector's armour – the armour he had taken from Patroclus – protected almost his entire body, except for the neck. As the Trojan charged forward, Achilles thrust his spear at the exact spot – a terrible wound, but not enough to kill him immediately. Hector fell to the ground, choking on his own blood, and Achilles stood in triumph over him. 'Did you think you could get away with killing Patroclus, you swine? The dogs and kites will rend your body, while the Greeks honour Patroclus.'

In a bubbling whisper, Hector begged Achilles not to dishonour his body, to let his father ransom it, but the Greek victor refused. 'Ask me nothing, you whining cur! I hate you with such passion that I could hack chunks from your body and eat them raw! No amount of gold will stop you feeding the crows.'

So Hector died at the hands of a pitiless man. But inside Achilles something slumped, and he spoke to himself: 'It is done. Now I can accept my own death when it comes.'

He called on his fellow Greeks to return to camp, leaving only a token force on the plain in case the Trojans tried anything. After stripping Hector of his armour, reclaiming it as his own, he pierced the dead man's ankles, drew strong cord through the holes, and tied the body to his chariot. So he drove back to the Greek camp, defiling the body of his foe, dragging it over the rocky plain, breaking every one of its bones, disregarding the laws of gods and men.

Priam and Hecuba, looking down from the walls, saw their son's death, and collapsed to the ground, broken by grief. But Andromache still knew nothing. She was in the chambers she shared with her husband, drawing a bath for him to enjoy when he returned from battle. But then the sound of Hecuba's wailing reached her, and she ran in trepidation to see what had happened.

She arrived just in time to see Achilles dragging Hector's body towards the ships. The sight caused her to fall in a faint to the floor, but the wailing of her parents and the womenfolk roused her. She mourned equally for herself and her fatherless son. Neither of them now had anything to hope for. Their lives had fled with Hector's.

Two Funerals

Night fell and, with his vengeance complete, Achilles let grief possess him. In the night Patroclus appeared to him, begging for an early funeral so that he could cross the Styx into Hades. In his dream, Achilles stretched out his hands for his friend, but grasped only mist and air. And the next day the Greeks forgot war and devoted themselves to the funeral rites for one they had loved and honoured.

Men collected firewood and heaped it on the shore. Achilles' womenfolk prepared Patroclus' body, and Achilles himself bore it and laid it on the pyre. He cropped his hair in mourning and closed Patroclus' hands around the golden tresses. Sheep were sacrificed, and the corpse smeared with fat. Four horses were killed and their bodies added to the pyre, and two fine hounds, and all twelve of the Trojan youths Achilles had captured the previous day, their throats slit. Then Achilles thrust the burning brand into the pyre, and the hungry flames consumed all. And he swore that Hector's body should receive no such funeral, but should be food for dogs and crows.

The following day, the Greeks damped down the glowing coals of the fire with wine, sifted the ash for Patroclus' bones, and sealed them in an urn. Achilles reverently laid the urn in the ground and surrounded it with all those things that were dear to his dearest friend, and whatever he would need for his final journey. Then all the Greeks heaped up a vast mound of protective earth over the bones, and turned in his honour to athletic competition, as was the custom.

But the games did little to settle Achilles' anger with Patroclus' killer. Still his heart was racked with bitter grief. Time and again he harnessed his chariot in the dawn's grey light to drag Hector's body around the newly constructed tomb, seeking to calm his restless spirit that way. But each day Apollo refreshed and restored the mutilated corpse.

The gods looked on from high Olympus in abhorrence at this transgression of sacred custom. For a while, the opposition of Hera and her allies created a stalemate, but Zeus, as always, had the deciding vote, and he issued a direct command: Achilles is to return Hector's body to Priam. He summoned Thetis, to ask her to make her son see reason, or risk the anger of the gods. And he sent Iris to Priam, to tell him that the way was clear for him to ransom his dear son's body.

Thetis found her son still wrapped in inconsolable sadness over the death of his friend, and exhausted by sleeplessness and savagery. But he readily obeyed Zeus' command: he would let Priam have Hector's body. He put aside the thought that he was somehow doing Patroclus a disservice by returning the body. Meanwhile, Iris told Priam to go alone and secretly to Achilles' tent, with valuable gifts for the ransom, taking only a driver for the cart; and she told him not to worry about the danger, because Zeus would send Hermes himself, the wayfinder, to guide him.

She found the king begrimed with dust and earth that he had poured over his head and body in his grief, and all the womenfolk of the palace in deep mourning.

Hecuba thought her husband had lost his mind, but, trusting in Zeus, Priam was determined to go. He ordered a great wagon loaded with bolts of the finest cloth, ten talents of gold, tripods, cauldrons, and a gorgeous golden cup of the finest Thracian workmanship. When they reached the ford across the Scamander, they were met by Hermes in the guise of a young Myrmidon from Achilles' camp. Safely he guided the old man through the Greek picket lines, by the simple expedient of putting the sentries to sleep.

So Priam completed his terrifying journey and entered Achilles' quarters. The son of Peleus greeted him kindly, and the old man dropped to the floor and tearfully begged the warrior to pity his old age and grant him the right to take his son's body back to Troy. Achilles gently raised the old man to his feet and bade him sit down, but Priam said that he could never rest while Hector's body lay unburied and dishonoured.

Achilles' temper flared at the suggestion that he had acted in a dishonourable manner, but he accepted the ransom and had all the valuables taken from the cart and stored in his quarters. Then he had his womenfolk bathe and anoint the corpse, and dress it in fine linen. He suggested that Priam spend the night in his quarters, and wait for daylight to make his way back across the plain to Troy. And for the first time since his son's death Priam felt able to sleep for a few hours, calmed by Achilles' assurance that the period required for Hector's funeral rites should be an armistice, untainted by war.

But in the middle of the night, while Achilles lay asleep, Hermes appeared again to Priam and urged him to arise and leave, in case word reached Agamemnon or one of the other Greek officers that the king of Troy was in their camp, and could easily be taken. Priam got ready in silence, and Hermes guided him back to the Scamander, where he took his leave and returned to Olympus. Priam, head bowed and covered, drove the cart slowly home along familiar lanes.

At the sight of Hector's body, trundling towards the city in the dawn's early light, all gave in to grief and mourning. Women tore their hair and raked their nails down their cheeks, while sighing bitterly when they thought what they had lost and what the future held for them. Andromache was utterly disconsolate, and young Astyanax wailed constantly, oppressed by the mood and his mother's tears.

Achilles arranged a truce as promised, and the citizens of Troy piled up wood for nine days. On the tenth they carried Hector out of the city gates to his pyre and burnt him with all honour. With tears streaming down their cheeks, they gathered his bones and sealed them in a jar of gold. They placed the jar inside a deep-dug grave, and heaped up stones and a mound of earth over the remains. And so they buried Hector, breaker of horses.

The Death of Achilles

All too soon, after the funeral truce, armour was once again donned, weapons once more straightened, sharpened, and burnished. Now reinforcements were arriving for the Trojans from the ends of the earth. From the north came a contingent of the wild warrior women, the Amazons; from the south came Memnon of Ethiopia. The war was not over yet.

The Amazons were led by Penthesilea, a daughter of Ares,

who was eager for glory in a war against men. She and her troop displayed great valour on the battlefield, and took many Greek lives, but then Penthesilea met Achilles. The duel was brief: Achilles' spear soon found her breast. But when the Greek hero removed the dying woman's helmet, he fell in love with her. He refused her burial, and kept the body by his side in his tent. Thersites, the crude troublemaker of the Greek army, made lewd suggestions about what Achilles got up to with the corpse, and paid for his insults with his life. But Diomedes was Thersites' kinsman, and he and Achilles fell out over the murder, until their fellow officers and aristocrats reconciled them. They did not want to see Achilles go off in another sulk. Nevertheless, he had to leave for a while, to be purified for the murder.

Memnon of Ethiopia was a giant of a man, the son of Eos and Tithonus, equipped with armour made especially for him in Hephaestus' workshop. He and his men cut swathes through the Greek troops, and confined them once again to their encampment. In the course of the Greek rout, Paris wounded one of the horses of Nestor's chariot team. The old man couldn't make it back to the Greek lines; his charioteer was dead, and he was caught in no-man's land. Just then, Memnon approached, and it seemed as though the Greeks would lose their most respected counsellor – but Antilochus, Nestor's son, stepped up and took Memnon's blow in his father's stead, and his head rolled in the dust.

Antilochus' sacrifice gave Achilles time to rescue Nestor from Memnon. The two heroes faced each other, battle fury disfiguring their faces. As they hefted their spears, up on Olympus the two mothers were begging Zeus for the lives of their sons. Once again Zeus raised the golden scales of fate. The death of Memnon was heavier, and Achilles slew him. Eos had not been able to save her son's life, but she implored Zeus for a special boon. And the father of gods and men turned the smoke from Memnon's funeral pyre into birds, which fought in mid-air, and fell dead into the flames as offerings to the hero.

But the slaying of Memnon was Achilles' last great deed. His death had often been foretold. He knew it, and he had made his choice, the heroic choice. After Memnon's death, the Trojans had no fighters to match the remaining Greek heroes, and they found themselves hard pressed. Achilles burst into the city at the head of his men, and the city seemed certain to fall – but this was the day of Achilles' doom, not Troy's. Apollo the archer himself took the form of Paris, no mean bowman even without the god's help. Paris aimed for the body, but Apollo knew better, and steered the fatal dart onto Achilles' ankle, the only place where his skin could be pricked. And though it was only an ankle wound, all his vulnerability was located there, and his life ebbed away on the threshold of the city.

A terrible fight arose over the hero's body, with every Trojan determined to win for himself Achilles' fabulous armour. Glaucus, the leader of the Lycians since Sarpedon's death, beat back the Greeks, wounding even Diomedes in the fracas, and managed to attach a rope to Achilles' leg; but even as he was dragging the body deeper into Troy, Ajax struck him dead with one mighty thrust of his spear. On and on the battle raged, until night was drawing near, and Zeus sent a thunderous storm to break it up. Then at last mighty Ajax managed to bear Achilles, armour and all, back to their camp.

Antilochus was buried with all honour, while Achilles' body lay long in state. All the Greeks paid their respects, but Thetis and the Muses keened and wailed by the fair corpse, on which no mark of a wound could be seen. After his body had been cremated and his bones collected, they were placed in the same urn as those of Patroclus and covered by a great mound of earth. For the funeral games, Thetis extracted prizes from the gods themselves. And ever after Achilles is worshipped at the site of his tomb as a hero.

But a far more bitter contest awaited the Greeks as a result of Achilles' death. Both Odysseus and Ajax coveted his armour, and each claimed a right to it on the same grounds: that he was the foremost warrior in the Greek army. In order to decide the quarrel, the army assembled and heard both Odysseus and Ajax state their cases. Trojan prisoners bore witness that Odysseus had done them more harm than Ajax, but even so the Greeks' vote was exactly tied. There was nothing to tell between the two of them in terms of valour. But Athena was the presiding judge, and she decided for Odysseus, her favourite.

This loss was more than Ajax could stand; it drove him out of his mind. He left the assembly staggering like a drunkard, and everyone kept out of his way in fear. They watched as Ajax fell on a flock of sheep, butchering the defenceless beasts in their pen, for he saw them as his enemies, those who had cheated him out of his prize, and was determined to have his revenge. When the hero came to his senses and saw what he had done, the disgrace was the final straw. On the secluded beach, he planted his sword hilt in the sand and fell forward onto the blade.

The Wooden Horse

Now Troy's end was close, and the Greek army had complete control of the plain. The Trojans were bottled up inside the city, too scared to show their faces, anticipating death or slavery within a few days. Odysseus captured Helenus and forced the soothsayer to reveal the final conditions that would have to be met before Troy could fall. First, Neoptolemus would have to be fetched from the island of Scyros, and Philoctetes from Lemnos; second, the city's magical talisman would have to be stolen.

Neoptolemus, the son Deidameia had conceived while Achilles was hiding, would act as a kind of substitute for his father, for though very young in years, the gods had smiled on his youth and had raised him well before his time to the prime of young manhood. Philoctetes was needed because he was the bearer of Heracles' bow, passed down to him by his father Poeas, and it was foretold that Troy would not fall except with the help of Heracles' bow. But more difficult than fetching either of these two was Helenus' other condition: Troy could never be sacked as long as the Palladium was safe inside its walls. This was an effigy of Athena that had fallen long ago from the skies, and was the most sacred object in Troy. It was kept in the heart of the city, and cast a protective ring all around.

Odysseus fetched Neoptolemus from Scyros. On arriving, the young hero spent several hours of silent grief at the tomb of the father he had never known, and ended by swearing revenge. In battle, he performed great deeds of valour, and put heart into the Greek troops, for he was the very image of his golden father. Odysseus gave him Achilles' armour, and the young man blazed on the battlefield like a savage new star.

With Neoptolemus in action, Agamemnon felt he could spare Odysseus and Diomedes to go and fetch Philoctetes. Now, Philoctetes was a mighty warrior, and had sailed as eagerly as any Greek to do battle at Troy. But on the way, when the fleet stopped at the island of Lemnos, he had been bitten on the foot by a snake, and the festering wound became so foul and smelly that the Greeks abandoned him there.

Ten years later, then, Diomedes and Odysseus returned to Lemnos to bring Philoctetes to Troy. They found him still in agony, with his foot still oozing evil-smelling slime. Nor was he pleased at having been left for so long on his own, and over the long years of bitter waiting he had fanned the flames of resentment of Agamemnon and the other Greeks. So while Diomedes hid, Odysseus appeared to Philoctetes as a stranger, with Athena's help. He won Philoctetes' trust and sneaked the bow away to Diomedes when the opportunity arose. Philoctetes was furious at the deception, but Odysseus, now revealed in his true form, assured him that, if he accompanied them to Troy, he would win great fame, and his foot would be healed.

And so it happened. Philoctetes was greeted with great joy by the Greeks, and once Machaon had healed his wound, he was put immediately to work. In the course of their very next assault on the city, the two great bowmen, Philoctetes and Paris, squared off against each other. Thick and fast their arrows flew through the air. But in the hands of Philoctetes Heracles' bow was invincible, and Paris fell, his corpse bristling with arrows. There were those, even in Troy, whose tears were blended with relief that the cause of the war had been punished. At any rate, with Paris' death, the heart went out of the Trojans. Heracles' bow had effectively brought the war to an end.

Troy was now under close assault, the end inevitable and imminent. But first the Greeks had to gain the sacred Palladium. Odysseus and Diomedes volunteered to enter the city and try to steal it. Their disguises had to be perfect: they both dressed in rags as beggars, and Odysseus even had himself beaten up for the occasion. They approached the city by night and, while

Diomedes kept watch outside, Odysseus crawled through a drain that ran out under the walls.

But fear of the future was keeping Helen awake, and she too was out in the streets at night. She bumped into Odysseus and recognized him in spite of his disguise. But she saw a way to ingratiate herself with the Greeks, into whose hands she was sure she would soon fall, and directed Odysseus to where the sacred relic was kept. First and last, Helen was the bane of Troy. Odysseus carried the effigy out to Diomedes and together they bore it in triumph back to the Greek camp. Trojan morale plummeted even further at the theft, but in order to calm their fears, Priam gave out that it was not the real Palladium that had been stolen, but a fake.

Now the Greeks were ready for their final ruse; now Zeus' will would be fulfilled. It was Athena's idea, whispered in the mind of Odysseus. The Greeks constructed an enormous horse out of wood, big enough to hold the cream of their heroes. Odysseus, Diomedes, Neoptolemus, Menelaus, and many others took their places inside, in eager anticipation. The Greeks then burnt their camp and sailed away out of sight – but only just out of sight: they hid on the far side of the nearby island of Tenedos, and waited for the signal.

After some hours of inaction, the Trojans cautiously emerged from the city to see what was going on. They were astonished to find the Greek camp abandoned and destroyed. The only solid structure standing amidst the litter was this enormous wheeled horse. What was it? What should they do with it? Now the next part of the trap was sprung. The Greeks had left behind a man called Sinon, who was, as planned, taken prisoner by the Trojans.

Feigning terror, Sinon told them that he hated the Greek nobles, and was so hated by them in return that they had left him behind. To the Trojans' questions about the horse, he replied that it was an offering to Athena, and that the Greeks had made it so large to prevent its being taken into the city. An oracle had told them, he lied, that if the horse entered the city of Troy, it would keep the city safe for ever.

The Trojans debated what to do. The majority wanted to bring the offering inside, to keep the city safe, but there were dissenting voices. Cassandra knew it for what it was, and tried to warn her fellow citizens, but as usual her truths were taken for the ravings of a madwoman. And Laocoön, Antenor's son and the priest of Apollo, was so suspicious that he hurled a spear into the side of the horse. It stuck there, quivering, and the structure emitted a hollow clang, but nobody recognized what that meant.

Then two vast serpents emerged from the sea and coiled their sinewy strength around Laocoön and his two sons, crushing them to death. That seemed decisive. Laocoön had died, people supposed, because he had opposed the will of the gods. No more talk of setting fire to the horse, or pushing it over a cliff. Now they were resolved to bring it into the city. They pulled down a section of the walls to allow the thing to be trundled inside – that is how sure they were that the war was over. In actual fact, what had been foretold was that the city would never fall unless by a kind of suicide. The Trojans themselves had to be responsible for their city's fall.

The Fall of Troy

The horse was left for the night in the main square of the city. Among the curious sightseers were Helen and Deiphobus. Three times they circled the strange structure, and Helen called out to each of the Greek leaders by name, making her voice sound like those of their wives. But inside the horse, under Odysseus' leadership, the men maintained strict silence. They were not even wearing metal armour. The Trojans, all unsuspecting, gave themselves over to wine and celebration, and slept well. But Helen knew what would happen on the morrow, and spent the night with her maids, preparing for departure.

In the silence of deep night, the Greek fighters silently opened the secret doorway set into the horse's side, let down a rope, and slipped into the dark streets of the city. Stealthily, the assassins went their separate ways. Meanwhile, alerted by the beacon Sinon lit at the tomb of Achilles, the Greek forces silently returned from Tenedos. As the numberless stars wheeled overhead, the Greeks poured in through the new, self-inflicted breach in the walls.

Neoptolemus sneaked into the royal palace, and found everyone asleep, from the king down to his servants, whom he cut down at their posts. Alerted by the noise, Priam raced on aged legs to take refuge at the altar of Zeus, but Neoptolemus dragged him away. He forced the old man to his knees, pulled back his grizzled head, and drew his blade sharply across the exposed throat.

Meanwhile, Odysseus and Menelaus went to Deiphobus' house. They would find Helen there, for, in accordance with Trojan custom, she had been awarded to Paris' brother after his death. While Odysseus engaged Deiphobus, Menelaus drew his sword to dispatch his former wife – but in her terror she let her robe slip from her creamy shoulders, and lust stayed his hand. He dragged her instead back to his ship – and the same thing happened all the way down to the beach: any who took up stones to harm her let them fall from slack hands at the sight of her loveliness. After a hard fight, Deiphobus succumbed to his wounds and bled to death on the floor of the chamber that he had shared so briefly with the most desirable woman in the world.

The Greeks gave themselves over to bloodlust. The frustration and fear of ten long years of warfare afforded them terrible energy. This too was justice: the Trojans had to pay. Very few survived the slaughter. One was Antenor, his door marked by Agamemnon for safety, in gratitude for his protection of the ambassadors ten long years before, and for his known opposition to Paris. Another was Aeneas, who escaped with his crippled father on his back. He had taken Laocoön's suspicions to heart and fled early to the hollows of Mount Ida, from where he looked down on the burning city and dimly heard the screams of the dying.

Neoptolemus snatched Hector's son Astyanax from his screaming mother's arms and hurled the innocent baby to his death from a high tower: Andromache was his prize, and he wanted no whelp of Hector's in his household. The women were spared, but not out of mercy: they were hauled off to captivity and slavery and unwelcome concubinage. Cassandra sought refuge at the altar of Athena, and was raped in the very sanctuary by Ajax of Locri, a crime for which the Locrians are still paying. Then she became the prize of Agamemnon.

The most terrible fate awaited Polyxena, the fairest of the daughters of Hecuba and Priam. After the sack of the city, she was not assigned as booty to any Greek chieftain, for the ghost of Achilles appeared to the senior Greek officers in a dream, demanding that she be sacrificed to him, as the price of their departure, just as Iphigeneia's death had released them from Greek shores ten years earlier. Ruthless Neoptolemus eagerly slaughtered the innocent maiden on his father's tomb.

Aethra, the mother of Theseus who had been forced to serve Helen, was found safe and returned to the bosom of her family after so many years.

Hecuba joined the entourage of Odysseus, but she and some of the other women escaped at the first stop of the Greeks' journey home, in Thrace. She had sent her youngest son Polydorus to King Polymestor there for safety during the war, so that Priam's line should not altogether die out in case of disaster; but on hearing of the sack of Troy Polymestor murdered the young man, and now Hecuba found his corpse washed up on the shore. Feigning ignorance, and knowing the Thracian king's greed, Hecuba enticed him and his children into an ambush with a tale of Trojan gold.

She and her friends slaughtered his children before his eyes, and then blinded him with their brooches. For this she was turned into a dog – but the former queen found this preferable to servitude, and thus she was saved from the hazards of Odysseus' tortuous journey home.

10

Odysseus' Return

Trouble on Ithaca

Muse, beginning where you will, tell of wily Odysseus, king of Ithaca, most resourceful of the warriors who assaulted the walls of Troy. His was the clever trick that opened the wide gates of the city in the tenth year of the conflict. The story of his return voyage is one of woe and disaster at every turn, with Death his constant companion. But for the protection of the grey-eyed goddess Athena, Odysseus would have fed the fishes many times over.

In assembly with the other immortals who dwell on high Olympus, Athena made her case before almighty Zeus for the son of Laertes. She argued that now, after twenty years away from home, he should be allowed to return to the arms of his devoted wife Penelope. In the absence of Poseidon, who nursed a grievance against Odysseus, the assembled gods decided in favour of Athena's suit. Swift Hermes was dispatched to Ogygia, isle of golden-haired Calypso, divine daughter of Atlas. On behalf of the cloud-gatherer, Hermes commanded her to release Odysseus from the island where she had held him for seven

long years. In fear of the almighty father of gods and men, the
nymph Calypso reluctantly obeyed. 'You Olympians!' she complained. 'You can't stand it when any other immortal takes a
mortal lover.'

Odysseus was sitting slumped on the shore, looking out over
the restless sea with tears streaming down his cheeks as he prayed
unceasingly to be allowed to return home. His wife Penelope
was nothing compared to Calypso – a mere mortal beside a
nymph endowed with eternal youth and beauty – and yet he
was compelled by his love and his duty to return to her. Calypso
approached and sat down beside him in the sand, the long plaits
of her golden hair brushing her shoulders. Speaking gently, she
told him to lay aside his cares, for she would help him leave at
last. 'Come,' she said, 'build a raft, and I will see that it is well
stocked with provisions.'

At first Odysseus suspected another trick, but she reassured
him. The raft he built was frail enough, but he trusted in his
skill and in the favour of the gods to see him safely home to
distant Ithaca. After one last night of divine passion, he set sail.
For seventeen days he travelled over friendly seas, and his spirits
rose. But then the lone sailor caught the attention of Poseidon,
who had been away receiving the worship of the Ethiopians.
The earth-shaker was annoyed by the sight of this hated mortal
boldly pitting himself against his watery realm. With a growl he
lowered his trident and stirred up the seas around Odysseus,
tossing him to and fro on rising waves until the raft was in
danger of breaking up.

But the nymph Leucothea, who had once been Ino, the
daughter of Cadmus, saw Odysseus' distress and came to him,
alighting on his storm-tossed wreck. She warned him to strip
his clothes off and abandon the raft. It was better, said the White

Goddess, to strike out for the shore of Scheria, island of the seafaring Phaeacians. She loaned him a magic scarf, which she said would protect him from injury or death. Odysseus hung on to the failing raft as long as he could, but finally wound the scarf about his waist and dived into the raging sea, trusting in Leucothea's words. Poseidon laughed, sure that he had seen the last of the puny man.

After two days and nights, clinging to a timber from the raft, Odysseus reached the safety of dry land by a river delta. Naked, exhausted, and uncertain where he was, he found a copse of trees near the water's edge. He made a bed of leaves beneath the trees and covered himself with more leaves for warmth in his nakedness. At once he fell into a deep sleep.

Meanwhile, back on Ithaca, trouble was brewing in the house of noble Odysseus. For some time the palace had been occupied by a gang of local noblemen who daily saw fit to demand that they be fed the good things provided by Odysseus' royal estates. Droves of livestock were slaughtered and sweet wine drunk by the cask, all at the expense of the absent king, whom they believed dead. The aim of each young man was to take for his bride Penelope, Odysseus' queen. To keep the suitors at bay, the lady made excuses and tried to trick the men so that she could delay making a choice.

For three years she had kept them waiting with a single ploy. She claimed it was necessary before she left the home of her first husband to weave for her aged father-in-law Laertes an elaborate shroud, so when he should pass none could say he had not been given the honour due to a well-loved patriarch. Daily she and her women sat at the loom, weaving the marvellous cloth, and every night in the upper chamber they unravelled by lamp-light all the fine work of the day. But a disloyal maid revealed the trick to the suitors, and once again Penelope was pressured to make a choice.

Witness to all of this was Telemachus, the noble son of Odysseus. Penelope had only just been delivered of the boy when his father was pressed into joining the expedition to sack Troy. Nearly two decades had passed and Telemachus was mature enough to resent this violation of his inheritance, but he lacked as yet the wisdom and strength to redress it. But Athena, the aegis-bearing daughter of Zeus, was looking after Odysseus' son, as well as Odysseus himself.

Athena appeared before Telemachus in the guise of a family friend, a trader from abroad, who advised the young prince to call an assembly of the men of Ithaca, to solicit their support for his efforts to oust the suitors from his home. She also urged the prince to journey to the Peloponnese, to seek out wise Nestor of Pylos, and Menelaus, king of Sparta. They might provide news of his long-lost father.

Telemachus agreed, and called the men of the region together to discuss the violation of his father's house. For the first time in his life, the young man took the speaker's staff in his hand and addressed the assembly of Ithaca. He explained the grievance he held against the suitors, but Antinous, a leader among those suing for the hand of Penelope, responded with spiteful words. He called on Telemachus to expel his scheming mother and send her back to her father's house, where she could be properly courted and dowered. 'It's time for her to choose,' Antinous insisted. 'No more deception: she has kept us at bay for three years by pretending that she would soon finish her embroidery. Now she must admit that Odysseus is dead: she is husbandless, and must choose one of us!'

In anger Telemachus replied that he would not for a moment

consider throwing his mother out of the house, to earn her curses and the displeasure of the immortal gods. And he promised to destroy the suitors if they persisted, calling on Zeus, father of gods and men, to witness his oath. As the words passed his lips, Zeus sent two eagles from the distant mountain. They hovered over the assembly and then attacked each other, clawing with their razor-like talons, before swooping off to the east.

A senior member of the assembly read the omen: Odysseus would soon return and there would be a reckoning against the wastrels who spent their days stuffing themselves on the fruits of their absent king's estates, and courting his lady. Antinous and the other suitors laughed in scorn.

Still in her disguise, Athena followed Telemachus down to the port. She encouraged the young man, spurring him to action so that the crew could get under way swiftly, without attracting unwanted attention. And so, without telling his long-suffering mother Penelope, Telemachus headed out to sea, to find what word he could about the fate of his long-lost father. And the grey-eyed goddess accompanied the son of her favourite, to protect and support him on his journey.

Telemachus' Journey

Telemachus' first stop was Pylos, the kingdom ruled by Nestor, who had arrived home from Troy safe and sound. The wise old king maintained his regal bearing, despite the burden of his years and the many losses he had endured in his long lifetime. He was tall, with flowing white hair and silken beard, and his dark eyes flashed with sagacious mirth. He welcomed Telemachus, who accompanied Nestor to his palace and listened with rapt attention as the old man told him of his return from Troy.

'There's little I can say about Odysseus' voyage, since he and I parted company almost immediately after leaving the shores of Troy. After many days of sailing we reached the rolling Argive lands, where Diomedes steered his vessels to shore, and made his way safely home. However, I have heard that his days of sorrow did not end there. Discovering his wife's infidelity, forced upon her by Aphrodite in retaliation for the wound he gave her at Troy, he left Argos and wandered far from his homeland. In foreign lands, he aided a king against his enemies, but was repaid with treachery and death. It is said that in their great mourning his men caught the attention of the gods on Olympus, who transformed them into herons, and still they keep watch over his tomb.

'I sailed on for Pylos. And although I made it back in one piece, it was a bitter-sweet return for me. My own dear son, brave Antilochus, had fallen before windy Troy, as had so many others. We lost Ajax of Salamis, the most able of the Greeks after Achilles, who fell on his own sword out of shame and never saw home again. Patroclus lost his life to mighty Hector before the walls of Troy as he led the Myrmidons in defence of the Greek ships. And Achilles' life-thread was cut there too, as he knew it was destined to be. Many of the Greek host met death in those long years of war. But their fame lives on, for in the wide halls bards sing of their deeds, and that is the only immortality attainable by man.'

After finishing his tale, Nestor offered Telemachus the use of a fine chariot and team to carry him swiftly overland to Sparta, where Menelaus ruled with Helen at his side. To accompany Telemachus on his journey Nestor chose his own son Peisistratus, and together the two young men set off with the rising sun in their eyes.

The companions stopped for nothing. Even the rugged and gorge-riven Taygetus mountains didn't slow their pace, and two days later they reached the rich lands of Sparta in the Eurotas valley. The palace of the red-haired king was filled with the sights and sounds of revelry, for it was a time for weddings. Hermione, the lovely daughter of Menelaus and white-armed Helen, was being prepared for her journey to far Phthia. She was betrothed to the godlike son of Achilles, Neoptolemus, king of the Myrmidons. The gallant Megapenthes, Menelaus' son by one of his concubines, was also to be married in the palace; and so the halls echoed with the sounds of music and good cheer.

The noble travellers were made welcome. Peisistratus introduced Telemachus to Menelaus, and the Spartan king was overjoyed to see him, for he glimpsed a young Odysseus in his guest's face. Just then Helen descended from her upper chamber to join them at the banquet, and her beauty dazzled all present into momentary silence. The evening passed, and the young guests were regaled with tales of the exploits of the Greeks at Troy, and especially of wily Odysseus, until dawn approached and the eastern sky was tinged with a fresh rosy glow. For earlier Helen had slipped a drug into the wine that had the property of banishing care and grief, for a while.

Later in the day, after all had taken their rest, Telemachus rejoined Menelaus in the great hall and, giving him a full account of his troubles at home, pleaded for news of his father. In reply Menelaus recounted for Telemachus the tale of his own return. 'My brother Agamemnon and I,' he said, 'parted ways on the sandy shore of Troy. I sailed my ships down the rich Phoenician coast, where we stayed long in the luxurious courts of those merchant kings. For seven years we tarried, Helen and I, but at last I felt compelled to see once more the peaks and plains of home.

'High winds swept our ships over the seas, until we made land in far-off Egypt. But when we sought to depart from there, the gods forbade us a swift voyage home. I had offended them by failing to honour them first, as is their due. Inviting the wrath of the gods will surely bring a man nothing but a grievous end. Take, for example, Locrian Ajax, that intrepid warrior, who, I'm told, met his fate in the surging sea. Athena punished him for his violation of ill-fated Cassandra in her own holy sanctuary. Zeus loaned the dread goddess his thunderbolt to hurl at the fleet, and her aim was unerring. Ajax fell overboard, but he clung to some rocks, all the while jeering at the gods: "You can't kill me!" Poseidon had wished to spare him, in spite of Athena's ire. But even he became annoyed by the reckless hero's raving. With a single stroke of his trident, he split the rock, and the brave son of Oileus was dragged down to the depths, his lungs filling with brine. Only fools mock the gods.

'But I was not stranded long in Egypt, thanks to Proteus, the Old Man of the Sea, and his wise daughter Eidothea. On Pharos Island I learnt from them of my transgression and the duty required of me before I could return home. In reparation, we made rich sacrifices to all the gods and prayed for aid along the way, so that Helen and I might return with all the fabulous wealth gained from our travels in foreign lands. And at last we made a happy homecoming, unlike my royal brother, proud Agamemnon, who was destined to return only to schemes and murder.

'Now to answer your question,' continued the Spartan king. 'Proteus also shared with me some news of your father, long-suffering Odysseus. He said he had glimpsed him pining on the shores of Ogygia, Calypso's isle. She held him there as her captive, a slave to her own purposes. Without ship or crew he had no chance of sailing for home.'

The news at once depressed and cheered Telemachus. His father was probably still alive, but there was no telling when or if he would get home. It was therefore up to him, Telemachus, to take care of the troubles at home. He refused Menelaus' invitation to stay longer. Until his home and hearth were free of the wasteful and arrogant suitors it was best he should not tarry. Menelaus felt proud for Odysseus, that he should be the father of such a son, and prayed that soon he might be restored to his family.

Presently Helen joined them, and lavished upon Telemachus rich guest-gifts to enhance his reputation and household. The shining chariot and team were prepared, and the princes sprang aboard. With a flick of the whip they set off back to sandy Pylos. Telemachus told his hosts there that he would sail immediately for Ithaca. They bade one another fond farewells, and the pilot set a course for home.

Odysseus on Scheria

While Odysseus slept on the island of Scheria under the trees near the river's mouth, his divine ally, Athena, went into the palace of Alcinous, good king of the sea-faring Phaeacians. Disguised as a childhood companion, she appeared before Nausicaa, the royal princess. Nausicaa was as sensible as she was beautiful, and each of the young noblemen of the island dreamt of having her for his wife. Athena put the idea into her mind to go to the river's edge with her maids and do the laundry. She asked her father to call for a wagon and mules, and when all was prepared the young ladies trundled off to the washing pools.

Odysseus was roused by the sounds of splashing and gay laughter issuing from upriver not far from where he had his mulchy bed. He rose and crept forward, keeping to the trees for cover, and spied the band of girls on the bank of the river. The maids and their mistress, lovely Nausicaa, had finished the washing and laid out the garments and fine linens to dry on warm rocks lining the river bank. While some bathed themselves in the stream, others played a ball game with the sparkling-eyed princess, and still others set out on a cloth on the ground delicacies and sweet wine mixed with clear water.

Pricked by his great need, Odysseus crept forward, all naked as he was, and knelt at the feet of the princess. Never one to panic, the young woman responded graciously to his pleas for help, although her girls had taken fright at the sudden appearance of the filthy stranger in their midst. She had her women take him off to bathe in the river, and then they dried him and rubbed him down with olive oil, while she chose a soft tunic and fine cloak from the freshly washed clothes. Once he was dressed, Athena made him seem taller and more handsome than ever, and the women were amazed. Nausicaa realized she had given aid to no common man. Then the modest princess advised her noble suppliant to follow her as she made her way back to town in the wagon. She warned him, for modesty's sake, to separate from the company of ladies when they approached the gates. He was to enter alone and ask for directions to the palace of Alcinous, her father.

Shrouded in mist by Athena, Odysseus found his way to the palace. Once inside, he strode briskly to the seat of Queen Arete, royal wife of Alcinous. As he knelt down and clasped her knees in supplication the mist dissipated. The queen was amazed at the stranger suddenly in their midst. Looking him over, she couldn't help noticing that he wore clothing she herself had spun, and she guessed he had received aid from Nausicaa. She smiled at her husband, who was sitting by her side, and welcomed Odysseus with kind and honest words.

Without offering his name, nimble-witted Odysseus related the tale of the shipwreck that left him at the mercy of Calypso, until after seven long years she released him. He told how he left the island on his raft, only to be shipwrecked again on the shores of Scheria, where Nausicaa had found him. He shared his fervent desire to return once again to his homeland, to sit once more before his own hearth, with his loyal wife at his side. Alcinous and Arete were moved by his heartfelt words, and agreed without hesitation to aid him in his quest. They were not so impolite as to ask him for his name, for he was clearly a man of standing and deserved their discretion and their hospitality.

The following day King Alcinous called a meeting of his counsellors. He ordered a fast ship to be manned and equipped to carry their long-suffering guest back to his homeland. The assembly agreed with one voice to the plan, and the work was immediately set in motion. When all was ready, the good king next called the ship's crew together with the noblemen of the realm to join him in the palace where a sacrifice was prepared to honour the gods, as is proper for those who seek safe passage across the vast expanse of the hostile and restless sea. After the ritual and the appropriate prayers to Zeus and all the immortals, a feast was prepared, and the bard, Demodocus, was summoned to sing of heroic deeds of times gone by.

When Demodocus had finished his lay, the good king called the men to demonstrate their prowess in games of strength and skill for their noble guest. Odysseus was invited to join in, but the travel-weary warrior politely refused. Yet he was goaded on by another young nobleman, Euryalus, who rashly incited the hero's anger with his insults and sarcasm. 'Yes,' he said, 'I never took you for a noble, worthy to join our games. You look more like a sailor, thinking only of risk and profit.'

Quick-tongued Odysseus eloquently stunned the offender into silence and, following words with deeds, grasped an enormous discus and hurled it aloft. It sang in the air as it hurtled beyond the marks of the others lately thrown by the competitors. Athena, disguised as a spectator, marked where the stone landed and declared Odysseus the clear winner.

After the games, Alcinous commanded that the ship be loaded with gifts appropriate for a royal guest, and called for a celebration in his wide hall as a proper send-off for crew and passenger. Euryalus approached Odysseus with a fine sword of bronze as atonement, which was graciously accepted. In good humour, the banqueters sat down to the delicious feast laid before them. The bard was again summoned to ply his trade, as only those gifted by the Muses can.

The tale the inspired Demodocus told was that of the final ploy of the Greeks to enter the bronze gates of Troy. The stratagem was conceived by crafty Odysseus himself. Within a hollow wooden horse of monumental size crouched the concealed Greeks, ready for ambush. The bard's song brought tears of remembrance to the eyes of the stranger in their midst, and Alcinous called for silence. He spoke gently to his guest, questioning him at last about his identity, his parents, and his homeland. And Odysseus launched into his tale of woe.

The Cyclops Polyphemus

'I am Odysseus, son of Laertes, commander of men. Home for me is sea-girt Ithaca, though I have not set eyes upon her welcome shores for many years. Nor do I know what fate has befallen my wife and son, who was a mere babe when I reluctantly set out for Troy. Not even the womanly wiles of golden-haired Calypso or the sorceress Circe could persuade me to forget home and hearth, where all good men yearn to be if, by the will of the gods, they are kept apart from their loved ones.

'Home was uppermost in my mind when with twelve ships I at last set sail from the shores of Troy. With an eye to further enrichment we sailed first to the land of the Cicones in Thrace, where our raids netted us many oxen and sheep, and captive women to warm our beds. For showing him mercy, a priest of Apollo there, Maron, gave me some of his very finest wine. This vintage would serve me well in later days. But some of the men lingered over their feasting and drinking. Soon local reinforcements swarmed down from the hills in retaliation against us. Before we could take to the fast ships dozens of men were struck down, and we lost most of our plunder. It was with considerably lowered spirits that we continued on our way, mourning our lost comrades.

'The helmsman's skill and fair weather brought us near to home, but at Cape Maleas the north wind blew up strong and sent us far off course, out into open seas. After ten days my crew and I arrived at the strange land of the Lotus-Eaters. The magical fruit they eat makes men forget everything, and fills them with the desire only to eat lotus and more lotus. On first sampling the fruit, our landing party nearly succumbed to this evil. It took a great deal of effort to hustle them aboard, and even then they had to be restrained from jumping ship and swimming ashore.

'Next we reached the land of the Cyclopes, those lawless, one-eyed giants, who disdain the gods. Each acts as a law unto himself and recognizes no authority but his own. We beached our ships on an offshore island rich in produce and grazing lands for sheep and goats. With renewed optimism we slung our weapons over our shoulders and set out to hunt. In no time a large herd of goats appeared and we picked off dozens of them. With hindsight I see that we should have sailed on straight away, without investigating further, but curiosity got the better of me.

'After a night of feasting and healing sleep, we woke just as dawn began to glow in the east. Little knowing what we were about to encounter, I told the men that I would take my ship and crew across to the mainland to seek out any inhabitants. As we glided across towards the mainland, we spied a flock of sheep and goats near a large cave. Outside the cave we could make out the silhouette of an enormous being. Still I was not to be put off – I wanted to know what sort of people these were. With twelve men and a large goatskin of the rich wine given me by Maron, I set out to see for myself.

'No one was home when we reached the cave. All around us were young sheep in their pens, separated by age, bleating for their mothers to come from the pastures. Soon they arrived, udders swinging from side to side with the weight of the good milk inside. Their master followed, whistling and clicking his tongue at them in the language they understood, and we caught our first sight of the hideous features of the Cyclops, with one huge eye filling the space above his nose. Once the entire flock was inside the cave, he rolled a massive boulder across the entrance to the cave. We were trapped! Then he took each ewe aside and milked her, before letting the lambs suck.

'When he caught sight of us inside his cave the creature roared with displeasure. The men were panicking, but I strode forward and confronted the Cyclops. I said that we were survivors from a shipwreck, throwing ourselves on his mercy in the name of Zeus, patron of suppliants. He replied that he cared nothing for men's rules of hospitality or even for the gods themselves. He proceeded then to scoop up two of my men and eat them, washing his gory meal down with buckets of fresh ewe's milk. We cowered in horror at the ghastly sight, and were sickened by the sound of our friends being crunched in his mouth. If we didn't escape soon, none of us was going to make it back to the ship.

'Just before dawn, the Cyclops rolled the gigantic stone away from the entrance to the cave. He scooped up two more of my men for breakfast, and washed the vile meal down with milk, before going about his chores. He released the sheep from their folds and herded them outside, but blocked the mouth of the cave with the stone as he departed. We were trapped for the day.

'In the Cyclops' absence, we searched for some means with which to defend ourselves. Lying in the sheep pen was a long beam as broad as a tree trunk. We cut a section of this and sharpened one end to a fine point. We thrust that end into the fire, turning and hardening it in the blazing coals. Soon we had a weapon and a picked team to hoist the stake and help me thrust it home, into that single great eye in the forehead of the Cyclops. But we still needed to get past the massive stone in the entrance.

'In the evening, when the sun began its slow descent, the Cyclops returned. He rolled away the stone and herded the ewes back inside, milking them and placing them with their young, as on the night before. He scooped up two more men for his gruesome supper. I stepped forward quickly with the great flask of wine before he could gulp the milk. I offered him a bowl filled to the brim with the sparkling liquid, and he drank deeply. He held out his bowl for more and asked me my name. "I'm Nobody," I told him as I refilled his bowl. He gulped it eagerly and took more again, bowl after bowl until he passed out on his side by the fire.

'We sprang as one to the stake we had prepared and raised it up. We lunged forward as if we stood before the gates of a great city with a battering ram, determined to break open the bronze doors. The point sank through the giant's closed eyelid and deep into the orb, sizzling like roasting fat when it runs off the skin of a spitted piglet onto the glowing coals below. The monster shrieked in anguish, so loudly that his neighbours, some distance away, called out in concern. "What's the matter?" they cried, and Polyphemus shouted back that "Nobody" had attacked him, and so they left him alone to his fate.

'Our escape was not yet assured, and despite the searing pain of his blinded eye the monster squatted down at the mouth of the cave, hoping to catch us one at a time by feel as we tried to sneak past. But I conceived a plan to save us all. I ordered the men to grab some sheep from the surrounding pens. I lashed three sheep together for each man, burying the rope deep in their shaggy hair. The men clung on to the woolly undersides of the middle sheep, and were protected from the Cyclops' groping hands by the other two. I myself gripped for all I was worth to the underside of a huge ram. It worked! The suffering Cyclops suspected nothing as the beasts ambled from the cave, and continued his torrent of threats against us as if we were still inside.

'Once we had cleared the cave, I untied the men from the sheep and we drove the flock down to the ship. As we headed back to the islet where we had left our companions, I hurled insults back at the Cyclops, igniting his rage. He tossed a boulder which landed near the bow, and its wave nearly washed us back to the point from which we'd set off. But the oarsmen cut the water with a will and we were soon out of range. I hollered back my true name as we sped away, and Polyphemus bellowed after us, calling down upon me the wrath of his father Poseidon. And Poseidon heard his son's curses, and has tormented me ever since.

'We rejoined our comrades. After dividing the flock fairly among the men, we made a sacrifice of the great ram which had carried me safely from Polyphemus' cave, thanking Father Zeus for our lives and imploring all the gods for safe passage across the moaning sea. A great feast was prepared there on the shore near the ships, and we partook of the fine meats and fragrant wine until fatigue overcame us and we lay down to sleep. As rosy-fingered dawn began to glow gently in the east we set sail, hoping for the best.'

Aeolus, the Laestrygonians, and Circe

'Over and over again, in our joy at escaping from Polyphemus' cave, we regaled one another with tales of the exploit. Next we made land on the floating island ruled by Aeolus, steward of the winds, whose six sons are married to his six daughters. On Aeolia there is unceasing feasting and celebration, day and night, and we were lavishly entertained in the palace for a month. When we left, Aeolus generously bestowed upon me a leather bag containing the swirling powers of the storm winds, so that only fair breezes might speed our voyage. Refreshed and hoping for the best, we set sail with gentle Zephyrus blowing astern.

'But my men snooped in the cargo hold, eager to see for themselves if I might be concealing some fabulous gift given me by Aeolus. The fools discovered the great leather bag. They unwound the silver thong that sealed the sack, releasing with a great rush all the winds trapped inside. The storm that arose buffeted the ships back the way we had come. We found ourselves once more on the shores of Aeolia, but our welcome this time was not so warm. Aeolus blasted us with cold words, refusing further assistance to men who were so clearly out of favour with the immortal gods. So once more we set off, this time with heavy hearts.

'For a week we sailed steadily on these strange seas, until we came to the land of the Laestrygonians, where the coastline forms a secure and well-sheltered haven for ships. The other vessels in our company sailed straight in, but I moored my ship outside the harbour mouth, and sent three men on ahead to discover what kind of people dwelt there.

'It soon became clear that this was not a hospitable place. As soon as my men encountered the chieftain of the Laestrygonians, the mountainous man made his hostile intentions plain by snatching up one of them to be put aside for dinner. For the Laestrygonians were vile and gigantic cannibals. In shock and horror the remaining two men sped away from the place and sprang back aboard my ship. But the other ships were trapped in the harbour, and the Laestrygonians pelted them with boulders that they tossed as easily as a child skips a stone across the still surface of a lake. In the blink of an eye my crew was rowing with a will away from that cursed place. But we were the only survivors; all the other ships were lost. We sailed on, mourning our lost comrades, terrified lest fresh disaster strike.

'Next we came to Aeaea, Circe's isle. After beaching the ship on the shore, we ate and rested, and then I detailed my best men to investigate the area. The rest remained with me, to guard the ship and be ready to take to the sea in case of danger. We didn't have to wait long before Eurylochus, the leader of the reconnaissance party, burst from the trees and ran down to the beach.

'Pale and quaking with fear, he answered our anxious questions. The scouts had come upon a villa in a clearing of the wood. Strangely, there were wild beasts rendered tame, lions and wolves, wandering about the grounds. They wagged their tails and approached the men like dogs who greet their master after a long absence. From within the house they heard a sweet voice singing. They called out to the occupant and a beautiful woman emerged. It was the witch Circe, daughter of Helios and sister of Aeëtes, ruler of Colchis. The sorceress welcomed the new arrivals and offered them hospitality. All but Eurylochus heeded her friendly summons and entered. But none came back out.

'At this fresh disaster I grabbed my sword and made for the clearing Eurylochus had described. Near the villa a stranger crossed my path. It must have been a god, perhaps Hermes, for he offered good advice. He told me to beware of the food and drink that Circe would offer me as her guest. They were tainted by a potion that was designed to transform men into beasts. He gave me a dose of moly, a special antidote to the witch's evil brew. Then clever Hermes, if that's who it was, told me how to get the sorceress to release my men from her magic spell. I took his advice to heart and made my way through the trees to Circe's villa. What I saw there shocked me to the point of despair.

'My good comrades were all together. They were penned into a sty, and all had been transformed into pigs. They rooted and snuffled the ground, or rolled in the soft mud, grunting and squealing. But clearly they still retained their wits, because when they caught sight of me they raised a terrific din in their attempts to warn me off, or to plead for their release. With anger in my heart I strode forward and called out to the occupant of the house.

'The radiant Circe emerged and bid me welcome. She led me to a chair, and offered me a golden cup. It contained her potion, of course, but I had taken the antidote, so with an internal smile I drank it down. She was astonished that it had no effect upon me. Following Hermes' advice, I drew my sword and made as if to strike her, and she cowered in fear and confusion. Seeming humble and submissive, she invited me to her bed – another trick, for she bound men with her sexual charms, but Hermes had told me what to do. After making her swear that she would play no more tricks, I happily accepted her invitation, for it was only if she was sexually satisfied that she would release my men.

'After we had enjoyed the sweet delights of love, she reversed the spell cast upon my men, and they were restored to themselves. As soon as the men back at the ships learnt the good news, they joined us. We remained for a year on Circe's isle as her welcome guests. And the lovely nymph and I found comfort together, but never did her charms erase from my heart the memory of my own dear wife Penelope, or my longing to be reunited with her.

'The men too began to yearn once more for their homes, and I appealed to Circe for aid in our time of need. The sorceress revealed to me what she knew of the trials that lay ahead for us. I and my men were to journey to the underworld, the dark realm where the shades of the dead pass eternity. Once there I was to question Theban Teiresias, who alone of all who dwell in Hades' halls retains his wisdom unimpaired. As I lay beside her in the soft bed, the beautiful witch told me how I was to summon the dead so that the seer would approach and tell me all I needed to know.

'When shining-haired Dawn arose in the east I called my men together in the hall of Circe's villa and announced our departure. There were shouts and laughter as the men made ready, gathering their gear and preparing to return to the ship beached on the shore. One of my men was on the roof, sleeping off the several flagons of wine he had consumed the night before, and he woke unsteadily to the noise below. Bleary-eyed and off balance, unlucky Elpenor fell from the roof and broke his neck. My comrades and I knew nothing of it, so we left him behind when we departed. His body lay there, unburied and unmourned, with his shade lingering uneasily at the edge of the underworld.'

The Underworld

'Divine Circe called forth a following wind as her parting gift, and we cut a wake through the foam-topped swell. I gathered the men on deck and announced our destination. They responded with exclamations of disbelief and fear, their hopes of heading straight for home dashed in a moment. Were we really sailing for the ends of the world and the home of the dead? But we remained true to the course I set and at last arrived on the far western shore of the great Ocean which encircles the world. The men and livestock disembarked, and I chose a ram and a black ewe that Circe had added to our stores, elements of the ritual necessary for calling up the shades of the dead.

'When we reached the place the witch had described, I knelt down and with my trusty sword carved a shallow trench. Into it I poured the proper libations of honey, milk, wine, and water.

I sprinkled white barley over all, and made prayers and invocations. I slit the throats of the victims, and the blood flowed into the narrow trench and sank down into the thirsty earth. Instantly the place was swarming with the insubstantial spirits of the dead, agitated by the presence of the blood and greedy to partake of it. But I held them back with my brandished sword. In the meantime my men went about the business of preparing the sheep and ram for sacrifice as burnt offerings to fearsome Hades and august Persephone, dread rulers of the underworld.

'The first of the dead to approach me was unlucky Elpenor, my own comrade who had lately fallen from the roof of Circe's house. I exclaimed in surprise at the sight of him, and after he had told me his sad tale I promised to return to Circe's isle and see to his burial.

'Just then the Theban prophet Teiresias approached. He recognized me, and when he had drunk the blood he revealed for me a homeward voyage filled with yet more dangers. Poseidon would dog my trail, intent on revenge for the blinding of his son, the Cyclops Polyphemus. In forbidding tones he warned me to control my men, especially when we came to Thrinacia, where the cattle of the all-seeing sun graze the wide green pastures of that island.

'As if all this weren't bad enough, the seer went on to tell me that my arrival home, after so many years of suffering and homesickness, would also be fraught with trouble. My home had been invaded by a band of insolent young nobles, eager to consume my wealth and woo my queen. He predicted that I would set things right in the end and there would be a reckoning for the suitors, but warned that my wanderings would not be over even then.

'In order finally to appease the wrath of Poseidon, he told me, I was to travel far, carrying with me an oar, seeking a people who knew not the sea. I would come to a place where the oar was identified as a winnowing shovel by some unknowing soul, and there I was charged to erect a shrine to the earth-shaker. Only then could I make my way safely home. The one piece of good news he shared with me was that I would meet my life's end in great old age, at my own hearth, surrounded by my loved ones. Then he departed, making his way back through the crowds of mirthless dead.

'I saw the shade of my beloved mother Anticlea, and she spoke briefly with me. I had not known she was dead. Though I wanted desperately to hold her in my arms, just once more, my hands grasped nothing but the insubstantial air, and her ghost moved away finally to join the other wandering shades. Other great women and men approached, and after I let them taste of the blood, they spoke to me.

'Of those who addressed me it was Agamemnon, son of Atreus, who came forward first. He shared with me the tragic story of his homecoming, how his scheming wife Clytemestra and her lover Aegisthus murdered him in his own bath, before the oars of his black ships had even begun to dry. And he told me how they took the life of ill-starred Cassandra, his war-prize, and killed all his loyal companions too. The once-great king held my eyes and warned me to approach my home shores secretly, even in disguise, and not reveal myself until I knew what I was facing. I took his advice to heart. For some time we stood together, though separated by the shallow trench of dark blood, and we reminisced over lost comrades-in-arms, many of whose shades milled about before me, anxious to drink and exchange words with a living man.

'There was Ajax of Salamis, who still begrudged me the arms of Achilles, and refused to speak to me. The Greek heroes Antilochus and Patroclus drew near, and then Achilles strode forward and took a sip. Recognizing me, he demanded to know what tricks I was up to now, making my way to the underworld while still a living man. Was this not the crowning exploit for any hero? "Not so," I replied. "For no one is recognized as a greater hero than you. You were admired as the greatest of the Greeks in your lifetime, and now you have high honour among the dead."

'But Achilles replied in sorrow that he would prefer to be a peasant labourer in the world above than king of the listless dead. Nevertheless, I was able to console him somewhat with news of his son, Neoptolemus. With words that cheered the mournful shade I described to Achilles the bravery of his son at Troy. At the end of the war, with his plundered wealth loaded into his ships he set sail from the wind-swept shores of Troy, and made for the Thessalian coast. There, on the advice of Thetis, he burned his ships and continued over land for home. As far as I know, I told him, he rules now in Phthia, home of the valiant Myrmidons. Achilles' shade thanked me for my words and strode proudly off, a new spring in his step.

'I saw too the ghosts of others, famous or infamous. There was Tityus, who paid a dear price for lusting after Leto. His vast bulk is lashed to the ground, and there, with arms outstretched he exposes his belly to the vultures that daily peck away at his liver. Tantalus too I spied, tempted as he is unceasingly by food and drink that remain for ever out of reach. Cunning Sisyphus of Corinth was there, labouring at his endless task, a punishment for his transgression against the immortal gods. For it is a fool who takes the gods in heaven lightly.

'I saw the wise king Minos there, dispensing justice among the dead along with his brother Rhadamanthys, as they were the first to dispense laws to god-fearing men. Last of all I spied the wraith of long-labouring Heracles, whose mortal self was burned away on the pyre at Trachis. His immortal self dwells now on Olympus, and he has Hebe, daughter of Hera, for wife. He recognized me, and shook his shaggy head in commiseration at my unease here in the presence of the dead. He recalled his own encounter in the underworld while still a living man, when Eurystheus commanded him to go down to Hades' halls and retrieve Cerberus.

'I might have waited longer for other heroes of the past to approach, but suddenly the press of disembodied souls, eager to taste of the bright blood, disconcerted me and filled me with fear. I turned and made my way quickly back to the ship and the familiar company of living men.'

Dangers at Sea

Peerless Alcinous and his noble queen were transfixed by Odysseus' tale, as were all the banqueters in the spacious hall, hung with fine tapestries. The weary wanderer pleaded fatigue and declared his intention to go and sleep on his ship until its departure, but they begged him to refresh himself from the board, take a draught of sparkling wine, and continue his story. In the meantime, Alcinous commanded that more gifts be added to those already bestowed upon far-travelled Odysseus, and all the nobles of Scheria sent porters down to the black ship waiting in the harbour and added their own presents to those of the king and his lady. After taking some refreshment the unhappy hero again took up the thread of his tale:

'We set sail in haste, the better to get away from that dreadful place, and a following wind sent us swiftly back the way we came. We arrived in good time at Circe's isle, and after we had rested on the sandy shore, we set about retrieving the body of poor Elpenor, our lost companion. We buried him properly and heaped a mound over his remains, with his oar on top to serve as a grave marker. Circe joined us for the meal that followed the mourning.

'The nymph and I sat apart from the others, and she offered me further advice. She warned that our route would take us by the lair of the Sirens, terrible creatures, half bird and half woman, whose captivating song lures men to certain death. Circe told me that, when we drew near, I should take some beeswax and soften it between my fingers. I should use it, she said, to plug the ears of my men, so that they might row past the Sirens without hearing a note of their tempting song. The only way I could hear their melodies for myself, if I were foolish enough, was to have the men lash me tightly to the tall mast of the ship. No matter how much I cried out to be released, the men would not heed my demands – they could not, with their ears plugged. I took shining Circe's words to heart, and listened closely as she continued.

'Once we had passed the lair of the Sirens, we would have to brave the passage where the fearsome monsters Scylla and Charybdis made their home. It was impossible, Circe warned, for us to get by these dread creatures unscathed. And yet, if we made it through the passage at all, there remained another challenge for us to face. The island of Thrinacia lies beyond the strait where Scylla and Charybdis await their victims. This magical isle is the pastureland for the cattle of all-seeing Helios, which are tended by his daughters. It would be best, the witch sternly warned, if I and the men sailed past this isle. If even one of his fine, fat cows were hurt, the wrath of the sun-god would fall on my ship and crew.

'At dawn my comrades and I put to sea once again. What should I say to prepare the men for the evils we were to face? I needed their cooperation to get past the Sirens, so I warned them about this danger, but I held my silence about the strait beyond, lest they panic. When I judged that we were close to the island of the dread Sirens, I had every crewman place softened wax in his ears, so that he would remain as immune to the lethal song as he would to my pleas. Me the men lashed firmly to the stepped mast of the ship.

'As soon as the coastline appeared I began to hear a melody wafting from the shore. The creatures called to me by name, enticing me to stop for a while and listen as they sang me tales of the heroic deeds of great men living and dead. Their voices were . . . indescribable. Every thought and emotion fled from my heart and was replaced with the pressing need to join the company of these sweet singers. They seemed to promise eternal bliss. In my enchantment, I strained mightily against my bonds, and I demanded to be set free, gesturing urgently to my deaf crewmen with my brows. But the men only tied me tighter, as I had ordered. I am the only man who has heard the deadly chorus and lived to tell the tale. We sailed past, my men freed me, and I steeled myself for the next encounter, which lay just ahead of us.

'The waters before us churned and there was a terrific roar from the echoes of waves crashing against the high cliffs that framed the strait. On one side Charybdis sucked down the waters in a vortex so powerful that at its bottom the sea-bed was visible. Then with a mighty upward thrust all that had been sucked

down was spewed forth again in an awesome jet. The gaping
men ceased rowing in their terror, but I ordered them to take
up their oars and cut the water with a fury, so we might get
through in one piece. Seeing that Charybdis was impassable, we
hugged the opposite side closely, while I kept a careful watch
for Scylla, who has the bark of a puppy but the bite of a six-
headed beast. She shot out of her cave in a flash, taking us all
by surprise. Half a dozen snaky necks writhed above the ship,
and in the blink of an eye the creature had six of my men. Their
pitiful screams will haunt me to the grave.'

The Cattle of the Sun

'We passed through the straits, rowing with all our might to
distance ourselves from the evil, and our hearts were heavy with
grief for the loss of our comrades. Before long we approached
the isle where the daughters of Helios tend his lowing cattle,
and although I too felt in need of rest and recuperation, I urged
the men to row on and seek another place for shelter. I shared
at last the stern warnings of Circe and Teiresias, that to destroy
even one of the cattle of Helios would mean disaster for us all.
But I was gainsaid by one of my outspoken comrades, who
argued for taking shelter on the island, since the men had had
enough. I extracted a promise from my men to avoid the sacred
cattle. We beached our good ship and set about preparing a
meal from the stores we had on board.

'But a god sought to test my men. A contrary wind rose, and
we were trapped on the island for many weeks. Our supplies
ran out. The men took to hunting and fishing, but their mood
became desperate. I went apart to a sacred clearing to make
offerings and supplications to the immortal ones for a change

of weather. Some god must have put me into a deep sleep, because I heard nothing – none of the noise and commotion as my men weakened and killed some of the cattle. I woke to the aroma of spitted roast, and my heart sank. I hurried to the shore, shouting at them to desist from their folly, but of course the damage was done.

'Before our terrified eyes, the flayed hides of the slaughtered beasts began to crawl about the campsite, and the spitted meat over the coals bellowed its pain. These portents made us desperate to leave the island, but for days we remained stranded there by the unceasing gale, and my comrades continued to gorge on the forbidden meat. Dejected, I sat away from camp, sure in the knowledge that they were doomed. When Zeus finally had the winds change, I ordered the men aboard. We shoved off with a dark cloud hovering over our vessel and my heart.

'Before long ferocious winds began to blow with astonishing force from the west. In a moment the mast and stays were split like tinder and the yard crashed down, striking the helmsman a deadly blow. Zeus hurled a thunderbolt, and it struck us amidships, shattering the hull. The men and their dying screams were swallowed up by the raging sea. I alone survived, clinging to the upturned keel and the remainder of the mast.

'To my horror I found myself floating back through the straits to confront yet again those twin terrors Scylla and Charybdis. My only hope of safety lay in perfect timing. When the swirling vortex began sucking at my makeshift raft, I lunged for the cliff-face, and clung for all I was worth to a fig tree jutting precariously out over the churning water. An eternity passed before the monster belched the mast and keel back out. I leapt into the swirling current and gripped them tightly again, keeping my head low as I drifted beneath dread Scylla's lair. I lay exposed on the unforgiving sea for nine days until at last I came ashore at Ogygia, immortal Calypso's island home. My sad tale concludes here. You know all the rest.'

Odysseus Reaches Ithaca

All the banqueters went their separate ways to sleep, and the next day King Alcinous was pleased to escort his guest to the harbour, where he oversaw the stowing of Odysseus' many guest-gifts. The traveller thanked his hosts with typical eloquence, and offered a blessing to all the people for their kindness and generosity. They cast off with the chariot of the sun descending in the west.

Lying on the deck Odysseus fell into a deep sleep, a magical sleep, while the Phaeacian ship sailed on beneath the sparkling stars. While it was still dark, they reached Ithaca and beached in a remote cove. Quickly and quietly, the crew gently brought the exhausted warrior from the ship and set him down on the sand near a sacred cave. Next they unloaded all the gifts he had received from the noble folk of Scheria, and set them nearby. All the while Odysseus slept as one who was dead.

Meanwhile, Poseidon learnt of Odysseus' safe arrival home. The earth-shaker was annoyed to learn that the Phaeacians had assisted the king's return. He complained to Zeus, threatening to raise an impassable mountain chain around their island kingdom. But the cloud-gatherer persuaded his furious brother to make an example only of the ship that had carried Odysseus home, rather than take more drastic measures. When the ship hove into view, the Phaeacians onshore rejoiced to see their countrymen returning. But just at that moment Poseidon struck the ship with the flat of his mighty hand, and instantly it turned to stone. There it sits today, a reminder of the consequences of crossing the gods, who are quick to anger.

Odysseus slept on, unaware that he was home at last on Ithaca. Athena came upon her favourite as he slept and hid him in a fine mist. He woke at last, looking about but seeing nothing that recalled home. The long-absent king groaned in dismay and set about checking his treasure, suddenly suspicious that his Phaeacian hosts had tricked him by abandoning him on a strange shore and taking back their fine gifts. He had suffered so much already that nothing would surprise him.

There he stood, muttering to himself, surrounded by golden goblets and three-legged bronze cauldrons. But grey-eyed Athena stepped forward in disguise as a young shepherd, and told him where he was. Valiant Odysseus rejoiced to hear he was finally on home soil, though he carefully refrained from revealing himself to the shepherd. He said instead that he was a Cretan noble, in exile for killing the son of Idomeneus. Athena indulged him as he spun his tale, taking pleasure in her incorrigible favourite. She touched his cheek, and as she did so her shepherd's guise fell away, and she stood before him in her divine loveliness.

After reassuring the long-suffering Odysseus that he was indeed home, the wise goddess prepared him for his next ordeals. She warned of the danger within the palace, and advised him to make his way to his swineherd, Eumaeus, who had remained loyal, and shelter there among the fatted pigs until he came up with a plan for revenge. Together they concealed the fine gifts in the sacred cave. Then the goddess disguised Odysseus as a wrinkled old beggar, and dressed him appropriately in filthy rags.

Athena sent him on his way to the farmstead beyond the town, while she swiftly made to intercept Telemachus, who was at that moment close to home on his way back from the sandy shores of Pylos. Athena warned him that a band of the wicked suitors was lying in ambush for him at the main port, so he asked to be let off elsewhere, explaining that he wished to inspect his estates and make his way back to town on foot. The ship sailed on without him around to the port of Ithaca. Alone, he began walking towards the humble hut of Eumaeus the swineherd.

At the Swineherd's Hut

Much-travelled Odysseus made his way to the farmstead, where he was welcomed and fed by his old servant. Over their humble meal, Eumaeus related to the stranger the story of how he came to be in the service of the royal house of Ithaca. His family was noble, from a far-away place called Syria. One day, when Eumaeus was a mere boy, a disloyal maidservant made off with him on a pirate ship. The men aboard sold him to Laertes, who raised him with a gentle hand, almost as a member of his own family. He was taught to care for the pigs and given his own small place.

Eumaeus smiled at the memory, but then his face darkened. His present master, the great Odysseus, had gone off twenty years before to fight at windy Troy, and had never returned. How the estates had suffered as a result! The presumptuous suitors, who returned daily to feast, were consuming all the best things for themselves. 'I can hardly bring myself to go into town these days,' he said. 'I can't bear to see the destruction of my master's wealth by those arrogant bastards.'

In his beggar's disguise, Odysseus spun a false tale to Eumaeus of his own background. He claimed again to be a noble Cretan, but this time one who had served in the company of Idomeneus when he was called by the Greeks to fight at Troy. Years of adventure on the seas had finally seen him shipwrecked near the shores of Thesprotia. He was saved by the son of the king, who offered him hospitality. It was in the grand halls of the king's palace in Thesprotia, he said, that he learnt of valiant Odysseus' fate. Ithaca's king had gone to the sacred grove at Dodona to learn the will of Zeus, and would soon be safely back in his own country.

But, the beggar went on, he himself had suffered more misery when the crew of the Thesprotian ship he joined robbed him and tied him up for the slave market. Nevertheless, when the ship reached Ithaca, he had made his escape, and now he sat before Eumaeus, his generous host.

The good swineherd cocked his eye at the beggar's story, discarding with a shake of his head the bit about the king's imminent return. If he had a bushel of grain for every time he'd heard such a rumour, he'd be a wealthy man. He rose and prepared a simple meal, and after they had eaten and drunk they lay down for the night in the shelter of the hut.

Early the next day, Odysseus, still in his beggar's disguise, heard the sounds of the dogs fawning over someone, thumping their tails on the ground and whimpering in recognition. In a moment, the handsome face of Telemachus appeared in the doorway. With a cry of delight the loyal swineherd dropped everything and folded the young man in his embrace, tears stinging his eyes, and ushered him into the humble dwelling.

After the men had eaten and drunk their fill the young prince questioned Eumaeus about the stranger in their midst. The kindly swineherd reported what the old beggar had told him the night before. Odysseus, who had stepped outside, overheard this exchange, and saw an opportunity to get things moving in the direction he wanted. He went back inside and declared his indignation that the suitors should get away with their scandalous behaviour.

'You're right, of course, stranger,' said Telemachus. 'But what can I do? I am one man, with no available allies, and they are many. Once they've consumed all my father's wealth, they'll turn on me. I have no hopes for a long life.' He turned to Eumaeus and told him to go down to the town and announce his return to patient Penelope, but to no one else. The swineherd nodded and set off briskly on his errand.

Wise Athena appeared just then in the open doorway of the hut and cocked her brow at Odysseus, who followed her outside. It was time, she said, for him to reveal himself to his son. As she did so the beggar's rags were miraculously replaced with splendid clothes and the king stood before her looking more regal than ever. Odysseus stepped back into the hut and stood before his son. Telemachus cried out in amazement, for he had not seen the goddess work her magic on the beggar. He piously shielded his eyes, believing himself in the presence of a god. With gentle words Odysseus assuaged his son's fear. 'Have no fear,' he said. 'I am no god. I am, in fact, your father.'

At first, Telemachus refused to believe it, thinking the gods were tricking him, but Odysseus explained how Athena had effected his transformation. They locked into a strong embrace, each shedding tears of joy and pain on the shoulders of the other.

When father and son could speak again, their talk turned to revenge. Odysseus swore Telemachus to secrecy, and together they hatched a plan to take the transgressors unawares. Telemachus would allow a 'wretched beggar' some small corner within the palace halls, as is proper for those who honour the laws of hospitality. Just as the Trojans were taken unawares when the Greeks burst forth from the Wooden Horse, so the suitors would be ambushed by the wiles of Laertes' son.

Meanwhile, the suitors had received word that their attempt to kill Telemachus had failed. Somehow the young man had slipped through their fingers. Seething with frustration, the impious band gathered to discuss a new plot. But they were overheard, and news reached the queen in the women's quarters of the palace just as the loyal swineherd Eumaeus arrived to announce Telemachus' safe arrival.

Queen Penelope decided to take action. She summoned her maids. Together they descended to the hall where the suitors lazed about. Penelope confronted them with stinging words, especially the ringleaders, and accused them of plotting to murder her son. They chided her for her baseless accusations, and argued that whatever men plan, for good or ill, the gods will have their own way. If they had only known how truly they spoke! The indignant queen withdrew in disgust, back to her chambers, where she gave way to bitter tears.

Eumaeus arrived back at the hut before the sun sank in the west. The king was disguised again, back in his beggar's rags, so that the swineherd still had no idea who he was. The three shared a meal together and lay down for sleep. Prince Telemachus was up with the first glow of dawn and ready to make his way to the palace. He told Eumaeus to escort the stranger to the town later in the day, where he could beg from people as he saw fit.

In the Palace

The prince arrived at the palace to a heartfelt welcome from the household. His dear mother flew to his side, tears of joy streaking her cheeks. She gently upbraided him for leaving her in the dark about his journey, but rejoiced at his safe return. She ordered delicacies and sweet wine be served. Telemachus took a polished chair and sat down beside Penelope while she questioned him about his journey.

Later in the morning, the swineherd Eumaeus and Odysseus set out for town. The king, still in his pathetic rags, carried a worn staff loaned to him by his faithful servant, who still had no idea who this beggar really was. They came to the public fountain just outside the city, where another of Odysseus' herdsmen, Melanthius, passed them on his way to the palace with fatted livestock for the suitors' midday feast. He heaped abuse upon their heads, and even landed a kick on the beggar's backside. Proud Odysseus remained passive, but took note of his servant's disloyalty.

The companions walked on towards town. As they passed the dung heaps piled on either side of the road near the gates, Odysseus heard a whimper. In the ordure lay an old hunting dog, covered in flies. The decrepit hound raised his head in recognition of their voices, and Odysseus saw that the dog was his favourite, Argus, who had shown such promise twenty long years before. At the sight and scent of his master, valiant Argus struggled to lift himself out of the filth in which he lay. But the effort overwhelmed him and he fell back, breathing his last. The hound's loyalty touched the king deeply, and he weighed it in his heart against Melanthius' treachery, and the insolence of his enemies.

Within the palace, preparations for the banquet had begun. The smell of roasting meat hung in the air. A lyre twanged as it was tuned. Eumaeus arrived at the door of the palace with his charge, and went inside to find Telemachus. Meanwhile the king-as-vagrant seated himself on the threshold of his own palace, where he was given a morsel of meat and a heel of bread. Later he went around the long table in the wide hall and begged from each of the suitors, sizing them up as he passed.

Disloyal Melanthius sat among the suitors and continued his verbal abuse. The mood in the hall became tense. Antinous, one of the ringleaders, went so far as to lob a footstool at the beggar, which struck him in the shoulder. But patient Odysseus did nothing and kept his humble place near the threshold. He knew his enemies' fate was sealed, and that he himself was the agent of its fulfilment.

The feast was nearly over when the bard took up his lyre and the banqueters turned to drinking and dancing. Another vagrant arrived at the door of the palace. It was despicable Arnaeus. He made a career of begging, and resented any weary travellers taking his place in the town. He accosted Odysseus, in his disguise near the threshold. Odysseus' long-held anger needed venting, and it was the misfortune of Arnaeus that he arrived on the scene when he did.

The two beggars bandied insults, circling like wrestlers in a bout. The suitors were amused to see the tramps going at it. They even offered a prize to the victor of the comical contest. Cowardly Arnaeus tried to escape, but the suitors tossed him back into the ring. The fool soon exposed himself. Odysseus punched him hard under the ear and sent him sprawling. Justice was at hand in the palace of Odysseus.

The news of the fracas spread through the palace and at last reached the good queen. Penelope called Eumaeus to her chamber to question him about the new beggar in their midst. She asked to see the stranger later in the evening, when they could converse in peace. Then Penelope, with her maids, went down to the hall, and the grey-eyed goddess enhanced her already prodigious beauty. The queen covered her face with a sheer veil as she entered the room, but her loveliness was as impossible to ignore as the sunrise.

First she gently chided her beloved Telemachus for allowing such rough behaviour within the palace halls. But the ringleaders, Eurymachus and Antinous, spoke boldly to the queen, extolling her beauty. She responded curtly that her beauty had long since dimmed from years of longing for her beloved husband. But now, she declared, the time of waiting was finished. Every man who sought her hand was to cease wasting the wealth of Odysseus and bring her from his own house proper bride-gifts. Eagerly the suitors sent squires for the best their estates could offer, but they made it clear that, until she had made her choice, they would remain feasting in the palace, eating and drinking all they wanted. Penelope retired in dismay to her chamber.

Penelope Meets the Beggar

Braziers were lit in the palace, for day was quickly fading. Odysseus remained in the hall to suffer the abuses heaped upon him by the disreputable suitors. Thus his ire was stoked even as he tended the fires of his own palace hall. Finally, when they had had enough of debauchery, each of the suitors left for his own home to sleep it off.

Telemachus and his father were alone at last, and finalized their plans for vengeance. Odysseus told his son to collect all the weapons and armour and lock them safely away from the suitors. Meanwhile, still disguised, Odysseus returned to the hall to face his interview with the queen, his own beloved Penelope.

The long-suffering queen entered the hall preceded by her maids, and a chair was brought up for the vagrant to sit by her side. They talked long into the night. Though he was reluctant to tell more lies to his wife, she pressed him to explain himself, and in response he began to spin yet another yarn. He said that he was a son of the royal Cretan house. When Idomeneus departed for Troy, he had stayed behind as regent, and in that time he had met Odysseus, who with his ships and men had been blown off course by a gale and made land at Crete. He claimed to have entertained her husband for many days before Odysseus sailed on to Troy.

Lonely Penelope guilelessly opened her heart to the strange beggar with the noble demeanour. In her grief and longing she begged him to describe for her what Odysseus' bearing was like, what clothes he wore, all those years ago when he had been driven onto Cretan shores. Proud Odysseus thought to brighten her memory of him by painting himself in the most flattering light. She gasped at his description of a beautiful purple cloak attached at the shoulder by a large brooch wrought of gold. In tears, she recounted how she had herself packed these things among Odysseus' belongings before he left so many years ago.

The stranger then made a prediction for the weeping queen: that her resourceful husband was, at that very moment, on his way back to home and family, with great wealth gained abroad. At the stranger's earnest words, grieving Penelope smiled through her shining tears, and prayed that his words might come to pass. Then she called Eurycleia to come and wash the feet of their humble guest, as he would allow none of the younger women to touch him and prepare him for bed.

The old nursemaid Eurycleia knelt at the beggar's feet and began bathing them in the copper basin of warm water. She was already surprised by how much the stranger reminded her of her long-lost master – and then on his left knee she spied a scar that the young Odysseus had earned hunting boar on Mount Parnassus years earlier. She glanced up at the old beggar, pain and joy passing through her heart and over her features. 'But . . . you . . . you are Odysseus!' she murmured, and tears started in her kind old eyes. But Odysseus urged her to silence until he gave the signal, and she agreed to keep the secret.

Athena had distracted Penelope from hearing their exchange, but in a moment the queen returned to her humble guest. She related to him a dream about an eagle destroying a flock of gaggling geese. He interpreted the dream for her. It was obvious, he said. The gods had revealed to her that Odysseus' return was imminent, as was the destruction of the suitors by his hand.

She prayed again that the beggar's words might come true. But in the morning, she told him, she would summon the suitors for a test founded upon the prodigious skills of Odysseus himself. Twelve axe-heads were to be lined up in a row on a table, and the archer who shot an arrow through all twelve – through the holes where the handles would go – would win her hand in marriage. Only Odysseus had been able to perform the feat in the past. What's more, they were to use the king's bow, left behind when he sailed from Ithaca's shores.

When bright Dawn appeared on her golden throne, quick-witted Odysseus was up and preparing for the fateful day that lay ahead. It was a festival day sacred to Apollo the far-shooter, and the palace bustled with activity. Servants scrubbed and polished floors and tables, or ground grain for bread. The herdsmen came driving beasts before them – Eumaeus with choice pigs, Melanthius with fine goats, and finally Philoetius, the master cowherd, with the pick of the royal cattle. This good man took notice of the beggar in his rags standing by the gate. He strode over with his hand outstretched in greeting, despite the vitriolic words that Melanthius spat in their direction. Wily Odysseus took note that the cowherd could be valuable in a fight.

Noble Telemachus returned from the assembly and sacrificed in honour of Apollo. All the suitors had arrived earlier, seeing no reason to stay for the full rite as pious men do. They hurried back to Odysseus' palace to renew their debauchery. Just as the prince passed the threshold a cow's hoof, hurled by one of the despicable suitors, whizzed past him. It struck the wall near the poor beggar, who merely turned his head slightly to avoid the missile. A look full of the promise of doom for the suitors passed between father and son.

Vengeance

The goddess with the flashing eyes, Athena, inspired courage in clever Penelope, who called her maids to attend her. Together they went to the storeroom where her husband's most precious belongings were stowed under lock and key. She drew forth his awesome bow in its case and the quiver of swift arrows. The maids picked up the bronze axe-heads, and followed their mistress back through the dark corridor to the light-filled hall.

The lady Penelope veiled her lovely cheeks and confronted the men. They told her that they had brought their bride-gifts, and reminded her, insolently, that today she was to choose one of them to be her lord. In return, she challenged them to emulate the feat of mighty Odysseus – to string the great bow and shoot an arrow through the twelve gleaming axe-heads. The winner would gain her as his wife.

At the sight of the king's wonderful bow and the gleaming axes the herdsmen Eumaeus and Philoetius grieved for their long-lost king. But Telemachus gestured at the suitors to step forward, and he himself was the first to attempt to string the bow. Three times he tried and failed. On the last attempt the bow was nearly strung, but Odysseus, still in his place by the entrance, caught his son's eye and signalled him to desist. With a dramatic groan the prince gave up and set down the bow. One by one the men took their turn, and each suffered sarcastic abuse from the others as he failed. Disgusted by the sight of such unsuitable men handling their king's favourite bow, Eumaeus and Philoetius left the hall. Quick-witted Odysseus dashed after them and, to their joy and amazement, revealed himself to them. Like Eurycleia, they recognized him by the scar on his knee. He quickly enlisted them in his plan for revenge.

Finally the bow came around to Eurymachus, one of the ringleaders of the gang. Try as he might, he could not string it. Pouting, he thrust the bow aside with a scowl. The revellers rationalized that on the festival day of Apollo, it was improper to string a bow anyway. Tomorrow would be better, they decided, after they had sacrificed a goat and burned the fat and thigh bones as an offering to the archer god. With that the suitors returned to their cups.

Then the beggar offered to entertain them by trying himself to string the magnificent bow. The rude suitors mocked, threatened, and heaped insults upon him. But queenly Penelope stepped forward and overruled the men, offering the vagrant new clothes and passage abroad if he should manage the feat. Telemachus concurred, and then suggested to his dear mother that she go about her household duties in the women's quarters. He knew that things would soon get ugly. Meanwhile Eumaeus went to warn Eurycleia to lock the maidservants' rooms, which she did at once.

Odysseus took up his bow and examined it, looking for signs of woodworm or ageing over the past twenty years. The suitors cried out in mockery: 'Ha! So now this beggar is an expert bowman, is he?' But to their amazement and shame, the beggar bent the bow and strung it, with no sign of effort. He plucked the taut string, and it responded with a twang. His lip curled with satisfaction at the balance of the weapon in his hand. The suitors sat stupefied. The beggar picked up the arrow at his feet, levelled the shaft, and notched it. He pulled back, took aim, and let fly. The arrow passed cleanly through all twelve of the axe-heads. A thunderclap burst overhead, and the king knew he had the blessing of Father Zeus.

With a shout brave Odysseus revealed himself to the suitors. Telemachus sprang to his side. Odysseus took swift, sure aim and an arrow pierced the throat of foolhardy Antinous. The rest scattered about the hall, seeking cover. No weapon or piece of armour was to be found anywhere, and they had to defend themselves with stools and tables. Haughty Eurymachus offered restitution, believing he could escape death with honeyed words. His speech fell on deaf ears, and in the end he drew his sword and leapt towards Odysseus. Another arrow flew from Odysseus' bow, and Eurymachus fell dead in a pool of blood.

The avengers too were short on weapons and armour, so Telemachus ran to fetch them, while Odysseus continued to pick off the suitors one by one with his swift arrows. Just as the quiver's load was spent, Telemachus returned with spears, swords, and shields. They quickly armed themselves, and stood back to back, father and son, ready for the foe.

But Melanthius suspected where the arms were concealed. He ran to the storeroom and brought out various pieces of equipment for the remaining suitors. Odysseus called on Eumaeus and Philoetius to capture the traitor and bind him strongly. The two faithful servants complied, and then took their places at the side of Odysseus and his noble son. Athena joined them, disguised as an old friend. Missiles rained down on the heroes, but the goddess made sure that none of the suitors hit their mark, while every shot or thrust by the avengers was successful. For the cowherd there was a satisfying moment when his spear pierced the breast of the lout who had earlier lobbed a hoof at the king. He stepped forward and braced himself on the dead man's body, jerking his weapon free. Before long, bodies were heaped one upon another and the hall ran with their blood.

Reunion

Justice had been dealt to the impious suitors. Odysseus ordered Eurycleia to fetch those of the household maids who had betrayed their master with the unscrupulous suitors, and they and the herdsmen were given the job of clearing the hall of bodies and washing away the gore.

Then the disloyal maids were herded to the back of the palace, where Telemachus strung them up by their necks with a rope. Their dangling feet jerked briefly, and then they breathed their last. Finally Melanthius paid for his treachery. His nose and ears were cut off, and after that his genitals. Then he was dragged beyond the palace walls and his hands and feet were hacked off as well. It took him some time to die.

Stalwart Odysseus called his old nurse to attend him. Sulphur and fire were needed for a purification of the hall. When this was done, the king sent for his faithful queen, who had slept a god-induced sleep throughout. Now all the household servants came forward to the king, many weeping with joy at the sight of their long-lost lord. It was almost too much for the weary wanderer to bear. He had steeled his emotions for so long. He wanted to weep with them, and rejoice. But there was still the most important task to complete.

Penelope woke to the old nurse Eurycleia hovering over her, shaking her gently and calling her name.

'What's the matter, Eurycleia, my dear? Why the fuss?' long-suffering Penelope groaned as she woke. 'Oh, what a dream I had! I saw Odysseus, and he was on his way home to us, as I've dreamt so many times before. It all seemed so real! He and his men were shipwrecked, and my suffering husband floated on, alone and half drowned. He came to the island of Calypso, who held him captive for years. Then he endured the sea alone on a sturdy raft, but mighty Poseidon was angry with him and caused him trouble. I dreamt that he was rescued by the sea-going Phaeacians, who bore him back to Ithaca's shores and left him near a sacred cave with a hoard of fine gifts. How a lonely woman's mind turns to fancy! I swear that I could almost hear him planning with Telemachus the revenge he sought against the unwelcome suitors! Oh, pity me! I think my mind is turning! The long years of waiting and hoping have taken their toll.'

The old woman was falling over herself in her haste to find her mistress a suitable gown and veil from the strong cypress chest in which she stored her best clothes. 'It's no dream, my dearest lady! No dream this time!' exclaimed Eurycleia, her face beaming, the wrinkles around her eyes creased by her grin. 'It's all come to pass! The king – he's here, in the palace at last! And he's calling for you now! You must make haste, my lady!'

'But this cannot be,' replied the cautious queen. 'Where is the herald to announce his return? We've had no news here in the palace. The only visitor – apart from those presumptuous suitors, curse them! – was the unfortunate beggar to whom my son gave hospitality.'

Eurycleia smiled and said, 'No, he's here, all right. And what's more, he's rid us of those cursed suitors, one and all! And the disloyal servants – all delivered to the fate allotted them by the gods. But now, please, my lady, *please*! I promised to bring you down to him straight away.'

'I'm still dreaming, that's it,' mused Penelope. 'All right, nurse dear; I'll come along as you insist. I am anxious to converse with my long-lost husband, even in a dream.'

She had her maids dress her and arrange her hair. Athena ensured that she would appear lovelier than ever, to dazzle Odysseus with her grace and beauty. She descended the long staircase with her attendants and took a seat in the hall near her son and the poor beggar with whom she had spoken before.

The queen sat staring at the stranger, silent, waiting. In his frustration Telemachus rose and stood between them, and there were harsh words on his tongue for his mother: 'Well, mother, here he is at last! Have you no word of welcome for your husband and king? Come now, any man has earned a joyful reception from his loved ones after a long journey! How much more does my father deserve, after twenty years of suffering and loneliness?'

Penelope spoke nothing but gentle words in response to her

son's admonitions: 'Dearest Telemachus, it's not that I'm not glad. The shock has left me speechless. If this were only a dream or a trick of the gods at my expense I wouldn't be surprised. I nearly lost all hope of seeing my beloved husband again, your dear father, after so many years apart.'

Odysseus patiently allowed her to finish speaking and then said to Telemachus: 'Leave us alone, my son. There are things that a couple share only between themselves, and it is through these things that we shall know each other at last. Go on, there's nothing to worry about.' He smiled encouragingly at the young man, who took the hint and left. Then Odysseus turned back to his circumspect wife, who eyed him warily from her polished chair.

'Perhaps, dear lady,' he said, 'I should bathe and dress appropriately before we speak again. In the meantime, preparations for a feast should be made ready, and all the sights and sounds of a celebration should emanate from the palace, the better to distract the community from discovering the carnage of the day before we've come up with a plan.'

When he returned from his bath it was as though he had been transformed. It was not just that he had shed his beggar's rags. Before Penelope stood a man glowing with strength and virility. He seemed somehow younger and more handsome than ever, and her heart lurched in her breast as he seated himself once more across from her.

The smells and sounds of celebration filled the air around them. Yet the queen eyed him with suspicion, still believing that she dreamt or had simply gone mad. When she still had nothing to say, the godlike Odysseus shook his head and sighed wearily: 'Well, then, if you have nothing to say, I'll have a maid make a bed for me in the hall.'

'Please, you must understand that this is all very hard to believe!' cried Penelope in distress. 'So many years of waiting, longing, hoping for your return! I had almost given up, and was steeling myself for the unpleasant task of choosing a new husband. And now here you are – or so you claim. Come, I'll have the women move your old bed out here, so you can sleep at last in some comfort, and I will retire to my chamber, to ponder all these amazing events.'

'You dare to say such a thing to me?' cried lion-hearted Odysseus. 'With my own two hands I crafted that great four-pillared bed. One of the posts was the trunk of a living olive tree, around which I built the entire room. If you can move our marriage bed then you have struck me a stinging blow by cutting that tree.'

In a moment Penelope had flown to her husband. She threw her arms around his neck, showering kisses on his neck and shoulders as the tears of joy streamed from her eyes.

'I'm not dreaming . . . not dreaming,' she sobbed. With shining eyes she met his gaze, softening now because he understood that he'd been tested. And he was filled with admiration for this woman who had waited so long, so patiently, out of duty, respect, and love. His heart melted and he held her in his arms, and finally he wept, joy and relief filling his soul. They held on tightly to each other even as they ascended the stairs to their bedchamber.

Eurycleia the wise old nurse had summoned the housekeepers and together they had strewn the floor of the chamber with sweet-smelling herbs, and laid the bed with fresh linen as if it were once more the royal couple's wedding day. Odysseus and his queen entered the room, and the servants withdrew.

The lovers held each other close through the night, and the wise goddess Athena instructed golden Dawn to stay her approach, in order to give them more time to renew their love in each other's arms.

11

The End of Hope

Pandora

So the heroes lived and died as playthings of the gods. The greater the hero, the greater his suffering. Heracles was tormented by fits of madness that led him to kill his own children; Achilles and countless others died young in wartime agony; those who survived Troy lost sons and brothers, and returned to find families torn apart. Generation after generation, the curses afflicting the noble houses of Mycenae and Thebes created men with monstrous minds, weaving evil schemes against their own kin. Banishment from home and family, hard travel, uncertainty, wounds, the frequent prospect of imminent death – these, not just their human or inhuman opponents, are the obstacles that heroes face and strive to overcome. Heroes must be better than themselves, and prevail against the most powerful natural and supernatural forces the gods hurl against them. But many do not return. In truth, life is a vale of tears.

Why should it be like this? Why are we born, only to suffer and die? All things are the gods' doing, and this is no exception. When Prometheus ensured the survival and continuation of the

human race by stealing fire from heaven, he knew the consequences. He was a Titan, one of the old gods. He knew that his
human wards would be punished and tormented no less savagely
than he, but he still saw this as the preferable course. He knew
the obstacles and difficulties that the gods would place in the
way of human life – but he also knew that it was only in the
fire of transcending these obstacles that we humans could purge
the dross from our souls and, perhaps, emerge as heroes ourselves. Our founding father Prometheus enjoins us not to
become bogged down in the soul-sucking mire of moaning and
complaint, but to seek always to enlarge our lives.

Zeus, for his part, did his best to bury and embroil us in so
many woes that we would forget our potential as human beings
and live our lives at the level of dumb beasts, looking only to
the gods, not to ourselves, for salvation. And he found an
exceptionally economical way to go about this. He didn't want
to spend his time constantly inventing new woes for humans
– disease one week, famine the next, and so on. He found just
a single instrument that would do it all at once, and he made
it so that, far from trying to avoid their bane, men would
actively seek to embrace it. And when he had dreamt up his
device, he laughed out loud, and the roots of Olympus shook
at his mirth.

He ordered great Hephaestus to fashion dumb clay and
imbue it with all the faculties that Prometheus' men already
had, with one difference. This new human was to be female,
not male, patterned on the irresistible beauty of the Olympian
goddesses. Athena taught her the womanly skills and Aphrodite
shrouded her with grace and allure, but, on Zeus' orders, cunning Hermes gave her the mind of a lying bitch and the
temperament of a thief.

When all the gods had finished their work, the beautiful product stood there motionless, a lifeless mannequin, until our common father Zeus breathed life into her. And he named the beautiful bane Pandora, 'Allgift', for all the gods had made her and all mischief in the lives of men was her gift.

Prometheus had stolen fire as a way of making up for his brother's mistake in failing to assign humans the powers they needed to survive. With Prometheus out of the way, pinned to the Caucasus mountains, his brother, Epimetheus, had no one to protect him from himself. Prometheus had warned him not to accept any gifts from the Olympian gods, for a great gulf of enmity was set between them and the Titans, but when Zeus sent him fair Pandora, to be his wife, Epimetheus forgot his brother's words and gladly took her in.

Up until then, men had lived free of crime and labour and illness, under the reign of Cronus. But Pandora, the first woman, with the malign curiosity of a thief, removed the great lid from the jar of evils and let them out into the world. All the human emotions – constructive, destructive, and futile – were released, except for hope alone. Only hope remains in the jar, by the will of Zeus, so that men live without the promise it brings. And this was the cruellest act, for Prometheus' gift of fire had offered us hope.

There can be no better future. Just as every day the eagle ate Prometheus' liver, so each new dawn brings fresh toil and pain for mortal men in an endlessly repeating cycle. The Titan is bound no longer, but we are pinned by Pandora, now and for ever, to the endless, wearisome cycle of procreation and production, of domesticity and death. Nevertheless, from time to time within this bitter existence a sweet fire blazes – a life that burns more brightly with a lust for glory, adventure, or vengeance, and is branded on the collective memory of humankind. These are the stories the Muse inspires in the hearts and minds of bards, to ignite our imaginations and allow us to bring our audience relief, however brief, from a world run by fickle gods. Praise be to the Muses, daughters of Zeus! Praise to all the gods!

SELECT BIBLIOGRAPHY

The myths were formed early in Greek history – between, say, 1500 and 500 BCE. On the whole, then, and wherever possible, in this book we have stuck to the earliest extant versions of the stories (starting with Homer in the eighth century BCE), and have used later authors (such as the Roman poet Ovid, a brilliant storyteller from the beginning of the first century CE) sparingly and with caution.

Good, or adequate, translations of the ancient Greek and Roman authors who preserve or reflect the myths – such as Homer, Hesiod, the *Homeric Hymns*, Pindar, the tragedians, pseudo-Apollodorus, Hyginus, and Ovid – are readily available, especially in the Oxford World's Classics and Penguin Classics series. Gaps in these two series may be filled by the Loeb Classical Library, published by Harvard University Press, though the Loeb translations may be old-fashioned. Pseudo-Apollodorus' *Library of Greek Mythology* is the most thorough source (though written late, perhaps in the second century CE), and there are three newer translations: Keith Aldrich, *Apollodorus: The Library of Greek Mythology* (Lawrence: Coronado Press, 1975); Michael Simpson, *Gods and Heroes of the Greeks:*

The Library *of Apollodorus* (Amherst: University of Massachu-setts Press, 1976); and – containing two of the most important texts – R. Scott Smith and Stephen Trzaskoma, *Apollodorus'* Library *and Hyginus'* Fabulae (Indianapolis: Hackett, 2007). There is also a good anthology, containing extracts from many literary sources in translation: Stephen Trzaskoma, R. Scott Smith, and Stephen Brunet (eds), *Anthology of Classical Myth: Primary Sources in Translation* (Indianapolis: Hackett, 2004).

General Reference

Simon Price and Emily Kearns (eds), *The Oxford Dictionary of Classical Myth and Religion* (Oxford: Oxford University Press, 2003). This consists of lightly edited essays extracted from the third edition of *The Oxford Classical Dictionary*, ed. by Simon Hornblower and Antony Spawforth (Oxford: Oxford University Press, 1996), which is a treasure trove of information on all aspects of the ancient world.

Greek Religion in General

Louise Bruit Zaidman and Pauline Schmitt Pantel, *Religion in the Ancient Greek City*, trans. by Paul Cartledge (2nd edn, Cambridge: Cambridge University Press, 1997).
Jon Mikalson, *Ancient Greek Religion* (Oxford: Blackwell, 2005).

The World of the Heroes

Moses Finley, *The World of Odysseus* (London: Chatto & Windus, 1956).

John V. Luce, *Homer and the Heroic Age* (London: Thames and Hudson, 1975).

Barry Strauss, *The Trojan War: A New History* (New York: Simon & Schuster, 2007).

Ancient Sources for the Myths

The standard reference work on the iconography of ancient Mediterranean myth is the 16–volume *Lexicon Iconographicum Mythologiae Classicae*, popularly referred to as *LIMC* (Zurich: Artemis, 1981). Far more accessible are:

Gudrun Ahlberg-Cornell, *Myth and Epos in Early Greek Art: Representation and Interpretation* (Jonsered: Paul Åströms, 1992).

Thomas Carpenter, *Art and Myth in Ancient Greece* (London: Thames and Hudson, 1991).

Timothy Gantz, *Early Greek Myth: A Guide to Literary and Artistic Sources* (Baltimore: The Johns Hopkins University Press, 1993; 2–vol. paperback edn, 1996).

H. Alan Shapiro, *Myth into Art: Poet and Painter in Classical Greece* (London: Routledge, 1994).

Later Artistic Reception of the Myths

Apart from what can be found online, the following books are recommended:

Colin Bailey, *The Loves of the Gods: Mythological Painting from Watteau to David* (Fort Worth: Kimbell Art Museum, 1992).

Jane Davidson Reid, *The Oxford Guide to Classical Mythology in the Arts, 1300–1990s* (2 vols, Oxford: Oxford University Press, 1993).

Maria Moog-Grünewald (ed.), *The Reception of Myth and Mythology: Classical Mythology in Literature, Music and Art* (Leiden: Brill, 2010).

Discussion

Jan Bremmer (ed.), *Interpretations of Greek Mythology* (London: Croom Helm, 1987).

Richard Buxton, *Imaginary Greece: The Contexts of Mythology* (Cambridge: Cambridge University Press, 1994).

Ken Dowden, *The Uses of Greek Mythology* (London: Routledge, 1992).

Ken Dowden and Niall Livingstone (eds), *A Companion to Greek Mythology* (Oxford: Wiley-Blackwell, 2011).

Lowell Edmunds (ed.), *Approaches to Greek Myth* (Baltimore: The Johns Hopkins University Press, 1990).

Richard Gordon (ed.), *Myth, Religion and Society: Structuralist Essays* (Cambridge: Cambridge University Press, 1981).

Fritz Graf, *Greek Mythology: An Introduction* (Baltimore: The Johns Hopkins University Press, 1993).

Geoffrey Kirk, *The Nature of Greek Myths* (Harmondsworth: Penguin, 1974).

Helen Morales, *Classical Mythology: A Very Short Introduction* (Oxford: Oxford University Press, 2007).

Martin Nilsson, *The Mycenaean Origin of Greek Mythology* (2nd edn, Berkeley: University of California Press, 1972).

PICTURE CREDITS

INDEX OF NAMES AND PLACES

INDEX OF SUBJECTS